I0611758

Golden Age

The Unexpected Conflict

By Michael Robert von Blucher-Altona

01-October-2024

Copyright @ 2024 by Michael Robert von Blucher-Altona

Library of Congress Control Number: 2024920286

ISBN: Hardback   978-1-7637277-1-7
           Paperback   978-1-7637277-0-0
           Kindle   978-0-6459906-9-0

This is a work of fiction. Names, characters, places and incidents either are the product of the author's imagination or are used fictitiously, and any resemblance to any actual persons, living or dead, events, or locales is entirely coincidental.

First published 2024

Books by Michael Robert von Blucher-Altona

ForkBraid
Book 1: ForkBraid   – The Price of Peace
Book 2: ForkBraid II   – The Cost of War
Book 3: ForkBraid III – Just Rewards

Golden Age
Book 1: Golden Age   – The Unexpected Conflict
Book 2: Golden Age II – The Great Explosion
Book 3: Golden Age III – The Outer Satellite Insurrection

This book has quite a long history to it.

I'm going to divulge that long history to you here.

Make of it what you may.

This book was originally written way back in 1987 during an economic downturn and period of unemployment. The book was never published, although several attempts were actually made at that time. Australian publishers back then did not publish science fiction novels, to this day, they still don't.

The book was written on an older style personal computer called a Hitachi Peach Level III Computer, using Word Processing software known back then as Hi-Writer. The manuscript was stored on 5.25" Hitachi Peach Level III floppy disks. The Hitachi Peach, purchased in 1982, did not possess a hard drive. The original twenty one chapters were later transferred from those 5.25" floppy disks to an MS-DOS personal computer. That process took place around 1990.

The transferal process required writing an MS-DOS Quick Basic 4.5 program called "capture.exe" and the files were copied down an asynchronous RS-232C line, then Captured into MS-DOS files. Another Quick Basic 4.5 program call "stripper.exe" was written to remove all of the non-alphabetic, non-numeric and non-punctuation from the those files, effectively rendering each chapter file as text.

Some time around 2004, those same files were finally imported into an early version of Open Office and saved as open office ".odt" files, after which they were then archived for future use. Of course, it is now 2024 and those files have sat archived and fallow for this inordinate and extraordinary amount of time. So I decided to drag out those twenty one chapters and rewrite the book. Dovetailing the book into the Forkbraid saga and universe, as an odd kind of prequel, 37 years in the making.

Two terraformers, a Martian and an Alien walk into a bar.

The terraformers buy the Martian a drink.

The first terraformer says to the Martian

"Your worlds all messed up. We can fix that up for you."

The second terraformer, a women, says to the Martian

"Yeah, it sure is. We'll do a really good job. Make it real pretty."

The Martian, also a woman, replies

"What are you talking about? Your worlds all messed up!"

The Alien, turns around to face the trio

"Who said they were your worlds. Muahahaha."

What Calendar would our future Martians use?

On Earth

For 365 ¼ Days

Thirty days hath September, April, June and November.

All the rest have thirty one, Excepting February alone,

And that hath twenty eight days clear.

And twenty nine in each leap year.

On Mars

For 687 Earth Days

Fifty six days hath September, April, June and November.

All the rest have fifty eight days, Excepting February alone,

And that hath fifty-seven days clear.

Or are the Days on Mars, Sols (Martian Days)

For 669 Sols (Martian Days)

Fifty five days hath September, April, June and November.

All the rest have fifty six days, except February alone,

And that hath fifty seven days clear.

When we get there, someone will come up with something, I'm sure.

A fulcrum is the pivotal point,
around which a lever works.

The Folcrom are the pivotal points,
around which reality is wrought.

Folcrom Tafazah. Summer Solstice 2040

Table of Contents

1. Eros - A World within a Rock............8
2. State of the System Report............18
3. The Martian Report............31
4. Assault on a Law............44
5. Manoeuvring Little Worlds............57
6. Instant Atmosphere............65
7. The Seeding of Life............81
8. Martians............90
9. Alien Birds............102
10. The Mimas Incident............115
11. Eros Decides............130
12. Captured in Transit............138
13. Quick Kill............155
14. Battling the Ice Moon............172
15. The Unthinkable............183
16. The Battle for Mars............197
17. Transference............212
18. Mimas Moves............231
19. The Response............241
20. Mobilisation............254
21. A Change of Course............271
22. Two Sides Meet............286
23. What's a Man to Do............303
24. Under an Alien Sun............317
25. Immanent Danger............335
26. Confrontation............344
27. The Purging of Mimas............361
28. Options and Complications............374
29. Assessing the Renovations............386
30. Barriers............402
31. The Exodus............413
32. Reverse Course............430
33. The Council of Shadows............441

1. Eros – A World within a Rock.

The alarm sounded and Doctor Gideon Reas awoke to face his last few hours aboard the interplanetary liner Hyperion. The Hyperion's powerful ion drive had long ago started its deceleration sequence as it approached Eros. A hollowed out asteroid, that had been moved into an orbital position at Earth Sun Lagrangian point five, sixty degrees behind the Earth in its orbit around the Sun.

Gideon had never been to Eros or to the Earth for that matter.

All of his life had been spent in high Martian orbit, in its largest O'Neil-style cylindrical colony, Aries. An immense pair of cylinders with a population of nearly a quarter of a million people each. His life had been spent studying Mars for the purpose of developing a suitable terraforming plan to transform the planet into a place where Earth life could survive and thrive. With him, he carried a report to the Colonisation Committee of Sol, for the committees twice a decade, State of the System Report, but a lot more was on his mind as he prepared for the day's events.

Gideon's preparation was complete, he relaxed and watched the liner's approach on his cabin's view screen. Eros, once an asteroid, now a colony, a twenty-mile-long rock, six miles wide. The interior took nearly a quarter of a century to hollow out to a diameter of four point seven five miles. It's kilometre thick crust fused from the inside to form a solid rock shell. Much of the Eros's outer details are hidden as the liner makes its way to the nearest end of the asteroid. However, the surface structure of Eros appears to be close to its original state. Ancient scars and impact craters were quite visible, although slightly obscured by Eros's rotation rate.

As Hyperion approached one end of Eros, the surface changed abruptly.

The once-rounded end was flattened, with an assortment of buildings and small craft landed at small spaceports. There were six in all, set in a hexagonal arrangement around a large central interplanetary spaceport. The whole spaceport system sitting perfectly motionless in the centre of Eros, while Eros itself continued to rotate at nearly point five revolutions per minute. Giving the inner land regions within, the equivalent of a little over one g of gravity through centrifugal force.

Six large panels slide out of view, leaving a large circular opening nearly one hundred and twenty meters across. The liner Hyperion approached and then manoeuvred towards the opening. The four-hundred-meter-long liner slowly entered the space port. Once inside, massive gantries locked onto the Hyperion's hull and manoeuvred it to the side, towards the docking facilities.

Doctor Gideon Reas and all of the other passengers began to disembark the liner and enter the port of Eros. Gideon's passport, travel papers and carry bag were all checked, then he was soon on his way by the rapid transit system towards the vast interior of the asteroid Eros itself.

"Quite puzzling", Gideon thought to himself, *"How does this vehicle translate from the stationary port to the rotating interior of Eros?"*

The answer, he reasoned, was quite simple, *"On the port, at the inner section between the port and the interior, there must be some kind of a ring. First, this ring is in a fixed position. The transit vehicle moves into it and then the ring rotates to match Eros's rotation. When it's matched to the rotation rate, the vehicle enters the interior of Eros. It had to be something of that nature."*

The transition from the spaceport to the interior was very smooth. Gideon had hardly noticed it. He considered it an excellent example of modern engineering. The engineers who had designed and built Eros had done a brilliant job. Every bit as good as the newest and the largest of the colony cylinders at Cis-Lunar L-Five, which were using the newer more modern techniques. Gideon waited patiently as the transit vehicle zipped along. He was wondering what the interior of Eros would look like.

The transit vehicle came to a halt, one point five miles inside of the asteroid. As the passengers stepped into the terminus, a voice came over the intercom.

"You have just passed from the spaceport, through the light industrial complex that services Eros, you are now in the interior. Elevators are to your right. These will take you to the ground level. For those who are seeing Eros for the first time, the viewing windows ahead, will give you the most marvellous views. I must caution you, that as you are close to the axis of rotation the force of gravity here is extremely light."

Gideon walked over to the large clear aluminium viewing windows. He gasped at the sight before him. He was thirty six hundred meters above the ground and the vast carved out cylinder, that was the interior land region of Eros, stretched out beneath him.

Right down the middle, along Eros's centre of rotation, ran a bright beam of light, illuminating the entire interior of Eros, cutting through a crystal clear blue sky. About six hundred meters above, below and to the sides of the illuminating beam were scattered clouds.

In one region, Gideon could even see light rain falling, *"Yes, of course, a colony this size would develop its own weather patterns"*, he thought to himself.

Gideon noticed a woman, also new to Eros, obviously an Earthling. The woman was not used to the horizon curving upwards to meet at the opposite side of the cylindrical land. Trees were growing upside down and, most intriguing of all, at right angles to her. The rain was falling sideways to the ground. Trees were also growing sideways to meet the falling rain. It was quite disorienting.

With the low-gravity environment and the disturbing vista before her, the woman leant forward, pressing her hands against the clear aluminium windows to steady herself. Obvious signs of vertigo.

"I recommend taking a seat. This kind of view can be quite disorienting if you're not use to it", Gideon advised her.

The Earth woman nodded in acknowledgement, then slowly and carefully, with Gideon's help, walked over to some nearby seating. Gideon, a colonist and spacer from the Aries colony, the largest in high Martian orbit, was used to seeing vistas like this. Totally artificial and far smaller than Eros, nonetheless, the cylindrical horizon was exceedingly familiar. People from the Earth, however, were not.

Gideon's attention was caught by the sheer scale of Eros's interior. About eight miles away in the very centre of the cylinder, running around the entire circumference, was a small sea, about two miles wide. Stretching towards him from the sea was a body of water, about a mile wide. It was about six miles long, he noticed it extended about the same distance again on the other side of the central sea.

Where the two seas met, in the middle, there was an island. It was in the shape of an eight-pointed star and covered with many buildings. The tallest building reaching nearly five hundred meters in height. This was the capital of Eros. Gideon noticed that one hundred and twenty degrees around the cylinder on either side of him, there were two other seas. These were about five miles long and one mile wide and each was separated from the central sea by about a mile of land. This pattern, he noted was repeated on the opposite side of the central sea.

In between the seas from their coasts, plains swept inland. Near the central regions, these grew into small mountains about fifteen hundred meters tall. A light scattering of snow was visible on their peaks. On the plains, crops could be seen growing in large patches and at the base of the mountains, small towns and villages were clearly evident. Along the coasts themselves, built around small bays, small towns were clearly visible. A network of roads crisscrossed the lands in every direction. In the land separating the isolated seas, Gideon clearly saw canals and waterways.

After nearly twenty minutes, Gideon moved over to an elevator and stepped in. As soon as it started down, glass windows were opened and the view was once more in sight. However, this time he was watching as the elevator approached the land below. The horizon curving upward ever more steeply as he approached the lower levels.

Being a terraformer scientist, Gideon wondered about the energy required to light the interior of Eros and at the design and size of the recycling plants to purify its air and the water for the colony.

"They must be enormous, the overall power required must be phenomenal."

The elevator came to a halt about fifteen hundred meters above the cylinder floor. Gideon stepped out of the elevator and onto a sheltered platform. The air was crisp but not overly cold. On the platform, just beyond the shelter, hoverbuses were waiting, their various destinations sign posted. Further along the platform was a hover taxi bay.

Gideon walked towards the taxi bay and climbed into the first waiting taxi.

Gideon then instructed the driver where he wanted to go, "Eros Central, please, Colonial Hotel, via the scenic route if you don't mind. I'd like to have a look around."

"Hey buddy, you're the boss", came the swift reply, "Are you one of those big noddy scientists, coming for that colonial committee report?"

"Why yes, how did you know that?", questioned Gideon.

"Most colonists from the outer colonies try to get into that Hotel. With this colonial report business, it ain't hard to guess your line of work. I figure you'll be charging this trip to a government expense account, right?"

"Quite right. I guess you know a lot about what goes on here, a regular wealth of information."

"In the taxi business you pick up all kinds of info. Now I'd better get you to where your going, scenic route, wasn't it?"

"Sure was", came Gideon's reply.

The taxi began to hover about five feet above the platform, then moved towards the edge. Gideon could see that the platform was built into a ring of mountains at the colony's end. He noted the gravity was only about point six g's and he couldn't see any snow on the slopes below.

"Doesn't it snow up here?", he enquired.

"No, it doesn't snow on either of the Ring Mountains. The weather patterns won't allow it", the taxi driver replied, adding, "They do get mists and rains from about the twelve hundred meter mark and down Though."

Over the edge the taxi slid, then zoomed down the rough and barren slopes, clearing the ground by about ten meters. The taxi driver was right, at about twelve hundred meters, the taxi slid into a thin cloud bank and further down, rain began to lightly fall. Mountain grasses and vegetation could be seen on the slopes and the driver increased the taxi's clearance to fifty meters as the first trees approached. They were the same as most of the trees grown throughout the solar system, developed on Earth, then genetically altered for their new man-made environments.

Near the bottom of the Ring Mountains, the taxi levelled off at two hundred meters, gliding effortlessly over undulating hills and wide rolling plains. A greater variety of trees were visible now and on the plains, fields of rice, wheat, corn and barley could easily be distinguished.

Swiftly the taxi passed the over coast and above the long sea, leading to Eros Central. On either side, in the distance, the mountains were quite visible, with their upper reaches covered with light snow. Closer at hand along the coast, beaches and coves could be seen. Birds could be seen flying in small flocks. Gideon thought that they might be seagulls, but at this distance, it was hard to tell for sure. However, a small number of pelicans could be seen as well. Something unheard of in the Aries colony.

"Obviously genetically modified specifically for Eros", Gideon thought to himself.

Small towns passed by as they travelled toward the Central Sea. Far below the hover taxi, pleasure craft of many kinds were sailing. People, dolphins and porpoises could be seen swimming together in the clear crystal blue waters.

"Dolphins? Porpoises?", Gideon thought aloud and that was also unheard of in the Aries colony.

"Yes, we have both", the taxi driver who had heard remarked, then added, "I sometimes swim them as well. I even bought myself one of those new headset translators. Dolphins can be really chatty."

"Chatty! I didn't know that", Gideon replied, this was the first time he'd seen dolphins or porpoises in real life.

The island at the intersection of the two seas was rapidly approaching and the tall buildings were clearly visible now. The tallest building was in the centre. Overhead, the cylindrical geometry of Eros was quite evident. The bright beam of light ran down its centre of rotation and beyond that, the land on the other side was slightly obscured by clouds. Very much reminiscent of a typical O'Neil style cylindrical colony, but without the immense strip windows to let in the light.

Eros Central approached quickly, small docks for pleasure and transport craft ringed the island city. The hover taxi approached the buildings and was soon flying in between them. The Colonial Hotel then appeared and the hover taxi came to a swift halt on the landing bay.

"Here's my expense card. Thanks for the ride", Gideon offered.

"Thanks buddy", came the drivers quick reply as he put the card through his transaction processor and then handed it back, "You have a good time while you're here."

"I certainly shall, thanks again", Gideon replied as he stepped onto the platform, carry bag in hand.

The air felt fresh and clean, with a pressure of about one point two atmospheres and a very high oxygen content, around twenty five percent. The same as with many of the larger colonies. Colony atmospheres were maintained to very high standards and all were very similar in terms of pressure, content and even freshness and smell. This was because the same basic air scrubbers and purifiers were used by all of the colonies. Gideon walked into the hotel and up to the counter.

"My name's Doctor Gideon Reas. I have a room booked", he told the receptionist.

"Why yes, of course, Doctor Reas. Room two zero six five, here's your entry card. If there's anything you require, please ask. All of our rooms are equipped with Compucomms", came her swift reply.

Enquiring further, "My luggage, has it arrived yet?"

"Why yes, Doctor Reas, it arrived about twenty minutes ago. The Spaceport luggage transport systems here are very efficient. You'll find your luggage in your room ready and waiting for you. One of our guide robots will lead you there", she replied while pointing to the guide robot.

"Thank you very much", Gideon replied.

The guide robot automatically came to Gideon's side as he moved away from the counter. He punched in his room number into the keyboard at the top of the small wheeled robot and it began to lead him quickly to his room, stopping occasionally to allow Gideon to catch up.

Once inside his room, Gideon unpacked his luggage and then went over to the Compucomm.

"Standard equipment", he thought to himself as he pushed a button on the desktop.

Automatically a keyboard slid out of the desk, then on the keyboard's right, a telecommunications unit. A large screen raised out from the back of the desk and the system was operable within seconds. Gideon called up the communications directory and then searched for the phone number of Colonel James J Bannon, whom he then called.

The screen lit up and the Colonel's face quickly appeared upon it, "Gideon. I see you made it here. Are you ready for that report tomorrow?"

"Yes, Colonel. I certainly am, the council has to be told."

"Yeah, that's for sure. You know they've scheduled you last."

"Yes, I heard that. I just hope that they'll listen to what I have to say."

"I hope they do too, Gideon. Something has to be done."

"Yes, I know. I'll see you there tomorrow then, Colonel."

"Okay then, Gideon, let's hope it all works out. See you tomorrow."

The screen then went blank and so Gideon set it to display random background images of interstellar gas and dust clouds.

The conversation was finished and so Gideon then decided to get to know more about Eros. A detailed map of Eros appeared on the screen. Gideon could see that most of the industry on Eros, was built into the ends of the asteroid and built deep into the crust. The entire region between the spaceports and the interior was taken up by power generation and air and water recycling systems. They were on a scale that Gideon had never seen before.

The crust in the cylindrical interior section of Eros had housing and light industry to a depth of two hundred metres. The light industry being towards both ends of Eros and the housing being towards the Central Sea. All of the towns and villages of Eros were of a set size. They weren't allowed to grow and expand as towns and villages on a planet could. Although Eros was huge compared to most colonies, it was nonetheless a colony itself and limited in land area. Much of Eros's living areas, shops, offices and entertainment complexes were all underground.

This underground structure surfaced at the villages, towns and Central City. It was all serviced by a highly efficient rapid transit system. After studying the structure of Eros, Gideon could see how easily the asteroid could house a population of over five million people.

Eros was truly a world within a rock. After hours of studying Eros, Gideon decided to hit the sack.

2. State of the System Report.

The committee meeting soon began. Officials and scientists from various parts of the solar system were seated in a large arc in front of the committee. The three speakers of the committee sat behind a table facing the gathering. A constant chatter was filling the room.

"All quiet please!", the Central Speaker bellowed out loudly, a swift silence then fell across the entire room.

"As the Central Speaker for the Colonisation Committee of Sol. I hereby declare this, the thirteenth session of the Colonisation Committee, State of the System Report open. I note here that this is the sixth session since the founding of Eros."

"Progress reports shall be summarised in person. All written reports have been passed to the committee for further study and assessment by our scientists here on Eros."

The Central Speaker then shuffled his papers, "Let me see, the first report is to made by our Earth representative, Doctor Gerald Danzig. Whenever you're ready, Doctor Danzig."

Doctor Danzig began speaking, "As most of you may be aware, our mother planet, the Earth, has had its population stabilised at just above six billion people. It is the constant outward expansion, through our colonising program, in conjunction with various population and birth control methods, that has enabled this."

"However, it has been predicted that in the very near future. Say in the next few decades or so, there will be a large, to put it simply, *'Baby boom'*. This will, if it occurs, create an extremely dangerous situation for the Earth, as it did during the late twentieth and early twenty first centuries."

"Those of you who know your history will, of course, remember that at that time, the Earth's population had increased to a very large eight billion plus people. Our people were luckily able to avoid a thermo-nuclear war, which would have destroyed our mother planet."

"Yes, Doctor", the Speaker on the left interrupted, "We are all aware of our history, could you avoid the basics and get to your point?"

Doctor Danzig began to explain, "It isn't international rivalry that the United Nations of the Earth and Earth Gov are worried about. It is the biological factor. Within the first fifty years of the twenty first century, we had a number of viral outbreaks that threatened our population before we were able to gain control of them. A great many millions of people died as result of those viral outbreaks."

"Yes, but what has that got to do with now?", enquired the same Speaker on the left.

"Other viral outbreaks will occur. We are still finding viruses in the wild that have the potential to threaten millions of people. The point is, if the Earth gets that over-crowded once again, we may not be able to isolate viral outbreaks fast enough. We could have more world wide pandemics on our hands."

"Speakers, representatives to this committee, the Earth will need to send out much greater numbers of colonists. Venus and Mars will both have to be terraformed in time. The usual colonies we develop and build may not be enough. We need our two nearest planets terraformed and we need them terraformed sooner rather than later."

"Doctor Danzig, the report made by the United Nations has basically demonstrated this and it has been duly noted. Please wait patiently, the reports on the proposed terraforming of Venus and the proposed terraforming of the planet Mars will be made shortly. Copies will be made available to your people by both the United Nations and the Earth Gov", the Central Speaker added in.

"Sir, those reports will be greatly appreciated. Our own scientists may even be able to add to them or at least improve on them. Thank you, Sir", came Danzig's reply.

Dr Danzig was extremely interested in these two reports. He sat back down and waited patiently, wondering if the rumours, he and the others had heard about Mars were true. Rumours about Mars and the problems that had occurred recently. Most of the representatives had dismissed the rumours as just that, rumours, but there was always some truth to rumours.

The Central Speaker then began, "The United Nations report will be available to you all, as will all the reports yet to be made", he then added, "The next report is to be made by Mr Jonathan Smythe of the Confederation of Lunar colonies."

Mr Smythe stood up and addressed the members, "Speakers, fellow scientists and officials. At this moment on the Moon, we have over a hundred thousand people. About fifty percent of these people are in the mining and construction industries. The remainder are mostly dome farmers, medical staff, scientists and of course our retailers and politicians, just to list a few."

"Over the past decade, many new ore deposits have been discovered. Our scientists have developed new mining, new processing and transport techniques. These will, of course, enable us to increase production and shipping of lunar materials by twenty to twenty five percent over the next decade."

"In addition to this, new techniques in our low-gravity farming domes have been developed and we should be fully self-sufficient in about fifteen years. A proposal has also been put forward to treble the size of our small industrial export program."

"All the facts and figures can be found in our detailed report. Thank you for listening. I hope you find it to be interesting reading."

"Thank you for your report, Mr Smythe. No doubt, like most reports from Lunar, it will probably be short, concise and correct, as always. Now moving along, the next report is to be by Mr Frank Johnston of the Federation of Cis-Lunar L-Five colonies. Whenever you are ready, Mr Johnston."

Mr Johnston was a true spacer, having never set foot on a planet or even a natural satellite.

He began, "L-Five is expanding very nicely. We have at the moment, some five hundred and thirty four Cylindrical, Toroidal and Bernal sphere colonies now built or under construction. These colonies range from the massive O'Neil cylinders, with populations between one and twenty million, like Colonial Central Command, to the smaller, older colonies with populations of ten thousand to one million."

"We are constantly upgrading and developing our colony construction methods. The larger cylinders are becoming easier, cheaper and faster to make. We are using ever stronger materials and alloys."

"As we do complete the newer larger colonies, we find that a lot of the citizens from the smaller, older colonies transfer to them. We also import colonists from the Earth. We have gotten to the stage where some of our older, smaller colonies are actually being dismantled and recycled. In some cases, they are even transported to the outer colonies in the Asteroid Belt and beyond."

"Large cylinder construction has come of age, ladies and gentlemen. Now, we only produce the smaller colony structures when requested to do so for use as corporate colonies, which only require smaller populations. Some of our large cylindrical colonies are favourites of the Jovian and Saturnian colonists, to whom we export our plans and schematics."

"So far, we have managed to increase our population to around half a billion and still maintain our self-sufficiency. All of the details are in our report. Many of the new developments in colony construction will be of special interest to the outer colonies."

"No doubt they will, Mr Johnston, thank you. Now, who's next? Ah yes, Ms Indra Shek of Venus."

Ms Shek was on her feet and promptly talking, "In the Venusian orbital zone, we have only fifteen O'Neil cylinders with a combined population of seventeen million people. We have also been building floating sky cities in the Venusian skies, fifty kilometres above the surface of Venus. The first of which, Venusville, came online just recently. We expect to build a great many more floating sky cities."

"Our work on the terraforming of Venus is problematic and currently well behind schedule. Our geneticists have yet to develop any living organisms that are capable of surviving in the Venusian atmosphere with its extremely high temperatures and sulphuric acid clouds and rain. It is currently considered beyond our capacity to terraform Venus at this point in time."

"Instead, we are recommending building new colonies in the Venusian Sun Lagrangian points one, four and five. We believe that if sufficient asteroidal materials can be manoeuvred into those orbital regions, we can accelerate the process of colony construction. That and the construction of the new Venusian sky cities should provide for millions of future Venusian inhabitants."

"Well Ms Shek, that should make the United Nations happy I think", stated the Speaker on the Central Speaker's right.

"Yes, I assume so. It may not be the terraforming of Venus, but we are endeavouring to build new habitats for humanity", Ms Shek replied.

The Central Speaker took over once more, "The Venusian report and all relevant information will be made available later. So, let's move on, shall we? Next on the agenda is Mr Harold Jenson from the Asteroid Belt. This should be interesting, we rarely hear from the Belters."

Mr Jenson stood up and began, "The Dwarf Planet Ceres, along with the twelve largest asteroids have all been colonised. They all have had mining facilities on them for quite some time now. As have their manufactured Moons, that were created from nearby smaller asteroids. Recently, to increase population, the smaller twin cylinder O'Neil-style colonies have been replaced by thirteen larger colonies, each supporting up to a quarter of a million people."

"We have begun to intensify the mining of these asteroids and have since started mining operations on many of the other asteroids in the local vicinity. Exploration continues unabated."

"Some of the older colonies of Cis-Lunar L-Five have been modified to increase mirror surface areas and concentration. These colonies have been manoeuvred into many regions of the Asteroid Belt. These colonies are used to set up mines, grow food and eventually, build further colonies of similar design and even larger colonies."

"Some of our colonies are indeed similar to Eros. We've cored out some of the smaller asteroids. Some eight miles long and four to six miles wide, to use as colonies. Collectively, these we find can and will support millions of people in the future. At the moment, we have completed and colonised only two. There are another eight or so in the process of construction. We will require many immigrants to live in and run these colonies when they are finally completed and brought online."

"The asteroid belt now sustains close to three million people. We will need to expand this by thirty percent over the next ten years. You see, my friends, you might not be able to terraform an asteroid to create a planet, but they can provide millions of tonnes of ore to build new colonies. These are every bit as good as any colonies you'll find in Cis-Lunar L-Five and when asteroids are hollowed out, they make artificial worlds every bit as good as Eros."

"I'm sure they do, Mr Jenson and no doubt your report will be as informative and well documented as the one provided by Lunar."

Mr Jensen then added, "Perhaps even better, Mr Speaker. In the report is a concept being developed by one of our engineers. To hollow out an even larger asteroid with a length of twenty five plus miles and a width of over more than twelve."

"We expect it will take many, many years to complete. We will need the help of Cis-Lunar L-Five and the Earth's expertise and technology. It may be too big to be rotated. We may need to develop an artificial gravity generator of sufficient size and power to provide the gravity for this."

"Yes I see, Mr Jenson, but that would become an immense task. This project will have to be fully investigated by our engineers before a decision can be made on it", the Central Speaker was correct, any large projects of this kind would eventually have to go through Parliamentary processes.

"Right then, let us move on. The next report is to be made by Mrs Janet Keal of the Jovian System", the Central Speaker informed the delegates.

Mrs Keal stood up and addressed the meeting, "Speakers and members. The colonies of Jupiter were first started by moving small colony cylinders from Cis-Lunar L-Five to the Fore and Aft Trojan asteroids, sixty degrees ahead and behind Jupiter in its orbit. At these locations, we mined the asteroids and built somewhat larger colonies. Some of the smaller colonies were subsequently moved into closer orbits nearer to Jupiter."

"Since then, a fleet of four huge push ships, owned by the Horridian

Corporation, has arrived from the Cis-Lunar L-Five space and started to process the smaller moons of Jupiter itself. These moons are for us what the Earth is for Cis-Lunar L-Five and Venus. That is, the materials we can't get from the Trojan asteroids, we can obtain from Jupiter's smaller moons. In addition to this, we now have small mining colonies on both Ganymede and Callisto. We operate fully automated mines on Europa, Io and Amalthea, where various exotic elements can be found."

The mention of the Horridian Corporation caused loud whispers and murmurs across the conference room. The Horridian Corporation had been disgraced for using indentured servitude as an employment policy. The result of which was massive fines being levelled by Colonial Central Command against the Horridian Corporation. Crippling massive fines!

"The Horridian Corporation! They're a disgraceful band of thugs!", a delegate at the back shouted.

"Their standard employment policy was to use indentured servitude where ever possible!", another delegate shouted, "As a sovereign colony, they arrested their own people, even visitors to their colony, for the slightest infractions and sentenced them to indentured servitude! They are a disgrace!"

Another delegate shouted, "Call it what it was. Those Horridian bastards legalised Slavery!"

Mrs Keal responded, shouting back, "Whatever their past, the Horridian Corporation is helping the Jovian colonies to grow and expand!"

The Central Speaker banged his gable on his bench several times, then raised his hand and called for silence, "Enough of this! This is not the place for this discussion. Now, please move on."

The conference room became silent once more and Mrs Keal then continued.

Mrs Keal continued, "Humanity cannot yet live on Europa, Io or Amalthea due to Jupiter's intense radiation belts, but we can mine them. The four big Galilean moons of Jupiter provide stable orbital regions, Lagrangian points, where we will build massive colony cylinders, every bit as big as the largest as you have at Cis-Lunar L-Five. We will use the blueprints for Colonial Central Command as their basic design and then tailor them to the various Jovian environments."

"We have been working on our largest project for some time now. Hollowing out the inside of the largest Trojan asteroid, Hector. Some three hundred and seventy kilometres long and two hundred wide. The materials we mine from it will be used for building Jupiter's Galilean orbital colonies."

"From Jupiter's moons, we mine and utilise frozen gases, methane, oxygen and water, among others. Some we mine from Jupiter itself, from its own atmosphere using special probes of immense size. The entire Jovian orbital system provides for the needs of our four million people and it can and will provide for a great many more."

"A massive amount of material is exported. From our colonies, we also export to the Asteroid Belt. Frozen gases from the moons of Jupiter and Jupiter itself. We also export to Saturn, materials and ore from inside of Hector itself and from our other larger Trojan asteroids. So that the Saturnians can build their future colonies."

Mrs Keal broke off for a second, looked at the people around her and then explained their major project.

"Why, you may ask, do we hollow out an asteroid the size of Hector? The answer is that it will be a gigantic version of Eros, an immense celestial citadel. We don't know that we can rotate a world as large as Hector, to provide the centrifugal force to create the artificial gravity required. We, just like the Belters, also need to develop large-scale gravitational generating systems. If the scientists and technicians of the Earth can help us with this task, then we can continue to build and create places for the Earth's people to inhabit."

The Speaker on the left replied, "It seems, there are now two groups in need to develop large scale gravity generating systems. If it is at all feasible, no doubt Parliament will respond favourably. However, a special report will have to be made with regard these proposals."

"The reports are all entered into the computer network already. That should make the process somewhat easier for you", came Mrs Keal's slightly arrogant reply.

"Well now, the committee will try to push those projects through", the Central Speaker butted in, "Now, I think we'll move on to our next report, Mr Mark Spencer of the Saturnian System."

Mr Mark Spencer stood up, he was a pioneer and was born on Titan, the largest moon of Saturn. A moon wrapped in a thick nitrogen methane atmosphere, with over one point six times the Earth's own atmospheric pressure. A moon where methane and ethane rains fell out of the Titanian skies, forming vast, cold seas and lakes of hydrocarbons.

His report began, "Saturn's colonies haven't been around as long as the others, but we are developing rapidly. Nitrogen and methane mined from our large Titan colony are being exported to the Belters. We have also begun exporting from our new mining colonies on the smaller moons, Tethys, Dione, Rhea and Iapetus, again to the Belters."

"Most of the ore we use in construction, we have to import from the Belters and the Jovians. We are still expanding, though and fully intend to mine Enceladus as soon as we can open a mine there. We have also decided to make a complete survey of the small moon Mimas, for the purposes of opening up a new mine there. The Terraformers from Mars have also asked for our permission to do a radical form of mining. To aide in the transforming of the planet Mars. We currently support a population of well over a quarter of a million people, but can also support a great many more."

"Another project that we would like to put together, with the aid of the inner solar system worlds, is the opening up of the Uranian and Neptunian orbital zones to colonisation. We believe that if push ships full of colonists were sent out to Uranus and Neptune to build new colonies, it would alleviate any future looming population crisis that the Earth may be worried about. This is also in our report."

"Well then, Mr Spencer. I'm certain that Doctor Danzig will be very pleased to hear that and equally eager to read your report."

"Now ladies and gentlemen, as Mars is the next on the agenda, may I suggest that we here what our representative from Mars has to say. Apparently there have been some problems of some kind. That is why they are the last on our schedule", the Central Speaker told everyone.

"I hope these problems won't have any effect on the plans they've made for those two Centaur bodies", enquired Mr Spencer, "We have performed a lot of simulations on how to move those."

"We shall find out shortly, Mr Spencer. However, as the meeting has thus far taken up most of the morning, let us first call for a break and go to lunch", the Central Speaker quickly replied.

Within minutes the committee room was cleared and the representatives were moving off to another room, where food and refreshments had been set up. The topic of their general conversation was Mars.

"Problems? What problems could they possibly have?", was a common enquiry.

"You know that group of useless crack pots! They've failed in their job so many times before", was a common reply.

Doctor Gideon Reas was bombarded with questions and his lunch break was ruined, so he left for more peaceful surroundings. Colonel Bannon followed Gideon out of the room and soon caught up to him.

Shoving a plate of sandwiches at him, the Colonel told him, "Gideon, you'd better rip into these. You'll need all the strength you've got to face that committee."

"Thanks, Colonel. I was feeling a little bit hungry", Gideon replied, taking hold of the plate.

"Hey, look, don't let that mob back there worry you. I'm here to back you up, remember."

Gideon looked at the Colonel, "Yeah, well, that will help, but I don't know, this is a very difficult problem to explain."

"So it is Gideon, but we've got a security problem and this is the only way to get anything done about it", the Colonel replied.

"You're probably right, Colonel, but they'll freak out when they hear it", came Gideon's reply.

The two men then walked back towards the luncheon room. On walking up the two steps leading to the doorway of the room, Colonel Bannon misjudged his step in Eros's one g of gravity. His large, muscular frame came to a sudden halt on the floor, releasing a dull thud on contact.

"Fuck this low gravity bullshit, give me one and a half g's in a military training cylinder any day", he shouted.

Gideon was unable to contain his laughter, "Eros has a little over one g Colonel. That's pretty much standard. You spend way too much time in high gravity training", as he helped the Colonel to his feet.

First the Colonel was upset at Gideon's ability to laugh at his misplaced footing, especially as half a dozen on lookers were watching, but soon he was also laughing along with him.

"Hey, I'm sorry, Colonel, I couldn't help laughing", Gideon said apologetically.

"That's okay Gideon, it relieves a bit of tension", replied the Colonel, adding, "Let's get back in there and do the job. If they freak out, so what, let them?"

Gideon and Colonel Bannon continued back towards the luncheon room. As they approached, Gideon was again bombarded with more of the same questions. He remained tight-lipped and continued on his way to the room.

Gideon's only reply to the questioning was, "You'll all find out when I make my report, be patient."

3. The Martian Report.

With lunch over, the representatives returned to the committee room and took to their seats, this time, however, everyone was silent.

The Central Speaker stood up and started the proceedings, "Thank you ladies and gentleman, we shall now here the final report from Doctor Gideon Reas, Head of the Martian Terraforming Department. You may make your report, whenever you are ready, Doctor Reas."

Gideon stood up and looked around the committee room at the faces of the other delegates, they were all waiting patiently. There hadn't been any real problems in the colonisation program for many, many decades. Humanity had reached, what appeared to be a golden age of exploration and colonisation. In general, everything was running very smoothly.

The last problems had been when people first reached into space. Before the first of the artificial colonies was completed. Ever since then, technology has leapt forward in leaps and bounds. Scientists and engineers checked all of their calculations and plans until they were completely error-free. Things generally moved quite smoothly and without any major mishaps. They all looked at Gideon, patiently, but with utter disbelief, that is all but one, Colonel James J Bannon.

Gideon began, "As most of you already all know, we have tried many different methods to bring about a change to the Martian atmosphere. Most of those methods have had some effects, although not all of them were good enough for us to continue to persevere with them."

"Seeding the polar ice caps for example with genetically modified lichens to absorb solar heat, increased the atmospheric pressure from only six millibars to fifteen. However, then the pressure stabilised and we needed to develop another method."

"The next method involved beaming energy to the polar regions from large solar arrays. Although this method heated the polar regions and increased the atmospheric pressure to some fifty millibars, we were not able to cause the soil-locked ancient Martian atmosphere to be released. Even though liquid water could now at least exist on the surface of Mars."

Gideon stopped for a moment and looked around him, up to now, he had said nothing new.

Gideon continued, "Studies in the late twentieth century had shown that if Mars was perhaps seven percent rounder. It's rotational axis would increase from twenty five degrees to maybe thirty or thirty two degrees. Allowing more solar energy to strike the polar regions for a longer length of time."

"The Tharsis Bulge and related geological regions are responsible for eight percent of the Martian surface irregularity. To collapse these regions and subsequently alter the axis of rotation is possible and we have calculated that Mars's atmospheric pressure would increase to approximately five hundred millibars as a result. That we believe is the total soil-locked atmosphere of Mars. It would make Mars habitable, but we would like to increase this even further and to also increase it's quantity of surface water considerably."

This time when Gideon stopped he could hear quiet murmuring in the room.

The Central Speaker then raised his hand and called for silence, "Please people. We shall not continue until there is silence in this room."

The room became silent once more, "Thank you, Mr Speaker", replied Gideon.

Gideon again looked around the room and then began to explain what his people had planned for the planet Mars. This would be hard enough for the committee to believe and he hadn't even got to the problems yet.

Gideon began once again, "Delegates from the Aries colony have recently approached Saturn's Colonial Council for the purpose of purchasing two Centaur bodies. The Centaurs as everyone is aware come under Saturnian jurisdiction. We are talking about the Centaur bodies Chariklo and Chiron in particular. Chariklo with its diameter of two hundred and fifty five kilometres and Chiron with its diameter of two hundred kilometres, both contain a vast quantity of frozen volatile gases, useful to our purposes and also a considerable quantity of frozen water. Vast quantities of water in fact."

"We will manoeuvre both Chariklo and Chiron from their current solar orbits to a Martian orbit. Where they will be broken up by internally placed clean fusion charges. Those pieces broken off will then be placed into trajectories, which will enable them to be vaporised in highly controlled atmospheric air bursts, high above the Martian surface."

"Some of you may be thinking that we're going to collapse the Tharsis Bulge and its geologically related regions to alter the Martian rotational axis. No, we are not going to do that at all. We don't believe that we'll need to do that. Collapsing the Tharsis Bulge would likely create more problems than it would solve. We believe, that just those two centaur bodies alone, Chariklo and Chiron, will provide Mars with enough atmospheric gases and water to terraform itself."

The murmuring began once more, one delegate shouted out loudly, "Are you insane! Are you mad!", this time it took much longer for the Central Speaker to again restore quiet to the committee room.

Most of the people in the committee room had not heard of this plan. Even though it had been tabled in Parliament and passed, it was a well kept government secret. All of the the Speakers had read the report in advance and were well aware of the plan, to them it was no surprise.

"Proceed when ready, Doctor Reas", the Central Speaker requested when he had again brought quiet to the committee room.

"Thank you again, Mr Speaker", Gideon began and then continued, "These two Centaur bodies were chosen over all the others possibilities because of their sheer size. Centaur bodies have unstable orbits and their removal will have little effect on the Saturnian system."

"The technology developed to move these two Centaurs, has already been used to move similar objects around our solar system. Eros itself was moved into this location, at Earth-Sun Lagrangian point five. Chariklo and Chiron are of course very much larger, however, we believe that manoeuvring them into an appropriate position for their demolition should pose no problems whatsoever. We will be breaking them up, in Mars Sun Lagrangian point one and working with the much, much smaller individual pieces."

"These much smaller pieces will be further broken up on their final approach to Mars. The aim is for these pieces to explode as air bursts, long before reaching the Martian surface. However, some smaller pieces will get through and strike the surface of Mars. We will be directing those into regions where there should be minimal harm."

"This influx of volatile gases and more importantly the vast volumes of water will cause the soil-locked Martian atmosphere to be freed. These two combined, will, as our modelling has indicated, create an atmosphere on Mars, with a surface pressure of between fourteen hundred and sixteen hundred millibars."

"Martian gravity is point three eight gs. This new atmosphere will be large, massive and extensive. Over time, Mars will develop its own ozone layer and the greenhouse effect of the atmosphere will raise the overall temperature of the planet. The temperature at the equator should become similar to that of the Earth's temperate zones. The arctic zones will of course be colder than Antarctica."

"The waters frozen under the Martian surface and the waters added from Chariklo and Chiron, have been modelled and are expected to create an ocean in the Martian northern hemisphere. That ocean is expected to be well over six thousand feet deep."

"Smaller southern oceans in the Argyle Basin and the Hellas Basin regions are expected to be over five kilometres and eight kilometres deep respectively. The water in the Argyle Basin is expected to spill over into the lower land regions around the South Pole. This entire process is expected to stabilise very quickly and colonisation could begin in around two centuries. Perhaps less."

This time when Gideon looked around the room, he noticed that everyone was quite shocked by his proposals. Speaking about playing interplanetary billiards with huge icy asteroids, was apparently quite disturbing. No doubt there would be a lot of questions about this scheme and he still had to tell them of the problems they come up against. He decided to launch himself straight into it.

"We have been developing the systems to be used, including the craft to actually tow these two Centaur bodies into their correct trajectories and their final locations. Massive asteroid tugs. In design, they are very similar to the craft that manoeuvred Eros into its present location. Only these are much larger and much more powerful vessels. However, we've had some problems, namely sabotage."

That was it, the shit finally hit the fan, that last word was unheard of and the committee room burst into a chorus of shouting, talking and questioning.

"Order, order, can we please have some order in this meeting, please!", the Central Speaker bellowed as loudly as he could, before he started banging the bench with his gabble.

Ever so slowly the room became quiet once more and after a long silence, Gideon started to explain.

"Yes, sabotage, crucial assemblies being built for the asteroid tugs were deliberately blown to pieces. In the first cases, unidentified craft approached after the work was completed and ready for orbital transfer. Explosive charges were placed and the assembled parts were destroyed. So we increased our security significantly. This time our assembled parts were destroyed by small fleets of unidentified interceptors. So we called in the armed forces and they managed to track the unidentified craft as far as the Martian surface."

Gideon continued, "That's right, the unidentified craft landed somewhere on Mars. Somewhere south of the Elysium region. The same region in which the monoliths are found. The so-called Pyramids of Mars. It is also interesting to note, that at the time of the attacks. Energy readings in the area around those monoliths were very much higher than they normally are."

"Doctor Reas. Are you saying, that there is some connection between those so called Martian monoliths and the attacks on your installations?", the Speaker on the right enquired.

These details had not been put into Gideon's report, "That is absolutely correct Speaker", Gideon replied honestly.

"That is absurd! The very notion of the idea is ridiculous!", the Speaker on the right retorted, "Even if those crackpot theories about the ancient Martians are correct, those theories all stipulate, that the hypothetical Martians died out well over ninety thousand years ago, when the Martian biosphere collapsed!"

"Your facts are out of date, Sir. More recent research has it, that the hypothetical Martian holocaust was over ninety thousand years ago. However, it is evident, that they may have survived up to at least fifty thousand years ago. There is also some evidence that has been found, that shows that they may have still been alive, as little as twenty five thousand years ago", Gideon replied quickly.

"Even so, surely they are extinct now, no life forms can live on the Martian surface?", inserted the Central Speaker, who then quickly added, "Hypothetically speaking of course. The jury is still out on whether those Martians actually existed at all. Officially speaking, there never was a Martian civilisation and the Martians have never existed."

"That's right, but what about underground, what about inside those ancient monoliths? The Elysium Pyramids have never been explored. Most of the information we have is from the monoliths in the Cydonia region, on the other side of Mars", Gideon quickly postulated, adding, "We have never opened them up, we have never even investigated them, let alone been inside them. Those structures could house millions of people."

"Pareidolia!", the Speaker on the left shouted out loudly, "The mind sees that the mind wants to see! All of this Martian nonsense has been completely debunked many decades ago. Crackpot theories from pseudo-scientists. Nothing more. None of them worth their salt!"

Now the Central Speaker was starting to get angry. When ever and where ever, the Martian monoliths were mentioned, there was always a hot debate. He could very easily lose control of the committee room.

"The very existence of those Martian monoliths is a hotly debated topic. Are they even real? No one really knows! The official stance of every major government in our entire system is that they are not! Our laws state quite clearly, that those so-called Martian monoliths, are not to be touched or opened, until such time as we have a clear understanding, as to what they are and their significance to human society and existence. We will have no more wild theories about Martians! You call yourself a scientist Doctor Reas? May I remind you, that more than one scientist has ruined their career going down that Martian monolith rabbit hole!"

Colonel Bannon knew that this would happen and he was prepared for it. He had also prepared and entered his own report on the committee's computer network.

Now it was his turn, Colonel James J Bannon stood up, "May I approach the Speakers bench, Sir?", he forcefully enquired.

The Central Speaker noticed the uniformed Colonel for the first time and asked, "And who may I ask are you, Sir?"

"Colonel James J Bannon, Senior intelligence officer assigned to the Martian security problem, Sir. I do have identification papers on me, if you would care to inspect them", the Colonel answered.

A committee official passed the Colonel's papers to the Speakers, who inspected them.

After conferring with the other two Speakers, the Central Speaker then stated, "Your papers are in order. You may approach the bench, Colonel Bannon."

"Thank you, Sir", the Colonel replied and then approached the Speakers, "If you use these access codes on your computer console, you'll receive access to a special report compiled by myself, on the Martian problem. This will yield more light on the situation."

Colonel Bannon gave the Speakers a card containing the codes, then returned to his seat. The Central Speaker entered the codes to access the report and very quickly scanned the pages therein.

After a short while, the Central Speaker announced, "We shall need a short recess to study this report. I shall adjourn this meeting for one hour, thank you ladies and gentlemen."

The room was cleared and the three Speakers began to study the report. It contained details of the attacks by the unidentified craft and the damage they caused. The reports also contained details on the design of these craft. They were truly alien and this was stipulated in the report, labelling them as, *"of an unknown and unrecognisable design"*.

Attempts to follow the alien vehicles were also reported. In five out of six cases, the vehicles disappeared south of the Elysium region. In the sixth case, they disappeared somewhere in the south polar region of Mars. In each of the cases, the regions around Martian monoliths displayed an increase in their local energy readings. This report startled the speakers, so much so, that they decided to enquire further.

The meeting restarted and there was a cacophony of voices in the committee room, so the Central Speaker called for quiet and banged his gable harshly on the bench. The voices all quickly stopped.

The Central Speaker began, "Colonel Bannon. These craft have extremely unusual designs. Have you been able to identify the design or their designer?"

"Sir, as stated in my report, the design of these craft has never been seen before. There is either a secret colony on Mars, where these craft were designed and built or they are of a totally alien origin", came Colonel Bannon's reply.

"Colonel, in your opinion, do you believe that it's possible that the designers were Martian?", the left Speaker enquired.

"Mr Speaker, as far as we can tell, there aren't any secret human colonies on Mars. The design of the craft is not a human design either. We've come to the conclusion, that there's either an extraterrestrial, that is to say, alien colony on Mars or that the Martians themselves did not entirely die out", the Colonel emphasised that last option.

"Then, Colonel, you believe, that there are, in fact, Martians and that they are responsible?", asked the Central Speaker.

"As we haven't found any evidence of extraterrestrial aliens so far. We believe the Martian theory is the most probable. You might remember, that during the twentieth and twenty first centuries on the Earth, UFO sightings were very commonplace", informed the Colonel, continuing, "Those we believe were also of a Martian origin."

"Thank you, Colonel Bannon", the Central Speaker replied.

The Central Speaker then turned his attention to Gideon, "Doctor Reas, has the terraforming project been able to continue?"

Gideon replied, "The project is currently continuing. It appears that as the military are now keeping the Martian monoliths under very strict surveillance, the sabotage and the attacks have stopped."

"That is very interesting indeed, Doctor Reas. It certainly supports your conclusion that the Martians are very much alive", injected the right Speaker, adding, "It is as if they fear being positively sighted and identified, more than they fear your terraforming project itself."

"Perhaps Sir, but as we have this very antiquated law protecting all of the Martian monoliths, we cannot investigate further or even take action against them", Gideon stated, adding, "We can't even prove, that they exist."

"How you may feel about the law, Doctor Reas is irrelevant. Neither you nor I have the power to change it", replied the Central Speaker whilst rubbing his chin.

Turning to Colonel Bannon, the Central Speaker enquired, "What do you intend to do about the situation, Colonel?"

"There isn't much I can do Sir. I've ordered my people to keep tight surveillance on all of the Martian monoliths, but apart from that, my hands are tied by this blasted law", the Colonel replied.

"And if they try to sabotage the project again Colonel?"

"Then my troops have orders to engage the enemy, Sir. However, this will take place in space and from what we've been able to tell, the weaponry we will be going up against is far superior to our own."

"Has Parliament been informed of the attacks?", enquired the left Speaker. "No Sir, they have not", Colonel Bannon replied, adding, "Doctor Reas and I have decided that it would be better to get the support of this committee first, before going before Parliament."

The Central Speaker conferred with the others for a short while, then he announced, "Ladies and gentlemen, members of this, the fifteenth meeting of the Colonisation Committee of Sol. This problem with the Martian project must be kept in the strictest of confidence. There must not be any leaks. This is to remain a secret of the most sensitive nature. Classification. Top Secret. Understood!"

The members were all in agreement, if information of this kind were to leak out, there would be panic, mass panic. That was something to be avoided at all costs.

The Central Speaker then addressed Gideon and the Colonel, "Doctor Reas, Colonel Bannon. You will have the full backing of this Committee and we speakers. Thank you, gentlemen. I shall speak to you both later."

The meeting then ended. Usually the next ten days would be spent studying the reports, asking and answering questions with the other delegates and setting up smaller meetings to exchange data and information. For Gideon, Colonel Bannon and the Central Speaker, this would not be so. For them, their task would be to persuade Parliament, to change a law that was more than a century old.

Gideon and Colonel Bannon met after the meeting and they were soon joined by the committee's Central Speaker.

"Doctor Reas, Colonel Bannon", the Central Speaker greeted them both, then asked, "If we are going to discuss this Martian issue, it might be best to dispense with the formalities, don't you think?"

"Good idea, Sir", replied Gideon, "Is that okay by you, Colonel?"

"Sure is, Gideon, the names, Jim remember?", the Colonel replied.

"Apart from my formal title, the Central Speaker to the Colonisation Committee of Sol. I usually use the name Professor Daniel Forbes", the Central Speaker informed them, "Most people call me Dan."

With formalities out of the way, they began their discussion.

"You do know that your chances of getting to see Parliament and changing the law, to allow you to enter those monoliths are virtually nil?"

"We know that, Dan, but we still have to try", replied Jim.

"Without conclusive evidence, that those craft came from the Martian monoliths, it is going to be extremely difficult", replied Gideon.

"Gideon, Jim, conclusive evidence be damned. You would need a captured alien craft and a live Martian specimen as well, just to get their attention."

"If Jim keeps them under surveillance long enough, maybe they'll make a slip-up, then we'll have our proof, Dan."

"Yeah, Gideon, but that proof might be a long time coming. Who knows how long they'll lie low for", replied Dan.

"True, but if they do come up, my troops will be waiting for them", the Colonel replied.

"It could be a long wait Jim and we've been scheduled to go before Parliament in one week", Dan informed them both.

"One week! That's not very long. I wonder if they'll make a move", Gideon replied.

"Don't worry about it, Gideon. If and when the Martians make their move, my men will be ready and waiting for them."

"If they don't make a move, what then Jim?"

"Well, Gideon, we'll just have to do the best we can, perhaps Dan will be able to sway them."

"I will back you up all the way on this one gentlemen, but there's no guarantee that they'll listen."

"Well then, Dan, Gideon, let's just give it our best shot", Jim replied.

"Looks like all we can do", replied Gideon, a grim look on his face.

The three men continued their discussion, but there wasn't much they could do. With only one week to go before Parliament and no real proof, there would be no guarantee that the law would be changed.

They had to try, these Martians were a threat. They had to find out for certain, whether they existed and if they did, then confront them. Convince them, that they had nothing to fear from the terraforming of Mars. That it was also in their interests. There was no doubt in their minds, however, there could be no other explanation. However, they would still have to persuade Parliament. It would be no easy task and it had to be done.

4. Assault on a Law.

Colonel Bannon had been waiting for the latest report from Mars. There was only one day to go before they had to confront Parliament. Gideon Reas arrived at the Colonel's apartment and pressed the intercom. Colonel Bannon was quick to answer it.

"That you Gideon?", he enquired.

"Sure is Jim", Gideon replied.

The door slid open and Gideon entered, "The report here yet or am I too early."

"Not yet, but it's due any time now", replied Jim, adding, "What's your poison Gideon, the Bars open you know."

"No alcohol thanks. Fruit juice if you've got it thanks, Jim."

"Sure no worries. I forgot that you don't drink Gideon, me, I think I'll have bourbon and ice."

The Compucomm in the Colonel's apartment let out an audible ring, the report had arrived.

The Colonel quickly answered the call, "Urgent Interplanetary call for Colonel James J Bannon", the operator informed him.

"I'm Colonel J Bannon", the Colonel replied.

"This call was set for scramble, you'll need to use your identity card", replied the operator, the Colonel placed his Id card into the communications slot, "Okay Colonel, stand by."

The report was in the form of a recording, as the time delay due to the distance between Eros and Mars, meant that two way conversation wasn't practical. The top secret security report came through on the screen, the Colonel and Gideon listened intently as the Lieutenant made his report. The Colonel also had the report saved and filed for future reference.

"Colonel Sir. Surveillance of the Martian monoliths has been very tight. There has been no sign of activity visible from the surface or from in space. There's been no activity at present that indicates the attacks were orchestrated from the monoliths."

"That law forbidding access to the monoliths means that we cannot get close enough to them, to inspect them properly. The project hasn't had any more interruptions though and the scientists have assured me that it is now back on schedule. I hope you can knock that law out of the way, I'd like to know what's inside these structures. Report complete Sir. Over and out.", the report ended.

"Great, Gideon, nothing new. It looks like we're going to have a hard time convincing Parliament."

"At least the project is back on schedule. If the Martians don't want to be positively identified, they might stay underground for as long as we keep those monoliths under surveillance."

"Yeah, but their civilisation was there when our ancestors lived in caves. They're more advanced than us, Gideon. We're colonising the solar system now. Surely they must have done the same", the Colonel postulated, then continued, questioning, "What if they attack us from some other ancient colony that we haven't found yet? One that we don't know about?"

"Well, Jim, Phobos gives credibility to that possibility. They supposedly used it as a base and source of raw materials. It was destroyed long ago during their holocaust, probably one of the very first casualties. Even though it's not covered by the law and we've had access to it, it was so badly damaged that we didn't learn anything about them at all. It's even debatable that it was even a base. To make matters worse, our own governments deny that the Martians even existed and have legally locked off any access to the very sites that we need to investigate."

"Gideon, we haven't found any other evidence of Martian colonies. The solar system is huge, we haven't been everywhere yet, so really we just don't know."

"Well, looking at it this way, your troops have the monoliths cordoned off. Nothing can get in, nothing can get out. If they were going to attack us from somewhere else, they would have done so by now, surely. I think they've studied our terraforming project in more detail. That they've decided, that it isn't as dangerous as they'd thought after all."

"I wish I could be so sure, Gideon", replied the Colonel.

"Don't let it worry you, Jim, maybe everything will turn out okay in the end", Gideon assured him.

"Maybe so, Gideon, but we don't know that for sure, do we? And they did attack us, we should retaliate anyway!", Jim replied angrily.

Their conversation was interrupted by a call on the compucomm. The Colonel answered it and Professor Daniel Forbes was on the other end of the line.

"Jim, I'm afraid we have a change of plans", he informed him.

Jim's response, "A change of plans hey. Well then, you'll have to let us in on them then."

"Us, you mean, Gideon is there as well", replied Dan.

"Certainly is, saves you telling the story twice, Dan."

"Okay then, tomorrow we won't be going before Parliament. First, we'll be seeing the Security Council. If we can get their backing, then we get to report to Parliament", explained Dan.

"What if we don't get their backing, Dan?", enquired the Colonel.

"Then we won't get any further, Jim. The law won't be changed Jim, however, if we do get their backing, the chances of us launching an expeditionary force into those monoliths will be better than ninety percent."

"Then basically, we have to get their support or we're sunk", the Colonel replied.

"It won't be easy, how was the latest report from Mars, Jim?"

"No change, accept that the project is back on schedule."

"Then we're going to have a hard time convincing the Security Council. By the way, Jim, we've got to front up at nine o'clock."

"Okay then, Dan, we'll see you there, signing off", finished Jim.

After leaving the Colonel's apartment, Gideon hired a car and flew it to the mountains he'd passed on the way to Eros Central. He parked the car about two hundred meters below the snowline on a level area. The car hovered about two feet off the ground as he jumped out and walked through the trees towards the snowline. The air was crisp with a slight chill to it, as he was about a thousand meters up in the mountains.

He went there to think through the situation. Something he'd done so often at the Aries colony in high Martian orbit, going through the project in his mind.

"Terraforming Mars by crashing two large icy asteroids onto the planet, piece by piece. Instant atmosphere, instant water, both helping to free Mars's own soil-locked ancient atmosphere and melt its subsurface water, whole oceans worth of it."

Gideon Reas had a mind like a calculator, he went through all the calculations in his head, *"The new atmosphere could be expected to support life for well over a billion years, if of course the Sun remained stable for all of that time."*

He'd found no mistakes, no errors, everything checked out. All of their modelling had indicated the project would succeed.

His mind reasoned, *"At first the Martians would have thought the project too dangerous, after all, it does at first sound insane and hence they tried to stop it. They wanted to keep their own existence secret, so when the surveillance started, they hid. Then they fully checked out the project. Realised that it would actually work and was even to their own advantage. Their world would again be alive. They won't attack again, they wanted the project to succeed as much as we do. They want their world to be terraformed and just as useful to them as it will be to us."*

Once Gideon realised what the situation was, he was no longer worried about it. He decided to enjoy the mountain forest and walked further into the snowline to relax among the snow gums. Whilst Gideon had decided that the Martians were no longer a threat, Colonel James J Bannon was formulating plans to retaliate against them.

After all, it was they who attacked first and he was a military man. He wondered about the extent of their weapons technology. What would his men be going up against? Could human technology be defeated by them? How could the unknown Martian adversary be vanquished? Would the Security Council see this threat and take the appropriate action or decide that the monolith connection was just a mere coincidence?

Gideon arrived at the meeting and met up with Colonel Bannon and Professor Forbes. They entered the Security Council chamber together and then took their seats. The Security Council members entered the chamber. They took their seats on the other side of a long table that curved in an arc about the three men. There were eleven Councillors in all.

The Councillor in the centre stood up, he then began to start the proceedings. He looked at Gideon and then asked, "Please identify yourself before this council."

Gideon stood up and replied, "Doctor Gideon Reas, Senior Terraformer Scientist, Terraforming Department, Aries Colony, high Martian orbit."

Gideon sat down and the Councillor then turned to the Colonel, "Please identify yourself before this council."

Colonel Bannon stood up and answered, "Colonel James J Bannon, Senior Security Officer, United Nations, presently on secondment to the Aries Colony in high Martian orbit."

The Councillor asked the same question to Dan, who replied, "Professor Daniel Forbes, Central Speaker to the Colonisation Committee of Sol."

The Councillor then stated, "Gentlemen, we the members of this Security Council have read your reports. You have been asked here for the purpose of answering some simple questions."

The Central Councillor then motioned the third Councillor on his left who asked, "Doctor Reas, when did you notify the United Nations for help in regards to your security problem."

Doctor Reas answered, "We asked the United Nations for help shortly after the second of the interceptor attacks."

"Why didn't you ask for help before this? From your reports there were two cases of sabotage beforehand, even before the interceptor attacks?"

To which Gideon replied, "Our own security people thought they could handle the sabotage themselves. And they did, however, the sabotage was replaced by the interceptor attacks. For which we needed help."

"Doctor Reas, what can you tell us about the technology of the craft used in the attacks?"

"They had unusual designs, very fast, armed with high-powered laser and particle beam weapons. I would assess the technology that they used as far superior to our own", replied Gideon.

"Thank you, Doctor Reas", replied the Councillor.

The Central Councillor then motioned the fifth Councillor on his left who began, "Colonel, when did the attacks stop?"

Colonel Bannon replied, "Sir, there were six interceptor attacks in all. The attacks all stopped after the Martian monoliths were put under very tight security surveillance."

"Colonel, why was the surveillance set up and what are your latest conclusions?"

"Sir. After tracking the interceptors. We found that in each case they disappeared in or close to the regions where the Martian monoliths are found. It was also found that energy levels in those regions were higher than normal at these times. We concluded, that our enemy originated from those regions and so we cordoned them off and put them under extremely tight surveillance."

"Colonel, in your opinion, why did the attacks stop?"

"Sir, the interceptors could not be launched without being seen. We believe that the Martians do not want their existence positively proven. So rather than risk being seen, they are now lying low."

"Colonel, do you agree with Doctor Reas about the level of technology they have?"

"Sir. Their craft are better than ours. Much faster, with far superior weaponry. They can use deflector shields which neutralise our own particle beam and laser beam weaponry as well. We don't have any weapons to match theirs, Sir. They are extremely advanced."

"Colonel. Do you consider them to be a threat?"

"Yes, Sir. Indeed they are a threat. I believe that we haven't seen the last of them and that we should retaliate against them as soon as it is possible to do so."

"Thank you, Colonel Bannon."

The Central Councillor then motioned to the third Councillor on his right. This Councillor began to question Gideon, "Doctor Reas, why do you think that they, assuming they exist, attacked?"

Gideon replied, "It is not a matter of whether they exist, they do exist, Sir. I think that they attacked because they were afraid of our terraforming project. They may have thought that it was far too radical and too dangerous for them to allow it to continue. I can understand their fears."

The Councillor asked, "Why do you think the attacks halted?"

"Well, Sir. It was a combination of two things. One. They were unable to leave the monoliths without being positively identified. That is something they definitely do not want. Two. I think they examined our project concepts in far more detail and came to the conclusion, that it will work and would be in their interest as well."

"I take it, that you no longer believe the Martians to be a threat, Doctor Reas?", the Councillor asked.

"At this point, I believe that to be the case. Now that they aren't afraid of the project and know that it will bring new life to Mars. They probably want it to succeed as much as we do", replied Gideon.

"Thank you, Doctor Reas", the Councillor finished.

The Central Councillor then motioned to the fifth Councillor on his right.

He questioned the Colonel, "Colonel, do you agree with the conclusion of Doctor Reas?"

"No, Sir! It seems that Doctor Reas has changed his mind since I last saw him. I still think they are an ongoing threat", he replied.

The Councillor then asked, "How would you like to handle this supposed threat, Colonel?"

The Colonel then answered, "Sir! The threat is real and I would like to take an expeditionary force into those monoliths. Open them up and then take retaliatory action."

To this the Councillor then asked, "Even if they are able to defeat your forces? As you yourself have said, they do seem to have the technological advantage."

The Colonel then replied, "We won't know that for certain, Sir, until we send our armed forces into those monoliths to find out."

"Thank you, Colonel", the Councillor finished.

The Central Councillor then motioned the Councillor on his left.

This Councillor then questioned Gideon, "Doctor Reas. What is your recommendation for handling this situation?"

Gideon replied, "I would prefer to have access to those monoliths. We have to try to communicate with them. We do need to open up a dialogue with the Martians, Sir."

"What if they don't want to communicate, Doctor Reas?", asked the Central Councillor.

"Then we can either force them to communicate, which will probably make them attack us or do exactly what we're doing now and wait for them to communicate with us", Gideon replied.

The Councillor then asked, "Doctor Reas. Do you think that they'll make any further attempts to stop the project?"

"No, Sir. I now think that they want the project to continue", Gideon Replied.

"Thank you, Doctor Reas", the Councillor finished.

The Central Councillor motioned to the Councillor on his right who questioned the Colonel, "Colonel, how long can your troops maintain the surveillance on the monoliths?"

The Colonel replied, "My men can keep up the surveillance indefinitely if they have to, Sir."

The Councillor then asked, "Colonel. Have any Martians been captured yet?"

"No, Sir. We haven't even seen one yet", the Colonel admitted.

"That's what I thought, Colonel. Do we have any conclusive proof that the Martians attacked or that they even exist?", he then enquired.

"No, Sir. We haven't got conclusive proof, but all the evidence points to those monoliths", the Colonel replied.

"Colonel. Could these attacks have been perpetrated by an unknown, unregistered colony of people from the Earth? Not Martians at all, just our very own people?", the Councillor asked.

Colonel Bannon replied, "I doubt that very much, Sir. Their interceptors, their weapons and their overall technology is far superior to ours. "

The Councillor then finished, "Thank you, Colonel."

The Central Councillor then asked of Dan, "Professor Forbes. What do you make of this problem?"

"Sir. The evidence does seem to point toward the monoliths and I believe, that in itself warrants further investigation on its own."

"Professor Forbes. Is the Colonisation Committee going to support, Doctor Reas and Colonel Bannon with this issue?"

"Yes, Sir. We are supporting them. We should get to the bottom of this problem", Dan replied.

"Yes, the problem does need a solution Professor, but this law that protects the Martian monoliths will not be removed without totally concrete proof", the Central Councillor stated, adding, "We shall adjourn this council meeting for one hour, during which time, we Councillors shall make our decision."

One hour later, the three men sat in the council chamber once more, awaiting for the Security Council's decision. They didn't like their chances. The Councillors returned and they all took their seats, they were right on time.

The Central Councillor stood and stated the Councils chosen decision, "Gentlemen. We the members of the Security Council of Sol, having read your reports and having heard your answers to our questions, have decided that the matter shall end here. The Martian terraforming project is continuing on schedule and the attacks have stopped. So we will not be recommending the opening of the monoliths or the sending in of a military expedition force."

"Colonel. You will keep up the surveillance of the monoliths indefinitely. We feel that the Martians, assuming they exist, were motivated by fear. Their actions were understandable and no lives have been lost. We believe that sending in a military expedition force will only increase their fears and may end up motivating them into a full-scale war. We wish to avoid this possibility."

"Fear is a powerful driving force gentlemen and we would prefer to give them room to breathe. When they realise that we mean them no harm, they will surely contact us of their own accord. Also, in case your conclusions are wrong and these crafts originated somewhere else, your people shall investigate every other possibility. Including the possibility of unregistered human colonies on Mars."

"Officially. The Martians have never existed and so this meeting must remain in the strictest of confidence. The general populace must not find out, that there is even the slightest possibility, that there are aliens within our solar system. There would be system-wide panic if this information was to leak out. Gentlemen, assuming they do exist, we will wait for the Martians to communicate with us. This meeting is now over, good day."

Professor Forbes noted, "That meeting was never going to go our way. You know that don't you."

"I thought we were in with an even chance", Gideon replied.

"No. It was never going to happen. They are too afraid, Gentlemen", the Professor commented.

"Afraid of what? What are they so afraid of?", the Colonel asked.

"At the moment the official line is, that all of those monoliths are just cases of pareidolia, Gentlemen. The human mind looks for and sees patterns in everything", the Professor explained, adding, "That has been their official explanation for well over a century and a half now."

"Yes, but isn't it better to know the truth", Gideon enquired.

"Earth Gov and the Security Council don't believe our people can handle the truth, Gideon", Professor Forbes replied, adding, "They are afraid that those monoliths are real, that they contain real artefacts. Proof that we are or at least were, not alone in the Universe."

"That is one hell of a can of worms to open up", Colonel Bannon agreed, "They're worried about a mass panic setting in."

"And the fact that the Earth Gov and their Security Council will have been caught in a centuries-long lie", the Professor noted, "I bet that weighs very heavily on their minds as well, Gentlemen. They don't want to be caught in a lie."

Gideon wasn't worried about the result, it was a predictable outcome, "What a shame. I would have liked to have met the Martians. I can only imagine their technology. Just think of what we might have learnt."

"Gideon, to hell with what we might have learnt. What if they attack us again?", the Colonel was genuinely worried.

"I don't think they will, Jim. I don't think they will. They were scared by our terraforming project. After all, it is quite radical. After studying it in greater detail, they would have eventually realised it was okay. They won't attack again", Gideon assured him.

"Then it's a jolly good thing that the Martians all live in the Elysium region, Gideon", Colonel Bannon noted.

"Why is that, Jim?", Gideon enquired.

"I've read your terraforming plans, Gideon. Studied them in detail", the Colonel informed him, commenting, "Those other monoliths in Cydonia. Well, what can I say. That whole region of Cydonia is going to be inundated by the new Northern Ocean. So if you are right and the Martians are all good with this project, then those particular monoliths must be abandoned."

"To be honest, Jim. I hadn't thought about that, but you're probably be right", Gideon admitted and agreed, "If those monoliths are going to be submerged, they are likely abandoned."

Gideon and Colonel Bannon returned to the Aries colony in high Martian orbit. Gideon to oversee the terraforming project and Colonel Bannon to keep a close watch over the Elysium monoliths with his indefinite surveillance.

The project was almost ready to begin. The two massive space tugs were now assembled. Already they were being sent to their destinations. They were being sent to hook onto the chosen Centaur asteroids, Chariklo and Chiron.

These two new space tugs were also experimental craft. They were built with standard ion drives as most modern spaceships were, however, these space tugs had huge, newly developed nuclear fusion drive systems. It would not be long before the project was fully underway.

Professor Forbes remained on Eros. If it wasn't for his job, he might have joined the Terraforming team. However, Professor Forbes had other responsibilities on Eros. He did not see either of the other two men again.

5. Manoeuvring Little Worlds.

The space tugs had been sent to their respective targets. It took them quite some time for each of them to reach their respective targets, being they were both Centaur bodies. Icy asteroids orbiting the Sun in unstable orbits between Saturn and Neptune. The two centaurs in particular being, one o one ninety nine Chariklo and two o six o Chiron.

Upon arriving at their destinations, the space tug began coupling themselves to their respective asteroids. The space tugs then manoeuvred the asteroids into their launch positions using their powerful ion drives. The very same ion drives that had been used to power the tugs to the asteroids.

After doing this, they stabilised their positions and then switched off their immense ion drives. They now proceeded to start the operation of their fusion drive units. These were of a far newer design, having never been used before and also having never been tested, except in complex computer simulations. Those simulations had shown that the new fusion drives should function as specified.

Up until the creation of the two massive space tugs, most space craft used one of two types of drive systems or a combination of both. There had been the well-used tried and tested ion drives, which although being slower, were very effective, reaching immensely high speeds the longer they were used.

Ion drives were highly efficient, using far less propellant and were perfect for longer duration missions, where a gradual yet continuous thrust could be used to achieve enormously high speeds over time. Their downside was of course their low thrust, their slow acceleration and their significant electrical power requirements. The space tugs had two fission reactors each, one to provide power for the ship's electrical systems and a separate larger one just to generate power for the ion drives.

Then there was also the fusion impulse drive, being powered by the controlled explosions of tiny hydrogen, usually deuterium or tritium, bomblets. A concept that combined aspects of nuclear fusion and pulsed propulsion. Each bomblet would explode inside a reinforced reaction chamber with the impulse thrust being directed as necessary.

Fusion impulse reactions release a tremendous amount of energy, offering a high specific impulse. The energy density of fusion reactions is incredibly high, meaning that small amounts of fuel could produce significant amounts of energy. The energy levels being so high, that the reaction chamber itself and the directional thrusters were built of highly durable titanium alloys. Even then they had to be inspected after each flight and replaced at regular intervals.

This type of drive was able to accelerate a craft much more quickly, to reach far higher speeds. Only the larger transports could use this kind of drive, as it was inherently unstable, requiring extremely complex technology to precisely control the detonations and the directing of the subsequent thrust.

The two space tugs, however, had a new fusion drive system known as the fusion torch. In this drive unit, a controlled fusion reaction was sustained. Super heated helium and radiation was directed from the rear of the craft driving it forward. Powerful magnetic fields separated the super heated plasma and radiation from the walls of the reaction chamber and direction thrusters.

This design although more advanced and complex than the fusion impulse drives and was far more stable. This was because the energy of the controlled fusion reaction was delivered far more smoothly instead of being delivered with impulsive explosions. To move around large asteroids the size of Chariklo and Chiron, this kind of drive system was an absolute necessity. They needed not only the power and the thrust but also the smoothness of operation that the new fusion torch drives provided.

The Captain of the space tug Calypso was preparing to launch his ship and with it, its Centaur body Chariklo, toward Martian orbit, "Is the trajectory lined up yet", he enquired.

"Yes, Sir. We're all lined up and ready to go, Captain", his navigator replied.

"Okay then. Drive master! Increase the magnetic field to maximum and inform me when the electromagnetic constriction is optimal", the Captain commanded.

The drive master moved a few switch settings and adjusted his controls.

Then after a few minutes, "Electromagnetic field is at maximum. Constriction is good to go, Captain."

To which the Captain replied, "Prepare the lasers for initial giant impulse."

Again the drive master turned on some switches and then adjusted the dials.

"Laser power at maximum. Ready for initial giant laser impulse, Captain", the Drive master replied.

The Captain was pleased, everything was going well, "Good! Right then, drive master, switch the lasers to fire automatically and inject plasma into the electromagnetic constriction."

The drive master replied, "Switching lasers to automatic. Lasers primed and ready. Injecting plasma into electromagnetic constriction zone now, Captain."

The hydrogen plasma was quickly constricted and superheated as it travelled down the drive tube and into the reaction chamber. Then at precisely the right moment, the lasers fired down the length of the drive tube. The initial giant impulse of coherent light carried an enormous amount of energy. In far less than the blink of an eye, the hydrogen plasma was heated to super-critical levels, then the lasers switched over to automatic mode.

In the section of the reaction chamber where the electromagnetic constriction was at its greatest, hydrogen plasma pressure and temperature shot up well above the super-critical levels and the fusion reaction began. The fusion reaction was now self-sustaining, with hydrogen plasma being injected into the drive tubes in a continuous stream and the lasers firing automatically to keep the reaction going.   The space tug Calypso and its immense cargo, Chariklo, shot forward as a torch of super-heated helium and radiation shot forth from the fusion drives thruster system.

The space tug Calypso accelerated towards Mars at precisely one quarter earth gravity. The space tug, Calypso's sister ship, the Olympus fired her fusion torch and was soon on her way as well, delivering her own Centaur body, Chiron, to Martian orbit. It would take some time for them both to reach their respective destinations.

As they'd approached closer and closer to the Sun, their two charges, Chariklo and Chiron had become active, like giant comets. The warmth of the Sun's rays began to cause frozen gases and particles to vaporise from their icy surfaces. Gradually at first and then more quickly, the gas and dust particles vaporised, forming vast cometary comas around both Chariklo and Chiron.

The Sun's solar wind began to push the vaporising gas and particles away from Chariklo and Chiron, outward in the direction opposite the Sun. Vast quantities of gas and dust were streaming away from them both, forming long cometary tails pointing in the direction opposite of the Sun.

This had been expected and the crews of both space tugs had to adjust their drive systems and thrusters to compensate and keep them both on track towards Martian orbit. They would become like gigantic comets, so both icy asteroids had been coupled to the tugs to an extreme depth. Some of the engineers back at the Aries colony had thought that the coupling depth had been overly cautious and that only half the chosen depth was necessary. It was safe to say that the Captains of both space tugs, were happy that the coupling depth was as extreme as it was. It was more than necessary.

The two huge icy asteroids had developed enormous comas and long tails like comets and were now clearly visible from the Earth and the entire solar system. Chariklo and Chiron were largest and most spectacular comets to ever be witnessed by humanity. People everywhere across the entire inner solar system and even the asteroid belt colonies were watching the unusual man made event. The event was so spectacular that it was even televised across the inner system networks and news feeds.

A little over one week later and the two huge space tugs were now within ten million kilometres of Mars. They had already started the deceleration phase of their journey some three days earlier. They both scanned the Martian system before them and then began adjusting their course for Mars Sun Lagrangian point one, approximately one million kilometres from Mars in the direction of the Sun.

If everything went according to their plans, both space tugs would come to a full stop, close to the centre of Lagrangian point one. Then their cargoes, Chariklo and Chiron, could be carefully placed into stable orbital positions within the Lagrangian point, effectively orbiting the Sun a million kilometres from Mars. The gas and dust from their cometary comas and tails would in theory be flowing back towards Mars, where it was hoped, that much of it would be captured by the Martian gravity well. Waste not, want not, as Gideon would say.

Before the end of the following day, both Chariklo and Chiron had been manoeuvred into their new home positions in the Mars Sun Lagrangian point one region. The solar wind continued to push the vaporising gas and particles from both icy asteroids outward from the Sun. Now, however, those evaporating volatile gases and dust were flowing directly towards Mars and for the larger part, were being captured by the Martian gravity well. Everything was going to plan.

The two space tugs stayed on station with the icy asteroids, waiting for the demolition teams from the Aries colony to arrive. The demolition teams task was to put in place cold fusion detonators, that would fracture the icy asteroids, Chariklo and Chiron, into scores and scores of much smaller icy fragments. After which, the two space tugs were to hold and stabilise Chariklo and Chiron together.

Then many smaller space tugs moved in and one by one, the many icy fragments were to be separated from Chariklo and Chiron, then ever so carefully directed towards Mars, to explode as bolides in the Martian upper atmosphere. The larger icy fragments would be drilled and implanted with fusion detonators, to fragment them even further as they approached Mars, to ensure they disintegrated correctly in the upper atmosphere.

The trajectory of each and every icy asteroidal fragment was to be worked out precisely and only the very largest would actually reach the surface of Mars. Even then, those fragments would be directed into the deep basins of Argyle Planitia and Hellas Planitia, which at five point two and eight kilometres deep respectively, it was hoped, would minimise any untoward affects on the rest of the Martian Surface.

Chariklo and Chiron were to be broken up and dismantled in unison. As this was all happening in Mars Sun Lagrangian point one, any escaping gases from the detonations and any larger particles would be flowing into their comet-like tails, only to end up captured by the Martian gravity well. Thus, maximising the amount of material to be transferred to planet Mars.

All of the figures and preliminary computer simulations had predicted, that there would be no problems. However, as all of these processes could not be tested, there was really only one way to find out in the end. The ultimate test would be the actual breaking up of the first of the centaur bodies, Chariklo. If that all went well, then the next centaur, Chiron, would follow very soon after.

Doctor Gideon Reas checked his instruments, everything would soon be ready. Outside of the Aries colony in high Martian orbit, there was a constant stream of volatile gases and small particles. They appeared as a constant fine mist surrounding the immense O'Neil style cylindrical colony, drifting on their way outward from the Sun, to being captured by the gravity of Mars.

The Aries colony's attitude control systems and orbital thrusters were working overtime against the lite, but constant pressure was exerted by the cometary stream from the two icy asteroids, Chariklo and Chiron. With each fusion detonation, there would be a huge increase, a pulse of gases and particles streaming towards Mars and the pressure exerted by the cometary steam would increase significantly. Gideon had calculated in advance, that the Aries colony's attitude control systems and orbital thrusters could and would cope, under those conditions.

The greater problem was the timing of each icy fragment being manoeuvred from Chariklo and Chiron down to Mars. These icy fragments had to pass through precise windows of opportunity, whereby Phobos, Deimos and indeed, the Aries colony itself, were well and truly out of the way. These timing windows had to be adhered to precisely. There could be no deviations, no mistiming. Everything had to be perfect. The trajectories of each fragment of icy asteroid were checked, double-checked and finally triple-checked before releasing them towards Mars.

The entire process from start to finish had to work with clockwork precision. Gideon's people had already informed him, that all of the Martian colonists on Mars itself, *"the Tunnellers"*, as they were unofficially known, had been evacuated. They were called tunnellers, as their colonies were generally tunnelled into the cliff and rock faces, literally tunnelled and carved out of the rock and stone of Mars.

Indeed, all of the known colonies on the surface of Mars had been evacuated already and in theory, Mars would be empty of any human beings during this entire terraforming process. However, there had been many landings on Mars over the decades and not all of those landings were documented, registered or even known.

Many countries, groups of countries and even some private consortiums had sent colonists to Mars. Some of these colonies had failed and some of them had flourished. Some, if not that many, were not officially listed and as a result, could not be contacted prior to the start of the terraforming process. These were the unknown colonists of Mars and to them, what was to follow, would become known as and remembered as, the *"Falling Skies"* and the *"Long Rains"*.

Tales would develop, that would become legends in the centuries to follow.

In the not-so-distant future, students at Martian schools would brag, *"My ancestors were living here on Mars when the skies fell and throughout the long rains that followed, when Mars convulsed and released its ancient breath!"*, as badges of honour.

6. Instant Atmosphere.

The detonation team was split into two groups. One group left for the asteroid Chariklo and the other group left for Chiron. The two groups had precisely the same job to do, only on different asteroids. The surfaces of each asteroid were very carefully surveyed and then a series of deep bore holes and tunnels were drilled into them. Into each of these bore holes and tunnels was placed an electromagnetic linking unit.

When the units were activated, they would each link together with powerful lines of electromagnetic force. These would help to hold the two asteroids together, so that they wouldn't be blown completely apart by the cold fusion detonations. These devices being used were deemed to be relatively clean, in that they generated very little if any radiation.

Following this, another series of very deep tunnels were carefully bored into each asteroid. Each tunnel was bored at precisely the right location. At specific points throughout the tunnels, from the surface to the core of the asteroids, small cold fusion detonation devices were installed. These would be used to literally cut and shatter the icy asteroids into a myriad of smaller pieces so that they could be broken up far more easily. When the detonation teams were finished, they then notified the Captains of the space tugs, who awaited their orders to continue with the operation.

The Calypso would be the first to detonate their cold fusion devices. The Captain of the space tug Calypso read the dispatch that had just arrived. Inside it were the orders he had been waiting for. In only one hour's time, the detonations would occur and the time passed far too quickly for his liking.

This procedure had been modelled in complex computer simulations, but it had never been performed in practice. This first attempt would be the very first time this would be performed. The Calypso's Captain counted down the hour with a large degree of fear, uncertainty and doubt.

Over the ships intercom, the Captain's voice bellowed out for his entire crew to hear, "Strap down and stand by, ten minutes to detonation", then he repeated to make sure they had all heard, "Strap down people, you have less than ten minutes to detonation."

Within minutes the crew were ready and waiting. Now time appeared to be passing by much, much slower, almost unbearably slow. It was as if, each and every crew member was acutely aware of the ticking of the ship's chronometer.

Nine minutes passed by and the Captain of the Calypso gave the final one-minute warning, "One minute to go people. One minute to go!", he bellowed into the ship's intercom.

The last minute passed by very slowly, excruciatingly slowly and then the Captain of the Calypso pressed the detonation button.

All of the cold fusion devices positioned deep within Chariklo's interior exploded simultaneously and the icy asteroid suddenly shuddered violently. A great deal of fear gripped the faces of all of the crew members, as the space tug Calypso shook violently in response to the icy asteroid's shuddering. The scenes on the Captain's monitor were equally violent and frightening as the icy asteroid burst forth with an immense pulse of vaporised gases and dust.

The surface of the Chariklo ruptured into a series of vast cracks, deep fissures and chasms. From out of the depths of Chariklo's interior, burst forth huge torrents of volatile gases, dust and water. These quickly vaporised in the vacuum of space. These gases and particles burst out far into space with immense velocity. Chariklo and the space tug were now buried in a vast cloud of erupting and vaporising debris. The Sun's solar wind then pushed this cloud of volatile gases, water vapour and debris away from Chariklo, forming a vast tail that pointed away from the Sun and towards the Martian gravity well.

After quite some time, Chariklo stabilised. The web of interconnected electromagnetic linking units had worked. Chariklo had expanded somewhat in size, but it was still linked together, by a webbing of electromagnetic lines of force. Very slowly materials stopped spewing out of Chariklo's interior. A vast system of broad cracks, deep fissures and chasms were evidence of the cataclysm that had just been inflicted upon Chariklo. The icy asteroid Chariklo was now shattered into a multitude of fragments and ready for dismantling.

Now the only cloud surrounding Chariklo, was again due to the heat from the Sun's rays, vaporising its surface materials. The next phase of the operation then began. The dismantling teams moved in quickly, as soon as it was safe enough to do so. Chariklo was again surveyed and divided into sections. Each section being related to a sizeable fragment of the icy asteroid. A very large fleet of smaller tugs then carefully moved in. Each tug attached itself to a designated fragment and with great effort, heaved it free from the icy asteroid Chariklo.

These fragments were of immense size, but not so large that they couldn't be ripped away from their parent asteroid. Once freed from Chariklo, a tunnel was bored deep into the centre of each fragment, into which a cold fusion detonation device was positioned. Then the tugs, one by one, moved each fragment into their predetermined trajectories. Determined in such a way, that each fragment would pass safely by the Aries colony in high Martian orbit, the Martian moons, Deimos and Phobos, on a collision course towards Mars itself.

Then once on their way and the fragments were on course, the tugs detached themselves and let the ice fragments continue towards Mars alone.

They then returned to the icy asteroid Chariklo, for yet another fragment to process. As each of the fragments of icy asteroid debris approached Mars, their distance from the surface was monitored. Then at an altitude of between five hundred and one kilometres above the surface of Mars, the cold fusion devices were detonated. The precise altitude was calculated for each individual fragment based on their size and mass.

The immense fragments of the icy asteroids fractured and broke up into a great many smaller pieces. Each of them following their specific trajectories towards Mars, to vaporise as exploding bolides in the thin upper Martian atmosphere. As they did so, they each released huge volumes of volatile gases, dust and water vapour into the Martian atmosphere.

Some small, very small pieces made it to the Martian surface. Small in size and small in number, their impacts caused very little if any surface damage. Still, more and more fragments of Chariklo were processed. Each fragment was manoeuvred and then hurled towards Mars. The dismantling of the icy asteroid Chariklo had begun in earnest.

Then it was the turn for the icy asteroid Chiron. The Captain of the space tug, Olympus, read the dispatch that had arrived. Inside were the orders that he had also been waiting for. In one hour the detonations would occur and the time passed far too quickly. The procedure had worked well enough with Chariklo, but it was still largely experimental and this was Chiron, another asteroid entirely. Each asteroid was different and its behaviour upon detonation could not be precisely predicted.

Over the ship's intercom, the Captain's voice bellowed out loudly, "Strap down and stand by, ten minutes to detonation. Ten minutes people! Get ready!"

The last ten minutes passed ever so slowly. The Captain gave the final one-minute warning and then at the appointed moment, one minute later, he pressed the detonation button. All of the cold fusion devices exploded simultaneously and the icy asteroid, Chiron, suddenly shuddered violently, as had the asteroid Chariklo before it. As with the space tug Calypso before them, fear and uncertainty gripped the faces of all of the crew members of the space tug Olympus, which also shook violently in response to the icy asteroid's shuddering.

As with Chariklo, the dismantling of Chiron, had begun. The surface of the asteroid Chiron ruptured into a vast series of broad cracks, deep fissures and chasms. As with Chariklo before it, from out of the depths of Chiron's interior, shot forth huge torrents of volatile gases and water ice, which quickly vaporised in the vacuum of space.

Gases burst forth from the torrents and they too, burst far out into space with immense velocity. Chiron and the space tug, Olympus, were now buried in a vast cloud of erupting and vaporising debris. The solar wind pushed this vast cloud of volatile gases, water vapour and debris away from Chiron and towards the Martian gravity well, into which it was absorbed.

After Chiron had begun to settle down to far safer levels of outgassing, the surveyors moved in, dividing up Chiron into fragmented sections ready for dismantling. Another large fleet of smaller tugs then carefully moved in, each attaching themselves to a designated fragment. With great effort, heaving them free from Chiron.

Just as with Chariklo before it, the dismantling of Chiron was soon underway and had begun in earnest. Fragments of both Chariklo and Chiron were now being hurled towards Mars, one after the other, in almost a continuous stream. The only breaks in the process, were when the Aries colony or either of the Martian moons, Deimos and Phobos, were in dangerous and untoward positions in their orbits around Mars. In which case, the hurling of the fragments from both Chariklo and Chiron halted, until the path to Mars was clear once more.

It took more than nine months to dismantle and hurl the fragments of Chariklo and Chiron, piece by piece to Mars. Most of the fragments of the icy asteroids had been vaporised well above Mars in the Martian atmosphere. The larger fragments of icy asteroid, that it had been determined, would, in fact, reach the ground, were directed over the deeper southern basins of Argyle and Hellas. At over five point two kilometres deep and eight kilometres deep retrospectively, it was hoped that any surface devastation could be contained to just those two deep regions of Mars. Regions that were destined to be filled with water.

With each and every exploding bolide, the volatile gases and water vapour released quickly, spreading around the planet Mars and increasing the atmospheric pressure significantly. As the atmospheric pressure reached critical levels, vast quantities of water began raining down upon the surface of Mars in huge volumes. Rain began falling from the Martian skies continuously.

With water soaking deeply into the cold dry Martian surface there was a counter reaction, as the ancient soil locked Martian atmosphere began to be released. The newly formed, roiling Martian atmosphere, full of volatile gases from both icy asteroids Chariklo and Chiron continued to grow. It become thicker and denser, as Mars itself began releasing its own, ancient soil locked atmosphere, to mix with the newly introduced one.

What remained of the former centaur bodies, Chariklo and Chiron, their small rocky cores were then moved out of Mars Sun Lagrangian point one. They were each manoeuvred to Mars Sun Lagrangian points four and five, sixty degrees ahead and behind Mars in its orbit. In their new locations, they would both be mined by the local colonists that lived in those orbital zones, for their precious minerals and resources.

Slowly temperatures had begun to rise, eventually to levels where the ancient frozen seas and oceans of Mars, small though they originally were and currently covered in tens of meters of Martian regolith, began to melt. Vast regions of the lowland surfaces began to subside, as the Martian regolith sank and the ancient ocean waters of Mars resurfaced. These newly surfaced ancient Martian waters began mixing with the newly imported waters raining out of the newly created Martian skies. The entire northern lowland basin of Mars began to slowly fill with water, as did the smaller, yet immensely deeper Argyle and Hellas basins much further to the south.

Slowly, yet surely the skies of Mars would begin to clear of dust and debris. Slowly, yet surely, the atmosphere of Mars would find its new stable equilibrium. Complex computer modelling had predicted a final atmospheric pressure of around sixteen hundred millibars. Slowly, yet surely the oceans and seas of Mars would find their own levels, both in the northern and the southern hemispheres. Computer modelling had predicted a northern ocean, with a depth of over six thousand feet and Mars having an overall surface water coverage of just over thirty five percent.

Now the terraformer teams waited as the atmosphere began to clear. It took yet another nine months for the dust to settle out of the new Martian atmosphere to the point where they had reasonable visibility. Still, the continuous rains were flushing vast quantities of water out of the Martian skies in great torrents, that continued to flow into the new seas and oceans of Mars. These were slowly but surely filling, but would still take decades longer to find their final levels.

The Martian regolith was still releasing ancient atmospheric gases in vast quantities. The new Martian atmosphere was turbulent with immense cyclonic storms occurring on a global scale. Yet even at this very early stage, the terraformers were more than happy with their results. Mars now had a thick atmosphere, all they had to do was wait for that new atmosphere to settle down.

The process was long, slow and arduous and Gideon knew that he had decades longer to wait for the Martian atmosphere to fully settle down. It would be quite some time before the atmosphere stabilised, as massive torrential rains continued to flood the Martian surface. The terraformers waited and watched patiently, whilst monitoring their project. There was a lot to be done and Gideon waited patiently for each of the reports on the stability of the new atmosphere of Mars to come in. Gideon eagerly read each and every one of them.

Gideon Reas read the latest reports on the project, thus far all was well. Everything had gone according to plan. A good fifteen years had now passed since the icy asteroids, Chariklo and Chiron had been delivered, fragment by fragment, into the Martian atmosphere. He had enquired of Colonel Bannon many times over the years about the Colonel's endless surveillance of the Martian monoliths.

There was never any change and no signs of any Martians. Nothing stirred at all, not even when the monoliths of the Cydonia region, were inundated with water and began sinking beneath the waves of the newly forming Northern Ocean. Even the last Colonisation Committee reports had been totally without any great event. Everything in the solar system was proceeding according to plan and everything was proceeding on schedule.

In less than a year the Saturnians would begin mining the ice moon Mimas. The Belters and Jupiter's Trojan colonists had both sent scientists to Cis-Lunar L-Five, to work with the Earth's scientists to develop large scale gravity generators. These were needed for their huge colonies, that they had under construction and development. Everything was working well, but Gideon wanted a bit more excitement and he'd soon be getting it.

Over the past fifteen years, the new Martian atmosphere had reached a reasonable new stable equilibrium and done so incredibly fast. It was the Martian atmosphere that was important at this stage. Stable at one point six atmospheres, more than one and a half times that of the Earth's. The new Martian atmosphere was composed of approximately seventy one percent nitrogen and twenty five percent oxygen, with one percent carbon dioxide and one percent a mix of other gases, of which water vapour and methane had become major components.

The large percentage of carbon dioxide, along with the water vapour and methane increased the atmospheric greenhouse effect. So the temperatures reached at the equator were far higher than had been expected. Around thirty eight degrees Celsius at Martian perihelion and during the Martian summer. From space, around eighty five percent cloud cover was clearly visible. Mostly due to the continuing cyclonic storms that were still flushing large amounts of water out of the atmosphere. Some of those cyclonic storms could still join together and become global storms of great magnitude, especially when Mars was at perihelion.

Below the atmosphere the surface was greatly changed. Nearly the whole region above thirty five degrees north latitude, was now largely the Northern Ocean and it was still filling. It not yet reached is final level. This ocean extended all the way to the equator at both the Chryse Plains and the Amazonis Plains, just west of the giant Olympus Mons volcano and the Tharsis Bulge.

Also at ten degrees north latitude was a new sea in the Isidis Plains, which now formed a huge gulf connected to the Northern Ocean, the Isidis Gulf.

Another stretch of water, ran from the Isidis region to the Amazonis region, covering some ten degrees of latitude between the equator and ten degrees south latitude. This stretch of water formed a long strait, which effectively isolated the Elysium Plains as a separate sub-continent. The only sub-continent on Mars.

Around the north polar regions pack ice was clearly evident and this was expected to become a permanent Northern Ice Pack. In the southern hemisphere, there were three smaller isolated oceans. The largest one was in the Hellas Plains and it would eventually be eight kilometres deep, the Hellas Ocean. The Hellas Ocean was also still filling and had not yet reached its final level. This huge hole in the surface of Mars was expected to take decades to finally fill completely.

The other smaller ocean was in the Argyre Plains and that was expected to reach a depth of five point two kilometres, it was called the Argyre Sea. The Argyre Sea would eventually overflow its basin and be connected to the largely frozen Southern Ocean further to the south. Again it would decades for the Argyre Sea to fill completely. The Southern Polar Cap was expected to be a permanent feature on Mars and was expected to grow somewhat in size, with the largely frozen Southern Ocean between it and the Argyre Sea.

Many other smaller bodies of water had collected in the basins, craters and the shallows of a lot of other land regions, both in the northern and southern hemispheres. What devastation had been caused by the fragments of the icy asteroids that managed to reach the surface, was now underwater or had been partly washed away by the torrents of water from the long global rains.

The high mountain regions of the southern hemisphere were now covered with snow and in some places ice. Snow was also found on the peaks of the Elysium volcanoes. Most unique of all, however, was Olympus Mons. At more than seventy two thousand feet tall, its peak could easily be seen from space. The sides of the volcano from about fifty thousand feet down to eight thousand feet were covered with thick ice and snow.

At this lower level, the snow melted and cascades of water and ice plunged over the escarpment, nearly five thousand feet to its base. Some of this water then flowed west and north into the Northern Ocean. Much of the water flowed south in long rivers that eventually were turned back by the Tharsis Bulge, only to flow into the Northern Ocean once more.

The Tharsis Bulge with its three shield volcanoes also had flanks covered in thick ice and snow. The melt-water of which flowed in all directions. Some of its rivers flowed into the Northern Ocean, however, great volumes of rivers flowing south and east ending up in the Marineris Valley. The immense volume of water flowing to the Marineris Valley, first passed through a region known as Noctis Labyrinthus, before reaching the Marineris Sea proper.

The currents in the extremely long Marineris Sea were strong and the winds blowing off of the Tharsis Bulge equally so. The water flowed through the Marineris Sea for thousands of miles before turning north and eventually entering the broad Chryce Sea and thereafter, the Northern Ocean.

Olympus Mons and the Tharsis Bulge had an incredible effect on the Martian environment. No clouds could fly over them, every cloud flowed around them and all of the time they were surrounded by clouds. The vast quantities of water that flowed off of the Olympus Mons and Tharsis Bulge volcanoes, were continually replenished by snowfall from those very same clouds.

The Martian orbit isn't circular either, being more elliptical than all the other inner solar system planets. So when Mars is at its aphelion, more snow and ice is deposited on Olympus Mons and the Tharsis Mounts. Especially so if this coincides with the Martian Winter. When Mars is at its perihelion, the volume of melting snow and ice increases and becomes greater. Especially if this coincides with the Martian Summer. Olympus Mons and the Tharsis Mounts together, generated yearly flooding over a vast expanse of the Martian surface.

This wasn't the only cause of flooding across the surface of Mars either. The seasonal melting of snow and ice from the Southern Polar Ice Cap could cause the Argyle Sea and Hellas Ocean to swell and overflow. The outflow from each flooded the river valleys to the north.

The Hellas Ocean and its outflow, the Hellas River, eventually spilled out into the Isidis Gulf and from there joined the Northern Ocean. The outflow of the Argyle Sea, the Argyle River, continued its long journey north, through a multitude of flooded craters and a mix of regions until eventually spilling into the Chryce Sea and the Northern Ocean. So long was the Argyre River that some of the terraformers and the cartographers petitioned to rename it, the Nova Nile River.

This was what Gideon Reas lived for, turning Mars into a planet capable of supporting life. Now Mars wasn't the lifeless world that it had once been. Mars had been changed and now could support life. Gideon's job and of course the project were not yet finished, there was a lot more to be done.

Already teams of environmentalists had been sent to Mars. Their purpose was to make detailed studies of the new Martian environment and its possible future biomes. The Martian atmosphere still contained some toxic compounds and other exotic gasses, however, these were in relatively low concentrations.

Apart from giving the Martian air a vile gut-retching stench and a disgusting taste, it was quite breathable, although exposure had to be limited to only a few hours at a time at most. Longer exposure to the new Martian air would cause migraine headaches and possible lung damage, so re-breathers were considered necessary and surface exposure without re-breathers was banned. Gideon fully expected that these toxic compounds and exotic gasses would be flushed out of the atmosphere by the near-continuous rainfall. It was simply going to take more time, several decades at least. Fortunately, no harmful viruses or bacteria had been detected as yet.

The results of these studies would show what types of Earth life could be transplanted to Mars and in which regions these would survive and hopefully thrive best. For those regions that appeared to be to *rugged*, what kinds of genetic alterations might be necessary. This was the part that Gideon liked most of all. Watching his new world begin to flower.

Before life could be transplanted to Mars, however, the regolith of Mars would need to be transformed and made fertile. Many large transports had arrived from Titan. In them was a precious cargo, it was nicknamed, *the chicken soup*.

The chicken soup was a thick prebiotic organic sludge, which develops naturally in Titan's atmosphere, from the break down of methane, with nitrogen. Pools of it collected on Titan's icy continents and a thick layer was found at the bottom of Titan's ethane and methane seas. This *chicken soup* was loaded with prebiotic organic molecules and could be used as high grade organic fertiliser.

The environmentalists would locate regions on Mars where life could be expected to flourish. Into these regions, the chicken soup would be sprayed. Regions where deserts were expected to form would also be fertilised, but these would be done last. The most fruitful regions would be looked after first.

Across some of the desert regions, flowed rivers from the Tharsis Bulge and Southern Polar Ice Cap. The annual flooding would carry some of the carry *chicken soup*, from other regions into the flooded plains, naturally fertilising these regions. The transports were loading the *chicken soup* into specially designed spray craft in preparation for the fertilisation project, which was soon to begin.

The spray craft were an unusual vessel, they were basically large tanks to contain the *chicken soup*. Around this tank, the vessel took on an aerofoil design, so that they could glide effectively in the new Martian atmosphere. Under the wings, if you could call them wings, was a set of spray tubes through which the *chicken soup* would be released into the Martian atmosphere.

The *chicken soup* then mixed with the local clouds, eventually raining down to the ground, soaking into the Martian regolith and fertilising it. Some of the *chicken soup* that was released, managed its way into the rivers, lakes, seas and oceans. This was also required so that the organic material would be present to provide nourishment to any organisms that were later transplanted to them.

The spray craft flew into the atmosphere on predetermined flight paths, Gideon flew one of the ships himself. He adjusted his angle of entry. Then upon entering the upper atmosphere, the outer hull was slowly heated by atmospheric friction. The atmosphere became denser the deeper he flew, the hull was now red hot, but the ceramic heat dissipation plating was doing its job well. Again, Gideon adjusted his angle of decent, shallowing the angle off. His craft dropped deeper into the atmosphere, until reaching a height of ten thousand feet. At this altitude, he levelled off and adjusted his course. Then upon reaching the desired location, he switched on his pumps and the great many tonnes of rich organic fertiliser were sprayed into the air.

The *chicken soup* spread out, slowly falling toward the ground. Soon it would spread over a very large area and be quickly absorbed by the clouds. The clouds themselves would eventually become heavily laden with *chicken soup* and would burst forth with rain, rich in fertiliser, falling towards the ground. Gideon's tank was now empty and he fired his thrusters and followed his course back into space, for the reloading station.

Once back at the reloading station, Gideon docked his ship and met with the designer, Sandra Danker, "Sandra, you've excelled yourself this time. This thing worked perfectly!"

"So they should. The amount of time I put into them", Sandra replied.

"Yeah, well, you've done really well this time, Sandra", Gideon praised her.

"Don't I always", Sandra replied, then chastised, "I just wish you wouldn't test them yourself. We do have people for that you know?", her voice showed serious concern.

"Don't be silly, Sandra. I may be the boss, but I do like to have some fun occasionally", Gideon replied, before enquiring, "How about the planned modifications for the seeding project? Are they all going according to plan?"

"They'll be ready before the fertilisation stage is completed", Sandra replied.

"Excellent. I don't know what I'd do without you, Sandra", Gideon commended.

Gideon was pleased with her work. Sandra Danker was the best spacecraft engineer and designer in the entire solar system. Sandra was also a beautiful sight to behold as well and Gideon had noticed.

"I'm sure the human race could survive without me, but it's good to know that my work is appreciated", Sandra replied.

"Sandra, it certainly is, believe me, you are the best we have and you know it", finished Gideon.

Sandra and Gideon both looked at each other for a long moment, there was so much more to be said, yet neither of them could say it. They were both professionals and work colleagues and what was in their hearts remained in their hearts. Their true feelings remained unspoken.

Gideon returned to his office, the spray craft would be continually flying through the new Martian atmosphere. Reloading before each new run, they were fully reusable craft. After the fertilisation of Mars was completed, the spray craft would be retrofitted for the next stage, the seeding of life. The designs for the modifications to the spray craft, were in Sandra Danker's extremely capable hands.

7. The Seeding of Life.

After Mars had been fertilised with the *chicken soup*, the spray craft were then cleaned out and retrofitted for the next phase. Now, they were to deliver the seeds of life to Mars. The spray craft were to be refitted in two different ways, some of the vehicles were to deliver life to the oceans, some to deliver life to the lands.

The spray craft were all assembled together in Mars Sun Lagrangian point one. As the crew of each craft left the vehicle in small shuttles, a large swarm of small pre-programmed maintenance robots moved in. Within minutes they attacked the spray craft, each meticulously performing their particular duties in the modification process. Within hours each of the spray craft would be completely modified as per Sandra Danker's new blue prints. Everything was working without a single hitch or problem.

In the first instance the spray craft were modified so that they could carry and deliver a concentrated solution of micro-organisms to the Martian seas and oceans. In the second instance the spray craft were modified to deliver various seeds to the vast areas of the barren Martian lands.

While these spray craft were being modified to perform these two functions, their chief designer, Sandra Danker was working on the designs and plans for the next set of modifications. The step following the seeding, would require changes to the spray craft, turning them into vehicles capable of carrying and delivering larger organisms. They would each and everyone of them, become like little arks. A short time before adding the finishing touches, the seeding began.

Sandra and Gideon watched the beginning of the first stage of the seeding operation, which involved two steps. The modified spray craft were being loaded, this time with living cargoes of the genetically enhanced life from Earth. Living seeds were genetically altered to increase the rate of growth and fecundity and also modified to suit each of their designated Martian biomes.

For the rivers, seas and oceans, the cargo would be living micro-organisms, also genetically enhanced in a similar fashion as to the seeds. The rapid growth and the rapid procreation would only last until they had become completely established in their environments, then they would revert to normal. Other genetic changes that would allow them to survive in their new environments more efficiently, however, were more permanent and would allow them to adapt to any changes very quickly.

The spray craft entered the Martian atmosphere on their well planned courses. To the Northern Ocean around the polar regions just outside of the ice pack, a concentrated solution containing antarctic planktons, krill and many kinds of algae were released from around three hundred feet above the water level. The same kind of micro-organisms were also released in the entire Southern Ocean, which was largely polar in nature.

In the Hellas Ocean, the Argyre Sea, as well as the regions of the Northern Ocean between sixty degrees north latitude and the coastline, a different mixture of micro-organisms was delivered. The concentrated solution in these cases contained a variety of planktons, diatoms, algae and the larvae of small life forms such as sea slugs and sunbursts, amongst many others. They were also delivered from the same altitude as the first mixture. A simpler mixture was also delivered into the various smaller seas, larger lakes and rivers.

On the land, the seeding was simpler. In the desert regions of the planet, wild desert grasses and flower seeds were distributed. In the mountain regions, mountain grasses and flower seeds were distributed. All around the smaller Southern Ocean, arctic grasses and seeds of arctic flowers and Siberian tundra seeds were spread everywhere.

Grasses such as wild wheat, alfalfa and savannas were spread all over the hills and plains of Mars. Various wildflowers were also scattered over these regions. In the more swampy, watery areas, grasses from the Everglades and bulrushes of various kinds, even wild rice and sugar canes were distributed. Finally the whole surface of Mars was littered with grass and flower seeds of all possible kinds. Yet the task of seeding, still wasn't finished. The new biosphere of the planet Mars would also need forests of various trees, the seas and oceans also needed larger life forms.

The *chicken soup* had fertilised the lands and waters of Mars, but also various kinds of bacteria had been introduced along with it. These bacteria were the kinds that made the existence of life possible, like nitrogen fixing bacteria etc. This had laid down a good foundation for the many different kinds of grass and flower seeds.

Before the seeding was even completed, the first grass and flower seeds had already germinated. Grasses and flowers of various kinds were starting to sprout everywhere across Mars. The seas, oceans, lakes and rivers of Mars were also teaming with various kinds of microbial and small forms of life.

Now the next step was at hand. This time the spray craft were to deliver other seeds to the lands and waters of Mars. To the Northern and Southern Oceans, various large forms of seaweeds and kelp were introduced. To the Hellas Ocean, the Argyre Sea and the smaller seas, a variety of smaller seaweeds and such were introduced. To all the Martian lakes, both large and small, a large variety of freshwater weeds and plants were introduced. These were all genetically altered to be able to survive in fresh or salt water and to be able to adapt swiftly as the conditions changed.

These all soon flourished in their new environments and soon there after, the spores and eggs of a great many species of small fish and other aquatic life forms had been added to their respective waters of Mars. This was soon followed on the land with Stingless Bees being introduced to help pollinate the developing flowering plants.

While this was all happening, on the lands various other seeds were also being introduced. The seeds of various kinds of trees were being introduced. In the southern regions around the Southern Ocean, various types of Siberian pine seeds were scattered. In the region of the Tharsis Bulge, a genetically modified variety of sequoia were seeded everywhere. In the high mountain regions of the southern hemisphere, many different kinds of mountain pines, elms, oaks and birch seeds were scattered all over the place. Each and every seed was genetically modified to give them the maximum chance of survival.

In the vast rolling hills and plains of Mars, however, there were scattered a special variety of seeds, in order to see which one would take hold the best. These were seeds which had been produced from Australian eucalypti. They had been genetically altered to enhance their growth and survival. There were red gums, ghost gums, white gums, ironbarks and a variety of others and their seeds were scattered everywhere in the hills and plains.

In the smaller mountains of the southern hemisphere, which weren't prone to snow cover, the giant Karri gum had been seeded. On and all around the volcanic mountains in the Elysium Plains, snow gums were seeded along with a variety of other trees. In all of the regions where the eucalypti were seeded, various types of fern spores were introduced.

In the swampier regions of Mars like the Kasei Valles and Ladon Basin, trees such as various kinds of Willows, Cypress, Maples, Birch, Swamp Oaks and Sycamores were being seeded.

The whole of Mars was being seeded with life, however, it wasn't quite finished. In specific locations, stands of English Oaks were also seeded. In other locations Willows, in others English Firs and yet in other locations were seeded Norfolk Island Pines and some multitudinous varieties of flax plants. Then other tree seeds were scattered among the eucalypti, these were citrus and stone fruits of a great many different varieties.

On the whole, it would take many, many years at least, for all these trees to grow to their full heights, however, many had already started to germinate and very soon the beginnings of forests would be evident. Some of these trees would die off, that was expected and some of them would flourish. Assuming the terraformers had gotten their mix of seeds correct, the future forests of Mars would gradually fill every biome and niche that suited them.

Gideon had watched the seeding operations with great joy. Now the lands of Mars had many grasses and flowers growing everywhere. It hadn't taken long for them to grow and develop. Seedlings had emerged and would soon become saplings. In a few years, small forests would be everywhere.

Especially where the faster-growing eucalypti were seeded, other forests would take a little longer. One thing was certain, however, within Gideon's lifetime he would see trees growing hundreds of feet tall. This was made possible by the low Martian gravity of point three eight gs.

What had been done so far was good. Then there were the oceans, the seas and the lakes. Now they were all teaming with life, from microbes to plankton and algae, to sea and water weeds and even small fish and other life forms. The terraforming plan was working extremely well and Gideon wanted to see the developing biosphere from as close to ground level as he could get. That of course would require a field trip, to fly low over the Martian landscape.

Gideon appropriated a landing vehicle and then asked Sandra Danker to accompany him. The final designs for the conversion of the spray craft, into craft capable of transplanting larger life forms were now being completed. Sandra also wanted to see the Martian world blooming from up close for herself. Sandra was quick to accept the invitation and looked forward to flying low over the Martian landscape to see how the seeds had been sprouting. To see the results of their hard work up close. It actually sounded like fun.

"Gideon, it's working beautifully isn't it!", she exclaimed excitedly.

"It sure is. Can you imagine what it will be like in ten years or even twenty years?", he questioned.

"I have got some idea, but that's just about it", Sandra replied, "Can you imagine this place a century from now?"

Gideon had an excellent idea of what the Martian biosphere would look like. He knew how fast the trees would grow, as he had read all of the reports from his team of geneticists. They were all genetically modified, so that they'd grow at accelerated rates for at least the first century. Then the rate of growth would begin to slow down over the half next century to more normal growth rates. Gideon explained to Sandra what the new Martian world would be like.

"Sandra, there will be forests everywhere. They won't be fully grown, but they will be forests. Around the Southern Ocean, there'll be a large belt of Arctic and Siberian pines. In the tall mountains in the south, there be forests of mountain pines and many other trees."

"In the hills and plains, there will be vast Eucalyptus forests, with ferns and plenty of other trees, such as Citrus and Stone fruits, even English Oaks scattered amongst them. The Tharsis Bulge and the mountains of the Elysium sub-continent will be forested with Eucalyptus trees, there'll even be Snow Gums on the higher peaks."

"There will be open grasslands and savanna lands. In the Tharsis

Mountains, Sequoias will be growing, they won't be very tall in ten years, but one day they will be immense. On the Earth, they can grow to three hundred feet tall. Here, with thirty eight percent gravity, they will be up to eight hundred feet tall, maybe even taller. The same with the Karri gums, they'll be nearly the same height."

After a short pause Gideon continued, "In ten year's time, the next transplants will take place. Insects that are harmless to crops will be let free in the forests and fields. Once they're established, birds will released to feed on them. Honey eaters and nectar-eating birds will also be released, as well as insect and leaf-eating tree mammals, marsupials and reptiles."

"No amphibians?", Sandra quickly interrupted, "You know, frogs and salamanders?"

"That will be up to our biologists Sandra", Gideon replied, "but I'm sure there will be."

Gideon continued, "I very much doubt that cattle will be brought here though. They're too big and inefficient. However, there will be sheep, goats, small deer, domesticated kangaroos and wallabies and possibly even rabbits and pigs. We could even import some small wild cats to be carnivores in the forests one day."

"In the oceans, seas, lakes and rivers, larger fish will then be released. To feed off the weeds growing in them, we might even import manatees and dugongs. They produce meat as well."

"To feed off the fish in the oceans and seas, we'll probably import porpoises and dolphins. We will communicate with them via the new translators, maybe even hand-pick them as we do with our colonists. Imagine that! We'll bring chimpanzees and other apes here as our mascots, just as colonists do when they go to the outer colonial regions. This world will be made as much like the Earth as it can be. Except there won't be any of the more destructive life forms, except for us humans of course. Once fully transformed, Mars will be an incredible place."

"I've never been to the Earth Gideon", Sandra stated, "I can't imagine all of those sights."

"I haven't been to the Earth either Sandra. Eros was great, I must admit that, but it still has that cylindrical horizon like any other O'Neil-style colony", Gideon replied, adding, "but we'll be on Mars soon enough. We may even see the fruits of our labour within our lifetimes."

"Wouldn't that be wonderful!", Sandra replied excitedly, remarking, "The colonies of Cis-Lunar space are great and all, but they're not planets."

"You know, Sandra. I may have actually underestimated the stabilisation time for the new Martian atmosphere. We could possibly open up Mars for colonisation in under a century and start actual colonies down there. It really all depends on how quickly the exotic compounds and other volatile gasses are flushed out of the atmosphere."

"That soon! That would be incredible", Sandra replied.

"I expect we will have people working down there in less than ten years, in science and research stations. They will need to use re-breathers when outside of the actual stations, but they will be able to continue the project on the Martian surface. They'll be developing and tweaking the planet's new biosphere. At some point our engineers will start building colony structures well in advance of colonisation. We won't let the colonists land, however, until everything is ready for them."

Sandra remarked, "Well then Gideon. We'd better get a move on then if we're going to get our sneak preview of Mars's new biosphere."

"Your right you know, let's get to the lander and get going", Gideon replied.

"Gideon, as I said, I've never been to the surface of any planet. It kind of sounds scary!"

"Don't worry, girl, the closest I've been to the surface of any planet, is the inside of the asteroid Eros and it was just brilliant. It was absolutely breathtaking!", Gideon replied.

"Do you know, what the most interesting thing about this entire seeding process is Gideon", Sandra enquired.

"No, Sandra. I don't know", Gideon admitted, then asked, "What do you think the most interesting thing about this entire seeding process is?"

Sandra snickered and replied with a small laugh, "It is kind of like we're just tossing stuff everywhere and just waiting to see what sticks."

Gideon thought about that for a long moment and then he agreed, "You are absolutely right, Sandra. For all of the work that our biologists, geneticists and environmentalists are performing, in the end we are doing just that. We are literally tossing stuff everywhere and we are waiting to see what flourishes and what doesn't. Basically what sticks."

8. Martians.

Gideon and Sandra boarded the landing craft, waiting inside was their pilot.

"Welcome aboard, Doctor Reas, Ms Danker. I'll be your tour guide for this little joy ride. My name is, Carl Trigg", the pilot informed them.

"Tour guide. I thought you were Colonel Bannon's personal pilot?"

"That I am, Doctor Reas, but as I've taken the Colonel to the surface of the planet so many times, that I feel like a damned tour guide", Carl replied.

"Well then, let's go for our tour, Carl. I'd like to fly past Olympus Mons, then across the Tharsis Mounts and follow the Marineris Valley all the way to the coast of the Chryse Sea. From there over to the Isidis Gulf and finally to the Elysium sub-continent."

"The grand tour hey. Elysium! I'll take you low over those monoliths, we'll get a real good look."

"That's the idea, Carl. We'd like to land as close to those monoliths as the law will allow so that we can get a look at them from ground level", Gideon replied.

"Up close and personal hey, Doctor Reas. I can drop us down just outside of the perimeter", Carl replied.

Gideon and Sandra strapped into their seats and Carl launched the craft. There was a slight burst of acceleration then the craft coasted. Carl swung the lander around and Mars appeared on the screen. The red planet was no longer red. Mars was now a precious blue orb, not unlike the Earth, but a lot smaller and with far more cloud cover. Red patches of desert could still be discerned below that cloud cover.

Carl brought the lander closer towards the planet and then angled towards Olympus Mons. The volcano was massive, with a height of over seventy two thousand feet and a diameter of three hundred and seventy five miles. The peak of Olympus Mons and its complex caldera stood more than twenty thousand feet above the major cloud layers.

Around the lower fifty thousand feet of Olympus Mons, there were thick layers of white clouds. The flanks of the volcano were covered in thick ice and snow. On the top of the volcano, in the largest of its calderas, a small base could be seen. It was an atmospheric research station. Which was kind of ironic, as the research station was so high up on Olympus Mons and the Martian air was so thin at that altitude, that it was almost in vacuum, almost in space. Carl brought his lander about again, flying around the caldera for a good view, before changing course and cruising to the west and then to the south of the volcano.

When directly south of Olympus Mons, Carl's lander hovered for a moment, before dropping beneath the cloud layers. The visibility was extremely poor and the giant volcano Olympus Mons could not be seen, even though it was exceedingly close. Carl watched his radar carefully as he approached the volcano. At a mere one hundred meters the enormous volcano, Olympus Mons, became visible once more. Using his radar, Carl followed the slopes of Olympus Mons lower into the cloud layers.

"Sweet Jesus, it must be cold out there!", Carl exclaimed softly.

"You are not wrong, Carl", replied Sandra.

Gideon was studying the view screen very closely.

The sides of the volcano were covered with thick ice. This ice layer extended down to about thirty five thousand feet, where it became packed with snow. The slopes of Olympus Mons appeared to be the same all the way down. The cloud cover broke at around ten thousand feet and as the visibility was much better. Carl swung the lander further out for a better view. As they approached the five thousand foot level, the escarpment of Olympus Mons came into view. It was an awesome sight.

Vast quantities of water spilled through narrow gaps in the edge of the escarpment. Ice and snow was being washed over the edge of the escarpment as well. There were literally thousands of waterfalls. In some areas glaciers approached the edge of the escarpment and rivers of water poured out from beneath them, flowing swiftly to the precipice. A few glaciers reached the edge of the escarpment and a couple of them even hung precariously over it.

Gideon and Sandra had watched in awe, as one of the glaciers calved an immense iceberg. It broke loose from its parent glacier with a terrifying cracking sound, that was picked up by the lander's scanners and relayed to the speakers inside. The iceberg then plummeted to the base of Olympus Mons, five thousand feet below. The occupants of the lander did not hear the iceberg explode on the rocks far below, as the sound of the falling water, ice and snow was deafening. By far, these were the tallest, largest and most complex system of waterfalls in the entire solar system.

The Falls of Olympus Mons.

"I've seen photo images of this, but this, this is truly awesome!", Sandra exclaimed.

"I know what you mean, Sandra, but imagine, in maybe a hundred million years, much of Olympus Mons will have been washed away by all of that force. Flowing water is a powerful thing and that is a hell of a lot of flowing water", Gideon replied.

Carl looked at Gideon and stated, "You're probably right, Doctor Reas, but if anyone is still alive by then, they probably wouldn't remember it ever being here in the first place. So they won't miss it anyway."

Carl then flew his lander further to the south east, towards the Tharsis Bulge region. Soon they were flying over the Tharsis Bulge and between the

Tharsis Monts. These three mountains were shield volcanoes, Ascraeus Mons, Pavonis Mons and Arsia Mons. All three of these volcanoes were incredibly similar to Olympus Mons in every possible way, only somewhat smaller.

Smaller, but not by much. The tallest of the three, Ascraeus Mons being fifty nine thousand feet high and the smallest being Arsia Mons at thirty thousand feet in height. Pavonis Mons being in the middle in terms of height, at forty six thousand feet tall. Any one of these three shield volcanoes could easily be mistaken for Olympus Mons. The taller of the three, Ascraeus Mons was also like Olympus Mons, in that its caldera was also above most of the new Martian atmosphere. Olympus Mon and the three shield volcanoes on the Tharsis Bulge would easily tower over Mount Everest on the Earth. Although   Pavonis Mons, not by that much. For the future Martian colonists, the entire Tharsis region would be a navigational and flight hazard. More than likely, those future Martian colonists would choose to fly around the entire Tharsis region and not fly through it.

As they continued flying over the Tharsis region, dozens of high mountain lakes could be seen. As with Olympus Mons, the three shield volcanoes delivered vast quantities of water to the Tharsis Plateau. Many fast flowing rivers with waterfalls and cascading rapids fed into the many lakes. The outflows of which, created many rivers flowing to the east and to the south. As with Olympus Mons, given enough time, these powerful fast flowing rivers would erode the three shield volcanoes and the surrounding Tharsis plateau significantly.

Then they flew over the chaotic region known as Noctis Labyrinthus, with its labyrinth of many canyons and chasms, at the base of which were fast flowing rivers with longs stretches of white water. East of Noctis Labyrinthus, all of these rivers joined together and finally flowed into the vast Marineris Valley. The entire Noctis Labyrinthus region provided the major inflow of water into the Marineris Valley. Carl flew their lander eastward, following the course of what had become the Marineris Sea.

Many rivers flowed into the Marineris Sea, making it one immense and extremely deep, fast flowing river with a powerful current. The Marineris Valley was longer than the Mediterranean Sea on the Earth by two hundred kilometres, but with more than four and half times its depth.

Their lander's instruments told them, that the Marineris Valley was around twenty three thousand feet deep. Currently, the water depth of the Marineris Sea that had formed within it, was around eighteen thousand feet deep and as the Northern Ocean basin was continuing to fill, so would the Marineris Valley. The final depth of the Northern Ocean had been modelled and was expected to reach around six thousand five hundred feet in depth, so the Marineris Sea would eventually fill to its maximum depth of twenty three thousand feet.

The Marineris Sea was now like an immense, narrow sea nearly four thousand kilometres long, but it was flowing with an unusually swift current. The Marineris Sea was fed by the enormous volumes of water cascading off of the Tharsis Monts and Tharsis Bulge. All of this water flowed into the newly formed Chryce Sea, which itself was a branch of the Northern Ocean. As a result, the Northern Ocean basin was quickly filling, far quicker than had been anticipated.

As they flew much further to the east, the Marineris Sea began to turn northeast into a region known as Aurorae Chaos. Here the Marineris Sea became like a huge broad delta, its waters still flowing with a good current. Carl flew their lander further to the east and then turned to the north, following the flow of water in the sea below them. Was this really a sea or was it the greatest river in the solar system by volume, it was really difficult to tell.

At this point the Marineris Sea broke up into many large channels as it flowed through the valley towards the Chryse Sea. The coast of the Chryce Sea was now clearly visible. The Marineris Sea flowed into it at a great many points. The Chryse Sea appeared like a broad gulf leading to the Northern Ocean. The immense current of the Marineris Sea effected the entire expanse of the Chryse Sea and even extended deep into the Northern Ocean. Carl turned their lander towards the east.

After passing by the Chryce Sea and the lands to the east of it, they could now see the Isidis Gulf. The Isidis Gulf was like a large, almost circular gulf in the land that adjoined the Utopia Planitia Basin, now the Utopia Sea, yet another branch of the Northern Ocean. The Isidis Gulf itself was an immense flooded crater. To the north of it was a broad strait that led to the Utopia Sea and the Northern Ocean.

To the southeast of the Isidis Gulf was the Elysium Straits. These broad straits separated the Elysium sub-continent from the coastlines of Nepenthes Mensae and Aeolis Mensae to the south of Elysium and connected to the Amazonis Sea much further to the east. Elysium, a separate sub-continent by virtue of the fact that it was now separated from the rest of the Martian lands, by ten degrees of latitude of water, the Elysium Straits.

Their destination was to the southeast of the Elysium region, so their pilot Carl swung his lander lower and then to the east. They quickly crossed the straits to the Elysium sub-continent and after flying over the sub-continent, their lander reached the relevant longitude, one ninety eight degrees east. Carl turned their lander to the south. It was not long before they were approaching the area of the Martian monoliths. The monoliths themselves were only a relatively short distance across from the new southern Elysium coastline.

"The pyramids and the other monoliths are just south across the Amazonis Sea from the Elysium sub-continent", Carl advised them both,

"They're not actually in the Elysium sub-continent itself. When we get to seven degrees north latitude, we'll be right close to them."

"Good to know, Carl", Gideon replied, adding almost jokingly, "Navigating on a planet is not something that I'm used to. So no one had better ask me for any directions."

"It's kind of hard to tell how close we can get to the monoliths, now that everything's changed down there, but I will try to keep our distance legal", Carl stated as he looked around at Gideon and Sandra, then winked.

Gideon and Sandra just smiled back at him, knowing full well that he was going to break the law and that his statement was purely for the onboard flight recorders. They both kind of liked the idea. Their lander flew lower and soon four regular tetrahedral-shaped pyramids came into view. As their lander approached, Gideon estimated their bases to be about three kilometres on a side. There were other polygonal structures in the area and they appeared to be up to six kilometres across.

"Pareidolia?", thought Gideon to himself, *"or are these real? They certainly look real."*

Gideon informed Sandra, "You know that in the late twentieth century, a well known architect once said, that cities would be much more efficient, if based on large pyramidal designs."

"Maybe he got his theory from these pyramids?", inquired Sandra.

"Those pyramids were discovered long after he published his theories, Sandra", Gideon replied adding, "Those structures, if they're real, could support thousands, possibly even millions of beings."

Sandra then joked, "I wonder if they'll come out to play, Gideon."

To which Gideon replied, "Please be serious, Sandra. Did you know that in the twenty-first century, they had the first hint that the Martians were still alive?"

"Gideon, now you're the one who's joking", Sandra responded.

"No, I'm not Sandra. They once photographed a collapsed or incomplete pyramid in the late twentieth century. Then some fifty or sixty years later, they photographed it again. This time it was intact, whole, completed", Gideon stated.

"That's incredible. Why didn't they investigate it?", enquired Sandra.

"They didn't actually know. The two pictures were never compared. At least, not until I dug them up out of the archives anyway", Gideon explained.

"So you did the comparison?", Sandra enquired.

"Yep. I'll show you the photos when we get back", Gideon answered.

Flying around the region, many hundreds of smaller structures were below them. Further to the east, a pyramid on the rim of a crater could be seen.

"Doctor Reas. I think you'd better take a look at this?", advised Carl.

"Why? What is it, Carl?", enquired Gideon.

As Carl flew their lander lower for a closer look, they saw it.

"People, Gideon, there's actually people down there!", exclaimed Sandra.

"Yes, I see them, Sandra. They appear to be working around those structures", Gideon Replied.

As they flew over the structures Carl automatically banked, to come back around for a second look.

"Doc, there's hundreds of them! Literally hundreds of them!", Carl exclaimed.

"I know. I can see them, Carl", Gideon replied, adding and asking, "They look humanoid! Are these the Martians?"

"Gideon, we should be recording all of this", stated Sandra.

Carl interjected, "We are already, Ms Danker. It's the first thing I did when we approached the monoliths. It's standard procedure. Every flight over these monoliths and the other structures, is a surveillance flight, including this little joy ride."

"Colonel Bannon would love to see this. Martians in their hundreds!",
Gideon exclaimed.

On their second approach they flew much, much lower. The Martian
monoliths were directly in front of them. There was a sudden flash of light
and an small explosion, their lander shuddered for long moments. A second
flash of light and again, another explosion, their lander shook violently. The
emergency lights started to flash red and the computer gave warning.

*"Computer reporting. The main thrusters are inoperative. The main stabilisers are
inoperative. Altitude cannot be maintained. Crash imminent."*

*"Computer reporting. The main thrusters are inoperative. The main stabilisers are
inoperative. Altitude cannot be maintained. Crash imminent."*

Carl flicked a switch, turning off the computer's warning, "Well, I don't
really need that!"

Then to his passengers, Carl reported, "Doctor Reas, Ms Danker. Belts on,
we are going to crash!"

"Crashing is not on my schedule, Carl", Gideon noted.

"It wasn't on mine either, Doctor Reas, but he we are aren't we?", Carl
replied.

Sandra enquired, "Isn't there anything you can do, Carl?"

"Not really. I'm kind of a glider pilot now, but I might just be able to land
this bitch", replied Carl.

Gideon held Sandra's hand to comfort her, "Don't worry Sandra, he's the
Colonel's personal pilot. That means Carl is the best."

Carl manoeuvred their stricken lander back out over the Elysium Straits,
then he swung her south once more, back towards the coastline. The lander
glided closely above the water. Carl pulled her nose up as she hit the water,

their lander skipped, then came down again. She skipped a second time, then a third. After the third skip their lander hit the coastal beach, covered in Martian regolith. Their lander skidded along the ground and then flipped over, rolling four times, before finally settling on her side. Eventually, the lander came to rest and amazingly she was still in one piece. The three occupants were all unconscious.

Gideon gained consciousness first, immediately he checked Sandra and she awoke to his touch. Gideon asked her to remain still and she did so. Gideon then checked her over, making sure that she was not injured, before releasing her seat belt clasp. Carl had been thrown from his crash couch and was laying against the ship's inner hull. Having told Gideon and Sandra to belt up, he himself, had not. Gideon rolled his eyes and shook his head in disbelief.

Carl had received a head injury and was unconscious. Gideon checked Carl over, to make sure he was otherwise okay. Then he double-checked Sandra, she was alright and he allowed her to get up. Together, they both carefully carried Carl back to his pilot's couch. Upon locating the ship's emergency medical kit, Gideon bandaged the deep gash on Carl's forehead. Gideon then checked the lander itself and seeing that there was no danger of an explosion, he decided to leave Carl on his pilot's couch. Gideon then set the emergency beacon, before he and Sandra prepared to go outside.

Gideon and Sandra then left the crashed and stricken ship to have a look around at the new Martian environment. The new Martian air was thick, but also heavily oxygenated. It was also excessively humid, containing copious amounts of water vapour. The overly moist air left them both feeling wet and clammy. Many of the new Martian atmosphere's volatile gases and toxic compounds had yet to be washed out. The new Martian atmosphere also had a terrible smell and a positively vial taste to it.

Sandra almost retched and exclaimed, "Well, Gideon, you wanted to see Mars close up!"

Gideon replied, "This isn't quite what I had in mind, Sandra! Oh my god, this air tastes disgusting!"

Sandra replied with a very sour look upon her face, "Quite stanky in fact don't you think?", then she asked, "Is it meant to smell and taste this bad?"

"This is still the early days, Sandra. There are still a lot of exotic compounds and gases in the air", Gideon explained, adding, "Give it a few more decades and most of those compounds will have been flushed out by the cyclonic storms. The atmosphere is still evolving and eventually, it will smell and taste a hell of a lot better."

"These exotic compounds you're talking about, just exactly how toxic are they?", Sandra enquired.

"Only mildly toxic at these levels. It's all about exposure. We should be good for a couple of hours or so, but really, we should be using re-breathers just to be on the safe side", Gideon answered.

"Well, that is good to know, Gideon", an only slightly relieved Sandra replied, thinking to herself, *Where are those damned re-breathers?*

There was a low rumbling sound far off in the distance.

Gideon pointed towards the Martian horizon, "We'd better take shelter, that storm looks cyclonic and it appears to be heading this way."

"Perhaps we'd be better off sheltering in the ship", Sandra suggested.

"Yes, agreed. We'll probably find those re-breathers I mentioned in the ship as well", Gideon replied.

"Excellent. Well, at least we can see that the seeding has gone well", Sandra remarked.

"It certainly looks that way, doesn't it, Sandra", Gideon replied.

As far as the eye could see, everywhere grasses and flowers were slowly pushing up from what was once barren Martian regolith. As they looked closer, they noticed eucalyptus seedlings also popping up amongst the fields.

"In a few decades or so from now, there'll be a vast forest growing here", he told Sandra.

9. Alien Birds.

Sandra enquired, "Gideon, there haven't been any birds brought here yet, have there?"

Gideon replied, "Heavens no. That's a hell of a long way off, decades away. Why do you ask?"

Sandra began to look very pale, "Gideon, Gideon look, over there!"

Six figures approached, flying about fifty feet above the ground. They were big, almost humanoid in appearance and when they finally landed, they were only about fifty feet away.

"Martians?", Sandra enquired of Gideon.

"If they are, they aren't the ones that we saw as we flew over the monoliths", Gideon replied, adding, "I have seen drawings of these kinds of beings and read descriptions of them, but that was in mythological and religious books. The stuff of ancient legends."

"That's what worries me Gideon", Sandra replied.

The creatures watched Gideon and Sandra curiously, while Gideon and Sandra did the same. For long moments neither side made a move. Unknown to either group, the pilot Carl had woken up. Carl was delirious and too weak to move, but he could see the scene outside through the lander's viewport. He watched in silent fear.

The creatures were seven to seven and a half feet tall. They had short stocky legs that were slightly bowed. Their arms were long and gangly, reaching below their knees. Their bodies were long and also reasonably solid, thick and barrel-chested. From out of their backs protruded a set of great leathery, blackish-brown wings, tinged red along their outer edges.

Whilst at rest they were folded together and held tightly against their backs. They were covered with thick, coarse brown hair and wore uniforms that looked like shorts and tee shirts. A weapon of some kind was strapped to their bodies. All six began to laugh maniacally as Sandra's and Gideon's fears began to grow.

The design of these creatures bodies were frightening enough, but their faces were much more hideous. Not to mention, the fact that behind them was an extension of their wings and vertebrae. This extension formed what appeared to be a prehensile tail about five feet long, at the end of which was a pointed, spade like manipulative tip.

Their faces though were truly hideous, they had narrow pointed chins and long pointed noses and they had extremely high, protruding cheeks. Their eyes loomed dark within deep, wide sockets, above which were thick brow ridges. Their skin was pulled tightly back over their facial features. Their hair was thick, shaggy and coarse. From out of their foreheads protruded two short curved horns. Even worse was their teeth. Their canine teeth, both top and bottom, were long and pointed and they were stained a gruesome red.

Gideon looked at them, thinking they looked like a cross between a gorilla and a gargoyle. An angry gorilla and an angry gargoyle at that, with a distinctly demonic aspect to them.

The creatures seemed to almost knuckle walk like apes. Without any warning one leapt into the air, its great wings unfolded. In a split second, it had covered the distance between them and grabbed Sandra by the arm. Its grip was so strong that Sandra couldn't shake it. Gideon's reaction was pure instinct, in Mars's weak point three eight gs of gravity, he leapt at the creature, feet first.

With a great deal of force, his right foot struck hard into the creatures chest. There was a sharp sound like the cracking of rib bones and the creature shrieked loudly. Its grip was released and it fell to the ground in screaming agony. It was then that Gideon realised, that being accustomed to a much higher gravity would become an advantage. Gideon grabbed Sandra by the arm and they both turned and ran quickly towards the lander.

They were too late, two of the creatures had leapt to the lander ahead of them, blocking their path. There was a sudden flash of brilliant light and the ground in front of them erupted with a shimmering heat and turned molten. Gideon and Sandra both jumped sideways, falling to the ground. The remaining three creatures had drawn their weapons as well. Gideon and Sandra had only one recourse and that was surrender.

Within minutes they were in manacles. The creatures then picked them up and carried them off, leaping into the air and they were soon flying. Their great wings worked furiously to keep them in flight with their human captives. One of the creatures had also picked up its injured comrade and was flying along with them, although trailing somewhat behind them.

After a short while they approached the four main Elysium pyramids and upon landing, Gideon and Sandra were dropped unceremoniously to the ground. They were led to the nearest pyramid and entered through what appeared to be a large airlock of sorts. Once inside the pyramid, they found the air to be much better than it was outside in the new Martian atmosphere. The air smelt clean and it was pleasant to taste, it was obviously scrubbed and processed.

They passed through a one hundred meter thick wall, which contained all of the pyramids support structures and living quarters. Beyond this wall they were astounded, the pyramid was hollow and at its apex was a brilliant light which illuminated the entire region inside. The interior was extremely well-lit.

There was a huge hydroponics farm. Everywhere crops were growing and it seemed that Gideon's previous observation was correct. The creatures that had caught them were definitely not the builders of this civilisation. They must have come much later and they, somehow were now the rulers. They had enslaved the true Martians, but from where had they come from?

The Martians themselves were a totally different type of being and they were so close to being human that it was incredible. The similarities between the faces of this race and the face of Mars in the Cydonia region showed that they were its builders. These people were almost Gideon's height of six feet, perhaps an inch or two shorter.

They were much slimmer than Earth people though, but this might have been due to the lower Martian gravity or perhaps they were indeed Slaves and were only supplied minimal food rations. The Martians wore simple clothing, in fact, not much more than loincloths. The air inside the pyramid was warm and slightly humid, so perhaps they didn't need much more. Although for work outside the pyramids, they appeared to have well-designed pressure suits.

"These would have been used before the terraforming had begun", Gideon thought to himself.

Their skin was of a delightful golden hue, to which a colony tan could never compare. Their hair both male and female was long, braided and had almost a golden yellow colour. Two types of eye colour appeared to be predominant, a creamy purple and a bright emerald green. Their eyes were almost, but not quite almond shaped.

The faces of the Martians were gentle and quite attractive to look upon, with an air of authority to them that displayed an underlying strength. Their females were very beautiful and slim, but nicely curved. Their breasts, however, were large and full, giving the appearance of firmness. Gideon, being a man, of course, had noticed.

There was something else Gideon noticed about the Martians. They had hands, that had four fingers and a thumb, just like human hands. The other creatures that had captured them, however, had three sets of paired, clawed fingers on each hand, no thumbs at all. The aliens had three pairs of opposable fingers. Most surprising of all, the Martians it appeared, were telepathic.

Sandra had noticed it as well, their minds were being probed and spoken to, by every Martian that had noticed them. So many minds in fact that both Sandra and Gideon became almost giddy with the intrusion of their thoughts. The creatures that had captured them had also noticed that the Martians were communicating with them. They could not pick up the Martian's thoughts, but the expressions on Gideon's and Sandra's faces easily gave them away. The creatures quickly flogged the Martians harshly to disperse them. Yes indeed, the Martians were Slaves.

The language of these aliens was a kind of fast guttural dialogue, full of clicks, barks and grunts, that no human could possibly master. Translators would definitely be necessary. The Martians on the other hand didn't speak at all or at least that appeared to be the case. The Martians appeared to be completely nonverbal telepaths.

Gideon and Sandra were taken to a detention cell, where they waited there for quite some time. Sandra was silent and very frightened, almost in a state of shock, so Gideon comforted her. Eventually, an alien of high rank entered their cell.

Being taller than the other aliens, this one had to stoop to enter the cell.

"Perhaps height was a factor in status amongst the aliens?", Gideon thought to himself.

The alien stood and stared at them for a while, then he spoke to them in broken English, "You! Why do you come here?", in a very guttural voice.

"We didn't intend to come here, we were checking the progress of the terraforming", Gideon replied.

"The terraforming? Ah yes. We must thank your people for that. For bringing life to our dead world, after we subjugate them of course", the alien replied in its guttural voice.

"Subjugate us, just how do you expect to do that?", enquired Gideon.

"Our Slaves have great intelligence. They provide advanced technology for us. Much greater than any technology that your people have and far greater than that which we, ourselves can make."

"If that's so, then how did you make them your Slaves?", Gideon asked.

"Ha! We thought that they would fight us. So to defeat them, we destroyed their planet's biosphere. It turned out to be a complete waste of time and effort. They are unable to kill, even to defend themselves. They are weaklings!", the alien explained.

"That maybe so, but our people will fight you and we will not be easily beaten", Gideon replied defiantly.

"Your people have outlawed war. We will defeat them and drink their blood as well", the alien replied.

Sandra heard this comment and the alien saw her fear.

"That is right. We tax them regularly in blood for our nourishment", stated the alien, adding, "Normally we would use the blood of lesser animals, as we do at our main abode, but here the blood of our Slaves, an intelligent species is quite delicious. In exchange for this, we let them live."

The alien turned and left the cell, again stooping as he passed through the doorway. Sandra felt sick to her stomach and Gideon was quick to comfort her once again.

After a short while a Martian woman was pushed roughly into the detention cell. The woman was tall, nearly five foot ten, with an extremely slim build and golden-tanned skin like the others of her kind. Her long braided hair was a striking golden yellow and her eyes were an extraordinary shade of emerald green. Clad in nothing but a loincloth and with an ample bosom, she was a sight to behold.

The Martian woman was carrying a tray of unusual fruits and vegetables. It seemed that feeding time had come around. Without speaking a single word, she approached them both and then informed them telepathically that her name was Winchilly.

Winchilly placed the tray on a low bench and then explained to them which foods they would enjoy the most. The aliens did not come back for her. Winchilly explained that they had chosen to leave her in the cell with them, to facilitate communication and instruct them on how to behave. As captives, they were now both Slaves. Winchilly then began to explain the full situation to Gideon and Sandra.

This story started long ago in the very distant past. When the aliens had attacked, it was by surprise and unprovoked. The planet's biosphere had been badly damaged by massive asteroidal bombardment. The war had been very quick and brutal. Entire cities had been vaporised by incoming asteroidal fragments. Those fragments were sourced from the Martian moons, Phobos and Deimos. The aliens had manoeuvred them into their current orbits for that very purpose. There had, apparently been a third asteroid that the aliens had moved into Martian orbit, however, they had expended it completely during the Martian bombardment.

Gideon now understood why the aliens had sabotaged and attacked their terraforming efforts a decade and a half earlier. Moving Chariklo and Chiron into Martian orbit was very similar to what they, themselves had done over ninety thousand years earlier. At first, they may have thought it was going to be an attack on Mars, before later realising it was a terraforming project and in their best interests.

Most of the Martian atmosphere had been blown off into space during the bombardment, the remainder then froze out during the long cold winters that followed the war. The Martian Oceans on being exposed to vacuum, mostly boiled off into space as well. Finally what was left of the Oceans froze solid and was eventually buried under dozens of meters of Martian dust and regolith, by the many great dust storms that ravaged the planet over the intervening aeons.

A great many people, billions of Martians, had died. Many other Martians had fled to the neighbouring planet, the Earth. The much higher gravity of the Earth had made their survival extremely difficult. They could not restart a new civilisation and they soon returned to a more primitive state of existence. Eventually, the Martians on the Earth, whilst in their primitive state of existence, interbred with the Earth's humans, hybridising with homo sapiens. They were eventually absorbed into the Earth's human population.

This was made possible, because it was, in fact, Martian scientists, that had millions of years earlier created the Earth's first hominids from their ape-like ancestors. They had been slowly adjusting and tweaking those hominids genetically, right up until the war that destroyed the Martian biosphere. The early homo sapiens were the Martian's final efforts in tweaking Earth's humans before they were conquered by the aliens.

Winchilly then went on to modern times, telepathically explaining, that the aliens were an evolutionary dead end. They had enslaved her people to use their intelligence. The aliens wanted to subjugate the people of the Earth but also wanted to spare the Earth's biosphere. They were waiting for Earthlings to evolve to a stage where they couldn't or wouldn't resist or be able to fight back.

After the Earth's people had outlawed war, the aliens tested the Earth's people by sabotaging and attacking their infrastructure in Martian orbit. There wasn't any retaliation and they thought, maybe it was time. The Earth's people had merely put up tight surveillance and didn't even really bother to investigate. The aliens were now simply waiting for the completion of the terraforming project before taking over the Earth. In that way, they would have obtained for themselves, two viable biospheres, the Earth's and Mars's.

Now, however, Gideon had changed all of that. He had attacked and injured one of them, showing that the Earth's people would defend themselves. Now, when the terraforming project is completed, they will destroy the Earth, sacrificing its biosphere and then enslave all of the human colonies.

They needed the humans for their intelligent and industrious nature. Which if controlled, could be used to develop and maintain an empire. So the aliens, being both patient and ambitious, desperately needed to enslave the entire human species after the destruction of the Earth.

The young Martian women then went on to explain, that the aliens main base was well armed with Martian technology, but that the Martians had held back. They didn't give the aliens anything that couldn't be countered. The problem was that they couldn't fight, but they could interfere with the alien controlled weaponry on Mars.

The Earth's armies would have to attack Mars first. Upon liberating the Martians, they could obtain the weaponry with which they could vanquish the aliens. If the Earth were to fight the aliens alone, without help from Mars, they would surely be defeated. Winchilly stressed that point and drove it home. Martian technology was the key to defeating the aliens.

Carl Trigg was not captured by the aliens, they didn't even know he was there. He lay in his crash couch for twelve hours before he was finally rescued. When back in high Martian orbit and the Aries colony, he was admitted straight into a military hospital. Colonel Bannon enquired of his condition and was surprised by the answer.

"Colonel, he is quite delirious, he keeps rambling on about Devils, Demons and Martians", the doctor told him.

"How long will it be before he can tell us what happened, Doc?", Colonel Bannon questioned.

"He may not recover, whatever he saw was enough to send him into shock. If he does come around though, I'll let you know", the Doctor replied.

Colonel Bannon decided that it might be best to simply review the recordings taken during the flight. The black box flight recorder contained little relevant information, with the exception that it proved that the lander had been shot down. That in itself was unexpected. The surveillance recorders on the other hand contained far more important data.

The pilot Carl Trigg had recorded pictures and film of the monoliths as he flew over them. Standard procedure, all flights over the monoliths did so. Towards the end of the recording, however, something very important was captured. People had been filmed working on or around one of the Martian structures. It was quite obvious that Carl had brought the lander back around for a closer look.

That was probably why they shot him down. The rest of the tape from there on, only contained excellent footage of the crash landing, alluding to Carl's excellent piloting skills. It was obvious that Gideon and Sandra were unhurt in the crash and had been captured. What the Colonel couldn't understand was Carl's talk and ravings about Devils and Demons. Colonel Bannon immediately sent an urgent communique to Eros.

The Security Council of Sol spent two days deliberating over the report that they had received. So much for the need for an urgent reply, permitting Colonel Bannon to make his move. After the Security Council had deliberated, their reply was not even favourable. The Colonel read the reply, just what he expected from nameless bloody bureaucrats.

It read, *"We of the Security Council of Sol, feel that the Martian action was justifiable. We also feel that Doctor Reas is more than capable of handling this situation. Furthermore, we Councillors are of the opinion, that Doctor Reas will actually make an excellent ambassador to the Martians."*

"What the fuck!", was the thought that went through the Colonel's mind.

"No military action of any kind is necessary at this time and we don't believe it will be in the future either. Colonel, all of your troops are to be kept out of the monolith zones, however, surveillance of the monoliths, is to continue as per usual."

"Well, that's bloody great! We are to do nothing! Absolutely fucking nothing! Watch and wait! They've tied my bloody hands!", the Colonel shouted out loud.

"Colonel Sir, what about Doctor Reas and Miss Danker?", enquired Captain Hawk.

"They're on their own, Captain. The Security Council's got a very bad case of rose-coloured spectacles", the Colonel Replied.

"We aren't going to leave them there, are we, Sir?", the Captain enquired.

"There is nothing we can do. We'll just have to wait and see what develops", the Colonel replied.

Meanwhile on Mars, Gideon and Sandra were still imprisoned. The lovely Martian woman, Winchilly, was being used as their personal servant. Winchilly went out for their food and drink when required. When they were taken out for exercise, they were always under guard. However, Winchilly was always there to answer all of their questions and they had an awful lot of questions.

The aliens watched and studied them intently. The aliens did not appear to care that Winchilly was there. Winchilly was only a Martian female after all. She was also looking after them and their captives could not escape. However, Winchilly was also giving them a lot of information. Winchilly told Gideon and Sandra everything that they wanted to know and even some things that they themselves, did not even know to ask about.

From Winchilly, they both learnt that their treatment had been very lenient. These aliens were an extremely malevolent species. Regularly, about twice a month, the Martians were required to give blood to their masters. Refusal to do so meant death, by a very slow method of torture and bloodletting.

The female Martians had to contend with another form of the alien's evil. Anytime, anywhere, their masters felt like it, they would rape them, sometimes quite violently. Apparently, the aliens did this for two specific reasons. One was that they could not impregnate Martian women and two, their own females liked to watch the Martian women being violated. They even appeared to enjoy watching and egging their males on. In many instances, it was actually the alien females who chose the victims.

Winchilly had explained to them, that the aliens had been ordered, by their superiors, not to harm either of them. This information made Sandra and Gideon extremely worried. If these orders were to change, for any reason, Sandra would be at risk. What then would Gideon do? He couldn't allow Sandra to be harmed in that way. Then there was also Winchilly. Since Winchilly had been assigned to look after them, she had also been left alone. Gideon did not want to see her violently raped either.

From Winchilly they also found out that the entire area beneath the monolith region was riddled with tunnels and habitats, in which the aliens and Martians all lived. All of the monoliths were connected via the passages. In the time since the aliens had taken control, the tunnels and passages had been reinforced and extended.

From Winchilly, Gideon and Sandra were able to create a mental map of the entire complex, which they had decided to memorise. They both had a lot of information and they had to escape. There was a slight problem, however, Gideon knew all to well, they were on their own. Gideon could easily predict the Security Council's decision and he knew what it would be.

10. The Mimas Incident.

Titanian colonists had landed on Saturn's moon Mimas to build a new mining colony. Nothing unusual, mining colonies were being set up right across the entire Saturnian system. There was even a standard procedure for the process. It was just time for Mimas.

This moon, in the fifth position from Saturn, the next orbit out from the Co-orbital moons, has a diameter of only three hundred and ninety kilometres, just a shade under four hundred kilometres. It's small size placed Mimas down the end of reasonably size list, seventh place in fact.

Mimas is distinct from the other moons of Saturn, in that it has a crater close to one hundred and thirty five kilometres across. It isn't the size of the crater that was significant, so much as its size in relation to the size of Mimas itself. The impact that created that crater, Herschel, ought to have ripped Mimas apart. Mimas should have been smashed into smithereens.

It was improbable, that Mimas could possibly have survived the impact. So unusual did Herschel Crater look, that when photographed for the first time, that someone had asked, *"Is that the engine?"* Others had remarked that Mimas looked remarkably like the *'death star'*, from a popular movie at the time. Little did they know how close that statement was to the truth.

The new mining colony was in place and the mining had been going very well. Materials had been mined from both the surface and within the icy crust of Mimas. Several shafts had been dug into Mimas to a depth of nearly ten kilometres. The first of these shafts to reach that depth ran into severe problems. None of the miners had expected what they'd found.

Erving Smith had been a miner on the Saturnian ice moons for quite some time now. Erving had started with the very first mining colony, that had been set up along with the main colonies on Saturn's largest moon Titan. Before that, he'd be an asteroid miner working in the asteroid belt. In all of his long experience, he'd never had this happen to him before. The highly experienced ice moon miner was completely perplexed.

"This ain't bloody right, Tommy boy, this just ain't bloody right!", he had told a fellow worker.

"Why, what's so wrong about it?", his younger workmate Tommy asked.

"This bloody rock for starters, Tommy boy! This is an ice moon! For fucks sake, there ain't no bloody rock in it", Erving replied.

Erving was right, Mimas was supposed to have a density close to that of water. How could Mimas, an ice moon, possibly have a solid mass of hard rock this close to the surface? Erving decided to call in the boss. The situation needed to be checked out by someone well above his pay grade.

Timothy Harding was a busy man, he had no time for mucking about, he had stuff to do.

When he was called over to the shaft, he clearly stipulated, *"that it had better not be someone's idea of a joke."*

Upon arriving at the base of the shaft, where Erving and Tommy were working, he immediately saw what the problem was.

"Sweet Jesus! That isn't supposed to be there!", Tim Harding had exclaimed.

"Too bloody right it ain't, Tim!", Erving replied.

Looking closer at the obstructing rock, Tim stated, "It looks like it's been fused at an extremely high temperature. This bloody rock is vitrified! It's been glassed!"

Erving was pissed off, even he could tell that, "That's what I bloody well thought!", he replied with an ever so slight hint of sarcasm.

Tim then speculated, "It could have been a meteorite once. An iron meteorite probably. It must have melted and vitrified on impact, punching its way this deep. There can't be too much of it. It's probably just a small pocket of rock. Tunnel around the fucker and be done with it!"

That was Tim Harding's take on the matter.

Nearly forty eight hours later, poor old Tim Harding was doing back flips. Four other shafts had hit solid, hard, fused rock, at variously spaced locations. This meant that it was far too extensive to be a pocket of old meteoritic material. What was even worse, the rock seemed to be curved and their estimates of its curvature showed, that it followed the curvature of Mimas itself.

This meant that it was far more than likely a global structure and new seismic tests showed it to be a great many kilometres thick. The known density of Mimas as measured, simply did not allow for the existence of a global rock shell. It simply should not have been there. What was even worse, it meant, that the inside of Mimas had to contain something with a density far less than that of water. This problem was extremely puzzling, to say the least and their planetary geologists only made the problem far worse.

The geologists at the mining complex did not believe it either, the rock shell simply should not be there. On top of this, how was the rock fused? It was vitrified. It had to have been vitrified by intense heat. Further seismic testing of the rock shell, came back with results that showed it was probably at least twenty five kilometres thick.

This was a major problem, the mass of Mimas was long known, it had an overall density of one point two. The ten kilometre thick ice crust had a density of one. Below this was the shell of fused, vitrified rock, which had a density of three point five. The mass of Mimas was completely taken up. Within the fused rock shell, the little ice moon had to be hollow, this was only logical possibility.

"Bullshit!", Tim Harding exclaimed, asking, "Do you idiots actually expect me to believe that?"

"The results speak for themselves, Sir", the lead Geologist replied.

"Well, I don't believe it. An internal ocean maybe, but not hollow! That's just plain ridiculous!", Tim Harding told his team of geologists.

The lead geologist insisted, "Sir. We have run four separate sets of seismic tests. They all get the same results. Exactly the same results."

"And those results are consistent with Mimas being hollow", one of the other geologists added.

"Then we're going to have to drill through that fucking rock shell", Tim Harding decided, "I want to see this, this hollow for myself."

Upon hearing that the inside of Mimas had to be hollow, the mining company executives that Tim Harding reported back to, decided to test the fact. The miners working Erving's shaft were all asked if they'd ever used high-intensity laser tunnelling equipment. Most ice moon miners wouldn't have even seen this kind of equipment. They were used to using far simpler mechanical mining equipment, which was more appropriate for an ice moon.

It turned out, however, that Erving's mate Tom, who had recently worked in the asteroid belt, had used such machinery, the very latest in mining technology, in fact. The mining company instructed him further in its use and put him in charge of the tunnelling project, in advance of the equipment arriving at the mine.

In the meantime, a message was sent to Titan, advising them about the unusual development and requesting that they build the laser tunneller required to burrow into the rock shell. The necessary equipment was then manufactured using the latest designs and then it was sent to the mining station along with scientists to study the unusual formation. Within a fortnight, the equipment was delivered to the base of the shaft. All of the miners and scientists were eagerly awaiting to see what was on the other side of the fused rock shell.

Tom operated the laser tunnelling machine and at set intervals, both he and Erving took core samples to be analysed by the scientists. Without this machine, they wouldn't have a hope in hell of tunnelling through the fused rock shell. They progressed at a pace of five hundred meters per day and it was slow going, yet much faster than any other conventional methods would have been. In around fifty days, they would break through to the other side and see for themselves what lay beyond the fused rock shell. They needed to be cautious, as they had no idea what was on the other side.

After forty days, Tom finally reached the twenty kilometre mark. The rock ahead became molten and flowed beneath the machine leaving a fifteen-foot wide tunnel, through which the machine slowly moved. The walls and floor of the tunnel were soon hardened and one hundred meters behind them, a set of electromagnetic tracks were being laid by an automatic track-laying machine.

As the laser tunnelling machine bored deeper and deeper into the rock shell, Tom was suddenly shocked. His tunnel-boring machine had suddenly and unexpectedly broken into an already existing tunnel. Nobody was expecting this to happen. They had all thought, that the rock shell was solid, all the way to the interior of Mimas.

This existing tunnel crossed Tom's own tunnel at right angles and it was a good twenty five feet across. The sides of its walls indicated, that it had obviously been made by a very similar tunnelling technique. The air flowing from the existing tunnel appeared to be breathable. Both Tom and Erving gave out a small sigh of relief, the air could just as easily have been toxic. Tom and Erving quickly relayed this new information to Tim Harding, who was quite surprised by it.

Tim Harding wanted to see this new tunnel for himself and with him, he took a squad of his security personnel. After all, from the information provided by Tom and Erving, someone had to have carved out this existing tunnel. Someone with equally modern laser boring techniques of their own. Arriving at the tunnel, Tim found that he had been beaten to it by the scientists. They quickly informed him, that it appeared to be a deep ventilation and transport tunnel system. They also informed him that the tunnel system's atmosphere was quite breathable, quite similar in fact to their own requirements.

The security squad was split into two groups and each group was sent into the tunnel, in opposite directions. They were directed to check out the tunnel for a distance of one kilometre in each direction.

The first group came back without having anything to report. Tim Harding sent them back down the tunnel to keep a watch at a distance of five hundred metres. The second group came back and reported another tunnel crossing at right angles at two hundred metres, but nothing further beyond it. Tim then led the group off towards this intersection. This new tunnel headed off at right angles to the first one, just as the security team had reported, directly towards the centre of Mimas.

Tim Harding, Tom, Erving and the small group of security men moved off down this new tunnel, to investigate it. Other smaller tunnels spread out at right angles to this one, every five hundred metres or so. They all ignored these tunnels and continued towards the centre of Mimas. Tim Harding was overly eager to see what the hollow interior of Mimas looked like. Around five kilometres later they approached a large grill-covered opening. Tom and Erving working together, cut out a section of the grill and then they all climbed through the opening. Just like cats, they were all overly curious.

Past the grill, the tunnel went for a short distance, perhaps only fifty metres. For some reason they could no longer easily walk upright in this section of the tunnel. The ice moon's meagre gravity appeared to be changing its direction of force over the short distance from the grill to the surface. Over the short distance of ten paces, they found that the gravity was increasing and its direction of force was no longer towards the centre of Mimas. For some reason, gravity was now pushing them back down the tunnel at around point three gs.

The group carefully climbed to the tunnel's opening and viewed the area around them. They were now inside of the hollow interior of Mimas. Far above them, beyond the tunnel's opening, in the very centre of the Mimasian interior was a bright burning light. It appeared to be a tiny contained fusion reaction and it illuminated the entire interior of Mimas. The Mimasian *"Sunlight"* was hot, giving off a very good supply of both light and heat. The group soon climbed out of the tunnel opening and found themselves at the top of a small rocky knoll.

This immense, hollow inner chamber of Mimas was spherical, about three hundred and twenty kilometres in diameter. The gravity was being produced by an unknown source and found to be about point three standard gs. As far as the eye could see in every direction in this inner sphere, the land appeared to be either a semi-arid or arid desert. The air above the arid desert areas shimmered, showing that the temperatures in those regions was quite high. The temperature was high where the small group was on the rocky knoll and they began to sweat profusely.

There were mountainous regions inside of Mimas, but they were too far away in the distance to see them clearly. So far in fact, that they were barely noticeable. In several areas, however, a lattice of water-containing canals were clearly visible. These canals appeared to be fed by underground or in this case, under shell springs.

There were also a few small rivers that were fed by the same kinds of springs. In those irrigated areas there was a prolific growth of plants. There were trees and bushes of types that they had never seen before. In the more arid areas, there was only a sparse growth of smaller shrubs and bushes. In the centre of the latticed areas, there appeared to be unusual structures. These may have been towns or villages of some kind. Not even one large body of water in this entire inside-out world could be seen, although there were more than a few smallish lakes visible, probably also fed by undershell springs.

In the skies above them there were only scattered, thin, wispy clouds. Obviously, very little rain fell in this strange inside-out world. It was totally different to anything they had seen before. The Mimasian interior didn't resemble any world, not even the larger colony cylinders, nor even the hollowed-out asteroid, Eros, that any of them had ever seen.

In the distance, creatures could be seen flying. At first they could not tell what they were, but taking into account the distance, they knew they were quite big. More surprising yet, they appeared to have come out from one of the unusual towns and were heading straight towards them.

As they approached, Tim Harding and the others could see, that there were close to fifty of them.

As they flew closer and they were able to get a better look at them, Erving exclaimed loudly, "Oh my god, we've discovered Hell!"

The six security men quickly drew their weapons, then the whole group moved back down towards the tunnel entrance from whence they came. The aliens closed in and began to fire their weapons. The rocks around them burst explosively and blobs of molten rock flew through the air.

Two of the security men were hit. One had his chest completely blown out, the other was now missing his head. Erving and Tom quickly grabbed up their comrade's fallen weapons and they began to fire back at the aliens. As they reached the tunnel entrance, another of the security men was hit. His body was blown backwards down into the tunnel. The security man's body fell straight down at first, then curved strangely, to land against the tunnel wall. Tim Harding dove after the body and grabbed the fallen security man's weapon.

At the mouth of the tunnel, the six remaining men returned fire at the aliens. One alien was hit in the wing. It fell to the ground in screaming agony and landed with a dull thud. More and more of the aliens were hit, their bodies dropping out of the sky to land on the rocky ground beneath them. In the distance Tim had seen that there were more of them coming. There were also other aliens moving off to other rock formations, where they disappeared into the rock shell.

.

Tim Harding shouted to his men, "Get back down that fucking tunnel! Move it! Fucking move it fast! They're trying to cut us off!"

Harding's men were quick to follow the order and followed him back through the grill and back down the tunnel. Within seconds they heard the sound of flapping wings behind them. They all turned and fired at once. The aliens were too big to fit through the small hole in the grill. They were cut to bits by laser fire, as they worked feverishly to enlarge the hole. Alien flesh and blood exploded from one side of the tunnel to the other, as they were struck repeatedly by the laser fire. They continued to fire their lasers, as more and more aliens swooped into the opening.

When they had finally stopped firing their lasers, behind them at the tunnel entrance, pressed up against the grill was a mass of dark and tangled alien bodies. The pile of bodies was still steaming with burning flesh and blood. The rising stench was beyond belief and the men turned around and fled back down the tunnel, away from the sight and smell of the carnage.

They had run for a good three kilometres and nothing yet was behind them. Being exhausted they decided to stop for a few short minutes. Whilst resting, they heard something in the tunnel ahead of them. Erving got up to investigate, the others then followed a short distance behind him. From out of one of the smaller side tunnels, two aliens stepped into view to confront the frightened group of men.

Erving ran at them shouting, "Die you fucking evil bastards!", he then opened fire upon them.

The two aliens were cut down in a stream of laser fire. Upon reaching the smaller tunnel, Erving leapt into it and the sounds of a battle could be heard. The others moved up closer to it and Tom looked into the smaller tunnel.

Bright flashes of laser light were everywhere. Aliens were being cut down and killed ahead of the crazed Erving, firing continuously as he advanced. Erving was hit and yet he still advanced, firing continuously. Again and again, Erving was hit and again and again, he fired his laser. Erving's last shots were fired as he fell to the ground, dead, a smouldering mess of flesh and bone, his mining career permanently ended.

Tom jumped into the smaller tunnel, aided by Tim Harding. They fired continuously at the aliens. When the pair had finished the tunnel stunk of cooked death. The smaller side tunnel was littered with bodies for a distance of more than one hundred meters. Flesh and blood was dripping from the walls. Erving had killed nearly all of them. Tom and Tim had mopped up the last dozen or so, yet there were easily sixty to seventy dead aliens in there.

Tim Harding grabbed a fear frozen Tom and shoved him back down the tunnel, then they began running down the tunnel with the three remaining security men. After some time they approached the end of the tunnel and a group of security men that were positioned at the intersection. Close behind them were the sounds of flapping wings. They entered this tunnel and rested for a few brief moments.

Tim shouted at the new security men, "Don't ask any questions! If you want to live, just blow the living hell out of anything that moves down there!", as he pointed back down the tunnel.

The six security men entered the tunnel that Tim had pointed to and fired at the approaching aliens.

They were only two hundred yards from the tunnel that Tom had created. As soon as they had rested, Tim then decided it would be best to retreat.

"Come on, men, let's move!", Tim Harding yelled.

"They're still coming, Sir!", one of the security men shouted back.

"Fuck them, let's get the hell out of here! Move it! All of you!", Tim quickly ordered.

They all moved off, quickly down the tunnel once more. They had just made it to Tom's tunnel when the aliens reached the intersection from both sides. They again opened fire on the advancing aliens. It was then that they heard the sounds of battle from the other side of the tunnel. The group of security men that were stationed there quickly joined them. Tim Harding then decided to retreat back towards the surface of Mimas. That was their only option.

"Give me a couple of minutes, Tim", Tom yelled.

Tom rigged his laser tunnelling machine to work with remote control, then he moved it back down the tunnel some ways. After this everyone retreated to the electromagnetic tracks and boarded their transit vehicles. They were soon travelling swiftly towards the mining colony on the surface.

When they were about six hundred meters down the tunnel, the aliens had reached the end of it. Tom waited for a few more seconds for the aliens to get deeper into his tunnel and then he switched on the laser tunnelling machine. Instantly scores of aliens were disintegrated. After that, the other aliens didn't enter the tunnel and instead, they waited for the beam to stop so that they could attack the tunnelling machine. There was a sudden massive explosion and the tunnel started to collapse. The end of Tom's tunnel was now sealed off completely.

After reaching the ice crust, Tim Harding sent his security men back down Tom's tunnel to place explosive charges. The security men did this very quickly and when completed, they set the explosive charges off, effectively sealing Tom's tunnel completely. Then everyone left for the Mining colony back on the surface of Mimas.

Back at the mining complex, Tim Harding wasn't sure what to do in this situation. Being attacked by aliens wasn't exactly in the manual. The scientists all advised him, that it would be best to evacuate the mining complex. As the aliens might have access to the surface from somewhere else on Mimas and could still attack them. The aliens might also have the means to clear tunnels as well. No one was safe.

Tim Harding wasn't so sure, after all, Mimas had been surveyed and no access tunnels had been found anywhere on it. Instead, Tim decided to send Tom to Titan, to advise them of the situation personally. An audible sigh of relief was heard as Tom was given his orders to go. A very pleased Tommy boy had no intentions of hanging around. In addition to this, Tim sent a quick, brief report to Titan as well, ahead of Tom's arrival to let them know of their situation.

Tom had taken off in the small vessel towards Titan. Tom had been sent, as he and Tim Harding were the only ones who had seen the interior of

Mimas and were still alive. The remaining security guards who had been with them inside Mimas had all perished at the end of the tunnel. Tim Harding had to stay at the mining complex, as he was the boss. Tom was actually pleased with this decision. Tom had seen all he wanted to see of Mimas and was travelling as fast as his craft could take him towards Titan and its colonies.

As Tom was fast approaching Titan, the mining complex on Mimas had other problems to deal with. From out of Mimas on the opposite side from the large crater, Herschel, right near the mining complex, a fleet of interceptors emerged. They were soon picked up by the radar at the mining complex. Tim Harding had already sent out the order to evacuate, but it was far too late.

As the first evacuation ships were launched, the aliens struck. Particle beams and laser weapons flashed at the launching craft. One by one they burst and ruptured in flame-less explosions in the airless vacuum of space. Their debris drifted slowly back down to the surface of Mimas.

Tim Harding sent an urgent message to Titan, "Harding to Titan! Harding to Titan! Titan, we are under attack! Evacuation craft have all been destroyed. Aliens are attacking the mining complex. Help is required urgently!"

The mining complex shuddered violently and then the signal went dead. One by one, the alien interceptors flew low over the mining complex, with particle beams and laser beams blazing. There were countless explosions everywhere, as the structure was deeply holed.

No one could escape, the final blow was struck when their fission reactor's cooling unit was hit. The entire mining complex shuddered violently for the last time and then in a brilliant flash of light and a massive expanding orange fireball, the complex disappeared from existence. All that was left was a large crater in the icy crust of Mimas.

Mark Spencer had been an ambitious man. He'd very recently moved up from being Saturn's colonisation committee liaison man to becoming the colony's top man, the top job. Under his leadership, the colony was rapidly expanding, perhaps too rapidly. Before him, on his desk was the final communique from the mining complex on Mimas and in front of him stood its only survivor.

"You are, Thomas Kaine?", Mr Spencer enquired.

"Yes, I am, Sir", Tommy boy replied.

"Well, Mr Kaine, your story is intriguing to say the least", Mr Spencer had seen the recorded interview already, he added, "You said they came out of the hollow interior of Mimas?"

"Sir, that they did. They were the most malevolent, evil creatures I have ever seen. They looked like winged devils", Tom replied, adding, "Kind of like fucking huge gargoyles."

"Winged devils you say, gargoyles you say, are you sure, Mr Kaine?", Mr Spencer pressed further.

"Yes, of course, I'm fucking sure! I was there! They were Satan's own fucking evil spawn. Demons I tell you! Demons!", Tom shouted at him.

"It's okay, Mr Kaine, there is no need to shout! I believe your story and our doctors have assured me, that you are telling the truth and that you are quite sane", Mr Spencer replied.

"Then why does everybody keep asking me these same damned stupid questions?", Tom asked.

"Mr Kaine. We have to be sure. Put yourself in my shoes. Who do you think has to send this report off to Eros?", Mr Spencer answered.

Tom looked at him for a few moments, then burst out in tearful laughter, "I'm glad I don't have your job. They'll all think your fucking mad!"

Mark Spencer sighed, indeed they would think he was mad!

Mark Spencer was sceptical about the unusual description, but the facts were, that the mining complex was destroyed and testing indicated that Mr Thomas Kaine was perfectly sane. He decided to set up a surveillance perimeter around Mimas and put his security forces on permanent standby.

Administrator Mark Spencer then sent a full report to Eros, to both the Colonisation Committee of Sol and the Security Council of Sol. The report contained the recordings of the last transmission from Mimas and the interview with Thomas Kaine. The situation was terrible, two thousand lives were lost when the mining complex on Mimas was destroyed. Just how would Eros handle this?

11. Eros Decides.

The Saturnian report was received by Eros and taken directly to the Security Council of Sol. A copy of the report was lodged with the Colonisation Committee as well, but that was mainly just to keep them in the loop. This report was given top priority, the Security Councillors were all knocked out of their seats by it's contents. This was not something they'd been expecting and it was their responsibility to deal with it.

The Central Councillor spoke to the others, "Well then, we have quite a problem now don't we. More than two thousand lives lost and a five billion credit mining complex destroyed."

The fifth Councillor on his left stated, "This situation can't have been foreseen. There's no way anyone could have known of the existence of this alien colony."

"Yes that is true, but now they have made themselves known, in the most violent and warlike fashion possible. Let us remember that", replied the Central Councillor.

Another Councillor, the third on his right, interjected, "As this was basically an act of war, rather than a simple assault or a possible misunderstanding. We simply cannot treat this as we have treated those Martian incidents."

A Councillor, third on the left was far more cautious, adding, "Yes, this was an act of war, but we must not forget, that people from the mining complex had trespassed on the Alien's territory. They were provoked!"

Another Councillor, on the far left added, questioning, "These aliens didn't give any warnings to the miners at all. They simply attacked and violently killed everyone without any warning, without any questions being asked. Is this the act of a civilised culture? No. This act is an act of pure malevolence, an outright act of war and surely that negates our esteemed colleague's previous reasoning", there was a combination of sarcasm and vitriol in her voice.

A Councillor on the right then noted, "This alien colony has been there for quite some time. Based upon their descriptions, it is evident that they have visited the Earth, in our deep past. I state as evidence, various religious and mythological texts. All of which, describe the aliens as always being extremely malevolent and violent."

The second Councillor on the right added, "That may be so. However, it may not be wise to take into account, shall we say, legends and tales from antiquity."

"So we're calling them Demons now are we or are they perhaps Gargoyles? Why not just label them beasts and be done with it!", the third Councillor on the left enquired dryly, then he added, "I'm also disinclined to drag up myths and legends. We did trespass on their territory! Just remember that!"

To this another Councillor on the left stated strongly, "All possible data, from all possible sources, should be taken into account without any exceptions whatsoever. And as for our people trespassing on their territory, do we shoot first and ask questions later? No we don't! No civilised society would behave in that fashion!", she was livid!

The third councillor on the left then replied, "The aliens were provoked! If we provoke them further we may be starting a war!"

"Are you an idiot! Two thousand people dead and an entire mining complex was destroyed! For fucks sake! We are already at war!", the councillor on the far left replied heatedly, adding under her breath, *"Gutless fucking wonder!"*

"Enough!" the Central Councillor bellowed, "I'll not have this meeting turn into a shouting match!"

The room was silent for a long moment.

The fifth Councillor on the right then added, "There is of course another possible link, a link with the Martian monoliths. Let us not forget, the descriptions from Mr Carl Trigg, which I shall point out, is precisely the same as that of Mr Thomas Kaine."

The Councillor fourth on the left then added, "Yes, this is way too much of a coincidence. We must remember, that they attacked humans as well!"

The fourth Councillor on the right then stated, "In view of the extent of the losses, both human and economic. We should retaliate against these aliens immediately and in the strongest possible military fashion!", he was definitely a hawk.

The councillor on the far left replied, "Here! Here! Now there we have the right attitude! We cannot let this act of war go unanswered!", she was definitely a hawk as well.

One of the councillors on the right who had not yet spoken up remarked, "There must be another answer to this issue, a better way to handle this. Remember, we as a species have outlawed all war!"

Again the room was quiet for long moments.

The Central Councillor interjected, "In my opinion, it appears that we have a few options which we may utilise. One, we could take immediate and direct military action against both Mimas and the Martian monoliths. Two, we could leave the Martian situation as it is and we could retaliate, militarily against Mimas. Three, we could send reinforcements to both Mars and Saturn, step up surveillance and wait for further developments."

The Central Councillor then continued, "Reaction to any new developments would then depend on what those developments are. Our reaction to them, should be in the hands of the respective colonial leaders, even if that action leads to war!", he too, was starting to lean towards the hawkish side.

After that, the Central Councillor suggested that they adjourn for about four hours to consider their options before making any decisions. Soon the council room was cleared. The Central Councillor knew which option would be the best course of action. He expected it to be chosen and had already prepared for it. Asking the other Councillors to think carefully about their decision and putting those options to a vote, was just a formality.

On the return of the Councillors after their adjournment, some four hours later, the vote was cast, of course option three was chosen. Not all of the councillors were happy with this option, however, they did understand that human society was not prepared for a war. As much as immediate retaliation would have been preferred in their eyes, they chose the third option instead, just to be on the side of caution.

The Central Councillor then informed the other Councillors as to steps he had prepared for that option and asked if there were any objections to any of them. There weren't any objections to the his preparations. The Saturnian report was then added to the report by the Security Council and taken to Parliament for their final decision.

The next step was to put this report before Parliament, so a special meeting had been called. The Parliamentarians read the reports and viewed the data records. They then went through the three options that the Security Council had prepared. When they were finished, they were all in agreement with the council and so they allowed the council to implement their chosen option, however, with one extremely important amendment.

Parliament had decided, that contact had to be attempted with both Mars and Mimas. This entire process took them less than fifteen hours. Two communiques were then issued, one to the Aries colony in high Martian orbit, the other to Titan in Saturnian orbit. The communique to the Aries colony in high Martian orbit was received by, Colonel James J Bannon.

The Colonel read the communique as soon as it was decoded.

"Colonel Bannon, given recent developments on Mimas, of which you have been informed. We are sending you, to be placed under your command the following. Thirty new interceptors and thirty ground tanks, these are each armed with both high powered laser beam and particle beam weaponry."

"In addition to this, we are putting at your disposal, five thousand crack ground troops with a full complement of weaponry. These troops shall be put on standby. Communications shall be attempted with the Martians. If their reaction is favourable, refer all further decisions to Eros and our diplomatic teams. If the Martian reaction is unfavourable, you have orders to take whatever action you see fit. Good luck with your mission Colonel Bannon."

Colonel Bannon sighed with relief, he was more than pleased with the action now being taken.

"Captain Hawk, those lousy bureaucrats have finally decided to pull their digits out of their arses and do things properly", the Colonel informed.

"You mean we'll be taking action, Sir?", enquired the Captain.

"Not yet, we'll receive reinforcements first and then we will make a proper diplomatic approach", the Colonel replied.

"Then what, Sir?", the Captain asked.

"Well, Captain. The Martians will obviously reject it, probably they'll attack us and I have orders to take whatever action I see fit", Colonel Bannon replied.

The Captain looked at the Colonel and he then replied, "When it all goes down, Sir. I just hope that Doctor Reas and Miss Danker are still alive to be rescued."

"So do I, Captain, so do I", came the Colonel's worried reply.

The communique to Titan, when decoded was received by Administrator Mark Spencer, he read through the contents.

"Given the attack and destruction of the Mimas mining complex, it has been decided to reinforce your colony. Being sent to your colony are fifty of our new interceptors, armed with both high-powered laser beam and particle beam weapons."

" For possible use, inside of Mimas, we are sending thirty tanks, these are armed as with the interceptors. In addition to this, we shall also be sending you five thousand crack ground troops and a complete complement of weapons. These are to be kept on standby. You are to attempt contact with the aliens first. If their reaction is favourable, you are to open diplomatic relations. If their reaction is unfavourable, then you have the freedom of action to handle the situation in any way you see fit. We wish you good luck, Mr Spencer."

Mark Spencer was pleased with the reinforcements, however, he was not exactly pleased with the diplomatic side of things. He would have much preferred to simply retaliate against the aliens and destroy them. He saw no sense in attempting to talk to them or make friends with them. They were an extremely malevolent and dangerous species, so they should be dealt with accordingly. He fully realised that his train of thought would lead to a horrible conclusion and that the extermination of an intelligent species was not exactly an adequate answer.

However, taking into account their level of malevolence, he understood that allowing them to live could lead to an all-out war between humanity and the aliens. Such a war would lead to massive losses on both sides and should be avoided at all costs. Obviously, these aliens couldn't be allowed to spread across the solar system, considering their level of malevolence and their total disregard for life. Likely, as the aliens were a malevolent species, they would reject diplomatic negotiations out of hand anyway.

The reinforcements had been arranged with Saturn as the priority. This was because Saturn was the major flash point. The first to be sent would be the new interceptors, as they were needed most of all. Following up would be the transports carrying the tanks and the troops. For Mimas, any battle would be difficult. First of all the interceptors would have to defeat those of the Mimasians to gain access to the surface.

Then the tanks would have to be transported to Mimas, with pressure suited troops to enter the interior of the ice moon. Once inside and on the interior surface of Mimas, the battle would take on more conventional tactics. The overall aim of this strategy, assuming that peace could not be achieved, to defeat the Mimasians, but without destroying the Mimasian habitat. Eros obviously wanted the Mimasian's inside out world to survive intact. The defeated Mimasians would still require somewhere to live after all.

The reinforcements being sent to Mars, it had been decided would be sent after Saturn's reinforcements were sent. Again, they would be sending the interceptors first. Then the transports containing the tanks and the troops would follow. With Mars, the battle would be far more conventional, that is, again assuming that any potential peace talks fail. The tanks and the ground troops would be deployed and enter the battle, with the interceptors giving them air support.

The new Martian atmosphere would make the surface battle far simpler, although the troops would require re-breathers to filter out the toxic compounds and noxious gases. As the Earth's soldiers are used to a much higher gravity, they would have a great advantage in natural biological strength.

Meanwhile on Mars, increased aerial surveillance had shown little new evidence of any Martian activity. Apparently the Martians were once again on the defensive and not showing themselves. The same could not be said of Mimas. The region around Mimas was a hive of activity.

The surface of Mimas was now literally covered with new installations. The Mimasians had been extremely busy. New facilities and installations were popping up like mushrooms daily. Whether they were of a defensive or an offensive nature, none of the Saturnian colonists knew. For the most part, the surface installations were covered. Although there were hints, that these new installations were weapons batteries. The speculation was that they were high-powered laser beam and particle beam batteries. The Saturnian colonists were waiting and watching, all of their security forces on permanent standby. They hoped and prayed that their reinforcements would be quick in arriving.

Surveillance of the ice moon, Mimas, had to be performed from a safe distances. The dark, airless skies above Mimas were swarming with alien interceptors. They patrolled continuously, keeping any colonial craft away from Mimas. Many of the surface installations were quite likely interceptor launch tubes. The colonial craft stayed well clear and no incidents occurred across the Mimasian perimeter, that the Mimasians had set up.

Any colonial attempts to contact the Mimasians were all in vain. They either weren't capable of receiving the signals or were simply ignoring them. Administrator Mark Spencer was worried by this apparent snubbing of diplomatic approaches. He hoped their reinforcements would arrive very soon.

12. Captured in Transit.

The reinforcements hadn't yet left the Earth and the Saturnian colonists were keeping a tight surveillance on the small ice moon Mimas. The asteroid belt colonies were keeping a close watch on the situation from various colonies across the asteroid belt as well.

When Saturn was at it's closest approach to any of the very wide spread Belter colonies. That particular colony in question would turn it's attention to Saturn and take it's turn monitoring the Saturnian situation. So the older Belter colonies were doing their part, keeping a watchful eye over the far younger Saturnian colonies.

In addition to this, the Aries colony, in high Martian orbit was also monitoring the situation at Saturn. They were receiving information from both Saturn and the various Belter colonies. Soon Mars and Saturn were due to reach their closest approach in their orbits. Around the ice moon Mimas, the alien interceptors continued their patrols. They had set up a perimeter around the little moon. No colony craft attempted to enter it.

These patrolling vehicles were being monitored carefully, very soon it was noticed that one of these alien vessels exited the perimeter at extremely high speed. This interceptor had not been patrolling like the others, instead it had launched from Mimas and then punched through the perimeter at high speed on a course for the inner solar system.

The alien vehicle quickly accelerated after leaving Mimasian orbit.

Administrator Mark Spencer was immediately notified and his compucomm buzzed for his attention, "Spencer here, who's speaking?"

"Surveillance control Sir, an alien ship has left Mimasian orbit", came the reply.

Then Mr Spencer inquired, "What's its trajectory?"

The reply came back, "Sir, the alien ship is travelling on a trajectory towards Mars."

"Mars!", Administrator Spencer exclaimed, adding, "I'd better send word to the Aries colony", then he signed off.

Mark Spencer then went to the communications room where he directed the operator to send a scrambled message to both the Aries colony in high Martian orbit and the nearest of the Belter colonies.

The message read, *"Alien vehicle on route Mimas to Mars, please monitor. If possible intercept and warn all local authorities."*

The message was short, but straight to the point.

The message travelled to it's destinations at light speed, even at this velocity the journey took time. The first colonies to receive it were in the asteroid belt. The colony cylinders in orbit with the asteroid Interamnia, picked up the message first.

The Communications officer handed the decoded transcript to his superior.

After reading it he ordered, "Send a message to their local defence fleet, I want it to read. *'Message from Saturn received. Alien craft on course to Mars. Intercept if possible'.*"

He added, "I want a message sent to Mars as well, I want it to read. *'Message from Saturn received. Mimasian craft is on course to you. Intercept if possible'.*"

The local defence fleet was only ten million kilometres away. Upon receiving the message, they plotted the course of the Mimasian craft and launched themselves on an intercept trajectory. There were eight craft in all and they expected to intercept the Mimasian ship just near the inner boundary of the asteroid belt, some thirty million kilometres from Mars.

At high Martian orbit, Colonel Bannon received the messages from both

Saturn and Interamnia. His own people had been monitoring the movements of these craft as well, both the Mimasian and the Belters. Immediately he launched six of his own interceptors to intercept the alien should the Belters fail. The Colonel's own interceptors would intercept the alien's vessel at fifteen million kilometres from Martian orbit.

The Colonel called in Captain Hawk and commented loudly, "Now Captain, we'll see if Carl Trigg was right!"

The Captain replied, "Yes, Sir, we certainly shall."

The two men watched their interceptors launch, flying to their rendezvous with the Mimasian craft. The brilliant blue of their ship's thrusters blazed brightly as they accelerated towards the enemy vessel, a vessel that was totally alien to their own.

The eight Belter interceptors travelled towards their objective. The Mimasian vessel appeared on their view scanners. They adjusted their course slightly so that at the point of interception they would be flying parallel to the alien craft. Shortly thereafter, they had reached their objective.

The Belter ships came upon the Mimasian, four ships ahead and four ships behind, the alien was quite well boxed in. Without any warning and before the Pilots of the lead ships could even attempt to communicate with the Mimasian, the alien made it's move.

Swiftly adjusting his controls, Kildrark altered his course ever so slightly. The searing helium exhaust from his ship's thrusters swept across one of the Belter ships that was behind him. There was a brilliant flash of light and the Belter ship was no more, exploding so quickly its pilot had no time to react. Death came mercifully quickly. On his next move, Kildrark corrected his course slightly once more and swept his exhaust across yet another Belter ship. As with the first, it quickly flashed into non-existence. The pilot was caught almost completely unaware. Kildrark laughed maniacally.

Kildrark then switched on his communicator, in response Lieutenant Selter then opened the channel. In guttural English, Kildrark arrogantly gave his ultimatum, "Be gone humans or I'll crush you like insects. I will give you no further warnings."

Lieutenant Selter didn't have a chance to reply, Kildrark had signed off. Instead, he sent out a command to take evasive action.

The Belters at the rear had taken their ships out of the range of the Kildrark's thruster exhaust. Kildrark then quickly raised his deflector shields and activated his weapons console. The Belters had activated their weapons consoles as well.

Kildrark's particle beams and laser beams flashed into action. Another two Belter ships, this time in front of him were hit. Large punctures in the Belter ship's hulls exposed their crews to the vacuum of space. As their air vanished, the pilot's blood began to boil and then leaked through every exposed orifice. Large streams of stomach contents spewed from their mouths. Again and again Kildrark fired on the damaged ships, which then flared brilliantly and exploded before vanishing from view.

The Belters fired upon the alien craft, their laser beams and particle beams had little effect on Kildrark's shields. Kildrark retaliated, one of the Belter ships flashed into oblivion. Another Belter ship suffered on board explosions and was left dead in space. There were now only two Belter ships left, Lieutenant Selter sent an urgent message to Mars.

"Aries control, we have only two craft left. Our weapons are ineffective against the Mimasian vessel. We are going to drop back and monitor the Mimasian's course until your own ships arrive", Lieutenant Selter then signed off.

It was too late before either of the last two Belter ships could drop back, Kildrark opened fire once more. Both vessels were hit, exploding in immense flashes of brilliance, in very quick order, they both ceased to exist.

Kildrark was ecstatic with the outcome, he had won the battle and destroyed all of the enemy ships. Kildrark adjusted his ship's course again and was soon back on a trajectory towards Mars. Content that the danger was over, Kildrark then switched off his weapons console and deactivated his deflector shields to conserve power. Kildrark was completely unaware of the approaching interceptors, instead thinking that he had a nice, easy flight ahead of him. Kildrark was wrong, dead wrong, it would be too late when he finally checked his long-range scanners.

The Pilot of the Icarus received Lieutenant Selter's message. He watched the alien craft on his long-range scanners. Soon his ships will face this alien. He quickly decided upon his course of action and then informed the pilots of his other ships, of the course of action that he had planned.

Four of his ships dropped back and those craft swung in a wide curve to bring them alongside of the Mimasian's vessel. His two lead ships continued on course and increased their rate of acceleration. They all quickly approached the Mimasian vessel.

"Aim to disable the Mimasian vessel. I don't want it destroyed", ordered the Pilot of the Icarus, adding, "We want this bastard taken alive!"

The two lead interceptors were now travelling at a very quick two-point five gs of acceleration.

Kildrark was stunned when he suddenly saw the two interceptors on his view scanner. They were both travelling with immense velocity. Kildrark made a move for his deflector shield control, but it was already far too late. As the two interceptors flew past, his craft was rocked by four small explosions. Kildrark's ship wasn't yet holed, but he requested his computer's damage report anyway.

Kildrark was now in deep trouble, his deflector shields were now inoperable and his reactor was on the verge of instability. He would also have to limit his ship's velocity to less than a third of its maximum as a result. Kildrark slowed his stricken vessel down and considered his current situation. At least those two interceptors would take a long time in turning around, so he could still out run them or so he had thought.

Kildrark then checked his long-range scanners, "more problems", he snarled at the blips on the long-range scanner screens.

There were four more interceptors, two aside closing in on him fast. Kildrark then checked his computer's damage report yet again. All of his weapons systems were okay. He decided that he could still win this upcoming battle and activated his weapons console once more.

The four ships closed in on their objective. Kildrark adjusted his course and caught one of the enemy ships with his thruster's helium exhaust. The interceptor burst into non-existence with a brilliant flash of light. The remaining interceptors all retaliated, although following their orders, they aimed to damage the Mimasian vessel.

Kildrark's ship lurched violently, six small explosions rocked his ship. He retaliated quickly, laser beams and particle beams flashed out at his attackers. His aim was good, very good, two interceptors exploded and vanished from his screens. His last attacker then fired upon him once more and two small explosions registered on Kildrark's ship, it shuddered violently.

Kildrark fired upon his enemy and hit it squarely. The interceptor exploded in flash of brilliant light and the battle was nearly over. Kildrark again checked his computer's damage report. His reactor had shut down and he was now coasting. His particle beams were now inoperative, but he still had his laser beams. Worse yet, his ship was holed, the computer had indicated at least four slow leaks.

Quickly Kildrark put on his pressure suit, the section over his mighty wings greatly limited his movement, but he would only need it until he got to Mars. Getting back to his damage report, his long-range scanners were also inoperative. Kildrark would have to rely on his ship's short-range scanners.

Sitting on his crash couch, Kildrark watched his short-range view scanners for any signs of the first two interceptors. The Icarus and its partner Scythe, had decelerated and turned back to attack the Mimasian vessel once again. Both of the Pilots knew that their other ships were all destroyed. They also knew that the Mimasian ship had sustained severe damage. The two Pilots had conferred and decided to give the alien craft another volley of glancing blows.

The two interceptors approached and as Kildrark watched his scanners he saw them clearly. Reaching for his laser controls, his ship lurched once more. There were four small explosions and his lasers failed to fire. Air rushed around his ship as its hull cracked and his air was quickly sucked into the vacuum of space. Kildrark's ship was now completely disabled and disarmed. Kildrark himself was now completely at the mercy of the Humans.

Kildrark had lost the battle and he sat quietly in his crash couch watching the planet Mars. It was so small in the distance and slowly his ship drifted closer and closer towards it. Kildrark, as a last resort, flipped open a sealed cover and pressed the self-destruct button to scuttle his ship. Nothing happened, he and his craft were still there. The self-destruct had failed! Kildrark smashed both of his six-fingered fists angrily against the cold hard steel of his control panel.

The Pilot of the Icarus sent an urgent message to Aries control, "Mimasian craft completely disabled and disarmed, currently drifting towards Mars. We will take it in tow. Four of our interceptors have been lost. All Belter craft have been lost. All of their pilots have been lost", he then signed off.

The two interceptors then took the stricken Mimasian vessel in tow back to the Aries colony in high Martian orbit. Kildrark's ship accelerated steadily and Mars quickly receded from his view screens, while the twin cylinders of the Aries colony in high Martian orbit loomed ever closer. Kildrark sat there in his pressure suit, waiting to see the humans who had captured him. Kildrark was anything but patient. Perhaps, just perhaps if he was lucky, he would get a chance to tear out the throats of his adversaries.

At the Aries colony, Colonel Bannon had sent word to the Belters informing them, officially of the loss of their interceptors. The four pilots of his own four lost interceptors were all heroes. They had all died aiming their weapons to disable the Mimasian craft, when they could easily have aimed to destroy it. They had followed their orders to the letter and died in the process, this too, was something that Kildrark could not fathom.

Why had they not destroyed him? Why was he still alive?

Soon the two interceptors and the stricken Mimasian vessel were at the Aries colony. The Mimasian vessel was towed into the port facilities within the east cylinder. The Mimasian, Kildrark, did not make it to Mars. Sadly for Kildrark, he was in a disgraceful position for one of his kind, a prisoner of war.

Soon the outer hatch of his craft was blown open. A few minutes later they would be inside the airlock and working on its inner hatch. The inner hatch was eventually opened and the Colonial Troops entered with their lasers drawn.

Kildrark was ready, he cut down the first three Colonial Troops with his own laser. The fourth colonial trooper, however, was too quick, blasting the laser from Kildrark's six fingered hand. The heat from his melting laser forced Kildrark to immediately drop it. His laser fell to the deck plating, forming a melted splodge of metal and fused components. The Mimasian was then quickly overpowered, shackled and taken into custody. The process of Kildrark's apprehension had been very quick.

Kildrark had never considered how physically strong these Earth humans would be. Instead, Kildrark had mistakenly thought them to be comparable to Martian humans, used to only point three eight gs of gravity. These colonial troopers were not only used to a full g of gravity but had been trained in one and a half gs of gravity in military training cylinders.

In Kildrark's black pressure suit with his dark visor closed it was impossible to see what Kildrark actually looked like, although his large wings were clearly evident. Kildrark's sheer size, broad barrel chest, short legs and long arms were also clearly evident, although none of his facial features were visible at all.

The people of the Aries colony had stopped and stared at the ungainly looking figure in the black pressure suit, as he was taken to Colonel Bannon. Under his dark visor Kildrark carried a broad devilish grin. A grin born from his species delusions of grandeur and of their superiority over all others. A grin that would have clearly shown his red-stained teeth.

Colonel Bannon went over to the detention cell where the Mimasian was going to be kept, he entered the cell and waited for it. His Colonial Troops brought in the Mimasian. The Colonel looked at the creature and ordered his troops to remove its pressure suit. The troops slashed at the alien's pressure suit with their combat knives and then tore it off roughly.

They gasped in shock and horror, as they now stared at the Mimasian standing in its uniform before them. Kildrark laughed loudly and gutturally, at the shocked looks on their faces, he delighted in it. Mimasians relished fear, they enjoyed it immensely and it made them feel powerful and in control.

Colonel Bannon could easily see how his pilot Carl Trigg, had seen this creature and its kind as devils. The nearly eight-foot alien stood there on its short stocky legs, leaning on its long gangly arms. The alien looked like a large barrel-chested gargoyle, with a long prehensile tail and large black leathery wings. Its devilish face, horns and pointed fangs displayed an arrogance, that could only have come from the insane malevolence of its species. It showed absolutely no fear whatsoever!

This security cell was placed quite close to the east cylinder's axis of rotation. The gravity was the equivalent of about point two gs. Kildrark stood there quite comfortably and he had wondered why they had not put him in a cell with a far more oppressive gravitational environment. After all, Kildrark did fully expect to be tortured. He was fully expecting them to flay the skin mercilessly from his body, as his own kind would have with any captive.

The Colonel informed Kildrark, "We know you understand our language. We picked up your transmissions to one of the Belter craft."

Kildrark spoke, "Why did your warriors aim to disable my ship when they could have easily destroyed me?", his speech was guttural.

The Colonel replied, "They had orders to follow and they obeyed them."

"Even if obeying those orders meant their deaths", Kildrark replied, adding, "They must have been fools", yet thinking to himself, *"I must get word to my people about this. It will be a problem!"*

"Fools. I would not say that, you see, we now have a prisoner", stated the

Colonel, who then added, "And you shall give us vital information. Whether you like it or not."

Now Kildrark was beginning to understand, he stated boldly, "I, Kildrark, will give you nothing!"

Colonel Bannon replied, "Well Kildrark, you just did then. You just gave us your name. We also have your ship and we have yet to interrogate you. So far, I'd say we're doing very well indeed."

The Colonel left the cell and ordered a twenty four hour guard on the Mimasian. On returning to his office, he asked for the results of the search of Kildrark's ship.

Captain Hawk entered and informed the Colonel, "We have removed the ship's computers and we are attempting to hook them up to one of our own. This could take some time, however, if we're successful it should yield some valuable information, that is assuming that we can access it and translate it correctly."

"We've also found what appears to be some kind of diplomatic pouch. It was in a hidden compartment in his ship's cockpit. It contained several documents, but we haven't been able to decode or translate them yet."

"Have you scanned the documents into our computer network for analysis?", the Colonel inquired.

"We are doing that now Sir. Our computers should have results by the end of the day, touch wood. We might finally know what his mission was then Sir", replied the Captain.

"Good then, by the way, I want our scientists to start work on his ship straight away. Let's not waste any time", the Colonel ordered.

Captain Hawk acknowledged the order and then left.

Some many hours later the Mimasian documents were decoded, the contents were brought straight away before the Colonel. The Colonel read through them thoroughly, then he re-read them a second time, before calling in Captain Hawk. After the Captain had arrived the Colonel then explained the situation to him.

"Captain Hawk, it seems that the Mimasians are not going to make peace with us at all ", the Colonel informed him.

"How do you know that, Sir? The Mimasian documents?", the Captain inquired.

"Well, yes. According to these, they want more weapons to ensure our defeat. They want a quick victory", replied the Colonel.

"Colonel, I don't understand. It took fourteen of our interceptors, just to stop one of their craft", the Captain again inquired.

"Captain, their craft has only one advantage over ours and that's their deflector shields. Apparently, their weaponry isn't that much better than ours, neither are their drive systems."

Now the Captain was beginning to get the picture, "So, if we were to develop a defence shield of our own, we would be almost on an equal footing."

The Colonel replied, "We may be already Captain. On Mimas, a handful of ordinary security men with no special training, killed well over ten times the number of them. They appear to be seriously worried by our better ground fighting skills and our strength advantages. We evolved in one Earth g and they appear to have evolved in a more Martian like gravitational environment."

"Then we have to fight them on our terms, Colonel", replied the Captain.

"Perhaps, but it seems that they were also demanding a few other things from Mars. Longer range for their weapons systems and faster, more efficient drives for their fighters. Curiously, they were demanding a weapon to use against our minds. Something to make us unable to fight them or as near as the decoders can make out, a neural weapon of some kind or other."

"Then, Colonel, Sir. Mars must be their think tank. That should be where we fight them first", replied Captain Hawk.

"To right, Captain, to right. It is also possible that Mars is their industrial base as well, but we'll have to wait for the reinforcements first", the Colonel replied.

The Colonel was of course right, these aliens had a far greater number of fighter craft on both Mimas and Mars and they were also shielded. They also had a far larger number of troops. The reinforcements to be sent to Saturn and Mars were being built, the troops were being enlisted and trained, specifically for the tasks ahead of them. Then again, on both Mars and Mimas, their targets were protected by being underground. That did not help the situation at all.

The most probable targets in their own human civilisation were completely vulnerable to attack. The following day the scientists informed Colonel Bannon, that the Mimasian craft was too badly damaged to be useful. The laser beam and particle beam attacks on it had fused or disintegrated many of the useful instruments. So the Colonel decided to interrogate the Mimasian, Kildrark. He ordered the alien to be brought to him under heavy guard.

Kildrark was brought into the Colonel's office, the Colonel then told him straight up, "We have decoded your documents, Kildrark and we now know that Mars is a think tank for your species."

Kildrark was now quite stunned, he did not think these primitives were capable of doing that. He grinned evilly but said nothing.

The Colonel then demanded, "I want to know more about Mars and you are going to tell me!"

Kildrark replied loudly in his guttural voice, "I will tell you nothing, human!"

The Colonel then said to him, "You must be hungry, Kildrark. What do you eat for nourishment?"

Kildrark replied coldly and honestly, "I drink the life fluids of lesser beasts, human blood amongst other things. Human blood is our delicacy", he then grinned, showing his red stained teeth.

"Well, Kildrark. You just told me something then and if you want food, you'll have to tell me more."

"Nothing of any great importance will tell you, human!", again in his guttural voice.

"We shall see. We shall see. When was the last time you ate, bloodsucker!", his question was entirely rhetorical, "You should be getting hungry very soon, Kildrark and you must be extremely uncomfortable at the moment! Especially with your delicious delicacy, standing guard all around you!", stated the Colonel both coldly and forcefully.

Kildrark did not reply, he knew that this human was right, he was very hungry, ravenously so. The equivalent gravity here in the Colonel's office, in the outer shell of the Aries colony, was far greater than the Earth's at one point two five gs. More than four times that which Kildrark was use to. The alien stood there, he was growing weaker with every passing minute.

The Colonel on the other hand was use to this gravity, through his training in high gravity training cylinders. Colonel Bannon sat there, watching his enemy slowly break. First, the Mimasian's legs began to weaken. Eventually Kildrark's knees began to buckle and then finally he folded them underneath himself and quickly sat down.

The Colonel motioned to one of the guards. The guard then butt whipped

Kildrark harshly, with his laser rifle's butt. Kildrark fell to the ground with a loud screaming thud. The guard butt whipped Kildrark again and then Kildrark let out another loud scream and then promptly stood back up on his feet. With his deep, dark eyes, he stared coldly, even satanically, at his human adversaries, but he knew he was going nowhere.

This went on for hours, then about lunchtime, the Colonel decided to order something to eat. When his meal arrived, he ate it in front of Kildrark, who was getting weaker and weaker, suffering from the effects of the much higher gravity and his ravenous hunger. Then the Colonel requested some whole blood to be brought to his office, just in case Kildrark was a little thirsty. The Colonel knew that he was. Upon arriving, Colonel Bannon removed the package of whole blood from its refrigerated box and held it out in front of Kildrark.

Kildrark wanted it, he was excessively hungry, but instead, he stated, "No human! I would rather starve than give you any information!", although he sounded very weak.

The Colonel replied, "We shall see, we shall see", as he replaced the blood package back into its refrigerated cooler.

Eventually, Kildrark collapsed, not so much from his hunger, but far more from the effects of the higher gravity. Butt whipping him with a laser rifle butt, no longer had any effect, so the Colonel then ordered Kildrark to be taken back to his cell.

"Drag our pitiful gargoyle here back to his cell", the Colonel ordered, then added, "Let him have the blood when he's back in his cell. He's no good to us dead."

The guards did as the Colonel had ordered and as soon as Kildrark was in the lighter gravitational environment, he slowly began to recover. When the Mimasian was recovered enough, the guards gave him the blood package. They were watching in disgust as he drank the blood and then when Kildrark had finished, much to the guard's surprise, he leapt towards them standing in the doorway.

The first guard he grabbed by the throat, squeezing tightly with his clawed six-fingered hand. The guard collapsed to the floor with blood rushing from severed jugular veins. Before the second guard could react, Kildrark had ripped out his throat, savagely with his bare teeth. Kildrark then placed the bodies in his cell. He then took as much time as he dared to feed. Kildrark was ever so hungry, ravenously so. After this, he then grabbed their lasers and quickly made his escape.

Kildrark then moved off quickly down the corridor. Two colonists saw him, they were both completely unarmed, but he cut them down with the lasers anyway. Soon the guard's bodies were found in the cell and the alarm was set off. Meanwhile, however, Kildrark had worked his way out of the cell block complex to a balcony. Kildrark moved onto the balcony and quickly leapt into the air. Kildrark was now flying, armed security men watched from the balcony as he quickly flew away from them. They had been way too late to stop him.

Upon hearing the news, the Colonel quickly accessed the security camera feeds in that section of the colony. Soon the Colonel had the camera feeds he required.

The Colonel could see Kildrark flying like an eight foot gargoyle, *"Where could the alien possible go?"*, he thought to himself.

Kildrark flew towards the port facilities, the security forces sent out two hovercars to cut him off. Kildrark looked ahead to see a hovercar in front of him, he reacted quickly and began firing upon it.

The hover car burst into flames and plummeted out of the sky, exploding and on fire, before landing on an apartment building roof. The rooftop garden, with its occupants attending a barbeque, were horrified by what appeared to be a horrendous accident. It of course was not an accident.

Kildrark, however, was too late to see the second hovercar, which fired upon him immediately. He was hit and his right wing was shredded and quickly crumpled up. Kildrark fell to the ground far below. Flapping his left wing wildly, Kildrark let loose a deafening wailing scream, before landing in a park with a loud audible thud. Many people were in the park at the time and they gathered to look at the body, they were all shocked and horrified. A devil had literally fallen from the sky. Several of the citizens of the Aries colony even fainted at the sight of the devilish creature.

Colonel Bannon had possibly lost his most important source of information, Kildrark, but the little information that he had obtained was enough. He sent an urgent message to Eros. It contained a full report of everything that had transpired and requested that the reinforcements be sent to both Mars and Saturn, as soon as possible.

This report was treated with a great deal of urgency, it was only two hours before the reply came back. This reply was highly favourable. The reinforcements would be leaving for Saturn ahead of schedule. This in turn meant that his own reinforcements would be leaving ahead of schedule as well.

The Colonel was now very happy with the way Eros was reacting. There was now going to be a war! No two ways about it. Eros was now preparing to meet it, instead of saying that they could avoid it and bring about peace.

13. Quick Kill.

Mark Spencer received the communique from Eros and upon reading it, he found out that the long-awaited reinforcements were on their way and would arrive very soon. He then sent word of their departure for Saturn to the commanders of his own security forces. They were exceedingly pleased to hear the news. They then sent word around to their men, who all cheered at it. How could they have known how everything would turn out? How premature their little celebrations actually were?

From out of Mimas, a fleet of interceptors flew. The surveillance control centre immediately informed the Colonial Administrator. On Titan a compucomm buzzed with urgency.

Administrator Mark Spencer answered it, "Colonial Administrator Spencer here, who's calling?"

"Surveillance control, Sir. We have detected a fleet of Mimasian interceptors", came the reply.

"A whole fleet?", the Administrator considered, remembering the Mimasian ship that had flown towards Mars, "How many and what's their trajectory?", he enquired.

The reply came back, "Sir. About thirty craft on course to Titanian Lagrangian point five."

Mark Spencer simply replied, "Thank you", and then he quickly signed off.

Workers watched curiously as the Administrator bolted swiftly from his office, within minutes he was at the communications room.

Once in the communications room, he ordered, "Urgent message to our security command at Titanian Lagrangian point five. Thirty Mimasian interceptors are on course to you. Evacuate the colony if possible to do so.

Repulse the enemy at all cost."

The message was quickly sent to the colony at Titanian Lagrangian point five and then Administrator Spencer ordered him to alert all of the other colony outposts as well. The half-stunned Communications officer did as he was instructed. The Administrator then ordered him to send some other urgent messages. Messages were to be sent to the nearest Belter colonies, as well as to the Jovian colonies, the Aries colony in high Martian orbit and finally to Eros.

"Urgent security alert. A Mimasian fleet is on course to Titanian Lagrangian point five. A fleet of thirty interceptors. We need urgent reinforcements. Please hurry!", Administrator Spencer dictated, then when finished, he added, "And when you've done with that, put us on our highest alert status."

After that Mark Spencer went back to his office to await the outcome. There was little else he could do about the situation. It was now completely out of his control.

The Saturnian system had only been colonised fairly recently and the only colony at the Titanian Lagrangian point five, was a large O'Neil-style twin-cylinder colony with a population of around twenty five thousand souls. Their colony security command straight away launched their fifteen small interceptors towards their enemy. These interceptors were to meet with another fifteen interceptors that were being launched from the far newer O'Neil-style twin-cylinder colony, that was positioned at Titanian Lagrangian point four.

Trouble of this nature had never been considered nor expected, so the interceptors were few and far between. The colonies simply did not have enough of them. Titan's main colony on Titan itself, had twenty interceptors of its own and these were quickly launched in the hopes of defending the evacuating ships leaving the colony at Titan's Lagrangian point five. The task of evacuating the colony cylinders in time would be almost impossible, but it was being done nonetheless. Shuttle flights were bringing the refugees to the main colony on Saturn's moon Titan.

A force of thirty human interceptors fell upon the opposing thirty enemy interceptors from Mimas. A single formation of alien craft and two formations of human vessels. In the orbital path of Dione, the fleets commenced battle. Protected by deflector shields, the Mimasians had little to worry about. The humans had no such protection, they were simply flying to their doom.

The Mimasian fleet soon picked up the two formations of Saturnian interceptors, however, they did not alter course to fight them. The human vessels were soon within range and fired on the Mimasian vessels. Their lasers and particle beams had little effect on the shielded alien craft. The Mimasians returned fire, explosive flashes of light lit up the dark void of space. Of the thirty Saturnian interceptors, ten were lost on their very first exchange.

The remaining Saturnian craft turned around for another exchange. The Mimasians had not changed their course, they had all stayed on their original trajectory towards Titanian Lagrangian point five.

This time, however, another tactic was used. The human ships swiftly cut through the Mimasian formation. They did not fire upon them at all. Instead, they flashed by quickly and their plasma thruster exhausts caught fourteen Mimasian interceptors by surprise. This, the Mimasians had no shielding against and all of these craft were destroyed in brilliant flashes of light, however, in the return volley the humans lost another eight more of their own vessels.

There were now twelve colonial ships, to the remaining sixteen Mimasian vessels. The colonial ships came around for another exchange with the

Mimasians. The crews of the colonial ships prayed as they approached. The final battle between the remaining twelve Saturnian vessels and the Mimasian vessels was fierce. Plasma thruster exhausts were used by the Saturnians very effectively. Laser beams and particle beams flashed from ships on both sides. However, the outcome was predictable. The last remaining Saturnian interceptors were all annihilated, yet there were still twelve Mimasian ships left.

The evacuation ships had started to leave the threatened O'Neil-style twin-cylinder colony in droves. Each passenger shuttle was to off load refugees on Titan, then return to pick up more. In all, they had to transport nearly twenty five thousand people. The Saturnian colonies were relatively new and under populated. Each of the O'Neil-style twin-cylinder colonies could house in excess of fifty thousand people. They were extremely fortunate that the colonies were new and were not fully populated.

Very few refugees had landed on Titan when the last of the Mimasian fleet attacked. The twelve remaining interceptors had split into two groups, six apiece. One group went after the evacuating passenger shuttles, as the other group headed straight for the big O'Neil-style twin-cylinder colony.

One by one the Mimasians destroyed the fleeing craft. It did not matter to them that they were completely unarmed and only carrying civilians. They relentlessly tracked down and destroyed all of the passenger craft they came across. As the group approached Titan, the Titanian interceptors flew towards the aliens. There were only twenty in all.

As they flew toward the Mimasians, the last of the evacuation shuttles made it to Titan. Only twenty passenger shuttles had made it, very nearly two thousand people were carried by them and they made it to Titan safely. A greater number, a far greater number, had been destroyed along the way.

The Titanian interceptors entered the battle and the skies above Titan lit up with furious flashes of light, as laser beams and particle beams on both sides flashed into action. The six Mimasian interceptors were able to destroy six of the Titanian craft on this very first exchange. They then turned around and again they exchanged fire. Six more Titanian fighters were destroyed.

On the next exchange of fire, four of the Mimasians were disintegrated by plasma thruster exhausts, but again six Titanian craft were eliminated. The final two Titanian craft then engaged the last two of the Mimasians in this group. Laser beams and particle beams again blazed on both sides and all four of the craft annihilated each other during this furious exchange.

The other group of Mimasian fighters then attacked the O'Neil twin-cylinder colony at Titanian Lagrangian point five without any resistance. Only two thousand people had managed to evacuate, another five thousand people were murdered in transit, in cold blood and well over eighteen thousand people remained in the colony itself.

They were trapped as the Mimasian fighters blew hole after hole in the colony cylinders. Laser beams and particle beams flashed continuously. Explosions were everywhere and the air quickly rushed out of the massive structure through multiple holes and jagged gashes, into the cold vacuum of space. The corpses of men, women and children, even their pets, floated off into the freezing cold darkness. In the interior of the colony, the remaining colonists had shut the emergency airtight doors and bulkheads in an attempt to ensure their survival.

The massive damage done to the colony cylinders had left gaping holes and gashes in the exterior structures. The atmosphere had quickly rushed out and only the sealed emergency compartment structures had survived. In these, the many citizens of the Titanian Lagrangian point five O'Neil twin-cylinder colony, were still alive and holding out hope, praying for their survival.

Shortly thereafter, the remaining Mimasian ships split into two groups of thee. One group continued to pummel both colony cylinders with particle beams and laser beams, causing as much damage as possible. Their orders were quite simple. No human beings were to survive. They attacked anything that still appeared to be intact, carving gaping holes into any structure that looked as if it might survive.

The other group of Mimasians travelled along the full length of both badly damaged colony cylinders. They were looking for anything giving off strong power signatures. They found some. At the very end of each colony cylinder, at the very end of their long extension booms. They'd found the main colony reactor clusters. The Mimasians then fired their laser beams and particle beams strategically at the cluster of reactors, targeting their cooling systems and heat radiators.

The two clusters of seven highly efficient and powerful fission reactors sat at the ends of long extension booms at one end of both cylinders, designated the southern end. Laser beams and particle beams sliced through the vital reactor cooling systems and heat radiators. The two clusters of seven fission reactors began to overheat to critical levels very quickly.

The Mimasian interceptors then quickly flew off to a safer distance. Slowly flashes of orange light were seen flaring from the multiple reactors. Then with massive explosions of brilliant orange light, one by one, the two clusters of seven fission reactors each, exploded.

Secondary explosions then travelled down the long extension booms and into both colony cylinders proper. Arcs of blue lightning shot out of and across the colony's entire structure. Then there was another pair of massive explosions as the colony's southern end caps burst into oblivion. This was quickly followed by a series of massive explosions running along the full length of both main colony cylinders. Then finally this was followed by another pair of massive explosions, as the colony's northern end caps burst into oblivion as well.

The Titanian Lagrangian point five colony was a ruination of its former self. There wasn't much left of its former majestic structure. Finally, both main colony cylinders erupted in another series of massive explosions and tore themselves apart. The colonists of the other colonies spread across the Saturnian system, had all watched in horror and abject terror. Sadly, the O'Neil-style twin-cylinder colony, at Titanian Lagrangian point five, had not been in existence long enough to be officially given a proper name.

Surveillance control watched as the six remaining Mimasian interceptor craft all returned to Mimas. All of the Saturnian colonies were now in a state of fear and mourning after seeing the death of over eighteen thousand of their fellow colonists. With those colonists killed in transit during the evacuation, the total was actually closer to twenty three thousand.

A great many colonists were in a state of shock. The Colonial Administrator, Mark Spencer, was in a state of shock as well. However, he still had to send a communique to the other colonies of the solar system, even the Earth itself. They all needed to know about the absolute brutality of the Mimasians.

His communique read, "*The recent Mimasian attack has decimated a good fifty of our interceptors. We urgently need reinforcements in case of further Mimasian attacks. It is with deep regret and sadness, that I have to inform you all, that the O'Neil-style twin-cylinder colony at Titan Lagrangian point five is no more. The colony and around eighteen thousand people who once lived there have been annihilated. Murdered in cold blood! The people inhabiting our other colonies are in a state of shock and extreme fear. We need your help urgently, please hurry!"*

Upon receiving this communique, all of the colonies across the solar system had been shocked. The fifty new reinforcement interceptors were refuelled at the Interamnia Belter Colony. They were soon joined by another twenty local Belter craft and ready to fight. The Jovian colonies then sent word, that they were sending a fleet of fifty interceptors to join with this Armada. This Armada would contain one hundred and twenty craft when it finally arrived at Saturn, to help the endangered Saturnian colonies.

Before the Armada had even left Interamnia, Saturn was again plunged into devastating and soul crushing warfare. Another fleet of thirty Mimasian interceptors had left Mimas, the Saturnian Colonial Administrator, Mark Spencer had been alerted. He then informed the colony at Titan Lagrangian point four, to prepare for the worst and evacuate immediately. That was the Mimasian's next target!

"Do we have any remaining ships? Any at all?", Mark Spencer asked his Communications officer.

"I can contact our outer colonies, Sir", the Communications officer offered.

"Do so. Whatever they have, we need them now. Tell them to converge on Titan Lagrangian point four. Defend and protect the colony at all cost", the Colonial Administrator ordered.

The Communications officer then contacted every known colony, base, mining operation and research station within the Saturnian system.

After nearly thirty minutes, he quickly tallied up what he'd managed to muster and reported the tally to the Administrator, "Sir. We have around two dozen ships launched and on their way to Lagrangian point four."

"Sadly, that won't be enough", the Colonial Administrator noted.

The two dozen ships converged on Titan Lagrangian point four and the Mimasian fleet. Very soon the battle would begin. They all fully realised that they would not return. It was a suicide mission. They had all decided to give a good account of themselves.

Meanwhile, the colony at the Titanian leading point had begun evacuating their people. The colony was far newer than the already destroyed colony, that had been in the Titanian trailing point, but was identical in all other respects. Having seen how their sister colony had been destroyed, the colonists all prayed, that the interceptors could buy them enough time to evacuate.

The two opposing fleets met. On their first attack run, the colonial craft swept in fast and close, then swung away slicing their plasma thruster exhausts through their adversaries flight paths. The Mimasians were caught off guard. They didn't have a chance to return effective fire and twenty of their ships exploded in brilliant balls of light.

The colonial craft turned around to attack again. The cheers of their crews over their intercoms were picked by nearby colonies. On their second attack run, they decided not to get too close and picked only five targets. The interceptors concentrated their firepower on only those five targets. Four ships to each target, using both laser beams and particle beams at maximum power. It worked, five more Mimasian craft exploded. The colony craft then quickly swung away before their enemy could return fire. It appeared that the Mimasian deflector shields could not stand up against concentrated firepower.

This time the Mimasians altered course and took pursuit. The colonists turned back around to face their enemies. Again the colonists picked their targets to concentrate their firepower. This time, however, the Mimasians were ready to attack. Laser beams and particle beams flashed brilliantly on both sides. At the end of the exchange the last five Mimasian interceptors were gone, obliterated, but then so were five of the colonial craft. The remaining nineteen colonial craft headed for Titan.

While the colonial interceptors were heading back to Titan in victory, celebrations had started in the colonies of Saturn. This was just a little bit too soon, a tad premature. Just before reaching Titan, another larger fleet of Mimasian interceptors had left Mimas, fifty in all. The last of the colonial interceptors were ordered to again do battle with their enemy.

Fifteen against fifty, this was a definite suicide mission. This time the ship's crews knew for sure that they would not be returning. On approaching the remaining colonial interceptors, the Mimasians split into three groups. Two groups of ten interceptors each had peeled off from the main body. These two groups then flew in opposite directions, one towards Saturn's leading Trojan point and the other towards Saturn's trailing Trojan point, sixty degrees ahead and behind Saturn in its orbit around the Sun. The main body of Mimasian interceptors continued towards Titan Lagrangian point four.

The remaining nineteen colonial ships went into battle against thirty Mimasians. This battle did not proceed as well as the preceding one. The nineteen colonial interceptors would not be able to concentrate their firepower on this much larger enemy fleet. Instead, they swept in close to use their plasma thruster exhausts. This was effective, but not altogether so. They managed to catch five enemy ships with their ship's helium exhausts, which were of course destroyed. In this same action, however, they had lost an equal number of their own craft and the exchange was quite costly.

The two enemies then came around again for another exchange, this time the Mimasians were ready. They lost only three craft, all of the colonial interceptors but one was destroyed. This one last interceptor tried to lead the Mimasians away, he flew his craft away from Titan. As his craft flew quickly away, he noticed his hydrogen fuel cells were running very low. The Mimasians quickly followed. Soon his fuel ran out and his craft coasted along under its own inertia. He was eventually overtaken and blown out of existence.

The remaining Mimasians in this group then adjusted their course back towards Titanian Lagrangian point four and its O'Neil-style twin-cylinder colony. Another twenty five thousand colonists were now at risk. Whilst in the communications room, Mark Spencer was informed of the fleets destruction. He inquired of the Mimasian interceptors.

"Three fleets Sir. Twenty two vessels on course to Titan Lagrangian point four. Ten vessels apiece on course to Saturn's leading and trailing Trojan points", the Communications officer replied.

The Colonial Administrator stood there for a short time, then ordered the Communications officer to inform all endangered colonies to begin evacuating at once. He thought of the carnage that would soon follow. Fifty thousand people at each of Saturn's leading and trailing Trojan points. Another twenty five thousand people at Titan Lagrangian point four. A good hundred and twenty five thousand people facing total destruction and not a single thing he could do to stop it. The situation looked hopeless.

The evacuation from Titan Lagrangian point four was moving smoothly, but only ten thousand people had made it to Titan and safety when the Mimasians attacked. The twenty two craft had branched into two groups, with one of the groups flying towards the fleeing passenger shuttles. They quickly caught up with the passenger shuttles and began destroying them without mercy. All except those that had made it into Titan's thick atmosphere. Some, a few, had been lucky.

The other group flew towards the massive O'Neil-style twin-cylinder colony in Titan Lagrangian point four. They attacked it relentlessly, laser beams and particle beams flashing continuously. Explosions were everywhere and the fighters kept up their attack. Cruelly taking their time, when they could have done the job so much more quickly, simply by blowing up the O'Neil-style twin-cylinder colony's two clusters of seven fission reactors.

The people of the Saturnian colonies watched in horror. They were unable to help. There was nothing they could do. For hours on end, the Mimasians continued firing at both colony cylinders, now all but guttered wrecks. Even the colony cylinder's air-tight, sealed compartments and bulkheads couldn't have survived the onslaught.

Then the Mimasians left, there was nothing left to destroy and the immense colony was now a lifeless hulk. The bodies of well over ten thousand people floated in and around both devastated colony cylinders. Wild flashes of blue electrical arcs were seen in all parts of them. Eventually, after a few more hours, one by one, the components of the stricken colony exploded. First the southern end caps, then the northern end caps, followed by the two man colony cylinders. The massive explosions of brilliant blue lights signified their total and complete destruction.

Yet, this wasn't the end, after many hours of flight, two more fleets of Mimasian interceptors were now approaching the other two main colony zones in Saturn's orbital realm. Saturn's forward and trailing Trojan points. These two Saturnian Lagrangian zones had been setup first, shortly before the Saturnian system itself was colonised.

The evacuation of these colonies was well underway, people were fleeing in any possible craft available to them. Packed into every available ship like sardines, they all fled. They did not fly towards Saturn and Titan, that was where the enemy was coming from. Instead they coasted swiftly, but silently towards Jupiter and the nearest Asteroid Belt colonies. There at the Jovian and Belter colonies, they might yet find refuge. Their ships running dark and silent, they had only hope on their side.

These refugees were escaping successfully, the Mimasians hadn't noticed their flight. They didn't have the fuel to catch up with them either, even if they had noticed them. As they had more time to evacuate their people, more people could be saved.

When the Mimasians had finally arrived at their two target locations, very nearly fifty thousand people had been evacuated from each. Most but not all of their populations. Upon sighting the last of the fast-fleeing humans, they let them go, they hadn't the fuel to chase after them.

They went straight for the massive O'Neil-style twin-cylinder colonies in each zone. There was only the one massive colony at each of the locations. Relentlessly, they fired their laser beams and particle beams at the colonies. The colony cylinders were quickly holed and like the other two colonies before them, they were completely defenceless. Within no time at all, their atmospheres had been lost to the cold vacuum of space through gaping huge holes blown into their structures.

Those people who had not escaped, had sealed themselves in airtight emergency compartments, just like the people of the other two colonies, but this would not save them. The Mimasians were relentless, as again and again, they swept in and fired their weapons. Eventually even the air tight compartments were holed. The remaining colonists all perished, as had those before them.

Approximately three hours after the Mimasians had left, there was a series of immense, brilliant blue explosions at each of the Saturnian leading and trailing Trojan points. The people of Titan knew, that those two massive O'Neil-style twin colonies were no more. Nothing would be left but burnt and twisted metallic hulks, scattered debris and the bodies of the dead.

However, in these two cases, close to a hundred thousand people had escaped the Mimasian onslaught.

After this series of attacks and battles, the human death toll now stood at nearly fifty thousand. The damage to the Saturnian colonial system stood at four immense, O'Neil-style twin-cylinder colonies, which when combined were capable of supporting close to quarter of a million people. This was destruction on a scale that had not been seen since the World Wars, more than two centuries earlier.

The Saturnians were now totally at the Mimasian's mercy and the Mimasians had yet to show any mercy at all. Indeed, the enemy appeared to be totally incapable of mercy. The Saturnian system's seventy four interceptors were all destroyed. The thirty thousand people living on Titan and the mining colonies of the smaller moons of Saturn, were all in a state of near total shock and fear.

The seventy interceptors that had left Interamnia, were now, just far too late. The fifty Jovian interceptors that were on their way from Jupiter, were also, far too late. Soon these two fleets would join to form an Armada and the Armada would arrive at Saturn very soon. The Saturnians asked themselves two vital questions.

Would they be extinct before the Armada arrived?

Can the reinforcements even defeat the Mimasians?

These people were all living in great fear, they very had little faith left and almost no hope. Colonial Administrator Mark Spencer had sent an urgent message to Eros, Jupiter, the Aries colony and several of the larger Belter colonies. The contents of the messages informed the leaders of the colonies, as to the war that had begun. Again the Colonial Administrator asked for urgent help.

Soon the leaders of the all the colonies were in great fear, they did not want the Mimasians to win at Saturn. If they did, where would the enemy attack next. Eros was flooded with urgent messages from all sections of the solar system, petitioning for greater help. They wanted Eros to declare the entire solar system, to be on a total war footing.

Eros then decided to step up weapons production. Plans were being created for newly designed craft. Interceptor weaponry wasn't powerful enough to pierce the Mimasian deflector shields and the interceptors were too small to contain more powerful weapons.

The development of new classes of weapons was begun and new ships as well. Newly designed fighter craft, as well as the newly designed Battle Cruiser and the Dreadnought. These new classes of vessels would contain multiple laser beams and multiple particle beams, at the very least, ten times more powerful than those in the original class of interceptors.

There were, however, some problems with the new designs. They would need deflector shields, as would the new interceptors. The Dreadnought and Battle Cruisers would also need far more powerful and efficient plasma drives. Present human technology could not as yet supply these. Their scientists were working on these problems. However, they were many years away from any possible solutions.

All of the colonies had also demanded deflector shields. These too, were beyond the present level of any human technology.

The reinforcements for Mars would be ready for transport very soon. Hearing of the massacres at Saturn, Colonel Bannon demanded that their delivery be sped up. By his reasoning, he had to launch an attack on the Martian monoliths as soon as possible. They were the Mimasian's think tank, all of the technology needed to beat them was there, just waiting for them to take it.

Doctor Gideon Reas had once told him, *"Just think of what we might learn"* and Colonel Bannon now knew, he was right!

From Mars, the secret of the Mimasian's deflector shield might be learnt.

The entire solar system was watching the Saturnian system. Soon the reinforcements and the Belter interceptors would join up with those of the Jovian system. Then the Armada, one hundred and twenty craft strong would be on its way to take the fight to the Mimasians. The upcoming battle would be great and the fate of the whole of human civilisation could very well depend on the outcome. The very future of humanity was clearly at stake.

Colonel Bannon knew that this battle would begin before his own reinforcements arrived. He was also waiting to see the outcome of this battle. Although he didn't like the Armada's chances, without shields, they would have to fight very cautiously. Skill and tactics would be their only option to ensure their victory. A victory that was far from certain.

Meanwhile on Titan, the Colonial Administrator, Mark Spencer, had been busy setting up defences. Laser pillboxes and tanks were quickly being built. Fighter craft specifically designed for Titan's thick, nitrogen, methane atmosphere were also being built. These would have far greater manoeuvrability than the Mimasian interceptors in Titan's thick atmosphere. The whole colony and the population of Titan were now being placed on a total war footing.

The Mimasians, however, were not attacking Titan, nor any of the big mining colonies on the other smaller moons. Instead, they had set up tight surveillance around them and had them all blockaded. All of the colonised moons of Saturn were now completely isolated from each other.

Colony craft could no longer fly between the moons of Saturn and all communications were being jammed. Mimasian interceptors were patrolling all of the colonised moons and the Saturnian space lanes quite heavily. The enemy now completely controlled all of the local space lanes. Nothing at all could fly around in the Saturnian system that was not Mimasian.

They didn't send in any landing craft, however, nor did they land any occupational forces. They merely patrolled and isolated the Saturnian colonies. Keeping all of the colonists in a state of total fear, panic and expectation, crushing their morale. A powerful feeling of total hopelessness was gripping the colonists. More than a few colonists had been found dead, after having committed suicide. This further spread fear and panic, so the Saturnian Colonial Administrator, Mark Spencer, declared martial law, ruling by decree.

Many Saturnian colonists watched and waited for the approach of the Armada. They saw nothing, no sign of the Armada's approach could be seen. No one on Titan, not even the government, could detect the Armada's approach. Mark Spencer kept assuring his people, that they were coming, though even he, himself, wasn't entirely certain.

14. Battling the Ice Moon.

The Armada quickly approached the Saturnian system. At about forty million kilometres away, the one hundred and twenty craft switched over to their ion drives, after cruising most of the distance at high speed. This way they would be harder to detect, than if they had used their plasma drives.

Instead of heading directly into the system, the Armada split into two fleets of sixty interceptors each. Both these fleets flew around the outskirts of the Saturnian system in opposite directions. They flew under strict communications silence and did their best to avoid being noticed by the Mimasians. The fleet feared the worst when they could not detect any signals from the Saturnian colonies nor any of their outposts. Maybe they were too late to save them.

Flying around the Saturnian system in a wide circumference, the two fleets then slowly adjusted their courses into a trajectory that would bring them closer to the planet Saturn itself. After passing the orbital distance of Saturn, the two fleets then adjusted their courses again. This new trajectory brought them around behind Saturn at a distance of around five hundred thousand kilometres. Then the two fleets approached each other from behind Saturn in opposite directions, to eventually regroup.

Saturn's moon, Mimas was at the moment at its closest approach to the Sun, on the other side of Saturn from them. So the two fleets again separated once again. This time they flew slowly on courses above and below Saturn, as close to its upper atmosphere as possible. Coming down on the sun-ward side the two fleets then approached Saturn's rings, but with one fleet above and the other fleet below.

The two fleets then slowly flew across the rings, but as close to them as possible. After they'd slowly flown across D, C, B and A rings, the fleets then quickly flew across Saturn's F ring. From there, they quickly moved on towards the two co-orbital moons. The co-orbital moons were between the two fleets and Mimas. Each of the two fleets was hidden behind these two moons. They had slipped in close to the Mimasians without being noticed. They were undetected and had the element of surprise on their side. The two fleets then flew quickly towards Mimas, then when at a much closer distance to the little ice moon, they switched back to their plasma drives.

The Mimasians were caught by complete surprise. They had scaled down their operations when they saw how easily they had defeated the Saturnian colonists. Their surveillance of the mining colonies and of Titan itself required very few craft and their own security at Mimas was also scaled down. Only ten alien interceptors were in space around Mimas.

Fortunately all of the colonised moons had been on the sun-ward side of Saturn as the two fleets approached. One of the fleets two fleets flew directly towards Mimas. The other fleet split up into two groups. Thirty interceptors flew towards Titan, then the remaining thirty interceptors also split up. Six interceptors each had been sent to each of the other smaller colonised moons, Tethys, Dione, Rhea, Iapetus and Enceladus. Their carefully thought-out plan was being implemented.

With lightning speed, the first fleet fell upon Mimas and the Mimasians were outnumbered sixty to ten. They fell upon the Mimasian fighters before they even knew they were there. With all of their laser beams and particle beams aimed at their targets to concentrate their firepower. Six of the colonials to each Mimasian interceptor. The resulting clash destroyed all of the enemy craft, vaporising them utterly and very soon they were attacking the surface of Mimas itself.

The colonials picked out the ground installations and fighter launching bays. Any Mimasian craft that tried to take off from Mimas was utterly destroyed, as they attempted to launch. Immense explosions spread throughout the launching bays, ripping them apart.

Bright lights flashed across the surface of Mimas, as the colonial laser beams and particle beams blazed. Soon they had blocked and destroyed all visible launching bays. Mimasian surface armoured divisions were quickly destroyed as well. The colonials very quickly had complete control of the skies above Mimas.

After closing off access to space from the interior of Mimas, the fleet then went on to help the others, while leaving a small contingent behind to keep a close watch on Mimas itself. Six fighters approached the moon Enceladus and only one Mimasian vessel was detected. The six fighters came into battle quickly. They concentrated their firepower and quickly destroyed it. After carefully scanning   Enceladus, only human complexes were located. The Mimasians hadn't yet landed any ground forces there and as the craft signalled the colony, the people all rejoiced.

Those six interceptors then rejoined the main fleet, while at the moon Tethys another six interceptors came upon a single Mimasian ship. The battle was similar to that on Enceladus and the people of Tethys were soon rejoicing as well. Then those six interceptors also joined the main fleet. The same scenario played out at the Saturnian moon, Dione and then the Saturnian moon, Rhea.

These battles had been easy, as the enemy was badly out numbered and caught by complete surprise. The Mimasians had not believed that their human adversaries could muster their forces so quickly. This did not happen at Saturn's largest moon Titan, where thirty colonial craft came upon ten Mimasians ships and this time, they were ready for them.

There the battle went badly, the colonials couldn't concentrate their firepower effectively. During their first exchange the colonial craft aimed to strike only six of their enemy, by concentrating their firepower. They pierced the Mimasian's shields and utterly destroyed them, but in the very first volley returned by the Mimasians, they lost fourteen of their own craft.

In their next exchange, the four remaining Mimasians picked off nine colonials without a single loss. That left only seven colonial interceptors remaining in this group and the Mimasians quickly destroyed them on their very next exchange. By this time, the main fleet had moved up and the four remaining Mimasian ships were then quickly destroyed. The battle above the skies of Titan was then over.

The battle at the Saturnian moon, Iapetus, went as smoothly as with the other smaller moons and soon most of the remaining ninety colonial craft, had regrouped at Titan. Sixty remained in space and thirty landed on Titan itself for refuelling and for their pilots to rest. Refuelling of the remaining interceptors was yet to be arranged. The fleet's commander, Colonel Manson, straight away went to see Saturn's Colonial Administrator, Mark Spencer.

Mark Spencer was very pleased to see Colonel Manson, he offered him a seat and thanked him for showing up and beating back the Mimasians.

"Colonel, I'm glad you and your people have arrived. I just wish it could have been sooner."

"Yes, well, Mr Spencer, we got here as quick as we could. Most of these fighters had to be made from scratch and their pilots had to be trained, you do understand."

"Well, Colonel, I do realise that, but as you've probably heard, we've lost a hell of a lot of people out here. Those Mimasian bastards have a level of cruelty to them that is beyond belief."

"I know and I wish we could have been here sooner, but we just weren't ready."

"I know that, Colonel, neither were we. I don't know that anyone could have been ready for what's taken place out here. We did not know of the Mimasian's existence until we discovered Mimas was hollow and ventured into its interior. "

Their conversation continued, "Well now, Colonel. Now you're here, you have those Mimasians on the run."

"Not really, Mr Spencer. We've got them locked down for the moment and we have demolished their ground forces, but I don't how long they'll take, to clear out their launching bays."

"Then we'll have to be ready before they can dig themselves out, Colonel."

"That is correct, Mr Spencer, but at the moment my fighters have to be refuelled. It has also been a very long flight to get here and my pilots need some rest as well."

The thirty fighters that had landed on Titan were all quickly refuelled and their pilots were allowed six hours of rest, after which they were sent back into space. Colonel Manson had ordered these thirty fighters to patrol Mimas. Their mission was very simple, to prevent the Mimasians from launching their interceptors at all cost. The handful of interceptors that had been left patrolling Mimas were then recalled back to Titan for refuelling.

The next thirty fighters then landed on Titan and these were also refuelled, with their pilots being given six hours of rest as well. After which these thirty interceptors were also sent back into orbit around Titan. The last group of fighters then took their turn to land on Titan and be refuelled. As with the first two groups, their pilots were give six hour of rest as well.

Colonel Manson's strategy was to keep all of the Mimasian launching bays blocked up so that they couldn't launch any more interceptors. This in turn meant that the Mimasians could not launch any more attacks on the Saturnian colonies. It seemed to be a simple enough plan and the Colonel organised a rotation system for the three fighter groups.

After three hours of patrolling the skies above Titan from orbit, that group would then leave for three hours patrolling Mimas. The group that had been refuelled and their pilots rested on Titan, would then launch into Titanian orbit for three hours of patrolling the Titanian skies. The group patrolling Mimas, who had been relieved of duty would then return to Titan for refuelling, maintenance and six hours of rest. So each group would spend six hours in space and six hours on Titan.

If they could keep the Mimasians pinned down indefinitely, it would give Eros and the rest of the solar system time to respond. They needed this time, the solar system was basically unprepared for any kind of military threat. This conflict with the Mimasians was a completely unexpected conflict.

Thirty colonial fighters approached Mimas. The Mimasians had not yet completely cleared their launching bays and couldn't launch any of their fighters. The colonial fighters approached Mimas and upon detecting the almost cleared launching bays, they immediately attacked once again. Their laser beams and particle beams blazed once more, this time their targets survived the attacks. The colonials came around for another attack run. This time they concentrated their firepower and yet again their targets survived.

The very first thing the Mimasians had done on being able to access the surface, was to put in place powerful deflector shield generators. The Mimasians had protected their launching bays. Even though they weren't yet cleared enough to launch any interceptors. The shield generators they used, were much more powerful than those on their fighter craft and so the colonials could not break through even using concentrated firepower.

A message was sent to Titan from the colonial fighters patrolled Mimas. Colonel Manson and Mark Spencer received the Message, they were not pleased, it was somewhat unpleasant.

"What now, Colonel, they've shielded all their launching bays?", enquired Mark Spencer.

"I don't really know, Mr Spencer. They can repair their launch bays quite easily while they're shielded, but we can probably still pick them off as they launch", Colonel Manson speculated.

"I'm not a military man, Colonel. Just how does that work?", Mark Spencer enquired.

Colonel Manson replied confidently, "When they launch any craft, they'll have to shut down their shields or at least provide a hole to launch through. That's when we can hit them!"

Soon the Mimasian launching bays were cleared and ready, it had them taken them quite some time to repair them. This latest colonial fighter group had been replaced by a fresh team of thirty craft from Titan. The Mimasians began to launch their interceptors.

A small hole was monitored in the deflector shield of one of the launch bays, a colonial fighter was at hand. A few seconds later an interceptor was launched. The pilot of the colonial fighter reacted to the launch immediately. No sooner than the interceptor was clear of its launching bay and long before its pilot could switch on his own deflector shield, it was caught by the colonial's particle beam. The Mimasian interceptor flared brilliantly then disappeared.

Again and again from this and other launching bays, interceptors were launched, only to find the colonial fighters waiting for them. At one launching bay, a Mimasian interceptor tried to launch with its own shields already activated. Its deflector shields reacted adversely with the shields of the launching bay. The interceptor exploded before it could clear the launching bay and a massive explosion ripped through it, tearing it asunder. It appeared that the Mimasians would have to find a new strategy.

Soon the colonials had noticed even more activity around the entrances of the launching bays. Construction of some kind was taking place and these, like the launching bays themselves, were also protected by their launching bay shields. When the constructions were finally completed, the colonials found that they had very real and terrible problems.

The colonial fighters were prepared to meet the launching of any Mimasian craft, they waited and watched the launching bays like hawks. After a long wait, the deflector shield around one of the launching bays shut down completely. Then before the nearest colonial fighter could react, a high-powered laser fired and the colonial fighter was destroyed. Then the defence shield was reactivated once again, but not before the safe launching of at least one Mimasian interceptor.

This began happening at all of the launching bays across Mimas. They would deactivate their shields, fire on colonial fighters and destroy them. Then before other colonials could react they would safely launch one of their own interceptors. After launching their interceptor, they would then reactivate the defence shield once more, to protect the launching bay once again. The colonial fighters could no longer effectively stop the enemy from launching their own fighters.

In this way, all of the thirty colonial fighters patrolling Mimas were soon destroyed. Soon thereafter a fleet of sixty Mimasian fighters were on their way to Titan, equal in number to the remaining colonial craft. Colonel Manson and Administrator Spencer were informed of this new threat and straight away the thirty craft patrolling Titan were ordered to fly down to be refuelled. Upon being refuelled these and the thirty craft already on the surface, were then quickly launched back into space and battle. It was a worried Colonel who spoke to Mark Spencer over his communicator.

"Mr Spencer. I am not terribly confident about the outcome of the battle ahead. It would be a good idea to place all of your remaining colonies on red alert."

"Colonel I've already done that. If things do go badly, our people will give them a fight to remember. To defeat us they will have to utterly destroy us."

"I hope things don't come down to that. With luck maybe we'll prevail, but don't count on it, Mark."

"Okay, Colonel, we'll be prepared. I hope lady luck is on your side. I know your boys will give it their best shot. Good luck to you, Sir."

Their conversation ended and Colonel Manson lead his fleet of sixty fighters into battle. The Mimasians approached, their sixty craft fully shielded against attack. Colonel Manson ordered his fleet into a formation of twelve groups of five. He then ordered each group to fly as a unit and also to fire as a unit, fully utilising their plasma thruster exhausts and to concentrate their firepower as necessary.

The two enemy fleets met. On their first exchange, twelve Mimasians fighters were destroyed by concentrated firepower, another ten were destroyed by the use of their plasma thruster exhausts. In this exchange, however, the colonials lost thirty eight of their own craft.

The remaining colonial craft came around for another exchange. The colonial fighters couldn't hold their formations and the battle quickly turned into an all out dog fight. In the end the colonials were all destroyed and there were still twenty eight Mimasian fighters left. These fighters didn't continue on to Titan, instead they all returned to Mimas.

Something that Administrator Mark Spencer found quite perplexing, *"Why would they not push their advantage"*, he thought to himself.

A short time later, a larger fleet of one hundred fighters launched from Mimas. Forty went straight into a defensive patrol around Mimas itself. The rest of them split up, five groups of six went into patrol of the five smaller colonised moons. The remaining thirty fighters then went into patrol around Titan. The Saturnian colonial system found itself back its previous captive state. They were literally back at square one!

The colonies of Saturn were again isolated from each other and all communications between them was once again jammed. The Mimasians did not try to land or occupy them, however, they had more important plans to put into motion. They firmly believed that if they defeated the Earth and Eros, that the rest of the solar system would fall into despair and fall straight into their hands. All of humanity would surely have to surrender to them. The humans would be slaves.

Once the Mimasians had cut off the Saturnian colonists from the rest of the solar system, the leaders of all of the other colonies and also the leaders of Eros and the Earth, became very concerned. They did not know whether their fellow colonists were still alive or not. They did, however, know that the reinforcements had been destroyed and that Saturn was now in the hands of the Mimasians once again.

At the Aries colony in high Martian orbit, Colonel Bannon was eagerly awaiting the arrival of his own reinforcements. Along with these, he would also receive the ground troops and the tanks that were to be sent to Saturn. As the Saturnian colonial system had fallen to the Mimasians, Eros had decided, that now it was time to capture their think tank, Mars. There perhaps, they would find or capture the technology required to defeat the Mimasians. The liberation of Saturn would be dependent on a successful military campaign on Mars.

The fate of the entire human species may well depend on a land war on Mars and how it progressed. It was hoped that human beings, being use to higher gravitational environments, would have a distinct advantage in this more conventional kind of warfare. Colonel Bannon had a lot on his mind, the fate of the entire human species was clearly resting on his leadership, on his abilities, he simply had to succeed. There was no other choice!

15. The Unthinkable.

The reinforcements arrived at the Aries colony in high Martian orbit and Colonel Bannon began to put his plan into operation. The Colonel now had thirty new interceptors with the most advanced plasma drives to add to the seventy craft he already had. Eros had also informed him, that there would be more interceptors on their way as soon as they were completed.

Of tanks, he now had at his disposal sixty, including the thirty that were to be sent to Saturn. His army had received ten thousand men, including the five thousand that were also supposed to be stationed at Saturn. This swelled the ranks of his army to twenty thousand men, not including his officer ranks.

"Captain Hawk, is everything okay? Are we all set to go?", Colonel Bannon enquired.

"Yes, Sir. We're just waiting for the final order to go Sir", the Captain replied.

"Good then, Captain. Land your tanks in groups of fifteen at these four points, here, here, here and here", the Colonel pointed to four points marked on his map, "Set up a perimeter around the monoliths and spread our men out evenly. I want our troop transports close at hand, so we can move in our troops quickly if required. Keep the interceptors on standby in a parking orbit, I expect we will need them for air support. Make sure our commandos are prepared to infiltrate those monoliths. I want every Martian installation taken."

Captain Hawk acknowledged the orders, then left to put them in motion.

Meanwhile on Mars, Gideon and Sandra had been lucky so far, the aliens had been treating them quite well. Now, however, the aliens had finished studying the humans. Their treatment would definitely not be so lenient from now on. Winchilly sat in their cell with Sandra and Gideon, the three of them had just finished eating. Winchilly then informed them both, that Colonel Bannon's forces were going to attack the monoliths very soon.

Winchilly's people had been carefully monitoring the Colonel's surveillance people telepathically. There were very distinct indications that an attack by the Colonel's forces was imminent. The aliens didn't know and would be caught by complete surprise. Winchilly explained that although her people would not fight, they would do their best to sabotage the alien's weaponry. The three then decided that it would be best for them to escape as soon as possible. The information they had would greatly speed up the success of the attack that was soon to come.

The cell door slammed open and a high ranking alien walked in. They could tell the alien was high ranking by his height. He was far taller than most of them.

The alien stood watching them for long moments with an evil grin upon his face, then he spoke in a guttural voice, he demanded of Gideon and Sandra, "Your garments, humans. Remove them now!"

Gideon and Sandra looked at the Alien, then they looked at each other. They didn't understand what the alien meant, not just his guttural accent, but why would he demand their clothes.

Again the alien demanded, this time more forcefully, "Your garments, humans. I want them now!"

Gideon and Sandra again looked at each other, then slowly began to undress. Soon they were standing naked in their cell, as another, shorter alien gathered their clothes together. It then threw them a pair of loin cloths, before it and its superior, quickly left their cell. Gideon and Sandra were bewildered, quite perplexed, they put on the loin cloths and then looked to Winchilly for answers.

Winchilly had tears in her beautiful emerald green eyes, she fully understood what had taken place. Winchilly was not afraid for herself, she had lived her whole life here in this hellish place. Winchilly knew what would happen now and she feared for her human friends, whom she had grown to love very dearly during their short period of incarceration. Winchilly began to explain to them, that from now on, they would be treated just like her people and subject to exactly the same treatment.

Gideon and Sandra were both shocked by this news, they looked at their Martian friend. Gideon looked at Sandra and Winchilly as they quietly sat there almost naked except for their loincloths. Fear clearly showed on both of their faces. Gideon couldn't let anything happen to them, not now. These two women both meant more to him than anything. He loved them both dearly. Never could he choose between them and he'd do his best to protect them. Now they had no choice, they had to escape and they had to do so very soon.

Winchilly looked at Gideon, she looked deeply into his mind. Winchilly knew Gideon's deepest feelings and she fully understood them. Telepathically, Winchilly then talked with Sandra. The two women both felt very deeply for Gideon, they both loved him. They communicated silently for some time, eventually deciding to share Gideon between them. They would do their best to stay together, no matter what.

Colonel Bannon watched as his troops were deployed. His hope of winning this battle was to get his troops inside the monoliths. The Colonel's tanks would aid in this by forming four armoured columns. These would push forward, his troops quickly following. His interceptors would provide the necessary air support and also defend against any enemy interceptors.

Captain Hawk moved the troops and the tanks quickly and quietly into their positions. He noticed that the Martian air was thick, humid, awfully stanky, but also rich in oxygen. Fortunately his troops all had their re-breathers to filter out any harmful compounds.

The gravity was far weaker than the troops were use to, this would be an advantage in close quarter hand to hand combat. His men regularly trained in both high and low gravity conditions and were proficient in both. His men would find the fighting far easier here, than they would have on the Earth.

The only drawback was the lack of significant ground cover. There were many rocks littering the Martian landscape, behind which the troops could gain cover, but nothing apart from that and the aliens could fly. Trees would have been a handy thing to have, but as yet there was only a thick covering of small grasses and a lot of seedlings and small saplings. He had wished that the forests were more developed, but that was at least a dozen Martian years away. Captain Hawk now waited for the final order.

Gideon had watched in wonder as Sandra and Winchilly both moved their bunks next to his in their cell. It was nearing the sleep cycle of the Martian day. The two women then led Gideon over to the now-conjoined bunks. Gideon spent most of the night in Winchilly's and Sandra's embrace, before finally falling asleep in their arms. Sandra straightened her long brown hair then reached over and kissed Winchilly. Then they both curled up beside Gideon and soon fell asleep beside him.

The next day, the three had slept well into the Martian morning. Gideon awoke with Sandra on his left and Winchilly on his right. Both of the women were still asleep, curled up beside him, his arms were pinned beneath them, their heads were resting gently upon his chest. Gideon moved his arms to pull them closer to him and as the two women rolled closer to him, they awoke. They both smiled at him and he smiled back, looking from one to the other.

Gideon noticed a gentle, content, almost a purring in Winchilly's telepathic mind. Winchilly then pressed her face tightly to Gideon's chest, as if afraid to let go. As Winchilly did this, Sandra raised herself up on one arm, she looked at Winchilly and gently stroked the Martian woman's golden yellow hair. Winchilly's emerald green eyes looked back at Sandra and the Martian woman smiled. Sandra then rested her head upon Gideon's chest once more. The three then remained in their bunks, soothing their fears in each other's mutual embrace.

Sometime later the cell door slammed open and five aliens entered their cell. They all looked at the three on the bunks and then laughed loudly and raucously at them, before then ordering them to come with them. Gideon, Sandra and the young Martian woman Winchilly were then led through the maze of corridors and passages beneath the Martian monoliths. Winchilly informed her two friends, that she had never been in these particular passages before. These passages were unknown to her.

After nearly an hour of walking they entered a large chamber, a small light at the top illuminated the whole inside. High above them, there was a group of twenty or so aliens flying about the chamber.

Twenty females and one male to be precise, the male alien being the tallest of the aliens thus far seen. Winchilly then informed her friends, that they were in the Prince's chamber. The Prince was in control of the monoliths on Mars, as well as the local aliens and the Martians, although he was a subordinate of the Emperor.

Above them were the Prince himself, his first wife and his concubines. They were flying in a courtship formation. Gideon looked around the chamber and noticed at various locations, sets of manacles on the floor, he now became extremely concerned and worried about their current situation.

Captain Hawk received a scrambled communique from the Aries colony. Waiting by the decoder, he finally received the decoded transcript.

It read, *"The Sun is slowly setting, run fast and prop it up."*

This was the code phrase he'd been waiting for, the final order.

Captain Hawk gave his command and the four columns of tanks were set in motion, their objective the monoliths. He then gave the order to move his troops forward. Behind the tank columns, the men marched, a mighty army of highly trained and armed troops.

When reasonably close to the monoliths, the infantry began to fan out from the armoured columns. They were soon spotted by the alien's defences. Low flying interceptors came out to face the humans, their pilots quickly switching on their shields. With their shields raised they attempted to get closer. The tanks opened up, laser beams and particle beams blazed. Not one of these dozen attacking alien craft survived, their shields had all failed. The same thing had happened at the other three tank columns.

At the royal chamber deep under the Martian surface, three humans awaited their fate. While they waited, three more aliens rushed into the chamber. These new aliens straight away flew up to meet with the Prince. A quick exchange of guttural speech occurred. Then the three aliens quickly flew down to the group on the floor. They exchanged words with the guards in their guttural language and then the three aliens left with four of the guards following closely behind.

Gideon, Sandra and Winchilly were now guarded by only one alien armed with a laser pistol. Winchilly explained that the monoliths were under attack and their guards were needed elsewhere. Gideon regarded this as a better situation than before, only one guard, now if they could only escape.

They had to, there was no other choice. The flying aliens then flew down to the trio. Gideon quickly noticed that only the Prince among them was actually armed. Two weapons and only two male aliens to deal with. The situation was looking better for them, how wrong could he have been?

The alien Prince moved towards them, he grabbed at Winchilly and then pushed her aside, "I can have a Martian woman any time", he said in his guttural voice, characteristic of his species.

The Prince then turned to Sandra, "You, I shall have you, human!", he shouted at her.

All of the female aliens in the chamber burst out in what could only be described as an evil, maniacal laughter. They all had broad grins upon their devilish looking faces.

"Not gonna happen", Gideon thought to himself before going berserk.

Gideon dropped down low and then suddenly brought up his elbow sharply into the remaining guard's groin. As the guard doubled over in agony, Gideon grabbed the alien's gun arm, forcing it to fire into its own chest. Laser light flashed and the guard's chest exploded outward through its own back. Burning blood and guts flew everywhere, leaving behind a cauterised wound and a dead alien corpse.

Gideon wasn't finished and before the alien Prince could react, the terraformer scientist leapt. Gideon knocked the laser pistol from out of the alien Prince's thumb-less, six fingered hand. Then Gideon swiftly kicked the alien Prince straight in the groin. The alien Prince then doubled over in shrieking agony, bringing its head down closer to Gideon's level.

Then in rapid succession, Gideon threw punches at the alien Prince's head. Gideon was used to a far heavier gravity and his punches had an unexpectedly heavy impact. The alien Prince's head began to loll about loosely upon his neck. Then there was a loud cracking sound as the alien Prince's skull fractured and he dropped lifelessly to the floor. Upon seeing their Prince die, there were shrieks of dismay from the Prince's wife and his concubines. An extreme anger was clearly visible in their eyes.

Before the three could react any further, the female aliens had taken action. All at once, they flew at Gideon and Sandra. Winchilly, they completely ignored her, as she was a Martian woman and not a threat to them. Sandra was bashed roughly about the head and quickly knocked out. Sandra slumped unconscious to the floor. Winchilly ran swiftly to her side.

Gideon had other problems. The alien females had picked him up, then they flew to about twenty feet above the floor and dropped him. Fortunately, the Martian gravity was only point three eight gs. Gideon landed on the floor with a dull thud and although he wasn't injured, he did have the wind knocked out of him.

The deceased alien Prince's wife screamed out in her guttural voice, "Secure him to the floor! My Husband's lust for his woman was the cause of his death! I will use this human as she would have been!
Then you will all take your own turns! When we are finished, we will all of us, drink their blood!"

Gideon was then stretched out and manacled to the floor, he was unable to move. The female aliens stood all around him, watching the dead alien Prince's wife approach. Winchilly could not help, her kind could not perpetrate violence. Instead Winchilly tried desperately to awaken the unconscious Sandra. Nigh on the whole Martian species could feel the anguish of her mind, screaming out as she watched the angry alien females approach Gideon.

As a Martian, Winchilly could not use violence and was unable to stop them. Instead, she reached deeply into Sandra's mind. She had to wake her, only by doing this could she help Gideon. Deeper and deeper, Winchilly reached into Sandra's unconscious mind. Tears streamed down Winchilly's cheeks as she continued with her attempts to awaken Sandra.

Gideon watched as the alien Princess approached. The alien Princess crouched down beside him and then tore off his loin cloth. Then the alien Princess smiled showing her red-stained fangs. Gideon turned his face away from her, at the sheer unpleasantness of the sight.

Gently, ever so gently, the deceased Prince's wife stroked him until he was aroused. The other alien females all giggled and laughed amongst themselves, as they understood, that they would be next in turn when their Princess was finished with him.

Then the deceased alien Prince's wife climbed on top of Gideon. She carefully thrust down on Gideon, taking him inside of her. Then with a rhythmic motion of her wings, she increased the power of her thrusting. The other alien females all began to squabble amongst themselves, over who would be next, all the while their Princess screamed out in ecstasy.

Winchilly reached even deeper into Sandra's mind and there she found the tiniest spark of consciousness. Winchilly nurtured it, fed strength into it, eventually the spark of consciousness began to expand and grow. Sandra very quickly regained consciousness. Winchilly spoke quickly with her mind, telepathically explaining the full situation to Sandra. Then Sandra reacted with a swiftness and a harshness that surprised even herself.

Sandra rolled over to the alien Prince's laser, grabbed it and then carefully stood up, still slightly giddy from being knocked out. As Sandra stood up, the dead alien Prince's concubines then turned to face her.

Sandra began shooting at them relentlessly. The other alien females moved towards her. Without the slightest hint of mercy, Sandra cut each and every one of them down with the laser pistol. Their bodies dropped to the ground in screaming agony. Their alien blood flowed freely.

The alien Princess was oblivious to the carnage behind her, her mind was lost in the ecstasy of her perverted deed. Her wings suddenly began to flap wildly, soon her wings began to shudder and shake, then she collapsed exhausted on top of Gideon. The last of the alien Prince's concubines dropped to the floor, then the alien Princess realised, something was wrong, terribly wrong!

Quickly the alien Princess tried to fly away, but Sandra was too quick. Laser fire pierced her wings, tearing great gaping holes in them and she dropped to the ground some distance behind Gideon.

Sandra stared coldly at the alien Princess, screaming at her, "You're going to pay you fucking bitch! You're going to pay!"

The alien Princess spoke quickly in her guttural voice, tinged with fear, "No wait, wait, don't shoot! I can help you escape! Please! I can help you!"

Sandra inquired, "How do we get up to the surface?"

The alien Princess then replied with a trembling voice, "At the back of this chamber. In the royal quarters. There is an escape passage. It will take you to the surface!"

Winchilly was quick to scan the alien Princess's mind and she telepathically stole the necessary information. Then having done so, Winchilly told Sandra telepathically, that she had the information that they needed and that the alien Princess could not be trusted. Winchilly then went to help free Gideon who was still manacled to the floor.

Sandra then looked at the alien Princess coldly, "My young, Martian friend, has just taken that very information straight out of your head."

The alien Princess replied gutturally with great fear in her voice, "Don't shoot! I can still help you! I can still help you!"

Sandra's eyes grew colder as she replied, "To hell with you! You god damned evil stinking bitch!"

Sandra opened fire with the laser pistol at the alien Princess and she kept firing and firing relentlessly until the alien Princess was a burning mass of melted flesh and bone.

Sandra then looked over at Gideon, she burst into tears, dropped the laser pistol and ran over to him.

Sandra then took his head into her arms and held him to her breast.

Gideon was okay, Winchilly had found some water and cloth and was washing him.

Sandra enquired of this and Winchilly replied telepathically, *"Gideon was feeling unclean and ashamed. I thought cleansing his body might help him."*

Sandra then turned to Gideon, "Hey, this wasn't your fault! What could you possibly have done to stop them?"

Winchilly then reached into his mind once more and tried to soothe him from within. After a few long minutes, Gideon was on his feet and ready to move.

Quickly, they then moved to the back of the royal chamber and into the alien Prince's royal quarters. They were led by Winchilly's accurately stolen information. They soon easily found the passage they required and then followed it to the surface. At the end of the passage, there was a small chamber that contained space suits, the kind that would have fitted the aliens. The dust on the floor was inches thick. It was obvious this escape passage and chamber had never been used. Beyond that chamber, there was an airlock, beyond which was the surface of the planet Mars.

The airlock mechanisms were ancient yet functional and they easily managed to work them. Then they quickly traversed the airlock and they soon found themselves standing under the blue Martian skies. The air was unpleasant and stanky, it had a disgusting vile taste to it. Winchilly almost gagged and retched when she first breathed it in. Gideon and Sandra on the other hand, had breathed it before and were somewhat more prepared for it. Yet still they both gagged and retched.

Having lived underground all of her life, in the labyrinth of tunnels and chambers beneath the monoliths, Winchilly had never been outside of them. Winchilly had never thought that the surface of Mars could be so beautiful. Winchilly looked all around the Martian landscape in wonder.

Winchilly asked telepathically, *"It looks very nice out here, but is it meant to smell and taste like this? So unpleasant?"*

Sandra replied, "Gideon tells me that the bad smell and taste will diminish greatly over time."

"That would be a very good thing", Winchilly replied.

Gideon had not spoken since the incident in the royal chamber.

Upon reaching the surface he advised, "We'd better move, the army will need our information."

Winchilly scanned the surrounding plains with her telepathic mind. She then reported to Gideon, that minds similar to his were to the south of them. Gideon knew this would be the colonial army, he asked Sandra and Winchilly to follow. They did so, the trio travelling south across the plains of Mars. The group of four pyramids gradually grew smaller and smaller in the background, as they continued moving in the direction of the colonial forces.

In the weak Martian gravity, Gideon and Sandra moved very strongly and quickly. Their young Martian friend, Winchilly, was struggling to keep up the pace. Soon Winchilly was exhausted and collapsed to the ground. Her two companions stopped and ran quickly to her side. Gideon and Sandra should have realised, that they were running way too fast for Winchilly to keep up. They decided to take turns in carrying Winchilly and were soon travelling south once more.

"How can you be so tall, so thin and this light?", asked Sandra.

Winchilly replied telepathically, *"My people are naturally tall, thin and light, Sandra."*

"Well I must say then, Winchilly, I am truly jealous", Sandra admitted.

"Jealous? That is not a concept that my people have, Sandra", Winchilly replied.

"How can your people not have jealousy?", a more than curious Sandra asked.

"My people are all telepaths. We share our thoughts freely. Jealousy and jealous thoughts cannot be maintained amongst telepaths. Such thoughts atrophy and diminish", Winchilly attempted to explain.

After running for a long time they heard something in the distance behind them. They all stopped to look around. Several small interceptors were fast approaching them. Quickly Gideon hid Winchilly behind a large boulder, then he and Sandra hid behind the boulder as well, covering Winchilly.

As the interceptors passed, they fired their laser beams and particle beams. The ground erupted around them and then the interceptors were gone. They had missed their targets completely and overflown. Their weapon systems appeared to be unusually inaccurate, more Martian sabotage perhaps.

"Captain Hawk, Sir! Five interceptors heading this way, they were firing at something on the ground", the Sergeant informed him.

"Put them out of action, then take out a patrol. I want to know what the hell they were firing at", replied Captain Hawk.

Gideon and Sandra looked up, watching the interceptors as they began to turn around. The aliens were coming back for another strafing run. Suddenly without any warning, there were five bright flashes of blue light. One by one the five interceptors exploded in the blue Martian skies and then they were gone.

Winchilly raised her head up to Gideon and Sandra, her mind spoke to them, *"Your people are coming! We are safe now my friends. We are safe!"*

Gideon then leaned down and kissed the beautiful young Martian woman. Winchilly returned the kiss passionately for a long minute. Then the trio waited patiently for the arrival of the Colonial Troops.

16. The Battle for Mars.

It wasn't long before the patrol came to the area that the alien interceptors had been strafing. The Sergeant inquired if his men could seen anything, one of them said he'd seen an incredible mirage. Sergeant Kelly then checked the area with his own field glasses. He couldn't believe what he was looking at either. Sergeant Kelly decided to report straight away to Captain Hawk.

"Captain, Sir. You are not going to believe this", Sergeant Kelly reported to the Captain.

"Just tell me the facts, Sergeant", the Captain replied.

"Captain. There are people out there. Three of them. A naked man and two beautiful topless women. They all appear to be human, although one of the women looks a bit unusual", the Sergeant replied.

Captain Hawk then ordered, "Keep clear of them. Don't approach them. They are not to be harmed. I'll be there as soon as possible", then thinking to himself, *"I hope this isn't some kind of a joke."*

Captain Hawk quickly arranged for a large hovercar and requested that some spare uniforms be brought to him. If only his guess was right. The Captain's hover car quickly covered the distance to the trio and soon he was hovering above the group. A group of three people and luckily, he had been correct. Captain Hawk then ordered the patrol to investigate closer to the pyramids and report back to him later. The Captain landed his hovercar close to the trio and then he stepped out. The new Martian air smelt and tasted vile, but fortunately, he would be back in his environmentally controlled command post very soon.

"Doctor Gideon Reas, Ms Sandra Danker I presume. I'm afraid I don't know your mysterious new companion", commented the Captain, as he tried his best to overt his eyes from staring at the two beautiful, near naked women.

"You're right of course, Captain. Our companion here is, Winchilly. A Martian and a telepath", came Gideon's reply.

"I thought that the Martians all had wings and tails and looked like demons?", the Captain queried.

"Not at all, Captain. The actual Martian species is related to ours. They are very human and quite gentle in fact. The other beings on the other hand are totally alien and malevolent. They conquered and enslaved the Martians many aeons ago in the distant past", Gideon informed the Captain.

"Enslaved the Martians hey! Well, it must be their liberation day then. Climb aboard and I'll take you all back to my command post. You'll be much safer there and the air won't be anywhere near this disgusting", replied the Captain.

"Thank you, Captain", Gideon and Sandra both replied almost in unison.

The Captain pointed out, that the clothes on the rear seats were for them. Nothing fancy, just army greens, but they were better than nothing. Gideon and Sandra quickly dressed themselves. Then they helped to dress their friend, Winchilly, as she had never worn proper clothing before. Winchilly then thanked them both telepathically.

The Captain then passed back a first aid kit, "Doctor Reas, you'll probably need this for Ms Danker. That contusion on her forehead looks nasty."

"Yes. Thank you, Captain. We haven't had any time to even think about our injuries", Gideon replied.

Soon the hovercar had landed at the Captain's command post, an extensive complex of relocatable buildings that were all linked together and hermetically sealed with purified air. They entered the complex via a covered car parking bay and then went straight to the Captain's office. Here a large exchange of information was going to take place.

The Captain had many questions to ask them and he also had a lot to tell them. Gideon and Sandra had not heard anything at all about the fall of the Saturnian colonies or even of the existence of the Mimasians. To save time informing each other about the events that had taken place, Gideon requested Winchilly's telepathic assistance. As it turned out, her telepathic Martian mind was a godsend.

Winchilly used her telepathic abilities as a thought relay between Sandra, Gideon and the Captain. Soon the Captain knew all of the facts about the Martian situation and the events that had happened to Gideon and Sandra. Winchilly had censored personal events, like the relationship between the three and of course Gideon being raped by the alien Princess. Winchilly had automatically sensed, that Gideon wanted this to remain secret, which she fully understood. However, Winchilly did let Captain Hawk know that Gideon had killed the alien Prince during their escape. The aliens were now leaderless!

Sandra and Gideon were then shocked upon hearing of the destruction of the Saturnian colony cylinders and of the extermination of some fifty thousand people. They were also extremely concerned about the control that Mimas had over the entire Saturnian system and the fate of the tens of thousands of people on the colonised moons of Saturn.

Gideon and Sandra also quickly realised, that the alien Martian overlords were of Mimasian decent and heritage. They were the same creatures, both here on Mars and there on Mimas. When Winchilly had finally finished, her beautiful emerald green eyes were full of tears. It took her several minutes to compose herself. Such was the level of emotion the murder of so many people had stirred within her.

Winchilly then informed them all, that they could learn of the fate of the Saturnian Colonists, by the use of her telepathy. However, first she had to give the Captain a lot of information. This information would be more than useful. Using her telepathy, Winchilly gave Captain Hawk a nearly a complete layout of the monoliths and their underground labyrinth of tunnels and chambers. As much information as he could possibly need.

The Captain quickly mapped out these details, along with all of the known entrances to the monoliths Winchilly pointed out changes telepathically, which the Captain had not fully understood. Then the Captain copied the maps and had those copies sent to all of his field commanders. Along with these, was the order, that all humanoid beings were to be spared and not harmed.

A description of the Martians was provided along with those orders. Only the winged, demon-like Mimasians were to be targeted. The discipline of the Colonial Troops would be enough to ensure that the order was strictly enforced. Winchilly also informed Captain Hawk, that her people would work with his people, to help them in any way they could, without actually killing. Winchilly then stated that she would be a psychic link between her people and the Captain.

After this, Winchilly then decided to find out the fate of the colonists on the colonised moons of Saturn. Winchilly sat quietly cross-legged on the floor, concentrating. For some unknown reason, Gideon and Sandra had become sensitised to the psychic fields that Winchilly generated. They both had thought that this was Winchilly's gift to them. However, upon their capture by the aliens, the Martian Elders had tweaked them both psychically, to increase their psychic potentials, hoping they could silently communicate with them. The results of that psychic intervention were still unfolding.

Winchilly linked with as many of her people as she could without it being noticed by the Mimasians. Soon the large group of Martian minds all concentrated and began to spread quickly outwards, like the ripples in a pond, spreading further and further. These subtle ripples quickly reached as far as Saturn.

Gideon and Sandra could see, not feel that the colonists were alive and although not exactly well, they were not in any immediate danger. This news made them feel much happier and they informed the Captain of the status of the Saturnian colonists. After this, they were feeling quite fatigued as one would expect, so the Captain showed them to some sleeping quarters where they could all get some rest. Sandra then requested a room with a bath, as they were quite filthy from their ordeal. The Captain smiled and then quickly had an appropriate room provided for their use.

Captain Hawk then went back to his office and compiled a full report. He sent a copy to Colonel Bannon and another copy to Eros, via the scrambler. The Colonel would be pleased to hear that both Gideon and Sandra were safe and okay. He would also be pleased the hear that the Saturnian colonists, although isolated and under complete Mimasian control, were apparently not in any further danger. At least not for the moment.

Once in their room, they ordered some food. This time Gideon and Sandra explained to Winchilly what the foods were and which foods were the nicest to eat. Winchilly only ate the fruits and vegetables, she also ate eggs, as they had not been fertilised, but being a vegetarian, she didn't eat any meat at all, not even fish. Winchilly even telepathically joked, that she would turn Gideon and Sandra into vegetarians as well if it was the last thing she did. This amused them both immensely.

After eating they all bathed, Gideon allowed Sandra and Winchilly to bathe first. After they'd both finished, he climbed into the bath. Gideon still felt unclean from his ordeal and began to scrub feverishly at his skin. Winchilly sensed what Gideon was doing and she went to the bathroom, while telepathically calling for Sandra. The two women grabbed Gideon's arms to stop him, tears were streaming down his cheeks.

Winchilly looked deeply into Gideon's eyes, with her own beautiful emerald green eyes showing genuine compassion. Fully understanding his anguish, there was no need for words, her mind spoke to them both ever so clearly. Winchilly explained to them both, that she had been raped, many, many times by the Mimasian males. That she fully understood how Gideon felt and that it wasn't his fault, that there was absolutely nothing he could have done to halt their malevolent lust.

Gideon pressed his face into Winchilly's breast, he now cried not for himself, but for her and all that she had lived through. It wasn't too long before Gideon stopped crying. Sandra and Winchilly both saw that he was now okay. They both gently bathed him, after which they dried him off and led him to bed.

Their three minds were now all linked, all of their thoughts shared, three souls linked for all eternity. While they entwined in their mutual embrace with each other, outside in the Martian night the battle for Mars began in earnest.

Captain Hawk moved his tank columns forward towards the four main entrances of the monolith complex. The Colonial Troops fanned out on either side of the columns and prepared for the major battle ahead. At ten other smaller, less used entrances, the Captain dispatched his commando forces. While his main troops knocked down the front doors, his commandos would sneak around the sides and gain entry through the back.

More than one hundred alien interceptors flew towards the four columns.

As they did so, the Captain's interceptors flew towards the monoliths to give his troops air support. The alien interceptors pealed away to battle with the colonial interceptors. The alien switched on their deflector shields and flew in formation thinking they had little to worry about.

The colonials flew at them, when within range, both sides fired their laser beams and particle beams. The colonial weapons flashed into action and the enemy interceptors exploded left, right and centre. Their shields all failed, their laser beams and their particle beams all failed. It wasn't long before all of the alien vessels were completely and utterly destroyed. They were annihilated!

Another, larger fleet of alien interceptors was launched and they swiftly flew into battle. With their deflector shields on and weapons activated they attacked the colonial fighters. The same result, all of their shields and weapons systems failed. They too, were all quickly annihilated!

Again, a larger fleet of alien interceptors was launched. These too had been sabotaged by the Martian, but not as thoroughly as the others. On this exchange with the colonials, many were destroyed, their shields and weapons systems failing. However, some had not, these fighters fought against the colonials quite effectively. The colonial fighters then concentrated their firepower and eventually defeated this fleet as well, but not without loss. Fifteen of their craft had also been destroyed.

No more alien interceptors were launched and nearly four hundred and fifty had been destroyed by the colonials. Most of these vessels had been sabotaged and their pilots didn't have a chance. The Martian people had kept their promise. They had done extremely well but were unable to sabotage all of the alien interceptors. Some had survived the Martian sabotage attempts and had been used effectively, but not so many.

As the Sun began to rise over the Martian plains once more, the battle took on a new face. The colonial army looked towards the pyramids, as the full force of the alien army approached them. The tank columns prepared for battle. From out of the pyramids, a large number of hover vehicles approached. Behind them were the alien armoured divisions. Further in the distance was the bulk of the alien army. They moved along the ground in droves, a large, almost countless number of them. Some of the aliens flew high above the battlefields. Like scouts, making a very detailed reconnaissance.

As the small hover vehicles approached, the colonial tanks opened fire with laser beams and particle beams blazing. The alien hover vehicles then activated their weapons systems. Soil and rock erupted in front of the colonial armoured divisions. Many attacking alien hover vehicles were destroyed in mid flight as they approached the colonial troop positions.

Colonial interceptors swept in towards the battle fields. The ground beneath the alien hover vehicles erupted with molten regolith, as the Colonial interceptors fired down upon them. All of the remaining alien hover vehicles were annihilated in very quick order. Then the colonial armies pushed forward towards the alien's armoured divisions.

Again the Martians had helped out, the alien's deflector shields were malfunctioning. This now meant that the battle would be fought on a more equal footing. As the alien fighters had already been taken out earlier in aerial dogfights, the colonials had a distinct advantage.

The armoured divisions of both sides began firing, when they were within range of each other. The colonial fighters swept down and fired from above and the aliens were caught in the crossfire. After nearly an hour of this constant firing, all of a sudden, the firing halted.

When the smoke finally cleared, all of the alien armoured weaponry was destroyed. A large number of colonial tanks had also been annihilated. There had been a great many losses in the armies of both sides, dead and wounded lay everywhere, littering the battlefields. The overpowering stench of burnt flesh wafted on the Martian winds. Yet it was not finished, it was not over.

At the smaller entrances to the monolith complex, the commandos struck. Most of the alien forces were battling the main columns of the colonial forces on the plains. The colonial commandos found little resistance. Sergeant Kelly led his band of twenty men into the escape passage that descended down into the royal quarters. The details of which had been provided by Winchilly.

At the four main battle fronts the colonial forces now fought the unsupported alien armies. Laser beam and particle beam tanks leading the way. Around twenty thousand colonials met the advancing alien multitudes at each of the battle fronts. The alien hordes attacked from both the ground and the air. The flapping sounds of their great wings could be heard above the sounds of the battle.

Sergeant Kelly's men threw themselves into battle. A contingent of aliens had been stationed in the royal quarters. They were standing watch over the bodies of their fallen Prince and Princess. The commandos lasers blazed as they advanced into battle. Aliens were cut down by the dozen. They made it into the royal quarters and were trapped. They were unable to cross the large royal chamber. The aliens were firing from the one and only entrance on the far side.

On the battle fields above the war continued. The colonials fired both forward and above while advancing. Aliens fell from the sky, as their wings and bodies were shredded by laser fire. They fell to the ground slowly in the low Martian gravity, making a dull thud when they struck. Laser fire from above cut down the colonial soldiers as they advanced. Yet they continued forward as bodies began to litter the battlefields once more.

Soon the flying aliens began to swoop down to fight at ground level in hand-to-hand combat. A huge mistake on their part. The colonials shot them down as they approached. Then they smashed them to death with their laser rifle butts or stabbed them to death with their bayonets and knives. The humans excelled at hand-to-hand combat and had the advantage of far greater strength, due to their high-gravity combat training.

The two enemy armies were now thoroughly entangled in battle, the situation was now one of close quarters combat. The battlefields were now a thoroughly bloody sight, as the front lines of both armies were over lapping. Close up laser fire blasted living flesh and bone from the bodies of those unfortunate enough to be struck.

The aliens fought from the ground, occasionally leaping into flight to fight from above. As their great black wings took them into the air, the colonial soldiers would shoot them down. Sometimes the Colonial Troops, with their much stronger leg muscles, would leap up into the air, in the weak Martian gravity, to grab the flying aliens and drag them back down. They would then battle in mid-air, as the great wings of the aliens beat furiously to keep them from falling to the ground below. The Colonial Troops would slash at their wings with their knives and bayonets to bring them down and then knife them to death. For all their size, the aliens did not have the strength of the humans from the Earth.

Towards the end of the day the battles all came slowly to an end. The

Colonials had won! Detachments of men were then sent to support the commandos in the tunnels beneath the pyramids. Captain Hawk had a new command post set up outside of the pyramids. The Captain then sent out men to count their losses and to take a body count of the alien dead. He also asked for volunteers, to collect the bodies of Colonial Troops for transport back to the Earth and to bury the dead aliens in mass graves, first thing in the morning.

Sergeant Kelly received his reinforcements with open arms and then went back to the task of entering the monoliths. Smoke grenades were thrown into the royal chamber. Under the cover of the smoke they advanced into it. His men were soon at the far entrance and battling the enemy there. They fought fiercely and mercilessly, blasting and killing the aliens as they went through the labyrinth of tunnels beneath the monoliths.

Deep in the back of Sergeant Kelly's mind, he could feel something. Cries for help, his men had felt it too. They hurried quickly down the passages, killing all of the enemies that they came across as they went. They turned here and turned there, into various passages, where ever the passage felt right. About half an hour later, they approached a gigantic open pyramidal chamber, with a huge bright light at its apex. Brilliant like an artificial Sun.

Once on the inside of the pyramid, they saw extensive hydroponics systems. Their map indicated, that this was definitely one of the pyramids. The cries for help came from the far side, behind a thick growth of hydroponically grown plants. A tall vertical garden of sorts. Quickly and silently, the Sergeant moved to the other side of the pyramid with a small number of his men. Upon reaching the other side, he carefully looked through the thick growth of plants.

He was shocked by what he saw. There were tens of thousands of Martians, if not many more, all herded together by the aliens. He could see what was going to happen to them and he had to stop it.

The aliens were going to extract revenge for the Martians sabotaging their shields and weapons systems. Sergeant Kelly slowly and cautiously brought up his men, quietly he spread them out around on either side of the alien guards. He looked at the fear in the Martian's eyes, especially the younger ones, who were silently, telepathically crying.

"Don't worry!", he thought to himself, hoping that the Martians could hear him, *"We are here now! You'll all be okay!"*

The Martians, all being telepaths, did hear him, although Sergeant Kelly was completely unaware of this. The Martians stayed quiet and prepared themselves for what was coming next.

The Sergeant's men all moved in quickly and on cue. They caught all of the alien guards in a crossfire and soon it was all over. They had literally saved tens of thousands of Martians, well over one hundred thousand of them in all. Their minds were swamped with thoughts of thanks and praise. These tough, highly trained commandos, were all brought to tears.

This very same thing happened to all of the commando groups within the monolith complex. They'd be summoned by very large masses of extremely frightened Martians. Upon locating the Martians, the commandos would be just in time to save them from being slaughtered by the aliens, in cold blooded murder. Upon liberating a large group of Martians, the commandos would quickly be on the move yet again, as another large group of Martians cried out to them for help.

Once liberated, the Martians moved quickly, selected groups would disappear into the complex. They opened up the monolith's main entrances and let the colonial armies march in. Thousands of Colonial Troops entered the monoliths and the Martian people cheered telepathically as they did so. The Martians had all been liberated after aeons of slavery and degradation!

Once inside the monoliths, the colonial army only had to mop up the enemy troops. The Colonial Troops spread through out the complex and searched out their enemy. The Martians helped them, by finding the enemy using their telepathy. When they did locate the enemy, the result was always the same. The aliens fought to the death, even the females. Soon the whole of the monolith complex was secured and not one of the many thousands of aliens had survived. None were left alive!

Gideon, Sandra and Winchilly had watched the entire battle unfold. Winchilly's telepathic mind linked with the minds of her people. Gideon and Sandra could see the tens of thousands of Martians being saved and the thousands of aliens being killed. They were very pleased with the liberation of the Martians, but also quite upset that so many of the aliens had to be slaughtered.

Winchilly had shown them many things, her mind constantly raised Gideon's and Sandra's to higher and higher levels of consciousness. It wasn't long before Gideon and Sandra, under Winchilly's guidance, had changed. Soon they would be as telepathic as the Martians, but they would still retain their ability speak.

Winchilly informed them, that her people had chosen them to be representatives for all of their people. Winchilly's people had been tweaking Gideon and Sandra telepathically, slowly but surely, activating their psychic potentials. Although Gideon and Sandra were not natural born psychics, none the less, psychics they would become!

Colonel Bannon was soon to land on Mars, he wanted to see his two friends and also the Martian people. There was so much to be done, they had won the battle for Mars, but the war with Mimas wasn't over. If he was right and he was certain that he was, the Martians would help them. Their technology could help to defeat the aliens.

The Colonel viewed the scene below his landing craft as it flew low over one of the battlefields. It was a ghastly sight, mangled and wrecked armoured vehicles were strewn everywhere. There were thousands upon thousands of mangled and twisted bodies, both human and alien alike. Mostly they were alien, however.

The Colonial's soldiers helped by the Martians, were collecting the bodies of their fallen comrades for transport back to the Earth and burial. Alien bodies were also collected but were buried in mass graves on the battlefields. There they would fertilise the Martian fields and plains. The battle for Mars had been truly bloody.

Colonel Bannon could feel the minds of the Martians as they all reached out to greet him. Amongst this immense presence of minds and thoughts, the Colonel could feel something else, something that he did not expect. The minds of his two friends Doctor Gideon Reas and Sandra Danker, with another third mind so close to theirs, a Martian woman with sparkling emerald green eyes.

The Colonel was stunned by this new development and this telepathic greeting, but he passed it off as his imagination. He was surrounded by thousands of telepaths and instead, he was thinking it was his mind playing tricks on him. After all, he was eagerly wanting to see his two friends again. His landing craft swooped in for a landing close to the entrance designated by Captain Hawk. It wasn't long before his craft had come to a complete halt and a staff hover car quickly zoomed across the plains towards it. Colonel

Bannon watched as the hover car came to a swift halt in front of his lander, hovering one meter above the ground.

Colonel Bannon stepped out of the lander and approached his staff car. The stench of the now-finished battle hung heavily in the air. The bodies of the dead were already beginning to decay and the stench of death was so strong, it was enough to cover the awful smell of the new Martian atmosphere. The Colonel almost retched, even though he was using a re-breather, so strong was the stench of death!

"Take me to, Captain Hawk", he ordered the driver, as he stepped into the staff hover car.

"Yes, Sir", the driver replied and the car was soon moving swiftly back towards the pyramid from which it had left.

The bodies of the dead passed beneath the staff car's hover jets, as they thrust the staff car forward towards the entrance of the pyramids.

The Colonel looked left and right across the battlefield, at the carnage that remained and thought to himself, *"It will take days to collect all of the dead and even longer to bury them all."*

The colonial forces had won the battle, it had been extremely costly, but the war was yet to be won and its outcome was far from certain.

17. Transference.

Colonel Bannon met with Captain Hawk on arriving at the monolith complex, "Captain, it's good to see you survived. From what I've seen out there, it's lucky anyone did", the Colonel noted.

"Well, Colonel, it was far worse for our front line troops than for us at the rear", the Captain honestly admitted.

"What are our losses, Captain?", inquired the Colonel.

The Captain hesitated, then he replied, "We've lost, in all about three thousand men, Sir."

"That many dead, it must have been an absolute blood bath", the Colonel replied.

The two men went over the casualty figures and other losses, including their wounded troops, "Have we evacuated our wounded yet?"

"They're on their way to the Aries colony as we speak, Colonel", Captain Hawk replied, adding, "Slightly above six thousand wounded in all, Sir."

"That is a lot, Captain. I was hoping our casualties would be far less", the Colonel replied.

Soon the Colonel wanted to know about the enemy's body count.

"Well, Sir, the aliens were completely wiped out", the Captain stated.

"Completely wiped out? Just how many, Captain?", the Colonel inquired further.

"A lot of them, Sir. In the battle fields alone, the aliens lost more than twenty five thousand troops and that's just an estimate on the low side. They just kept coming and coming at us, like a horde of rabid beasts", Captain Hawk informed him, explaining "In hand to hand combat, they were no match for our Colonial Troops. No match at all."

"That's a hell of a lot, what about inside the monoliths?", the Colonial asked.

"Sir, inside the monoliths the aliens lost another ten thousand troops, including fifteen thousand females and about ten thousand young", the Captain replied honestly.

"I didn't know that our troops were ordered to kill women and children", the Colonel remarked, "That is definitely going to need some explaining, Captain."

"They weren't, Sir. The alien males fought to their deaths. They literally fought to the death. Their women folk took up arms as well and they too, just like their men, fought to their deaths. Although a great many of their females committed mass suicide, taking their children along with them", the Captain explained, thinking to himself, *"Should we even be calling them men, women and children, they are aliens after all."*

The Colonel thought about the alien losses, more than sixty thousand of them.

The Colonel enquired, "Captain, how many Martians did we liberate from the aliens?"

Captain Hawk replied, "We managed to save well over two and a half million of them, Sir. Nearly all of them, in fact. It was quite a miracle. The Martian slaves have all been liberated!"

"Thank Christ for that, at least they didn't suffer such great losses!", the Colonel exclaimed.

"Sir, the Martians have suffered for over ninety thousand years. Before the aliens conquered and enslaved them, they numbered in their billions", the Captain noted.

The pair continued talking, as Captain Hawk led the way to Gideon and Sandra, before going about his scheduled tasks.

Gideon and Sandra had gone back into the monoliths after the battle had been won. Winchilly had shown them to their quarters and all three of them were awaiting the arrival of Colonel Bannon. While they waited, Gideon and Sandra practised their newly acquired psychic abilities. Winchilly was pleased and yet surprised by how fast they were developing and truly astounded by another development.

Gideon and Sandra were developing their new psychic abilities into fields and regions, where even the Martians themselves could not. There was a knock at the door, Winchilly opened it and beckoned Colonel Bannon in. Gideon and Sandra greeted the Colonel telepathically, at first he was taken aback, then he responded.

"Gideon, Sandra, it's great to see you both again. I'm glad you're both okay", he replied, then he asked, "Was that my imagination or did you just talk directly to my mind?"

Gideon answered him, this time vocally, "No Jim, it's not your imagination. Both Sandra and myself have developed some new talents, psychic talents. By the way, that beautiful young lady who just let you in is our dear companion Winchilly."

Gideon then summoned Winchilly to his side. The Colonel then greeted the young Martian woman, who had then replied in return, telepathically.

The four of them then talked for hours, although the Colonel had trouble keeping up with the conversation. Sandra and Gideon were quickly going from vocal to telepathic communications and back again. They used telepathy to talk to Winchilly. When they did so, although the Colonel could sense them, the conversation was very quick and fluid, so it was hard for him to follow. With a lot of concentration, the Colonel could still follow the general gist and flow of their conversation.

During their conversation, Winchilly informed the Colonel that her people would start working with Gideon and Sandra to develop new weapons systems to counter any alien attacks. Winchilly was now specifically calling the aliens Mimasians, as the threat was now from Mimas. This pleased the Colonel immensely, as the new weapons systems would be needed and he knew it all too well.

Gideon and Sandra were a necessity when it came to the Martians developing weapons systems. The Martians could devise the theory and the technology, but to utilise these in actual practical weapons, they needed the help of others. The Martians had immense trouble coming to grips, psychologically, when creating weapons of war. Sandra, being a spacecraft engineer and designer, found the task somewhat easier, than her lover Gideon.

They took the basic designs for the Dreadnoughts and the Battle Cruisers, which Eros, the Earth and Cis-Lunar L-Five had come up with and started work.

Gideon asked of his Martian colleagues, *"Is their any possible way to increase the output of laser beam and particle beam weaponry, without increasing the actual bulk or size of these weapons? You know, scale up the power, but not the overall footprint they take up?"*

His Martian colleagues answered almost immediately, *"Yes, of course, there are ways, but we can only realistically double the output. Your current designs are extremely inefficient."*

Gideon was surprised by that last statement, but thanked them and asked them to work on the laser beam and particle beam problem. Soon they had developed new designs for their laser beams and particle beams. These were to be placed into the newly designed interceptors.

On these smaller interceptors, these weapons were placed into paired arrangements. They could fire together in unison on a single target or they were able to fire independently at separate targets.

The control systems were then altered, so that only one pilot was needed, instead of a crew of two. In addition to this, modifications to their plasma drive systems were to be made, making the craft much faster and far more efficient in fuel consumption.

When asked about weapons systems for the Dreadnoughts and the Battle Cruisers, the Martians then greatly increased them in size and scale to produce weapons a good ten times more powerful than the original ones. These much larger scale weapon systems were designed to be mounted into weapons blisters, which in turn were mounted into the fuselage of the Dreadnoughts and the Battle Cruisers.

These weapons mounted to the Dreadnoughts and the Battle Cruisers, had precisely the same paired arrangements, they also had the same versatility. However, they were much larger and much more powerful. Being placed in special weapons pods, called blisters, enabled them able to fire with a far greater range of movement.

These weapons blisters were to be mounted on the fuselage of the Battle Cruisers. One on the front, with two on either side towards the centre, with another two mounted on either side further along the hull, closer to the rear of the ship. Five weapons pods in all.

The Dreadnoughts, however, being much longer ships, were to have four extra weapons blisters. These were to be mounted two aside, along the hull inline with and between the other weapons blisters. All up total of nine weapons pods.

The Battle Cruisers were to be manned by a pilot, five gunners, four engineers, one cook, one ship's doctor and of course the Captain. The Dreadnoughts being much larger vessels, had four extra gunners. In addition, the Dreadnoughts also had larger, more efficient and more powerful plasma drives designed for the them.

Gideon and Sandra came up with another clever idea, the interceptors of course being small could not carry very much fuel. They would have to make use of refuelling stations on any long flights. Refuelling stations were not always as available as needed. They began to design another class of vessels. These were the Interplanetary Fighter Carrier and Armoured Refuelling Craft or IFC and ARC for short.

The IFCs were designed along similar lines to that of the Battle Cruisers. They were to have the same weapons arrangements, the main differences being, that those weapons pods were scaled up to be twice as powerful and the craft itself was also very much larger. Being designed to carry interceptors, they designed the IFCs to have four interceptor launch and landing tubes. Two of each, on each side of the vessel, in between the forward, middle and rear weapons pods.

On the interior of each of the launch and landing tubes were the interceptor bays. Each of these four interceptor bays held five interceptors. The IFC, being so large, also had four large plasma drives to power it. These much larger vessels had been designed for a crew of forty three, which included the interceptor pilots, the equivalent crew of a Battle Cruiser, plus ten engineering crew for maintaining and repairing the twenty interceptors.

The ARCs were an even larger vessel than the IFCs, although they were not designed as battle craft. This craft was designed to carry the same weapons as the IFC, but it's interior was designed to carry very large quantities of compressed precious fuel.

The Battle Cruisers, the IFCs and the individual interceptors could all refuel at these mobile refuelling stations. The ARCs would be able to refuel five to twenty craft at a time, depending on what class of vessels were being refuelled. An IFC was also designed to refuel its own interceptors at the same time as it refuelled.

The ARCs were also designed to collect hydrogen gas, using ram scoops by diving into the atmospheres of the gas giants planets. To do so required substantial radiation shielding. The ARCs were also powered by four enormously large and powerful plasma drives.

Martian technology then became incredibly important, they gave Gideon and Sandra the designs and plans of their deflector shields. These plans were for shield generators, more compact, more versatile and also more powerful than those of the Mimasians. They were also designed to be far more energy efficient, needing a lot less power to run them.

It appeared that across all of the many centuries, nine hundred in all, that all of the Martians had been enslaved, they had deliberately held back on the technology that they had allowed the Mimasians to have. Was this extreme Martian foresight, that the Humans they'd been genetically tweaking on the Earth, would eventually one day catch up to them in technology and eventually free them?

All of these newly designed vessels, the new Interceptors, the Dreadnoughts, the Battle Cruisers, the IFCs and the ARCs, were designed to utilise these deflector shields. Another variation of the deflector shields were specially designed to be used as a defence shield for space colonies. The very types of colony cylinders, that were so easily destroyed in the Saturnian orbital zone. The size of a colony dictated how many deflector shield generators were required for full coverage.

In addition to this, the Martians showed Gideon and Sandra how to use their existing colonial computer systems, to increase the effectiveness of the deflector shields. All of the deflector shield generators mounted on a vessel or cylinder could be linked together using computer networking systems.

The overall combined deflector shields around the structure could then effectively be manipulated, to greatly strengthen any given point in less than a microsecond. Even concentrated firepower could be effectively defended against, such that only minor damage might result if any damage at all. This would work equally well on the new ship designs as well.

The Martians also gave them the designs for small-scale gravity-generating systems. These would be extremely useful to colonists if they could be scaled up in size. No longer would massive hollowed-out asteroids have to be rotated to produce artificial gravity. They could produce it via gravity generators.

Sadly, the Martians informed Gideon that the generators would not scale to such a large degree. They could be used to give deck plating artificial gravity for spaceships, but large colonies would require far too many of them. The designs simply did not scale. The overall power requirements would be astronomical.

Gideon noted, that even without the gravity generators, the large hollowed-out asteroids could still be viable if spun up to the required rate of rotation, using the immense space tugs, Calypso and Olympus. Having successfully delivered Chariklo and Chiron to Martian orbit for the terraforming project, both space tugs were now on duty manoeuvring Earth-crossing asteroids into the Earth's forward and trailing Trojan points. Sixty degrees ahead and behind the Earth in its orbital path around the Sun. This was being done to both protect the Earth from possibly dangerous asteroids and also to provide asteroids for the colonies in those orbital zones to mine and process.

However, Gideon could see other possible uses for the gravity generators.

Gideon expressed his ideas to Sandra and Winchilly, *"We could use those gravity generators for a few other purposes perhaps."*

Sandra inquired, *"How do you mean, Gideon? As it's just been explained to us, they don't scale very well at all."*

Gideon replied, *"Well, we could perhaps, use a cluster of these gravity generators to produce an offset gravitational point, at a distance from a craft. It could be used for manoeuvring in flight, whilst coasting. Maybe? Potentially? It's just a thought."*

Sandra had caught on, *"Like a gravitational slingshot?"*, she queried.

"Exactly!", Gideon replied.

Winchilly passed this idea around the Martian scientists, most of them thought that this idea was completely impractical, a few of them, however, replied that it might be possible.

Gideon was pleased with this, he went on, *"This offset gravitation point if it could be made strong enough, could also be used as an extremely effective flight manoeuvre."*

Sandra played with this idea even further, *"It could be used to destroy an attacking enemy craft from within. If the gravitational point was generated inside an enemy's ship. Imagine what it could do to the fuel control systems or even their weapons systems. Just a thought."*

The idea was passed around by the Martian scientists, the overall answer, it was in theory possible, but not with present-day technology. Although some of their scientists insisted on attempting. Gideon was more than happy with that response, it was of course just one of his wackier ideas after all.

They were subsequently informed by the Martian scientists, that in theory a gravitational field could be generated with sufficient strength, that not even light could escape. It would flash out of this universe and become a miniature artificial black hole. If such a field could be manipulated correctly, it could possibly even be used as a method of worm hole transportation.

Those same Martian scientists also admitted, that it was well beyond even their technology at the present moment in time and would probably be a good many centuries before they would have a viable solution. Gideon asked them to work on it anyway, even though it would only be for future generations to use.

All of the submitted designs were compiled into categorised reports. Some reports focused on systems ready for immediate implementation, such as deflector shields, gravity field generators, weapon systems and advanced plasma drive units. Others detailed how to optimise the use of these technologies.

The big ticket items, like the IFCs and the ARCs were compiled into their own separate detailed reports, as were the recommended design changes for the Battle Cruisers and Dreadnoughts. Comprehensive analyses of the data were presented in separate reports, covering the designs of both defensive and offensive weapons systems.

All of these reports were then sent under extremely tight security and high priority to Eros. The Security Council of Sol was very pleased to receive them. From Eros, those same reports were quickly sent to the construction plants at Cis-Lunar L-Five, where they were to be implemented and all of the systems, including the spacecraft were to be constructed.

The Earth's engineers were stunned by the new designs and the technologies, so simple and yet so far beyond present human technology, yet now thanks to the Martians, a real possibility. The exact source of these new technologies, the Martians, was never divulged. That was a closely kept secret, kept ever so tightly under wraps. No one on the Earth or in Cis-Lunar L-Five would know of the Martian's existence.

The Security Council of Sol decided to build the new Interceptors, the Battle Cruisers, the Dreadnoughts, the IFCs and the ARCs. The shipyards of Cis-Lunar L-Four were going to be busy, very busy indeed.

The construction sites at Cis-Lunar L-Four were extremely versatile and could easily be redesigned to build the modified Interceptors. They would be the quickest of the new spacecraft to manufacture. Construction sites for the Battle Cruisers and the Dreadnoughts had already been planned and so those, in theory, wouldn't take too long to build, assuming there was enough time to do so.

The construction of the IFC and the ARC classes of vessels, would require totally redesigned sites and equipment. So they decided to concentrate on the IFCs first and if time permitted later, to consider the building of the ARCs. Before the building of these vessels could start, a lot of data had to be checked out. The components would have to be constructed and tested, before they could be installed.

For the construction of these craft, the engineers at Cis-Lunar L-Four would have to almost start from scratch. Their engineers had, over the years, developed an obsession for checking and rechecking everything. This habitual testing and checking could easily add excessive time to the construction of the newly designed vessels. These things were worrying Colonel Bannon, as he knew the way things usually worked and he also knew that Eros had not yet put the solar system on a total war footing.

"Gideon. I've been thinking about the new designs you sent to Eros", Colonel Bannon said to him.

"Yeah, I know. I have as well, Jim", Gideon replied.

"Just how long do you think it will take them before they have that new fleet ready, Gideon?", the Colonel asked.

"Going by how they usually do things at Cis-Lunar L-Four, I'd say way too long, Jim", Gideon replied.

Sandra then joined in, "You know, we still have all of those designs here. I'm pretty sure, that we could build a small fleet here at Aries. Trust me, we do have the capability and we have the capacity."

Gideon looked at Sandra with a curious eye, "You do know, of course, Sandra, that it is illegal to build a fleet of warships without Eros's approval?"

Sandra replied honestly, "Yes, of course, I do, Gideon, but we can do away with all of that excessive testing and have a small fleet ready long before Cis-Lunar L-Four could."

Colonel Bannon then added, "They don't have to be told straight away and I'm quite certain, we're going to need that little fleet very soon."

Gideon then replied, "In other words, Eros won't know until we're probably in battle and in that case, we'd all be heroes and they couldn't touch us anyway."

The Colonel agreed with Gideon and they decided to look into the construction of a small fleet of their own, a lot more seriously.

Gideon, Sandra and Winchilly, after looking into the details, then reported to Colonel Bannon.

The Colonel enquired, "Well then, will our little project get off the ground?"

Winchilly replied telepathically, *"We can assemble forty interceptors on Mars very easily, with the aid of your engineers of course."*

Sandra then added, "We can assemble three Battle Cruisers and two IFCs in high Martian orbit, but it will take a little bit of time. We won't worry about the Dreadnoughts or the ARCs for the moment. They're just too big and too complex."

Colonel Bannon then asked, "Roughly how long will it take?"

Sandra was in thought for several long moments, then she replied, "We can assemble them, in probably one third of the time it takes Cis-Lunar L-Four to build the main fleet."

"Considering that they have much better facilities than we do, that is quite incredible. Well then, let's get this little project of ours under way", the Colonel then replied.

Whilst at the Cis-Lunar L-Four ship yards, the mightiest space Armada ever to be created by humanity slowly started construction, at Mars, a far smaller and also highly unofficial, illegal fleet, began to take shape. The Martians were able to produce interceptors at very quick rates. Although, as there were weapons systems to be installed, they needed Earth humans to help construct them. The design of them was also more along human lines and quite unlike the Mimasian fighters.

In high Martian orbit, the construction of the larger vessels would take longer. The craft were of a totally new design and so new construction methods were needed. The components to be utilised in the vessels, were also being manufactured in high Martian orbit, to be more specific, at the Aries colony cylinder, under extremely tight security.

The transfer of technology from the Martians to Eros and the people of the Earth, had given a technological edge to the colonials. However, whether they would have enough time to take advantage of it, was another matter entirely. The Martians were also using their considerable intellect in other fields. The information they had would also be passed on to Eros, but for now, they had a priority, the war with Mimas and its evil hoards of winged Mimasian devils.

War was once such an easy thing for the humans of the Earth to wage, now in the many years since the near holocaust in the twentieth first century, it was not. All of the concepts of war had almost been lost. Eros knew that the war could not be avoided, but they still went about thinking, there was plenty of time or that somehow, even peace could be achieved.

In the outer colonies, the more adventurous colonials had a very much different opinion. The colonies of Jupiter and the Asteroid Belt were asking the Aries colony for shield generators. Eros had decided in its wisdom, that they would build them all at Cis-Lunar L-Four and then distribute them from there. However, only after out fitting their Armada and the colonies at Cis-Lunar L-Four first. This effectively meant that the outer colonies would be waiting many, many years.

Gideon and Sandra, upon hearing about this act of stupidity, decided that they would do things their way. Using a scrambler and a tight beam laser communications system, they sent all of the plans for the deflector shield generators, along with how to maximise their use, to the outer colonies. Sandra sent them a message asking them not to divulge to Eros that they had received those plans. Soon the colonies of Jupiter and the Asteroid Belt were quickly building deflector shields for their own colonies and fighter craft. They would be prepared for an attack if an attack did occur.

The construction of Colonel Bannon's private fleet had now begun. Gideon and Sandra were now able to spend more time practising their psychic abilities. Winchilly was helping them to reach their absolute potential. Winchilly found this occasionally difficult, as their potential was considerably greater than her own. This was something that Winchilly did not understand and neither did her people.

Gideon and Sandra sat quietly cross-legged on the floor. In this position they allowed their consciousness to expand outwards. Their Martian lover,

Winchilly, linked with their minds and joined in on this journey. Their subtle ripples of consciousness soon reached the Saturnian system. They had managed this on their own, without help from any other source. Winchilly had been carried along with them and was truly amazed at their newly found abilities. Winchilly was still at a loss, as to how this was even possible. This would not have been possible without many Martian minds helping them.

They monitored the situation on Titan. They could see that the Saturnian colonists on Titan had been preparing against the Mimasians. However, this preparation was limited mainly to Titan and even then, they could only prepare against attack. With the situation of enforced isolation, they couldn't get the necessary materials to build all of the weapons they required.

Gideon then led the way to Titan's central computer system, then he and Sandra psychically entered it. Winchilly watched them both, as they entered data in the computer's memory banks. Data about deflector shield generators and other newly designed weapons systems. After this, they psychically travelled outward to the other Saturnian colonies.

Colony by colony, they entered data about deflector shield generators into the computer systems of all of the colonised moons of Saturn. When they'd finished, they deliberately set the alarm bells ringing, so that the colonists quickly checked their computer systems. Winchilly wondered how they did this, it was another ability that her people did not have.

Mark Spencer on Titan received the news from Titan's computer control centre.

"Why'd the alarms sound off?", he inquired.

"Sir, someone has tampered with the main computer system's database", the operator replied.

"Do we know who? Have they caused any damage? Was it the enemy?",

Administrator Spencer inquired, he was particularly concerned about the last possibility.

"Well sir, we know exactly who did it", noted the operator, adding, "It was Doctor Gideon Reas and Sandra Danker of the Aries colony. Doctor Reas inserted data into our memory banks on the construction and usage of deflector shield generators, also data on several new classes of interceptors."

Administrator Mark Spencer looked stunned, he thought it had to be a sick joke, but he had the plans checked out anyway. Hope was a commodity that was in very short supply in the Saturnian colonies.

Soon the results came back, the plans were more than viable. The problem in his mind was, how in the hell were they put there? For now that didn't matter, the deflector shield generators needed to be built first and built quickly. The Administrator quickly approved their manufacture.

Winchilly then followed as Gideon and Sandra reached out further, this time to Mimas.

Winchilly's mind then began to give them urgent warnings, *"No, you must not! Please, it is too dangerous! It is extremely dangerous! My people never come here!"*

Gideon and Sandra decided to be cautious but continued. Soon their minds had entered the interior regions of Mimas. Winchilly was shaking almost uncontrollably with fear.

Gideon and Sandra could sense the heat blazing from off of the artificial Mimasian Sun, even though they were not physically present. They were able to see the inner structure of Mimas and the unusual Mimasian cities. They could see the Mimasians in their natural habitat and they found that the Mimasian society was highly decadent. They did little if any actual work and appeared to spend most of their time mutilating, specially bred, small fury animals before feeding on their blood. They were exceedingly cruel in the ways that they did this.

Gideon, however, could sense something else and he and Sandra quickly sent out tendrils of thought to investigate it. Soon they were close to the object of their curiosity. All of the way there, Winchilly kept asking them to return, to withdraw their minds. Gideon and Sandra did not, they were dauntless and continued on towards the unknown entity.

As they entered deep into the rock shell of Mimas, under one of the Mimasian structures, their fear began to grow. Their minds traversed so slowly through the passages, that they were able to memorise them in great detail. Soon they came upon a vast cavern, they slowly entered it and their minds perceived the colour red all around them.

The walls of this particular cavern had been painted in blood, old, decayed, Mimasian carcasses were flattened and stuck to the walls. It was an incredibly unpleasant place and Winchilly continued with her urgent warnings, she was frantic and frightened and wanted them to leave immediately.

Their combined consciousness could sense the entity they'd sought. It knew that they were there, from the far side of the vast cavern it approached. A single alien entity was approaching them. It walked, no glided above the ground, but without the use of its legs or its wings. Its eyes were rolled back in deep, dark, sinister sockets. The whites of its eyes showed clearly with bright red veins. In its right hand, it held a three-pronged sceptre, the prongs of which were all pointing upwards in an extended tetrahedral arrangement.

At a mere thirty paces from them, the alien entity stopped approaching. Gideon, Sandra and Winchilly reeled at the power of this creature. Its malevolence was palpable. All around the extended tendrils of their consciousness, the air began to swirl with its malevolence. They perceived its hatred, its anger and its supreme vileness, the pure evilness of this creature.

Fear began to reach deep down within them. The creature laughed loudly, maniacally, in their minds, its satanic nature delighted in their abhorrence of it. This alien's mind reviled them and began to approach them with its tendrils of supremely evil thought.

Gideon's and Sandra's minds froze, fear overwhelmed them, reaching deep into the very fabric of their being. Winchilly instinctively reacted, she locked her mind around theirs and with them both in tow, fled swiftly back to Mars, back across the vast expanse of space from which they'd come. Soon the three frightened minds had made it back to their bodies. All three of them were drenched in their own sweat, they felt cold and clammy, with skin like ice. They sat there staring at each other for a long time, still reeling from the shock of what they had seen. After many long minutes, they'd recovered enough to speak about what had just happened.

Gideon inquired, *"Winchilly, what was that thing?"*
Winchilly replied fearfully, *"That was the Mimasian's leader, their Emperor."*
Sandra asked, *"But we thought that the Mimasians didn't have any psychic potential?"*
Winchilly replied to the query cautiously, *"They don't. It has long been said amongst my people, that an entity exists within the Mimasian species. An evil entity!"*
Sandra inquired further, *"Winchilly, what do you mean by entity?"*
Winchilly replied telepathically, *"On death, the Mimasian Emperor's mind possesses, takes over, that of the current heir to the throne. His mind and only his mind alone, has any psychic potential amongst them. We suspect that it was not originally a Mimasian mind and that it was introduced from somewhere else."*
Gideon then stated, *"So this entity, has controlled the Mimasians for maybe, millions of years."* Winchilly replied, *"Yes. It is also the reason why their Emperor has never set foot in our world. His evil mind can not stomach our peaceful and benevolent*

psychic potentials."

They then went back to checking the progress reports on their small fleet. Everything was progressing according to their schedules and the fleet would soon be ready. Even if Eros wasn't ready to fight the Mimasians, the Colonists at the Aries colony would be. Ready to fight and to defend their human civilisation from destruction.

18. Mimas Moves.

Ahriman had watched closely as the interloping minds that had entered Mimas moved around the interior of his small ice moon. His evil mind sent out a subtle tendril of thought, just enough to entice them towards him and the interlopers followed it. His evil soul could perceive three minds, one a Martian mind, the other two were different, they were unique. He did not need the Martian, however, Ahriman could use these other two.

Ahriman's mind wandered backward in time, well over six million years in time. To the time when he first returned to the form of flesh, from his exile as a disembodied spirit wandering through deep space. His mind remembered how he'd drifted endlessly, as a malevolent entity in the vastness of deep space, drifting aimlessly for an eternity.

Eventually drifting past a pair of small insignificant stars, with their entourage of planets, amongst which he found a small world populated by winged humanoids. These people had originally been a gentle, peaceful species of beautiful beings on the verge of an evolutionary leap.

They were not a primitive species, however, they had a fair degree of intelligence and significant technology. A species with almost angelic features and an incredibly high degree of compassion. Then Ahriman came upon their peaceful little world.

The entity that was Ahriman had changed all of that. He had taken possession of the body of the leader of the largest nation on their planet. A peaceful kingdom with a very high level of technology. Shortly after that, he started a war to take over their entire planet and within three generations had succeeded. He gave his subjects new knowledge, then he created a special breeding program. Over the millions of years that followed, he had utterly changed the species, producing an enormous number of physical changes and none of them were good.

Their angelic features were lost and they had become devilish like gargoyles. Their smooth, pale skins had turned dark and grew thick, coarse brown hair. Their peaceful natures had become as malevolent as their leader. He had even changed their diets from vegetarian, to omnivorous beings, with a taste for raw flesh and blood. Then Ahriman had ran into problems, genetic problems at first and then later, problems of a planetary nature.

This race that Ahriman had ruled for so long had reached a dead end in its evolutionary path, mostly because of his own genetic interference and his lack of foresight. Ahriman could not increase their intellectual capacity, without undoing their totally evil nature. Ahriman found that there was a fine balance, a fine line between the intellects of his subjects and the behavioural characteristics, that he preferred them to have.

Ahriman bred the species, which he called Tarlaks, into three classes. The lower, shorter class were dullards who would act and not think. These were the majority of the species. The middle class, which were somewhat taller, were trained to be engineers or commanders. The final class were the nobles, who were the tallest of them all and from whom Ahriman would acquire his host bodies. The nobles were fewer in number and carefully managed, to ensure a good supply of suitable hosts.

Then there was the planet itself, millions of years of uncontrolled rampant exploitation, had almost completely destroyed its environment. As the planet's environment had slowly died, so did many of its inhabitants. So Ahriman had devised and created a means of escape and survival, a huge generation ship. A neighbouring planet's small moon was hollowed out and its outer crust completely fused solid as vitrified rock. He then had it covered in a thick shell of ice.

On the inside, Ahriman then created his new and yet artificial world. For warmth and light, Ahriman had built a crude but effective, controlled and contained fusion reaction Sun. This artificial Sun provided all of the heat and the light, that the generation ship would require. This artificial Sun burned steadily and brightly for many, many millennia, requiring refuelling only occasionally, with fuel acquired from the collection of interstellar hydrogen and helium gas.

For gravity, the small moon was made to rotate, creating artificial gravity by centrifugal force. For those smaller interior regions along the axis of rotation, where centrifugal force was insufficient, he had built a pair of crude but effective gravitational generating systems. They could only simulate low gravity and even then, only over those relatively small areas. Then he built an incredibly large and powerful ion drive system.

Once the generation ship was finished and after the planet's environment had almost completely died, Ahriman placed his little inside-out world into motion across the deep void of interstellar space. Not every one of his subjects went with him, as Ahriman selected only the best of his subjects and abandoned the rest to their fate.

So into the void Ahriman's generation ship flew, in search of a new home amongst the stars, whilst those left behind, were left to fend for themselves on a dying world. Not just his Tarlaks either, there were a handful of the original species from which they'd evolved, surviving in hiding, in the more remote and isolated pockets of the planet. Along with them, was another couple of species that Ahriman had considered inconsequential, he allowed his Tarlaks to hunt them for sport.

Now Ahriman's mind returned to the present, he watched as the interlopers approached. The Martian he could see was a female. She like the rest of her species, was so completely attuned to the benevolent side of the universal cosmic field, that they could never be turned away from it. As a result, the Martians would be slaves to his people forever, a workforce to design and build his weapons of war and not much else. Ahriman could control them, but never would he be able to possess them. The mere thought of doing so made him feel violently ill.

These other two were entirely different, they had evolved on the Earth and were another species of human altogether. They were a similar species as that of the Martian female and yet, they were very, very different. They were quite intelligent and industrious, but better yet, they still had slightly violent and warlike natures to them. They had very high aggression levels. Yes, he could certainly use the Earth's human species, these two, even had very high psychic potential. Very useful indeed.

Their potentials were powerful, yet raw and untrained, they still had enough links with their ancient animalistic and malevolent side to be turned. To become as himself, thoroughly and completely evil. As he approached them, he had considered the possibilities. They must not escape! Ahriman must keep them here! Ahriman must master and control them both! Then Ahriman could turn them to pure malevolence and return them to the Earth, to do his work amongst their own people!

Ahriman approached them slowly, ever so slowly, levitating slightly above the cavern floor. His evil presence encroached upon them as he slowly drew closer to them, red veins showing in the whites of his eyes. Ahriman needed these two Earth humans, he needed their entire species. Ahriman believed that, although they were striving towards the benevolent side of the cosmic field, their many older links to the malevolent side could be nurtured, strengthened and reinvigorated within them.

Ahriman believed that the Earth's entire population could be turned and become as with his own Tarlak subjects. To be ruled by him and to create an empire. An empire he could expand into interstellar space and the surrounding star systems, with an evil humanity as its main force. Something Ahriman could never achieve with the Martians.

Ahriman stopped a mere thirty paces away from the combined minds of the three interlopers. Ahriman gave them a small taste of his raw power and he was pleased immensely when they all reeled back in shock and horror. Ahriman then pervaded the very air around them with his malevolence, to keep their state of fear at a maximum, so that they would be shocked into total immobility. It was working, they could not move at all. All Ahriman had to do now, was make them submit to his will and then bring them physically through time and space to Mimas.

Ahriman reviled them, to suppress them into submission to his will. Ahriman's will reached deep inside them, forcing their wills into tiny, minuscule pockets within their own minds. Then Ahriman saw interference! Damnable interference! The Martian female was working quickly, she yanked them both back away from him and they were dragged swiftly backwards towards whence they'd come.

Ahriman pursued them, though he wasn't fast enough and they quickly fled Mimas, back all of the way to Mars. He quickly gave up the chase and he was enraged by the loss. He had lost hold of two highly intelligent beings with great psychic potentials and he now feared them and their developing consciousness immensely. They were now a danger to him and no longer possible assets!

Gideon Reas and Sandra Danker were members of a species capable of terraforming planets, changing them to make them habitable for flourishing life. As Gideon and Sandra were reaching into the realm of the universal cosmic field, they were on the verge of a new evolution, a psychic evolution beyond anything, that they themselves could presently comprehend.

If they progressed much further into the benevolent side of the cosmic field, they would soon learn to manipulate it. When that happened, they would find that instead of merely being able to change existing worlds, they'd be able to create them, entire systems as well, from scratch within the Realm of Universal Mind. The noumena from all phenomena was derived.

Ahriman had very good reason to fear such a development, as he could not wage a war against a fully developed psychic species. If he could not fully control these two humans, then they would have to be eliminated. This new evolution had to be stopped before it could develop a solid foundation. Then he could turn their entire species toward the malevolent side and make them like himself.

The complete opposite of any benevolent psychic species. His own species were the en-slavers of life wherever they found it. Perverting it, making it malevolent. If they couldn't enslave and possess it, they'd destroy it utterly and leave behind a dead planet or a dead star system.

Ahriman's original species had been destroyed by the combined efforts of six highly evolved psychic species, in a war that lasted many millennia. Of Ahriman's species, all that remained were scattered, disembodied, evil souls drifting forever, through the dark vastness of interstellar and intergalactic space. Ahriman himself had been very lucky to find a new host species.

Ahriman then summoned his commanders and they very swiftly came to his side. He looked at them, his Tarlak overlords, superior to the mainstream of their species, but nonetheless malevolent, then Ahriman spoke.

"We have lost the fourth rock world to the indigenous species of this system. Even now they are preparing to wage war against us. We must move fast! We shall move our world to the fourth rock world and do battle with them before they are ready!", Ahriman's voice was guttural, loud and forceful, the Mimasians listened to him with great fear.

One of his commanders then stated to him, "My lord, Ahriman. The ion drive has not been used in many scores of millennia. We must check it first my Lord, it could malfunction."

Ahriman stared at him, he was enraged, no one, absolutely no one was to give him advice, "There will be no checking, the ion drive system will work perfectly!", he screamed.

Ahriman then clenched his fist and the Mimasian commander who had spoken out, collapsed to the ground dying, blood gushing from his throat.

Ahriman then questioned his remaining commanders very clearly, "Are there any more of you, who would advise against my plans?"

They all answered in unison in their guttural voices, "No my lord. Your will be done!"

Ahriman then stated, "We shall first retake the fourth rock world. After which, we will then move onto the third rock system, where we shall destroy all of their detached colonies. If resistance from the third rock world continues, we shall totally annihilate it. Nothing shall be allowed to resist us. This system belongs to me and I shall reign supreme!"

Ahriman's decision now threatened more than six billion humans. It didn't matter to him, so long as the entire system was his after the war. It wasn't very long before the gigantic ion drive was activated, slowly it warmed up and was found to be in good working order. Over all of the millennia since it had last been used, its automatic maintenance systems had been in operation. Mimas was soon moving and on a course out of the Saturnian system, on a trajectory towards Mars.

On Titan, the colonial Administrator, Mark Spencer received a call on his compucomm, he was very quick to answer it, "Administrator Spencer here, what's the news?"

"Mr Spencer, security here, it's Mimas, Sir", the voice on the other end of the line informed him.

"Well then, what about Mimas?", Administrator Spencer inquired.

"Sir, Mimas is moving. It's leaving Saturn's orbit and is now on a course towards the inner solar system", he replied.

"That isn't possible!", exclaimed Administrator Spencer.

"Mr Spencer, Sir, it's true and Sir, the interceptors that were patrolling our colonies, are now all on a course to rendezvous with it", the voice replied.

Administrator Mark Spencer then went to double-check this new information and he found out that it was, in fact, correct. His engineers also told him, that Mimas appeared to be powered by an immense ion drive. Mimas's largest crater, Herschel, appeared to be an immense ion drive thruster exhaust system. Mimas was, in fact, a generation ship, that had been parked in Saturnian orbit for millennia.

Administrator Spencer then went to the communications room and asked if it was possible to transmit a message. The Communications officer told him, that all of the communications jamming had stopped and that it was now possible to both transmit and receive. He ordered the Communications officer to transmit a coded message to the nearest Belter colonies, as well as to Mars and Eros. The message was very simple and straight to the point.

The message read, *"The patrolling Mimasian fighter craft have all returned to Mimas. Mimas is on the move, on a trajectory towards the inner solar system. What's left of our colonies are okay for now, concentrate on defeating Mimas. The main interceptor launching tubes are on the opposite side of the crater, Herschel. Caution, they are protected by both deflector shields and high-intensity laser weaponry. Mimas appears to be powered by an extremely large ion drive system. The crater Herschel, is functioning as an immense ion thruster exhaust system."*

Administrator Spencer then ordered, "Repeat that message over and over, until you get a response from everyone you've sent it to. Then let me know they've received it."

The Belter colonies were the first to receive this transmission. They immediately began to increase their deflector shield production and then began fitting out their interceptors with them. Then they watched Mimas with fear as it approached the outer belt. It was found, however, that the small ice moon was actually following a trajectory, that would take it through the least populated regions of the asteroid belt. Only a handful of the smaller mining colonies were in Mimas's path and these were easily evacuated. This trajectory, however, would take the small ice moon directly to Mars.

At the Aries colony, Colonel Bannon received the Saturnian transmission, he had already been informed that Mimas was moving and that it was heading towards Mars. He quickly summoned Gideon, Sandra and Winchilly and they came as quickly as they could.

When they arrived, Colonel Bannon made inquiries about their fleet's progress, "Sandra, how is our little fleet coming along?"

Sandra replied, "It will be completed soon, Jim."

Colonel Bannon then asked, "Is there any way of speeding up the schedule?"

Sandra's reply was cautious, "I suppose we could, but why do you ask?"

The Colonel looked at the trio, then he informed them, "Mimas is moving and it's heading straight towards us."

A perplexed Sandra then asked the Colonel, "How can Mimas move?"

Winchilly interjected, *"The ice moon Mimas, is actually an immense generation ship. It contains a very powerful ion drive system."*

Gideon and Sandra then looked at Winchilly, she had not mentioned anything about this at all.

Winchilly then explained, *"I assumed that you already knew, that the Mimasians are not of our system. That you both had already realised, that they came here using Mimas, a generation ship."*

Gideon then replied, "We never considered the possibility, Winchilly. I guess we'll have to get our little fleet ready a lot sooner. We should have realised."

The Colonel then replied, "Thanks Gideon, Sandra. We'll be needing those ships for sure now."

The schedule for their small fleet was then moved up and the rate of ship production increased.

19. The Response.

Eros received the news from Saturn and they quickly sent word to Cis-Lunar L-Five to speed up production of the Armada. The reply they received back, was that they couldn't speed up production without cutting corners. To do so, they would have to dispose of some of their routine safety testing. They wanted the Security Council to take full responsibility for any possible mishaps.

The Security Council of Sol then met to decide on this problem.

The Central Councillor opened the meeting and stated the situation to the other Councillors, "Mimas is now moving on an intercept trajectory towards Mars and our Armada isn't even one-third completed. I have been informed that by cutting out a lot of routine testing, we can halve the remaining construction time. We have a problem in that Cis-Lunar L-Five would like us to take full responsibility for any decision on this, we of course appear to have no choice."

The Councillor, third on the right asked, "Can we put together a smaller fleet straight away to buy us some more time?"

The Central Councillor replied, "We haven't any craft ready as yet. It will still take time just to get a small fleet on its way. Time which we simply do not have!"

The Councillor, second on the left inquired, "If we cut out just the more routine testing, will the Armada be able to make it to Mars on time?"

The Central Councillor replied, "No, as things are, the Armada still won't make it on time. The situation may very well be hopeless."

The Councillor, third on the left then stated, "Then it really is irrelevant isn't it? Whether we cut out the testing or not. We still can't have the Armada ready in time."

A Councillor, fourth on the right replied, asking, "Even if the fleet can't be ready to save Mars, will it be ready to stop them before they reach Cis-Lunar Space?"

"That Councillor, we do not know. We can't predict how long it will take for the aliens to retake Mars nor how long they will stay in Martian orbit", the Central Councillor responded.

The Councillor, fifth on the left then stated, "What will happen if a major malfunction occurs, one that may have been picked in the routine testing? It would be a major disaster!"

The Councillor, second on the right then inquired, "If we cut out the routine testing on just a handful of craft, to create a smaller fleet, can we get it to Mars in time?"

The Central Councillor then replied, "According to the schedules, yes, but it would have to be a very small fleet indeed."

The Councillor, fourth on the left then stated, "That could buy us enough time to get another larger fleet ready, but again, we would have to cut corners on the routine testing."

The Councillor on the right then stated, "We'll be able to fight Mimas with successive fleets, each one of them growing in size. Fleet after fleet."

The Councillor on the left then stated, "We haven't even solved the problem of any unforeseen malfunctions yet, have we?"

The Central Councillor replied, "Our engineers know their work. We might assume, as they haven't made any mistakes as yet, that there won't be any unforeseen malfunctions."

The fifth Councillor on the right then stated, "Gentlemen, we've forgotten three very important factors. Colonel Bannon, Doctor Gideon Reas and Sandra Danker. These three people are not likely to put all their eggs in one basket and they are definitely not stupid. Those three, may very well have taken the initiative, to make preparations themselves."

The Central Councillor then stated, "Yes. I believe you may be right. Might I suggest that we find out what, if any preparations they may have made, before we make our final decision."

The meeting was quickly adjourned and an urgent message was sent to the Aries colony in high Martian orbit. Colonel Bannon received the message and then he summoned Sandra and Gideon.

"Sandra. How long till our little fleet is ready?", he inquired.

"Colonel, our fleet will be ready to fly in less than twenty four hours", Sandra replied.

"That's good, Sandra. Very good indeed. It appears that the Security Council of Sol wants to know if we are building any ships of our own", he informed Sandra.

Gideon stepped in and replied, "It looks like Eros needs a little help from us, Jim", adding, "Tell them, we've got a little fleet ready for combat and that we'll buy them as much time as we can."

The message was then quickly sent to Eros. The Security Council of Sol received the reply from Colonel Bannon and during their next meeting, the Central Councillor read it out to his colleagues.

"The Mimasian threat was not taken lightly here in high Martian orbit. Doctor Reas, Miss Danker, their Martian colleague Winchilly and myself, after looking into the enormity of the Mimasian threat, took it upon ourselves to make all possible preparations to meet that threat. We have created a small fleet, this new fleet contains forty of the deadliest interceptors we could devise."

"In addition to this, we have also built three Battle Cruisers and two Interplanetary Fighter Carriers. This small fleet will be launched on an intercept course to Mimas as soon

as possible, to intercept Mimas as it enters the Asteroid Belt. We fully intend to give Cis-Lunar L-Five as much time as possible to build the Armada. We will achieve this goal at all costs. Colonel James J Bannon."

The Councillor, fifth on the right then stated, "It seems that I was right about our three friends at the Aries colony. Never underestimate determined minds!"

Another Councillor, the second on the left then questioned, "Can we assemble a fleet of equal size to reinforce the Colonel's fleet?"

The Central Councillor then replied, "With the Colonel's fleet buying us time, it could be possible. We'd need to cut corners of course but it could be done."

The Councillor on his right then inquired, "Will we now have enough time to fully complete the Armada, without cutting back on the more routine testing?"

The Central Councillor replied to him, "Perhaps, perhaps not, it will all depend on how much time this little Martian fleet can buy us."

The Security Council meeting finished. They had decided to quickly assemble a small fleet to reinforce Colonel Bannon's fleet. The fleet would be equal in size and strength, but of course would not be ready in time to fight in the initial battle. They then sent word to Colonel Bannon, that the small fleet being built by them would be at his disposal as soon as it was built and launched toward Mars.

The Colonel received their second message and was pleased that they'd decided to assemble the small fleet. He definitely knew it would be needed before long. His own small fleet was ready for launch. He himself would be in the Captains seat of the command ship, a Battle Cruiser, which had yet to be be named. The Colonel quickly said goodbye to his three friends, who wished him luck and then he boarded the brand new Battle Cruiser.

Soon he and his small fleet were on their way. Gideon, Sandra and Winchilly watched as their fleet flew swiftly into the dark, vastness of deep interplanetary space. They watched as the fleet's plasma drives ignited. Five large vessels rushed towards Mimas at a swift acceleration rate. The forty new interceptors being carried inside of the two IFC's interceptor hanger bays. Their course was locked in and they were on their way.

The two IFCs carried a crew of forty two each, plus the ship's Captains. There were of course twenty pilots for twenty interceptors in the four fighter bays. Then there were the ten engineers for the twenty interceptors. Each being a specialist in interceptor maintenance and repair. Then of course, for the five weapons pods, there were five gunners. For the four plasma drives, there were also four engineers, these were also trained to repair any damage to the weapons systems on the craft as well.

Also on board was a cook, whose job needs little explanation and also a fully trained ships surgeon. They took care of both the crews nutritional needs and their medical needs, with the aid of complex computer and robotics equipment. The pilot also had a very complicated job, he flew the IFC when the Captain wasn't at the helm. He was also the ship's navigator and doubled as a computer engineer, both in the hardware and software fields.

The Captains of the IFCs, had a similar task to that of the Cruiser Captain. He co-ordinates all of the crew's activities, as well as being able to pilot the IFC. He was also responsible for all of the major decisions on board the craft, as well as the crew's safety and well-being, both physical and mental.

After the long haul from Mars, Colonel Bannon's small fleet had now began to decelerate, as they quickly approached Mimas, which was now entering the outer regions of the Asteroid Belt. Mimas was still too far away from the fleet for the fleet to appear on its long-range scanners. Colonel Bannon had a little trick to play on the Mimasians as well, it would be quite a surprise for them.

Soon, Mimas appeared on their long-range scanners, this also meant that the Mimasians had likely located them as well. Colonel Bannon placed his two IFCs in the van of the fleet, he then placed his Battle Cruisers in the rear flanks in a triangular formation. Swiftly they closed in on their enemy, an enemy who watched five ships approach. Two massive ships and three large ships, of a kind they had never seen before.

"What kind of ships were these?", the Mimasians thought to themselves.

One of Ahriman's commanders entered his chambers, "My Lord, there are five human vessels approaching us", he informed Ahriman in his guttural voice.

Ahriman inquired, "What kinds of human vessels?"

The commander replied cautiously, "We do not know, my Lord. We have not seen these types of vessels before. They are different! Very different!"

Ahriman did not like the answer, he decided, "I will come to the scanner chamber. I wish to see these new human vessels for myself."

Ahriman was in the scanner chamber, watching these strange new human vessels approaching, "They are indeed unique, new designs I believe. I wonder what the purpose of those two larger craft are in front. The smaller three at the rear are quite obviously warships, carrying many times the firepower of one of our small interceptors."

One of his commanders suggested, "They appear to be shielding the warships, my Lord."

Ahriman thought he had the answer, "Yes of course, shields for their warships, but more than that, they probably carry a vast number of fusion bombs. Yes! They intend to ram them into us, detonate them and then attack with their warships."

It made perfect sense to him, it was after all, something that Ahriman would have his own people do. He would sacrifice any number of his own people in a heartbeat!

Ahriman ordered twenty of his fighter craft to attack and destroy the lead ships first.

"Those two lead ships, must not reach the surface!", Ahriman warned his commanders.

Colonel Bannon watched as twenty interceptors launched from Mimas. He then gave his order to launch their attack. Without any warning, forty interceptors were launched from out of the two IFCs, which then peeled away from the attack formation. Now forty interceptors led the way to Mimas and the three Battle Cruisers followed, remaining in formation.

Ahriman watched the manoeuvre and he was enraged, "Fighter carriers! I should have known! I should have guessed!"

It was all too late. As Ahriman watched, the forty colonial fighters quickly destroyed his twenty interceptors, using concentrated firepower, with laser beam and particle beam weapons far more powerful than their Mimasian counterparts. What was even worse, these colonial fighters were also shielded. It was a brilliant dogfight and a nice victory, however, the battle did not go all their way.

As the colonial fighters fell upon Mimas for a strafing run, the large surface mounted lasers opened fire. These were powerful weapons and although the colonials were shielded, they simply could not stand up to this intense laser fire. Brilliant explosions lit up the void around Mimas. Eventually, all of the colonial fighters were destroyed, but not before they had caused considerable surface installation damage during their strafing runs.

The Battle Cruisers had moved up next, they opened fire on the surface of Mimas. This was then followed by the IFCs, which also opened fire on the surface installations. Another one hundred Mimasian interceptors had been launched. These all attacked the Battle Cruisers and the IFCs, which were pummelling the Mimasian surface installations.

The Mimasians flew in formation and concentrated their firepower. As they attacked, the weapons pods of the colonial vessels sent laser beams and particle beams blazing in vicious arcs through the void around Mimas. Mimasian fighters were being blown to pieces by the dozens, but they were causing a lot of damage to the colonial vessels as well, even with their powerful shielding.

In the end though, it was the big lasers on the surface of Mimas, that did the most damage. As they had fired upon the colonial vessels, the colonials vessels had fired back. A great deal of damage was being done on both sides. However, it wasn't long before both of the IFCs were badly damaged, then they were quickly destroyed by the big surface lasers in two massive explosions of brilliant blue light.

Colonel Bannon decided to try another tactic, this was his last resort. The Battle Cruisers had to attempt to manoeuvre around the very rear of Mimas, to its ion drive's vulnerable thruster exhaust systems. In previous discussions with Sandra and Gideon, they had decided that Mimas's ion drive thruster system was its Achilles's heal. As the three Battle Cruisers manoeuvred around Mimas, they were struck again and again by the big surface lasers.

The Mimasian interceptors had been severely depleted in numbers, but they still attacked. It wasn't long before one of the Battle Cruisers was destroyed. Colonel Bannon watched his view-port out of the corner of his eye, as the Battle Cruiser flared brilliantly and then vanished into cosmic dust. The last two Battle Cruisers continued and very soon they were approaching Mimas's ion drive thruster exhaust systems.

This was a very special, very vulnerable target. Colonel Bannon and his counterpart on the other Battle Cruiser picked their targets very carefully. They had to hit precise vulnerable regions. As the last of the Mimasian interceptors was slowly destroyed, the heavy ground lasers continued to fire. The two remaining Battle Cruisers responded by firing at their selected targets. There was a series of sudden explosions in the immense crater, Herschel. Mimas's massive ion drive automatically shut itself down, to avoid tearing Mimas apart. The ice moon Mimas was now drifting in space.

Another of the Battle Cruisers fell victim to the big ground-based lasers, vanishing in an enormous flash of brilliant blue light and only the Colonel's flagship remained. The Colonel was quick to order his pilot to withdraw from the battle and his craft retreated, as it was hit by yet another volley of laser fire. The Colonel's small fleet had caused an enormous amount of damage to Mimas and only his Battle Cruiser was left. He requested a damage report as he watched Mimas, now drifting slowly in space, dropping farther and farther into the distance.

"Sir. We've lost both weapons pods on our port side and our rear weapons pod on our starboard side. All three gunners were killed. Our plasma drives are okay and will continue to function quite well. We were very lucky, Sir. Our port deflector shields are down, as is our rear starboard deflector shield. Our rear and mid-port bulkheads have all been sealed. Our hull has been severely holed in those sections of the ship", the engineer informed him and then passed him the complete list.

Quickly reading through the damage report, the Colonel enquired, "Will we make it back to Aries?"

"We will make it home, Colonel", the engineer replied.

Colonel Bannon then ordered his pilot to lay in a course for the Aries colony in high Martian orbit. His Battle Cruiser was again quickly accelerating, but this time towards home.

Back on Mimas, Ahriman was enraged, he asked his commanders for their damage reports. One of them was elected to read them, he knew it would be the last thing he'd do.

"My Lord, our ion drive's thruster exhaust systems are all damaged and the ion drive itself has shut down. It will take quite a while to repair the damage and until then, our world is drifting in space. The laser weaponry on the surface is also severely damaged and will take some time to be repaired. We've lost one-third of our launch tubes, which will also need to be repaired. One hundred and twenty of our interceptors were destroyed and we will have to replace them as well."

Slowly, Ahriman's rage reached its peak. He looked at the elected commander who had delivered the reports, a bringer of bad news, he then concentrated on him. Slowly the commander's blood began to boil, he screamed in agony as his skin burst and flesh began to melt. Soon the commander's body had been reduced to a mess of melted flesh and bone. With a sweep of his clawed hand, Ahriman then telekinetically threw his commander's body against the chamber wall, where it stuck and began to fuse into the gross mass of gore that was already present there.

Ahriman spoke gutturally, "You have all seen my rage and you all know what I can do to you. I want all of the repairs made as quickly as possible. There shall be no mistakes! There shall be no errors! I want the surface armaments to be trebled, no quadrupled and the power of them to be increased. I want shielding to protect all of our surface armaments and to protect our ion drive's thruster exhaust systems. I want all of this completed by the time I am ready to move our world again. If you fail me, you shall all die and you will all die ever so very slowly."

Ahriman returned to his chambers, he wondered at the bold attempt to fight his world. These humans he had reasoned, had tried to delay him in his plans to retake Mars and to destroy the Earth. They had succeeded in that respect, but they would never be able to do so again. He would turn his little world into a fortress, bristling with weapons. He would make it too dangerous for any enemy to approach it and while keeping them at bay, he could destroy them. The Earth's solar system would then be his for the taking.

Colonel Bannon's damaged flagship was now approaching the Aries colony in Martian high orbit. He switched on his communications unit and put a call through to Gideon and Sandra. As he was now very close to Mars, the time delay was minimal. A mere four seconds at seven hundred and fifty thousand miles.

"Gideon, Sandra, we've managed to delay Mimas for a while", the Colonel informed them.

A few seconds later, "That's great, Jim. Will any other ships make it back?", inquired Gideon.

"No. We're the only one left, Gideon. Mimas has a hell of a lot of firepower", the Colonel replied.

"Well, Jim. You've done a bloody good job. Our surveillance has shown that Mimas is now drifting in space", Sandra then inserted.

"We also managed to do a lot of surface damage and closed quite a few of their launch tubes", the Colonel replied.

He then went on to describe the tactic he'd used and how they'd caught Mimas by surprise.

"Well, Jim. Now that they've seen our ships, you won't catch them by surprise like that again", Gideon remarked.

"Yeah I know, Gideon, but we'll have to use another strategy for our IFCs", the Colonel replied.

"Why, Jim? What's the problem with them?", inquired Sandra.

"Well, they're good in that we can transport our interceptors and not have to worry too much about fuel. However, in combat, they are extremely under-armed and need the support and protection of our interceptors. On their own, they are just too big and far too vulnerable. We lost a lot of good men on those IFCs. Hell, we lost a lot of good men, period!"

Sandra had been taking notes as the Colonel was speaking, she had already come up with a few ideas and was quick to relay that information back to the Colonel.

"I think we can improve on our original designs, Jim", replied Sandra and the discussion continued along those lines.

Eventually, their conversation finished and the intercom went silent.

Gideon and Sandra quickly joined Winchilly and began to put her ideas into actual plans. Within a short time, they had designed some simple modifications. The shielding could easily be doubled on the IFCs and the as-yet-unbuilt ARCs. It was simply a matter of incorporating extra deflector shield modules into their designs. Their weapons pods could be modified to contain, two large high-powered lasers and also two large high-powered particle beams, instead of just one of each.

Sandra adjusted her designs, so that they could be used as a single unit or in pairs or completely independently. A weapons computer system could be used to target and fire at the enemy automatically, with an accuracy and speed far greater than any human gunner. In addition to this, the Battle Cruisers and Interceptors could have their shielding doubled as well. It was only a matter of where to fit the extra shield generators. The weapons pods on the Battle Cruisers would be modified the same as with the IFCs, as well.

These modifications could easily be made, the extra shields could easily be added to the vessels. The weapons pods could be modified and fitted without effecting the actual ship's hull at all. Once they had finished, the reports were sent to Eros, under tight security and top priority. These were delivered directly to the Security Council of Sol, who then quickly convened a meeting.

20. Mobilisation.

The Security Council of Sol met to decide on the modifications to their ship designs.

The Central Councillor opened the meeting, "We now have a problem gentlemen. The IFCs have some problems during battle. This latest report explains that they are both under armed and require heavier shielding."

The Central Councillor continued, "Doctor Gideon Reas, Miss Sandra Danker and their Martian colleagues, have come up with some new modifications. These modifications apparently need to be implemented on every class of the new warships. It is up to us to decide upon this."

All of the other councillors had read the reports and fully understood the situation.

The Councillor, second on the left stated, "The modifications to the weapons pods, appear to be reasonably simple to implement and will not take terribly long. I say that we should do so."

Another Councillor on the right then agreed, "Yes, they would be easy to implement and after reading these reports on the extra shielding. I believe that these can be added without any great delay in construction. We should definitely implement theses new changes."

Yet another Councillor on the left then stated, "The Colonel's small fleet managed to halt Mimas dead in its tracks. Viewing this, I don't think we need these modifications at all. We need to save time and these changes will not help in that regard."

However, another Councillor, fifth on the right replied, "All of the Colonel's vessels except for one were destroyed and even that one surviving vessel was extremely badly damaged. We completely underestimated the enemies firepower!"

Then the third Councillor on the right quickly added, "Yes! That was so and we haven't any idea of the countermeasures being taken by the Mimasians. Our enemies will be taken action as well!"

It was at this stage that the Councillor, fourth on the left then stated, "The Colonel's fleet was obviously assembled without all of the excessive testing that occurs at Cis-Lunar L-Five. No malfunctions whatsoever have occurred. This indicates, these modifications could be made and our excessive testing cut out to some degree. We could definitely gain some time in doing so."

To this, the second Councillor on the right then stated, "This could be so, but we really have little idea on how much time we actually have. I suggest that a reconnaissance flight be sent past Mimas, to find out exactly what they're up to, before we reach any decision. We need to know!"

The Councillor, fifth on the left then inquired, "That small fleet we were creating for Colonel Bannon is already finished. Do we modify it now or do we send it as it is?"

The Central Councillor then spoke to them all, "We seem to have some problems, ladies and gentlemen. I'm recommending that we ask Colonel Bannon to send a reconnaissance flight past Mimas and that we send the small fleet to the Aries colony as is. It may yet buy us some more time."

So the Security Council voted on the Central Councillor's recommendations. They had passed it unanimously. Then they sent a communique to Colonel Bannon.

Colonel Bannon received their message, he then called in his three friends. Gideon asked, "Well Jim, what's the news from Eros?"

The Colonel replied, "Well, Gideon. We are going to get our small fleet and it will be equal in size and power to the one that we made."

Sandra asked, "Will it contain our modifications?"

The Colonel then replied, "No, it won't. Sandra."

Gideon then inquired, "What about the Armada?"

The Colonel replied, "Well, that all depends on the Mimasians. They want us to send out a reconnaissance flight past Mimas. Once they have more information on what the Mimasians are doing, then they'll decide whether or not they'll implement the modifications."

Sandra looked at the Colonel, "That's ridiculous, they're going to need those modifications."

James Bannon replied, "Yes, but they want to be sure they'll need them before implementing them."

Gideon looked towards Winchilly, he'd had an idea, "This fleet we are going to receive will have little effect on Mimas, but I was just thinking. Could we develop a method of cloaking our ships. Some sort of cloaking device to hide our craft from their scanners?"

Winchilly replied honestly, *"I do not know Gideon. I can pass the concept around to our scientists. They may be able to come up with something, but I cannot guarantee it."*

"Great, if we can hide our vessels from their scanners, even if it's just long enough to get up close. We'll be able to attack them with the element of surprise on our side once again."

It wasn't long before some designs were brought to Gideon, he and Sandra studied them intently.

Winchilly explained, *"This cloaking device is extremely limited. It could easily be placed inside an interceptor, but it would be completely ineffective on any larger vessels. In addition to this, it will only hide a craft from long-range scanners, short-range scans will see right through it."*

"How does it work, Winchilly?", Gideon asked.

"I must be honest, I don't really know myself", Winchilly admitted, explaining, *"but I have been told that the device negates their long-range scanners. Their long-range*

scanners were of course designed and manufactured by my people, so our scientists know precisely how they function."

Sandra asked, "Winchilly, we will need forty of these. Can your people have them ready in time?"

To this Winchilly replied, *"I believe we can, Sandra. Given more time, we might have been able to improve on their design as well."*

Gideon then noted, "Well, we will be using Jim's Battle Cruiser for the reconnaissance mission. I would have preferred it to have been cloaked. I guess we'll just have to make do."

Sandra replied with concern, "No cloak. That doesn't bode well for, Jim!"

Winchilly then asked, *"Has his Battle Cruiser been repaired yet? It was quite heavily damaged."*

Sandra replied, "Yeah. We had to almost rebuild it, but it is almost ready to go."

Gideon then stated, "I just hope they make it back."

Colonel Bannon boarded his Battle Cruiser and once on its bridge, he said goodbye to his friends over the communicator. Gideon, Sandra and Winchilly all wished him good luck, then they watched as his Battle Cruiser launched. Its plasma drives were soon ignited and its brilliant blue thruster exhausts shined brightly, as the Battle Cruiser flew towards their enemy in deep space, slowly drifting just inside of the Asteroid Belt. As they watched it fly away, Winchilly suggested that they practice using and developing their psychic talents.

Gideon and Sandra sat cross-legged on the floor, with Winchilly sitting in front of them. Their minds linked up and Winchilly watched, as they both moved into realms that her people could not. Winchilly's people appeared to have reached a psychic evolutionary dead end, perhaps caused by the

Mimasian's enslavement of her people. Only the future would tell if this was so and whether their liberation from enslavement would change their situation.

Their human relatives from the Earth, on the other hand, had not been subjected to Mimasian slavery and as a result, perhaps they were far more capable. Being highly telepathic to the point of being nonverbal and being able to astral project over large distances, was the Martian's highest psychic achievement.

Slowly at first and then with greater ease, Gideon and Sandra began to move objects around the room telekinetically. Winchilly was astounded by the speed with which they'd developed their telekinetic abilities. The pair did not stop with telekinesis either, after a short while, the objects stopped moving around. Then Winchilly watched in awe as Gideon and Sandra slowly lifted up from the floor.

A form of self-telekinesis, they were literally levitating and doing so with incredible ease. Winchilly's mind was linked with theirs, but still she could not understand nor fathom, how they had performed these feats. What was even harder for Winchilly to comprehend, was the feat that they performed next.

Winchilly followed, as Gideon and Sandra took their minds into the depths of space. This time they travelled towards the Earth's orbital zone. Winchilly followed with them as they moved their minds swiftly through space. Winchilly watched the Earth from close up with Gideon and Sandra. A small bright blue sphere in the vastness of space.

Then they slowly moved back away from the Earth and then moved towards Eros at the Earth-Sun Lagrangian point five. Sandra explained to Winchilly, that the gravity of the Earth would be far too much for her body to handle. Winchilly understood that Martian gravity was only three eight percent of the Earth's gravity, but didn't exactly understand what they had meant, but very soon she found out.

The trio quickly approached Eros and soon their minds penetrated the rock crust and entered inside the hollowed out Asteroid. Winchilly had never seen the inside of Eros before. It was a most beautiful sight. In the very centre of its long cylindrical landscape, there was the one mile wide sea, that traversed the full circumference of the inside of this cylindrical world. There were eight mile long cylindrical plains on either side of it.

Effective crossing this cylindrical sea, Winchilly saw another sea, also one mile in width and with a total length of about thirteen miles. Then there were the isolated seas, two on either side of the cylindrical sea. Each of these seas was about a third the way around the interior from the long sea. They were each five miles long and about one mile wide.

Crops and forests grew everywhere. The capital city, Eros Central, stood majestically on an island at the junction of the cylindrical sea and the long sea. Other little cities, towns and villages were visible across the landscape. From within Gideon's mind, Winchilly became aware that most of Eros's population lived underground, inside of the crust of Eros.

Their three minds now rested on the gentle slopes of a mountain, that Gideon had visited on his first day on Eros. He had relaxed at this very same spot. Their three minds were now inside of the snowline at around a thousand meters altitude from the main interior surface of Eros.

Within a split second, they were all physically there. Winchilly nearly fainted with the sudden shock of transference. Winchilly felt a slight chill in the air, her muscles had felt a slight strain. Winchilly quickly realised that her body was no longer at the Aries colony in high Martian orbit. There, close to the Aries colony's axis of rotation, the gravity had been around point three gs.

Here, the gravity was at least twice that, at about point six gs. Somewhat more than Winchilly was used to. Winchilly and her companions were now on Eros. Gideon and Sandra had teleported her there.

"How did you do that?", a concerned and excited Winchilly quickly asked.

Gideon and Sandra did not answer her yet. They merely smiled at her and asked her to enjoy the view of Eros. Winchilly could see that they were not ready to explain it, so she did not ask again and instead enjoyed her new surroundings.

"This is a nice place", Winchilly mentally noted.

Gideon and Sandra both seemed a little disappointed, so Winchilly asked them, *"Did I say something wrong?"*

"No, Winchilly. We just thought you might find this place, somewhat more exciting", Gideon replied.

"Oh", Winchilly replied, adding, *"This is a very nice place!"*

Gideon and Sandra both laughed and gave Winchilly a loving hug.

Winchilly asked them, *"Will my world be like this?"*, as she gestured towards the distance horizon and the lands outstretching towards it.

"Similar, but not quite the same", Gideon replied.

Sandra clarified, "Here, the inside of Eros is a cylinder and the horizon curves upwards. On Mars, more or less a sphere, the horizon curves the other way."

Winchilly nodded in understanding, remarking, *"Yes, I was aware of that ,Sandra, yet somehow I prefer this horizon."*

The trio could not have begun to guess how prophetic Winchilly's observation actually was.

The trio stayed there amongst the snow gums for more than two hours, relaxing in the crisp mountain air. Although they were above the snowline, the snow was quite light on the ground. Winchilly had never seen snow before and spent some time studying it. It was cold, it was wet and melted when she held it too long. Later their three minds combined once more and travelled swiftly back to the Aries colony, back in high Martian orbit.

Gideon and Sandra had brought Winchilly back with them, as easily as they had taken her to Eros in the first instance. They teleported across the vastness of space and soon Winchilly was again, close to the axis of the Aries colony, in a level of gravity to which she was far more comfortable.

Winchilly gazed upon her two lovers, telepathically she thanked them for the trip to Eros and again inquired, *"How did you do that?"*

Gideon answered telepathically, *"We don't really know, Winchilly. I just wanted to see Eros again and Sandra wanted to go there as well. We wanted you to accompany us and before we knew it, we were all there. I guess we got what we wished for."*

It was hardly an answer, but it was what it was and Winchilly accepted it.

Ahriman sat in his chambers, he felt a sudden huge surge of raw power in the local cosmic field. Two hours later, there was yet another huge surge of raw power. Now, Ahriman knew what it was, someone had manipulated the cosmic field, someone had teleported through space, twice! Ahriman could not tell where the starting point or the destination was, only that someone had done it, someone had manipulated the cosmic field and they'd done it twice!

Now Ahriman would have to strike quickly and he would also have to do so in the most soul-crushing way possible. Only by totally annihilating the entire third rock system, could he hope to crush the morale of humanity to the very core of their souls. As soon as Mimas was repaired, Ahriman would now go directly to the Earth, instead of retaking Mars. He would devastate the Earth, Eros and Cis-Lunar L-Five, after which all of the colonies of humanity would quickly fall into his hands. The sheer level of destruction and despair will have already defeated them for him.

Colonel Bannon's Battle Cruiser was now decelerating, but still swiftly approaching Mimas. Cautiously watching his long-range scanners for Mimas to appear on the screen. Colonel Bannon quickly prepared his reconnaissance equipment. Soon the Battle Cruiser would fly past Mimas. The Colonel had asked for an extra piece of equipment to be mounted to his ship. This was a special gravitational generator. It was Gideon's idea! It was also highly experimental and he had no idea if it would work. Colonel Bannon switched off his plasma drives and let his Battle Cruiser coast towards the little ice moon, Mimas.

Mimas now appeared much larger on the view screen. The Colonel switched on his reconnaissance equipment and activated his gravitational generator. Colonel Bannon then activated all of his deflector shields on maximum and ordered his crew to prepare for battle.

As he approached, ten interceptors were launched against him from Mimas. Laser beams and particle beams blazed and the attacking enemy craft returned concentrated firepower. The Colonel's Battle Cruiser shook violently, as its shields automatically adjusted to deflect the savage attacks from the Mimasian interceptors.

The attacking Mimasian fighters were blown into dust by the Battle Cruiser's blazing weapons pods. Soon all of the Mimasian interceptors were destroyed and his Battle Cruiser came within firing range of the big ground-based lasers.

Beams of blazing blue, coherent light shot up from the Mimasian surface and again the Battle Cruiser's weapons pods blazed. Particle beams and laser beams fired savagely, strafing the surface of Mimas. The Battle Cruiser suddenly lurched violently, as the computer-controlled shields feverishly adjusted themselves to deflect this extremely powerful laser attack.

Explosions rocked the Battle Cruiser's outer hull, the rear port side shields gave way and the corresponding weapons pod blew off into space. The Engineers quickly sealed the bulkheads and the Battle Cruiser continued its journey towards Mimas. The big Mimasian surface lasers continued to spit forth their powerful radiant beams of coherent blue light.

Colonel Bannon's Battle Cruiser was now side on to Mimas, he toyed with the gravitational field generator's controls. Soon, he had created what he needed, a small but strong offset point of gravity on the far side of Mimas. As the Colonel's Battle Cruiser coasted towards the far side of Mimas, his Battle Cruiser was suddenly hit by a massive broadside. All of the remaining port side deflector shields suddenly gave way. The outer hull was again rocked by explosions, the forward and central weapons pods blew off into space. The Ship's Engineers quickly sealed off all of the port side bulkheads.

The gravitational generator did its little trick, creating an offset gravitational point directly behind Mimas. Acting like a gravitational slingshot, the Battle Cruiser quickly swung behind Mimas, pivoting sharply around the offset gravitational point. The Colonel's Battle Cruiser was now heading back towards the inner solar system and Mars. A huge boost of momentum was passed to the Colonel's Battle Cruiser and it accelerated swiftly away from Mimas.

As the Battle Cruiser passed by the other side of Mimas, the Colonel adjusted his attitude control thrusters. The Battle Cruiser then suddenly rolled and quickly showed Mimas her starboard weapons pods. Their laser beams and particle beams blazed, ripping deeply into the icy surface of Mimas, with intense brilliant blue heat. Explosions erupted everywhere.

The surviving ground-based lasers fired back intensely at the now fleeing

Battle Cruiser. This onslaught caused the starboard shields to fail completely, the central and rear weapons pods blew off and disappeared into the darkness of space.

Again and again, the Colonel's Battle Cruiser was struck! Soon all of the starboard bulkheads had been sealed by the ship's Engineers. The hull was holed severely on both the port and starboard sides, even the ship's bridge was severely breached. Quickly the two Engineers, the Pilot and Colonel Bannon climbed into their pressure suits.

The Colonel reignited his plasma drives once again and super heated helium flames shot out of the Battle Cruiser's thruster exhausts. The Battle Cruiser lurched forward. The Colonel increased the ship's acceleration and laid in a course back to the Aries colony in high Martian orbit.

One of his Engineers quickly stepped forward, "Colonel, Sir. The plasma drives are unstable. You'll have to shut them down. Immediately, Sir!"

The Colonel moved quickly to shut down his plasma drives, but it was too late, far too late and the drives continued to burn their hydrogen fuel. Then he quickly moved again, this time to close the fuel inlet valves. Once the Colonel had done this, he blew his remaining fuel off into space by opening the safety release valves to the outer hull.

Depleted of fuel, the plasma drives all shut down, but not before four large explosions blew most of the ship's stern off into space. The stricken Battle Cruiser now somersaulted, head over tail through space, on a rough course towards the Aries colony in high Martian orbit.

Travelling at relatively high gs, the scanner display screens, showed stars rotating in spirals, as the Battle Cruiser flew in this ungainly fashion. The Colonel quickly shut down the scanners and the view screens, after one of his two Engineers threw up in his own helmet. The unfortunate man then began to choke on his own vomit.

The pilot moved swiftly, he quickly opened the man's visor ever so slightly, to allow the vomit to be released into the vacuum. He then slapped the visor closed again before too much oxygen was lost. The pressure suit's oxygen supply quickly made up for the small loss of oxygen and the Engineer began to breathe more easily, although the stench inside his helmet was hard for him to handle.

Colonel Bannon had seen the surface of Mimas, he didn't need to see the recordings, his only thought now was to get them back to Eros. He activated his ship's emergency beacons and hoped that the Aries colony would pick them up and be able to take his Battle Cruiser in tow. The Colonel then sat back and waited with his remaining crew members. It shouldn't take too long now and they had a lot of reserve oxygen in the Battle Cruiser's remaining oxygen tanks.

After some time, a tapping sound was evident on the outer hull. Colonel Bannon switched on the view screens. The star fields spiralling motion began to slow and finally stopped. Two vessels came into view, they were Belter craft. The man in charge informed Colonel Bannon, that they'd take them in tow and would deliver them to the Aries colony shortly. He explained, that they would have been quicker, but they had trouble decelerating his ship and slowing its rotation.

The Colonel and his crew let out sighs of relief. Soon the stricken Battle Cruiser was back at the Aries colony in high Martian orbit. The Battle Cruiser was a complete write-off. Gideon, Sandra and Winchilly didn't know how anyone could have survived. Luckily four people had and so had the all-important surveillance recordings.

Colonel Bannon was met by Captain Hawk as soon as he left his ruined craft, he mumbling under his breath, "We didn't even get to name her!"

Quickly they went to the communications room. The data recorder was put in place and Colonel Bannon quickly sent the contents of the recording to Eros, via scrambler and tight beam laser communications.

Captain Hawk queried, "Don't you want to see it first, Colonel?"

The Colonel replied, "No need, Captain. I was there. I saw plenty."

The Captain then remarked, "It looks like you were lucky to survive, Sir."

Colonel Bannon replied, "Damned lucky and some of us didn't quite make it."

The Captain replied, "Yes, Sir. I know, Sir. Jesus though, that ship of yours was a write-off. How anyone survived in that I'll never know."

The Colonel looked at Captain Hawk, "It was a bloody miracle, Captain. By the way, when this transmission is finished, I want all of our Officers to study this data closely."

Captain Hawk accepted the order and then Colonel Bannon left, he went straight away to see his three friends.

Winchilly beckoned Colonel Bannon into the apartment, he greeted her and once he was inside, he greeted Gideon and Sandra.

"Jim, it's good to see you again!", exclaimed Gideon.

"Yeah, Gideon. It's great to be here", he had replied.

"Well then, what's happening on Mimas?", inquired Sandra, straight to business.

"Mimas is being turned into a bloody fortress. There are shield generators and big lasers being built and installed everywhere", the Colonel replied.

"That should shock them into putting those modifications in place then", Gideon stated.

"Yeah, it should do, by the way, Gideon, you're a bloody genius", replied the Colonel.

"I take it that my gravitational slingshot worked then?", replied Gideon questioningly.

"It sure did, Gideon, perfectly. Saved my arse good and proper. We wouldn't have gotten back without it.", Colonel Bannon replied.

"We've sent the plans for the cloaking device to Eros", Sandra informed Colonel Bannon.

"That's good, I hope they mount them on all of the interceptors", replied the Colonel.

"If we didn't need to have those surveillance recordings, we could have done the reconnaissance by astral projection", Gideon stated.

"Winchilly would never have allowed us to do that, Gideon", Sandra quickly replied.

"It could have saved a few lives, Sandra", Gideon replied.

"I've been wondering, why is that, Winchilly?", Colonel Bannon inquired.

"If they allow their minds to come too close to the evil one before they have learnt enough. Then they would be mastered by him and become evil like the Mimasians. They must stay away from him for their own safety", Winchilly replied.

Gideon, Sandra and James Bannon looked at Winchilly in disbelief, yet they all knew, she was right.

At Eros, another meeting of the Security Council was convened. The recordings of Mimas were shown and the Councillors could see for themselves, all of the laser weapons and shield generators being installed. They could also see a large number of launching tubes being constructed as well. Mimas was quickly becoming a fortress and the Councillors could see that the modifications that had been developed, would definitely be needed, there were no two ways about it.

The Central Councillor Spoke, "I believe, that I can safely say, that we need not discuss this development. I would recommend that we cut out all of the unnecessary routine and repetitive testing during the construction of the Armada. I would also recommend, that all of the modifications that have been suggested, including the latest for the interceptor cloaking devices, be implemented as soon as possible. These changes appear to be absolutely necessary."

"Furthermore, I recommend that we ask the Earth Gov and the United Nations of the Earth, to start building as many big troop transport ships as they can supply. I also recommend that we raise and train an army of up to five million men, ready for action. This Mimasian threat is now far too great and we need to take the appropriate actions."

After the Central Speaker had spoken, he asked for a show of hands in favour of his proposals. Every Councillor at the table raised their hand in agreement. Eros was now moving closer towards a total war footing.

The Security Council sent a message to the Aries colony. Colonel Bannon received it, he called for Gideon Reas and Captain Hawk. The Captain arrived quickly, Gideon arrived shortly there after with his two woman, Sandra and Winchilly. Colonel Bannon read the message to the four people gathered before him.

"The small fleet, to replace the one so valiantly sacrificed, is already on its way to the Aries colony. This fleet will comprise of forty Interceptors, two IFCs and three Battle Cruisers. These craft are as per their original specifications and have not been modified. The Armada is now being constructed as quickly as possible and all modifications are to be implemented. This Armada will consist of fifty IFCs and one thousand interceptors, as well as two hundred and fifty Battle Cruisers. In addition to this, the Earth is constructing enough troop carriers to transport an army, which is currently being raised, consisting of

some five million troops. These troops will be fully trained and fully armed."

"Colonel Bannon. We require your presence here on Eros, to take command of the Armada. The army we are raising will be under the command of General Tilos T. Brennan-Chives. Captain Hawk will be placed in charge of all security in the Martian orbital zone."

"Well then, Jim, it looks like they're going to modify the Armada after all", stated Gideon.

"Yeah and I'll be in charge of it", Colonel Bannon replied.

"You don't seem too pleased, Jim?", Gideon replied questioningly.

"You know me, Gideon. I like to do things my way. I don't like the idea of being under some General's command", replied the Colonel, adding, "Besides, I'll miss you people you know."

They too, would miss the Colonel, he had been at Mars for many years and had many friends there.

Soon Colonel Bannon was on his way to Eros and Captain Hawk had taken command.

"As soon as your fleet arrives, Captain, we'll have the interceptors fitted out with the cloaking devices. It won't take long", Sandra informed him.

The Captain replied, "The cloaking devices will help, however, without the other modifications, any attack on Mimas would be suicide."

Sandra knew that the Captain was right, if they had time, she would have all of the vessels fitted with the extra shielding at least.

"If I'm ordered to launch this fleet against Mimas, then I'll be in command of the flagship", Captain Hawk told the other three.

"You can't do that, Captain. You are in charge of all Martian orbital security. You are required here at the Aries colony", Gideon reminded him.

The Captain smiled at them, then replied, "Doctor Reas. I cannot send my men on such a dangerous mission like this, without being there myself."

"If that's the case, then who'll be in charge here?", inquired Sandra.

"Why, Doctor Reas of course", replied the Captain.

"You can't do that, Captain. I'm not a part of the military", Gideon quickly replied.

Captain Hawk explained, "Doctor Reas. You know more about this colony and Mars than I ever will. You even no more about my job than I do, who else do you think I would leave in command."

The Captain was of course right. Gideon was more than capable of taking over command if he had to. For now, however, he'd rather not think about the possibility.

"Doctor Reas, don't look so shocked. I'll be performing my duty by placing the best man for the task in charge", the Captain remarked.

Gideon looked at the Captain for a long moment, then he replied, "My name is, Gideon, by the way, Captain."

The meeting then ended and the Captain then went about his duties, wondering when his final mission would come. It would only be a matter of time.

21. A Change of Course.

Ahriman's commanders entered his chambers, they had a report to deliver to him, this time the news would be good.

"Well, how are the repairs and modifications?", Ahriman demanded.

"My Lord, all of the repairs are completed and we have quadrupled the surface defences and weaponry", one of them informed him.

"Good, good, you are ahead of schedule. My ion drive system, is it ready?", asked Ahriman.

"Yes my, Lord Ahriman. Everything is ready, Sir", the commander replied.

Ahriman was happy, he smiled showing his red stained fangs, then spoke again, "Activate the ion drive, change course for the third rock system. I wish to destroy it."

"Yes, my Lord. Straight away my Lord", the commander then moved away swiftly to carry out his orders.

He had no intention of hanging around any longer than he had to.

Within a short time the ice moon, Mimas was again moving closer towards the inner solar system. Slowly Mimas's course changed and the generation ship was on its way, this time heading directly towards the Earth and its Cis-Lunar colonies.

Captain Hawk at the Aries colony was informed of the development, he straight away went to the communications centre to send a warning to Eros.

The Captain commanded his Communications officer, "I want to send an urgent message to Eros, now!"

"Yes, Sir", replied the officer, who was caught by surprise.

He then went on, "I want it to read, *'Mimas is moving again, its course has changed and it's now heading directly towards the Earth. Awaiting your orders, Captain Hawk'.*"

The message was sent and Captain Hawk then began preparing to carry out the order, that he knew he would soon receive.

Captain Hawk then summoned Gideon and Sandra and they came very quickly.

When they arrived, the Captain asked, "Sandra, have the cloaking devices been fitted to the interceptors yet?"

Sandra replied, "Yes, they have been. However, if you can give us another forty eight hours, we'll even double the fleet's shielding."

The Captain looked at her and replied honestly, "We don't have the time. Mimas is on the move again. This time heading straight for the Earth."

Gideon inquired, "Have you been ordered to attack Mimas?"

Captain Hawk replied, "Not yet. I'm still waiting for the order to come through."

The three looked at each other.

Sandra then commented, "It won't take long for that order to come through", and they all knew she was right.

The message was received at Eros and an emergency meeting of the Security Council was called. The Central Councillor quickly opened the meeting, "Gentlemen, members of this council, we have been summoned to this meeting, due to a new development in the Mimas problem."

One of the Councillors, fifth on the left, quickly stated, "When are we going to treat this situation properly? We don't merely have a problem with Mimas! We are at War with Mimas! These Mimasians are an existential fucking threat!", she was livid.

The Central Councillor replied, "Yes, we are all well aware that this is a war and now this war is about to escalate. The situation is getting worse!"

Another Councillor, the third on the right inquired, "What is this new development, this escalation?"

The Central Councillor then replied, "An urgent message from Mars has informed us that Mimas is moving again."

A Councillor, the second on the right then inquired, "How long will it take for Mimas to reach Mars?"

The Central Councillor then replied, "The message stated and the new calculations by our own people confirm, that Mimas has changed course and is heading directly for the Earth."

His ten fellow Councillors were all suddenly shocked, it was a quite few minutes before one of them spoke.

"How much time do we have before Mimas enters Cis-Lunar space?", the Councillor on the far left inquired, she had a very worried tone to her voice, probably because she herself was from Cis-Lunar L-Five and she had family still living there.

"Not very long at all I'm afraid, a week, perhaps two at the most", replied the Central Councillor.

The look of shock on the Councillor's faces began to grow.

The Councillor on the far left stood up as if to leave the council chambers, the Central Councillor quickly spoke up, "We understand that you have family and relatives back at Cis-Lunar L-Five, but if you warn them now, you risk starting a panic. Please sit down, Marlene."

The Councillor on the far left, Marlene, then reluctantly sat back down, she knew the Central Councillor was right.

Another Councillor, this time on the right, asked the question that was on the minds of all of the others, "Will our Armada be ready in time to defend the Earth and the Cis-Lunar colonies from Mimas?"

The Central Councillor answered honestly, "The Armada will be ready, but

Mimas will be within Cis-Lunar space before we can do battle with it. The fight will take place in the skies above the Earth."

A Councillor, the third on the left then stated, "The battle zone is far too close to our mother planet. The Earth is the industrial, economic and political centre for the entire solar system. Mimas must be stopped or at least slowed down until the Armada is ready."

The fifth Councillor on the left then agreed, "Mimas must be stopped at all costs and not just because I have family living at Cis-Lunar L-Five. The Earth and Cis-Lunar L-Five are the heart and soul of the entire solar system! If we lose that, then we lose everything!", she was of course correct.

All of the other Councillors were nodding their heads in agreement.

The Central Councillor replied, "We still have one option though, that small fleet we sent to the Aries colony. We will need to use it."

To this statement, the Councillor fourth on the right had stated, "We cannot, that fleet hasn't been modified. They won't stand a ghost of a chance."

Another Councillor, second on the left agreed, "That is correct. We'd be ordering Captain Hawk and his men to their certain deaths. What you're suggesting, is literally a suicide mission."

Another Councillor on the right then questioned, "Captain Hawk?"

The second Councillor on the left then replied sharply, "I know the Captain! He won't send his men on a suicide mission without going with them himself!"

The Central Councillor then stated, "Yes, yes, very commendable. What choice do we have though, his fleet may buy us enough time to prepare and we need that time!"

The fourth Councillor on the left then agreed, "That is so! We must remember that Colonel Bannon managed to buy us time, with a fleet he built illegally I might add. Captain Hawk will surely carry out the order, even if he does not like it and can predict the end result."

Finally, the fifth Councillor on the right then stated the obvious, "What good will it do to argue about the moralities involved with this order. We haven't got any choice in this matter, let's just vote on it and be done with it."

The Central Councillor then stated, "Basically we're in a position in which we must order good men to their deaths. To buy us time for the completion of our own Armada. We must do it! Like it or not, we have little choice in the matter!"

The eleven Security Councillors then voted, unanimously agreeing to send out the order. Within minutes the order was on its way to the Aries colony in high Martian orbit and to the awaiting Captain Hawk. Straight away, after receiving the message, it was relayed to the Captain and he called for Gideon and Sandra.

On arriving at his office he informed them both, "My orders have arrived."

Gideon looked at him, Captain Hawk's face was grim, Gideon then asked him, "Is it the order that you were expecting?"

Captain Hawk replied, "I'll read it to you."

The Captain began reading the order, *"Captain Hawk, given this situation. The Security Council of Sol has found it necessary to issue an order, that we would have preferred to have avoided. Your fleet must confront the ice moon. Mimas must be stopped at all costs. Mimas must not be allowed to enter the inner solar system beyond the orbit of Mars. It is with great regret that we must send this order, but we have no choice in the matter. Good luck to you and your men Captain Hawk."*

Gideon and Sandra looked at the Captain, Sandra then spoke, "They are right of course, they didn't have much of a choice."

"Yes, I know. Now I understand how Colonel Bannon must have felt going into battle with his fleet", replied the Captain.

Gideon and Sandra then wished him good luck and went with him to his Battle Cruiser. The Captain's had already assembled the small fleet's personnel. The fleet's crews were ready and waiting.

Before he boarded his own vessel, he remarked, "Gideon, I'm leaving you in charge now. The Aries colony and Mars are yours now. Do a good job."

Captain Hawk was soon aboard his Battle Cruiser, then a short time later, the small fleet was launched and on its way. As soon as his plasma drives ignited and they were on their way, Captain Hawk contacted the Captains of his other craft.

His orders had been simple, "My Battle Cruiser will lead the formation. I want the other two to follow behind me in a tight V formation. Further behind them, I want the two IFCs to follow, side by side."

"I want all of our interceptors prepared for launch long before we reach scanner range. When I give the word, I want all of our interceptors launched with their cloaking devices activated. Then they are to fly forward passed the two trailing Battle Cruisers. Split into two groups of twenty craft each and overtake my Battle Cruiser, to lead the formation. If everything goes well, the Mimasians won't know that we've launched our interceptors, until it's far too late."

The fleet then continued towards Mimas, an enemy with vastly superior firepower, an enemy they could never hope to defeat, but could they stop them dead in their tracks?

Gideon, Sandra and Winchilly sat watching the screens showing the telescopic image scans of Mimas, as it moved towards the Earth. The telescopic views, showed both the view of Mimas and the view of their small fleet, sent to slow Mimas down and possibly even halt the ice moon. These two opposing forces were still an extremely large distance apart. The view of Mimas, was showing a fuzzy haze around the ice moon and that fuzzy haze was growing.

As Mimas approached closer to the inner solar system, the Sun's radiation had begun slowly vaporising the surface of its ice shell. This formed a small thin cloud of gas and particles that surrounded the ice moon. The solar wind then pushed this cloud outward away from the Sun and off into space, forming a long tail that was continuously growing.

After some more time, the two forces had almost reached their mutual scanner ranges. Whilst the trio at the Aries colony had intermittently watched the two forces approaching each other, Captain Hawk on the other hand, had sat with his eyes glued to screens of his Battle Cruiser's long-range scanners. He watched and he waited in anticipation.

As soon as Mimas had appeared on his scanner screens, Captain Hawk sent out a simple message over the intercom, "Okay, let the lads loose."

Forty colonial interceptors were quickly launched with their cloaks activated and then they took up position at the lead of the formation. Their cloaking devices hid them from their enemy's long-range scanners.

While Ahriman sat in his chambers, one of his commanders cautiously entered.

Ahriman asked what he wanted, "Well then, for what reason do you dare to disturb me?"

The commander replied, his guttural voice slightly trembling, it was bad news, "My Lord, there is a small fleet of human vessels approaching us."

Ahriman enquired, "What kinds of human vessels?"

The commander then replied, "Their fleet contains the same types of vessels as the last one. Three warships and two carriers my Lord."

Ahriman then stated, "I shall come to the scanner chamber. I wish to watch this battle unfold."

The commander replied, "Yes, my Lord."

Ahriman then looked at the commander, he stated coldly, "We should defeat them easily this time. If we do not, then you shall surely die", he then bared his blood-red fangs.

It was only a short time before Ahriman was in the scanner chambers.

Ahriman watched the formation of warships approach and he noticed something different, "They fly in the opposite formation this time, the three warships in front of the two carriers! Why?"

The commander who had reported the approaching fleet to him replied, "My Lord, we know what the larger craft are. They cannot fool us a second time. This time, the humans protect them."

To this, Ahriman replied, "Yes, I know that, but these humans are tricky! Launch fifty interceptors."   The commander replied in his guttural voice, "Yes, my Lord."

Captain Hawk managed a wry smile as his scanners showed fifty enemy craft emerging from Mimas. They flew directly towards his small fleet as if nothing stood in their way.

Ahriman, however, was very surprised, "Why haven't they launched their fighters yet?", he inquired.

His commander answered honestly, "My Lord. I do not know."

The small human fleet kept coming closer and closer, Ahriman could not understand why the humans had not launched their interceptors yet.

"Why haven't they launched their interceptors?", Ahriman demanded to know, "They should have launched them long ago. What are these humans doing?"

Swiftly, forty colonial interceptors came within the range of the Mimasian short-range scanners. As if from out of nowhere, forty human interceptors now appeared on the scanner screens.

Ahriman was enraged, "Where the hell did they come from? This cannot be so! What is wrong with our long-range scanners?", he then turned to his commander.

"My Lord, please no! This isn't my fault. All of our scanners are operating perfectly", his commander pleaded in his now trembling guttural voice.

Ahriman didn't care, he pointed two clawed fingers at his commander, then concentrated deeply. His commander's eyes turned white, as they rolled backwards in their sockets. The commander then let out a long wailing scream and then his head exploded backwards across the scanner chamber's wall. Deep red blood, flesh, brain and bone slowly oozed down the wall, forming a pool on the floor next to the commander's fallen body.

The forty colonial interceptors fell upon the Mimasians before they even knew that they were there. The use of concentrated firepower destroyed twenty of them on their first pass. They then came around for a second pass and again their laser beams and particle beams blazed, again twenty Mimasian interceptors were destroyed. Then on their third exchange, all of the remaining Mimasian craft were cut to pieces by the colonial's laser beams and particle beams. The battle was going in favour of the colonials and Captain Hawk was happy with their progress so far.

Ahriman's rage grew to unfathomable levels and he bellowed out an order, "Do not launch any more interceptors. Use all of the ground-based lasers. I want all of these pathetic humans destroyed."

Ahriman turned away from the screens and faced the blood-stained scanner chamber wall. Ahriman raised both of his hands high above his head, splaying his six fingers on each hand in three pairs. Electricity discharged from all twelve fingers, like small bolts of lightning.

The lightning suddenly shot down into his commander's fallen body on the floor, forcing it up against the wall and burning into it. Ahriman didn't stop until the air in the scanner chamber was full of the stench of burning death. Ahriman laughed maniacally at the gruesome artwork that he'd created on the scanner chamber wall, then turned once more to watch the battle unfolding on the screens.

The forty colonial interceptors fell upon Mimas, the Battle Cruisers and the IFCs were not too far behind. Interceptor laser beams and particle beams spat blazing beams of intense, coherent energy down upon Mimas. From the surface of the ice moon, the big powerful enemy lasers spat back.

The Mimasian surface shielding withstood the interceptor's attacks, whilst the interceptor's shields failed. They simply could not stand up against the Mimasian surface laser's firepower. Colonial interceptors were quickly being shot down and blown into dust. One by one, they were destroyed until there weren't any more of them left. Sadly, Captain Hawk had expected this.

Captain Hawk brought in his Battle Cruisers and his IFCs in to attack, his weapons pods and those of his other vessels all blazing in unison. The surface of Mimas erupted violently as the beams cut deeply into its icy crust. Some of the surface installations were destroyed as their shields gave way. Most, however, were unharmed, as their heavier shielding protected them.

From the surface, the big powerful lasers blazed back at the colonials. Captain Hawk watched his screens, as the port side weapons pods of an IFC exploded outward into space. As he watched on, it was pummelled again and again, over and over, then there was a blazing flash of intense brilliant blue light. The colonial IFC then vanished from existence in a blaze of light and debris.

There was a sudden series of explosions at the rear port side of his own Battle Cruiser, a weapons pod exploded and flew off into space. The Captain rolled his Battle Cruiser and opened fire with his starboard weapons pods, the Mimasian surface shields held. He watched the screens as the shields on his remaining IFC finally failed, as it too was pummelled into oblivion by the big powerful surface lasers. Many beams of blazing blue coherent light had stuck it hard and it too, exploded brilliantly, in a huge flash of light and then it was quickly gone, leaving little but debris in its wake.

The Captain sent out an order to his other two Battle Cruisers, to concentrate their firepower and try to hit the Mimasian ion drive thruster exhaust systems. Their weapons pods blazed in unison and some of the surface installations erupted and exploded as their shielding gave way. Then the big powerful Mimasian surface of lasers suddenly blazed brightly, as they all concentrated their own firepower.

A Battle Cruiser disappeared in an immense, brilliant blue flash of light and debris flew past the Captain's scanner screens, some of it striking his own Battle Cruiser. Captain Hawk's own Battle Cruiser was hit badly, explosions severely rocked its outer hull. His own vessel now flew out of control, in the direction of the Mimasian surface.

Captain Hawk sent one final message to the Aries colony, "Gideon, Sandra, Winchilly. I'm glad to have known you all. My Battle Cruiser hasn't long to go. We gave a good account of ourselves, as did our entire fleet. Farewell my friends, I wish I could see you all....", then the message abruptly ended.

The transmission went dead as Captain Hawk's Battle Cruiser struck the surface of Mimas and it too exploded in a massive ball of brilliant blue light, leaving behind only a massive crater and debris where it had struck. The Mimasian surface installations in close vicinity of the crater were all wiped out and the surrounding regions of Mimas shuddered violently in response.

The final Battle Cruiser fought valiantly, as it flew in close over the interceptor launching tubes and its weapons pods blazed brilliantly in unison. A volley of return fire struck it hard and the Battle Cruiser shook violently as its shielding finally gave way. Then it was struck again and again, by the big powerful surface lasers, pummelled over and over. Then there was a series of large explosions, followed by one massive final explosion. Then the Battle Cruiser blew up in a ball of blue brilliance and then it too was wiped from existence.

Back at the Aries colony in high Martian orbit, Gideon, Sandra and Winchilly had watched the final image on the screen disappear, leaving only the ice moon, Mimas. They knew that the fleet was defeated, they knew that their friend was dead. It wasn't long before Captain Hawk's final message was delivered to them. After reading it, they spent several few minutes in silence, as a sign of respect.

Gideon noted, "Captain Hawk didn't take full crew complements along with him. He knew that this was a one-way trip, so he left behind anyone that wasn't needed for the mission."

Sandra solemnly replied, "By my calculations, the Captain saved forty four very lucky crewmen."

Winchilly commented, *"That won't stop them from suffering from survivor's guilt."*

Gideon and Sandra looked at Winchilly, she was right, the Captain may have save them by leaving them behind, but they were bound to suffer from survivor's guilt to some degree.

Mimas remained on course, the attack had little if any real effect. They'd caused a lot of surface damage, however, Mimas itself had only been slightly slowed down. The fleet had not even gotten close to its ion drive, let alone its thruster exhaust systems. The greatest damage was caused by the Captain's own Battle Cruiser crashing into Mimas.

Gideon walked swiftly to the communications centre and once there, he asked the communications officer in charge, "I'd like to send an urgent message to Eros, it is to be sent top priority, to the Security Council of Sol."

The officer set up his equipment and then waited for the message.

Gideon dictated it, *"The fleet sent to stall Mimas has been destroyed with all hands lost. They did manage to slow the generation ship down, but only slightly. It is still on course to the Earth and will be travelling at its previous velocity very soon. Doctor Gideon Reas. Aries colony. High Martian Orbit."*

The Security Council was called to an emergency meeting, they had all read transcripts of Gideon's message. They had also read a series of reports compiled by their own people on Mimas's current course and velocity.

The Central Councillor opened the meeting, "Ladies and Gentlemen. The fleet led by Captain Hawk has been destroyed. They did manage to slow Mimas down, but only slightly. However, our latest reports show that we have only perhaps, four to six hours of extra time, with which to complete our Armada's preparations. Our Armada and Mimas will meet in battle just outside the borders of Cis-   Lunar space, assuming we're lucky and can keep everything on schedule."

The third Councillor on the left then stated angrily, "We sacrificed that entire fleet and all of those good men, just to buy four to six hours! We would have done better to have spared them!"

The fourth Councillor on the right then quickly stated, "Four to six hours is better than nothing! We had little option at the time or don't you remember that? Now we have to concentrate on being prepared! We must concentrate on that!"

Another Councillor on the right then stated, "We do have a far older class of weaponry, which may become very useful."

The Councillor, fifth on the left then caught onto this idea, "Yes. We could very easily redevelop old fashioned high yield nuclear weaponry, as a backup plan", these were desperate times and she was feeling hawkish, especially with her, having family back at Cis-Lunar L-Five.

To this, the Councillor, third on the right reminded, "Do you forget, the last time nuclear weapons were built? We very nearly had a holocaust as a result."

The Central Councillor then quickly stated, "Deflector shielding can't stand up against high-yield fusion bombs. Might I suggest, that small high-yield fusion bombs, the type that we still use extensively in large-scale asteroid mining operations, can be modified as tactical weapons? To be fitted to small launch rockets and then carried by just a handful of our interceptors."

One of the Councillors, the second on the left quickly added, "They would have to be very small. So as not to be detected by their scanners!"

The Councillor on the left then stated, "It would not take very long to develop this primitive, yet effective weapon. They could be very useful as a backup plan, just in case our Armada has major problems during the main battle."

A Councillor, second on the right then stated, "As Mimas approaches our system, the Sun's radiation should turn it into a massive cometary like object. The ejected cloud of gas and other particles, will definitely effect their scanners, small missiles wouldn't be noticed at all."

A Councillor, fifth on the right then spoke, "Our colleague is as usual correct, but this cometary type cloud, will make battle with laser beams and particle beams more difficult as well. I suggest, that the Mimasians have a more deadly tactic to use."

The Councillor, fifth on the left now spoke once more, "Might I recommend that we assign the fusion missiles to one interceptor in each IFC. That these interceptors should carry two missiles each. I recommend a yield of two megatons for each missile. We should only need one hundred of them, to be used as a last resort of course."

The Central Councillor then noted, "We do not have enough time to discuss all of the possible solutions to this war with Mimas. The vessels in our Armada have all had their shielding doubled. The IFCs and the Battle Cruisers, have all had their weaponry doubled as well and the interceptors are fitted with cloaking devices. I now second the recommendation, that we approve the fitting of fusion missiles to one interceptor in each of the IFCs. Let us all vote on this now, without any further delays."

The Councillors all voted in favour of this new modification and then the engineers at Cis-Lunar L-Five were instructed to implement it. The Armada was now very close to completion. The very weapons, that had nearly brought humanity to extinction, were now being redeveloped to use against Mimas.

22. Two Sides Meet.

Mimas was now well within the orbit of Mars and already the Sun's radiation was causing its icy surface to vaporise. A vast cloud of gas and dust had formed, more than one hundred thousand miles across. The solar wind dragged this cloud outward, away from the sun, forming a tail many millions of miles long. The approach of Mimas was clearly visible from the Earth and the colonies of Cis-Lunar space. It was also visible from as far away as the colonies of Venusian orbit, Martian orbit and even the Asteroid Belt and the outer colonies.

This tenuous cloud of gas and dust particles would have an effect on the weapons of both the human Armada and Mimas. Laser beam and particle beam energies could be absorbed by the particles in the cloud, greatly limiting their range and destructive force. It would also affect the short-range scanners of both opposing forces and perhaps provide a shield for Eros's small nuclear missiles. However, Ahriman had some plans of his own.

As Mimas approached Cis-Lunar space, Ahriman watched his long-range scanner screens very closely. Already the humans would be massing their forces to confront him. Indeed, the Earth's Armada had already been launched and was currently on an intercept course to Mimas.

Ahriman gave his orders, "I want two small fleets of interceptors to be launched. Twenty craft each, one to attack the colonies there", he pointed to a certain point on the screen, signifying the L-Five colonies in Cis-Lunar space, "The other to attack the little rock world there", pointing out another spot on the screen, much farther afield, signifying Eros, at Earth Sun Lagrangian point five.

Within minutes the two small fleets were launched.

The Mimasians were stretching their long-range scanners to the limit, in an attempt to cover the entirety of the Earth's orbital system. At the very limit of their long-range scanner's range, a vast Armada was spotted approaching Mimas.

Ahriman stood in the scanner chamber, he asked, "How many ships have we detected?"

The commander in charge of the scanners replied in his guttural voice, "My Lord, it is not possible to say at this range."

On board Colonel Bannon's flagship, Mimas appeared at the very limit of their scanners, the image was extremely indistinct. However, on another screen, instead of a scanner image, there was a telescopic optical image. This was very much clearer, showing a cloud-shrouded Mimas. More importantly though, from out of this cloud flew two formations of Mimasian interceptors, easily seen by their plasma thruster exhausts. The Colonel sighted them, then he quickly calculated their trajectories and took the appropriate actions.

The Mimasian's targets appeared to be the colony cylinders at Cis-Lunar Lagrangian point five and the Asteroidal colony of Eros, at Earth Sun Lagrangian point five, sixty degrees behind the Earth in its orbit around the Sun. Based upon their plasma thruster exhausts, the two formations contained twenty interceptors a piece. These two enemy fleets had a good head start, so Colonel Bannon acted quickly.

Colonel Bannon contacted four of his trailing IFCs in the Armada, "IFC47, IFC48, IFC49 and IFC50, this is Colonel Bannon here, another development has arisen."

The captain of each vessel acknowledged his call and the Colonel continued, "IFC47 and IFC48, I want you to proceed to Eros at Earth-Sun Lagrangian point five. IFC49 and IFC50, I want you to return to Cis-Lunar

Lagrangian point five. Make haste. Fleets of Mimasian interceptors are heading towards both locations. Don't, I repeat, don't launch your special interceptors, you all know the ones I mean. Use your remaining interceptors to take down the Mimasians. Once your missions are completed, assuming you are successful, lay in an intercept course to rejoin our forces en route to Mimas."

The order was acknowledged and soon the four IFCs were on their way to their respective targets.

Two IFCs were now on their way to Eros at the Earth's trailing Trojan point, Earth-Sun Lagrangian point five, along with their forty interceptors, thirty eight of which were to be used to defend Eros against the Mimasians. Two other IFCs were now returning to Cis-Lunar space to the Earth-Moon Lagrangian point five, along with their forty interceptors, thirty eight of which were to be used to defend the Cis-Lunar L-Five colonies from the Mimasians. The remainder of the Armada continued on its course to intercept Mimas.

The Mimasians had a good head start, they would reach their targets before the defending human IFCs arrived. As Cis-Lunar L-Five had put all of its resources into the construction of the Armada, the many hundreds of colonies at Cis-Lunar L-Five and Eros at the Earth's trailing Trojan point, were not shielded.

The first of the small Mimasian fleets to arrive at its target, was the one sent to Eros. The asteroid Eros, now a hollowed out world and the main control centre for the solar system's colonisation program. Eros was literally unprotected and helpless in space, at the Earth's trailing Trojan point, designated on inner solar system maps as Earth Sun L-Five.

Gideon, Sandra and Winchilly had returned to Mars. From inside of the monoliths, their three minds were expanding outward. They expanded outward and reached towards Earth's orbital system. From the safety of Mars, with their minds reaching across space they watched the proceedings of the battle. They could see the Mimasian interceptors approaching Eros at the Earth's trailing Trojan point.

The Mimasian interceptors fell upon a completely undefended Eros, straight away attacking the asteroid. The one-kilometre thick fused rock crust of Eros was protection enough for the interior. The Mimasian interceptors, however, attacked the communications and spaceport facilities at each end of the asteroid that was Eros, which also contained Eros's attitude thruster control stations.

Laser beams and particle beams blazed, the spaceports were badly struck and explosions erupted everywhere. Within minutes, the six smaller local colony spaceports at each end of Eros, designed with the purpose of servicing the local colonies in the Trojan Point, were all destroyed. The interceptors then concentrated their firepower on the much larger interplanetary spaceports at each end of Eros.

These large central spaceports were quickly destroyed, massive explosions ripping deep into the hard rocky crust of Eros. Now the interior of Eros was effectively sealed off from the outside. The entire spaceport system at each end of Eros had been motionless, whilst the rest of Eros had been rotating at point five revolutions per minute. Now, however, both of the spaceport systems were fused to Eros's rocky crust and suddenly locked to the rest of Eros and they began to rotate. This caused the asteroid, Eros, to experience severe vibrations and shuddering, as sections of the rock crust suffered stress fractures. The millions of inhabitants of Eros began to worry that their little asteroid world would be doomed.

The Mimasians then attacked the rotation control stations at each end of

Eros. Laser beams and particle beams again blazed, the stations were soon demolished and massive explosions caused violent shuddering to the entire asteroid. These massive explosions caused Eros's rotational rate to increase. The millions of inhabitants began to feel the immediate effects of this devastating blow.

Then the IFCs with their colonial interceptors arrived and they flew straight into battle against the Mimasians. The Mimasians were severely outnumbered. The colonial interceptors opened fire with their blazing laser beams and particle beams. It didn't take too long for the colonials to destroy the twenty Mimasian fighters. They, themselves managed to lose only seven craft. However, the damage had already been done to Eros and the asteroid's rotational rate was still accelerating.

Gideon, Sandra and Winchilly had watched this battle, their minds could clearly perceive Eros's damage. Normally the gravity inside of Eros was set to a comfortable one point zero seven gs of gravity. Now, with Eros's rotational rate increasing, its interior artificial gravity, its centrifugal force, also increased. The centrifugal force had almost reached one point five gs and was still climbing.

Winchilly's mind quickly asked, *"What can we do? If the rotational rate keeps increasing, the people inside will be crushed!"*

Sandra's mind replied, enquiring, *"I don't know, Gideon what do you think?"*

Gideon's mind quickly replied, *"Sandra, we can help them"*, he then added, *"Winchilly, you may watch us, but Sandra and I must go to Eros, alone!"*

Without warning Gideon and Sandra had disappeared in a small, brief flash of bright light.

Winchilly's mind watched them re-appear, on a mountain inside of Eros. The equivalent gravity, inside of Eros had reached almost two point five gs and was still increasing and soon it would hit three gs. Gideon and Sandra sat cross-legged on the mountainside, concentrating on Eros's increasing rotation rate. They then focused the attention of their minds on Eros's many attitude control thrusters.

Winchilly could sense only the smallest smidgen of the power that her two lovers were manipulating. Winchilly's mind watched with both awe and wonder, as Gideon and Sandra triggered Eros's attitude control thrusters to fire and slow down Eros's rate of rotation. The pair used their concentration to control Eros's attitude control thrusters, using a source of power that Winchilly herself could not. Martians could perform telekinesis.

Slowly, Gideon and Sandra were bringing Eros's rotational rate back to its normal levels. Then they continued to concentrate on Eros's rate of rotational rate, until it was again stable at point five revolutions per minute, generating its normal one point zero seven gs of centrifugal force. Gideon and Sandra both rested for several long minutes on the mountainside. After which, they swiftly teleported back to Mars and in a small flash of brilliant light, were once more sitting with Winchilly.

Ahriman felt the sudden surge of power in the universal cosmic field. He also sensed the manipulation of the immense power that it contained and another sudden surge of power. Ahriman could sense what had happened. The two human souls that had invaded his world, before he launched it towards Earth, had begun to learn and evolve far too quickly for his liking. Ahriman had to win this battle and annihilate the third rock system very quickly. The total despair it would cause them would end their psychic evolution very swiftly.

The second small fleet of Mimasian interceptors had reached the L-Five colonies in Cis-Lunar space. The many hundreds of unprotected colonies, both small and large and of varying styles of construction, had been preparing. The colonists had sealed all of their air tight compartments, closed their bulkheads and shut down any operating fission reactors. With regards to power, these colonies were of a very different design, to those colonies of the Saturnian system.

As Cis-Lunar L-Five was far closer to the Sun, the main source of power was solar power. On each of the O'Neil style colony cylinders, there were three large flat mirror systems, to direct sunlight through three long strip windows, running the full length of each cylinder.

Inside each cylinder's main body, were three long wide land regions, in which the farms of the colony were situated. Other mirrors directed light through narrow, cylindrical windows, illuminating the hemispherical end caps, in which most of the inhabitants lived. Other types of colonies had their own style of mirror systems, used to collect, concentrate and distribute the Sun's rays, to provide efficient solar energy for the colonies to use.

The Mimasian interceptors flew from cylinder to cylinder, firing their laser beams and particle beams. These beams passed straight through the strip windows without actually damaging them. So the Mimasians had to aim at the land regions. Blazing beams of intense heat severely holed many colonies and their air rushed quickly into the vacuum of space, taking with it anything that could be sucked through the holes. None of the colonies had not been designed to take such an onslaught. The Interior habitats had been quickly destroyed and only the sealed air-tight compartments and the sealed end caps remained intact.

However, there were far too many colonies for the Mimasians to attack. So they decided to concentrate on only the ones they'd already damaged. They then fired their laser beams and particle beams in such a way as to destroy the colony mirror systems. To do this, they aimed at the supporting structures and eventually the colonies under attack, were left without any means to generate power. Their emergency stored energy systems were quickly switched on.

After this, they then turned their weapons systems onto the hemispherical end caps. These were soon severely holed and the air quickly escaped into space. Now, only the air-tight compartments inside the colonies were left. As these colonies only rarely contained fission reactors and the ones that did, had all been shut down, the Mimasians could not easily blow them into dust. The only way to totally destroy these colonies would be to keep on attacking them until all of their air-tight compartments were holed. This would be an extremely time-consuming process for the Mimasians.

The Mimasians simply didn't have enough time, so they then moved on to the next group of colonies. The two IFCs then arrived and launched their colonial fighters. They outnumbered the Mimasians and opened fire with their laser beams and particle beams. Using concentrated firepower, they destroyed fourteen Mimasian interceptors on their first pass. On their second pass, the colonial interceptors cut the remaining enemy craft to pieces. During this short exchange, the colonials lost only eight interceptors of their own.

The Mimasians had severely damaged some twenty seven colonies. Their atmospheres had been lost to space and their interior habitats were all destroyed. For all this damage, however, relatively very few lives had actually been lost. Most of the colonists had made it to the air-tight compartments and had survived the battle. Even though their farm crops and stock were destroyed, they could and would still survive. The damage to Eros at the Earth's trailing Trojan point and the twenty seven colonies at Cis-Lunar L-Five, being quite substantial, however, could nonetheless be repaired given sufficient time.

The four IFCs along with their remaining interceptors, sent to defend Eros and the colonies of Cis-Lunar L-Five, were soon on their way to rendezvous with the Armada. Accelerating quickly and then shutting off their plasma drives, this way they would reach high velocities and then quickly coast to their destinations, saving precious fuel for the main battle.

Gideon, Sandra and Winchilly had been watching the battle at Cis-Lunar L-Five. Gideon and Sandra found it very strange, that they could use their psychic abilities to actually save lives or do something that wouldn't cause harm to any living thing, but not to save life by taking life. So they were unable to use their psychic abilities to destroy the Mimasian fighter craft. This was the only aspect of their abilities, besides their telepathy, that Winchilly could fully understand.

Ahriman watched his scanner screens more closely. The Armada was still a long way off, but now rapidly approaching Mimas. Now he could see how many vessels it consisted of.

He asked his commander, "How many craft do you see on the screens before you?"

His commander replied, "My Lord, before me on the screens, there are three hundred craft."

Ahriman then replied, "You are almost correct commander. There are two hundred and fifty warships and fifty fighter carriers and within each fighter carrier, there are twenty interceptors. They may have already launched their interceptors, which can hide from our scanners."

Ahriman then asked his commander once again, "How many craft do you see now, Commander?"

This time the commander replied, "My Lord, I see two hundred and fifty warships and fifty fighter carriers. I know there are one thousand fighters in those fighter carrier's bellies or the space around them. Thus one thousand, three hundred craft are approaching us. It is a considerable sized fleet!"

Ahriman then stated, "You are assuming that all of the fighters are there. As we have sent out two fleets to their main colonies and their rock world capital. It is obvious, that they will have launched some of their fighters to defend them."

The commander replied, "Yes, my Lord."

Ahriman then continued, "If you make one more mistake, I will kill you myself and have you replaced. Is that understood!"

The commander then replied once again, "Yes, my Lord."

Ahriman waited for the Armada to come closer, he then ordered, "Launch one thousand fighters! Attack that human fleet! After that, I want two hundred fighters to break away. They are to set a course for their main colonies in the third rock system and completely destroy them. After which, they shall attack and destroy the colonies on their home world's moon."

"As soon as they break away. I want another five hundred fighters to be launched to attack the human vessels. Warn our pilots that the human fighters will not show up on their long-range scanners."

Colonel Bannon saw the Mimasian fighters leaving Mimas's shroud of gasses. The Colonel quickly counted the number of craft and then he gave the command to launch all interceptors, except those armed with the nuclear missiles. After this, he ordered his IFCs to slowly drop back, so that they would not be caught in the thickest part of the battle, as they were much more vulnerable. The Colonel's fighters travelled swiftly, they had their cloaking devices activated and their pilots were watching their long-range scanners, fully intending to concentrate their firepower.

The Mimasian pilots were unable to see the colonial interceptor fleet approaching on their long-range scanners. Almost without warning the colonial fighters appeared on the Mimasian's short-range scanner screens. Quickly their weapons blazed. They were far too late, the colonials had already opened up with their laser beams and particle beams. They flashed brilliantly in the darkness of space and the colonials had already passed them by. In this very first exchange, two hundred and twenty Mimasian interceptors were utterly destroyed.

Seven hundred and eighty Mimasian fighters now flew towards the Colonel's Battle Cruisers. As they approached, two hundred fighters began peeling away on a course for Cis-Lunar L-Five. Five hundred and eighty Mimasian interceptors then continued on their way towards the colonial Battle Cruisers. Ahriman's other orders were then carried out.

As Colonel Bannon watched his scanner screens, another five hundred fighters emerged from Mimas. There were now three enemy fleets to contend with. The five hundred and eighty fighters that were now flying towards his Battle Cruisers. Another five hundred interceptors emerged from Mimas and the two hundred interceptors headed for Cis-Lunar L-Five. The Colonel's own interceptors would soon be within range of the newest of the enemy's fleets.

The Colonel then quickly sent out an order to his own fighters, "This is Colonel Bannon here. I want two hundred interceptors to break away and follow the Mimasian interceptors heading towards Cis-Lunar L-Five. They must be over taken and destroyed at all cost. Colonel Bannon over and out."

Quickly two hundred of the colonial interceptors broke away and changed course for Cis-Lunar L-Five.

The Battle Cruisers all flew in a conical formation as the enemy fighters attacked. Their modified weapons pods opened fire, two massive laser beams and particle beams each, blazing away at their enemies. The Mimasian interceptors returned fire, but the Battle Cruisers with their extra shielding survived unharmed. With incredible ease, the colonial Battle Cruisers cut the attacking Mimasian fighters to shreds and blew them into cosmic dust.

The remaining Mimasian fighters quickly concentrated their firepower. With a remarkable swiftness, the computers on the colonial Battle Cruisers, then adjusted their shields to deflect these attacks. Only minor damage resulted and it was not long before all five hundred and eighty Mimasian craft were utterly and completely destroyed.

Ahriman had been watching the battle unfold and he was enraged, "There is something wrong! Those warships are different to the ones we have seen so far!"

Ahriman looked towards his commander, "What is different about these human warships, Commander?", he asked.

His commander replied carefully, "My Lord. These warships appear to have twice the number of weapons in their weapons pods and they are also far more powerful weapons. They also appear to have far better shielding as well."

Ahriman replied, clenching his six-fingered fists and holding back his anger, "You are correct! My fighters are useless against them!"

Five hundred Mimasian fighters then came upon the colonial craft. The colonial fighters outnumbered the Mimasians by nearly two hundred craft. However, they attacked with extreme efficiency, concentrating their firepower and using their plasma thruster exhausts. On their first pass, the odds were evened out. The two fleets of interceptors then came back around for another clash, this time the colonial fighters were far more prepared.

The colonials fighters went far beyond their enemy's short-range scanner range. Then they totally rearranged their formation, before coming back within the range of their enemy's short-range scanners once more. When the colonials appeared again, they were flying in groups of five. By using their plasma thruster exhausts and by concentrating their firepower, they destroyed many of the enemy Mimasian fighters. This battle then quickly turned into a dogfight, with laser beams and particle beams blazing on both sides. This light show lit up a vast expanse of interplanetary space ahead of Mimas.

By the time the colonial Battle Cruisers had moved up, there were only one hundred and twenty seven Mimasian fighters left, to three hundred and ninety colonials. In a very short time, all of the remaining Mimasian interceptors were annihilated by the big lasers and particle beams of the Battle Cruisers. Colonel Bannon then ordered his Armada to regroup before moving closer to the gas-shrouded generation ship, Mimas.

The two IFCs that were returning to the Armada from their defence of Cis-Lunar L-Five noticed something on their long-range scanners. A fleet of two hundred Mimasian interceptors heading their way and the colonials hadn't yet been spotted. The two IFCs then quickly activated their plasma drives and accelerated towards their enemy. They launched their remaining fighters at three gs towards the Mimasians. They picked their targets for the use of concentrated firepower and were preparing to use their plasma thruster exhausts. The gap between the two fleets was narrowing swiftly, thirty against two hundred.

Without warning, the colonial fighters appeared on the Mimasian's short-range scanners. Before the Mimasians could attack, the colonials opened fire with their laser beams and particle beams. Again and again, they fired, their weapons blazing. Then they swung away cutting through the enemy formation with their plasma thruster exhausts. They attacked and quickly withdrew before the Mimasians had a chance to return fire. On this exchange alone, the thirty colonial fighters destroyed seventy five Mimasian craft.

The thirty colonial fighters launched from the two IFCs had been travelling at such a high velocity, that before they had a chance to return to attack again, the pursuing colonials from the Armada appeared on their scanners. The two colonial forces then joined together. Now two hundred and thirty fighters strong, they were chasing down the Mimasian fleet of interceptors. They pushed their plasma drives to the limit, accelerating well above six gs. They soon started to overtake the Mimasian craft.

In a sudden blur, the colonials came upon the remaining Mimasian fighter craft. As they over took, their laser beams and particle beams spat intense energy at them. One hundred and twenty five exploding balls of blue brilliance appeared and were quickly gone, as were all of the remaining enemy craft in this fleet. The colonial fighters then decelerated and began to alter course to return to the Armada at Mimas.

Ahriman watched his scanner screens, the Armada was regrouping in the space around Mimas, outside of the effective range of his big surface lasers. Ahriman had lost one thousand five hundred fighter craft. He had an equal number left and he knew they were not capable of defeating the approaching warships.

Ahriman had another idea instead, he had to bring the humans closer to Mimas, closer to his big surface lasers. He had to lure them in! Ahriman decided to take a huge gamble and soon all his remaining interceptors were launched. His pilots had all been given orders, to leave the cometary cloud of gas and dust surrounding Mimas, only to entice the human warships to come closer in.

Colonel Bannon had regrouped his Armada and soon the two hundred and thirty interceptors and the two IFCs that were on their way to rejoin it, arrived. Their mission to Cis-Lunar L-Five completed successfully. The other two IFCs from Eros, along with their compliment of interceptors, were on their way back as well. The Colonel waited for them all to arrive.

Colonel Bannon had his remaining six hundred and sixty one interceptors all refuelled and formed into an attack formation. Behind these were his Battle Cruisers in their conical formation and further behind them were the IFCs.

Colonel Bannon ordered the fifty interceptors that were armed with fusion missiles to be launched with the cloaking devices activated. The Colonel then ordered them to remain behind, beyond the range of the Mimasian short-range scanners, where they were to await further orders.

As Colonel Bannon prepared to enter the cloud of gas and dust, he noticed on his screen, Mimasian interceptors flying out of it. These interceptors flew out, travelled a short distance then doubled back to return within it. Inside of this cometary cloud, the Mimasian fighters could be seen by their scanners, but they were partially obscured. Colonel Bannon ordered his Armada, except for his missile armed fighters, forward.

Slowly the Armada entered the cloud of gas and dust, one thousand five hundred Mimasian interceptors showed on the Colonel's scanners. Laser beam and particle beam fire was exchanged by both the colonial and Mimasian interceptors. The shields on both sides held, as the cloud of gas and dust absorbed some of their weapons energy, so very little damage was done to either side.

The colonial fighters tried to regroup to concentrate their firepower. Each time they did so, the Mimasians dispersed and moved in a little closer to Mimas. Colonel Bannon understood exactly what they were doing, but he had little choice in the matter, he had to follow with his Armada.

The Colonel ordered his interceptors to fly in groups of five and to follow the Mimasians swiftly but cautiously. In this formation, the colonial interceptors pursued their enemies. The laser beams and particle beams of both sides blazed once again. The concentrated firepower used by the colonial fighters, began cutting the Mimasian fighter craft to pieces. Blazing energy beams and brilliant explosions, caused an eerie glow throughout the cometary cloud of gas and dust.

The colonial fighters then came within the range of the big powerful Mimasian surface lasers. Blazing beams of intense energy leapt upwards from the surface of the Mimas. One by one, the colonial fighters began to explode in balls of brilliant blue light. The remaining colonial fighters withdrew to a safer distance from the surface of the generation ship. The Mimasian fighter craft did not follow. Instead the Mimasian fighter craft all stayed within the range of safety provided by the big surface lasers.

Colonel Bannon was now faced with a huge problem. Against the big Mimasian surface lasers, his IFCs and his Battle Cruisers had previously been cut to pieces. Although, now his craft now had twice the shielding and twice the weaponry of his previous vessels, they should be more effective and give the Mimasians a better fight. Another problem was time. The Colonel had to box the Mimasians in beneath their ice shell, so that the colonial troop transports could land and then the Colonial Troops could take hold of the Mimasian surface and interior.

General Tilos T. Brennan-Chives was already on his way to Mimas from the Earth, with the first wave of Colonial Troops. One million fully armed, fully trained troops, travelling in a thousand troop transport ships. All of them, already on their way. Colonel Bannon decided to take his Armada in close to Mimas, in an attempt to destroy those big surface lasers. The Colonel believed his vessels could defeat the surface weaponry of the ancient generation ship.

23. What's a Man to Do.

The Colonel ordered his Battle Cruisers and interceptors forward, leaving his IFCs at much safer distances. Within the cloud of gas and dust, his forces closed in on Mimas. His fighters were flying in groups of five and ordered to take care of any enemy craft that they came across. The Colonel's two hundred and fifty Battle Cruisers concentrated their weaponry on the Mimasian surface installations. Their main targets, the big surface lasers and the ion drive's thruster exhaust systems.

The colonial fighters let their weapons blaze at the Mimasian fighter craft, clearing a path for the more powerful Battle Cruisers. The Battle Cruisers quickly followed and moved in closer to Mimas, their weapons pods, equipped with powerful dual laser beams and particle beams began blazing away.

Brilliant blue explosions lit up many small regions of the gas cloud, as the Mimasian interceptors were destroyed. The icy surface of Mimas erupted as the colonial Battle Cruisers attacked. Their weapons pods spat high-energy laser beams and particle beams at the big Mimasian surface laser installations. The big surface lasers returned fire and the Battle Cruiser's computers worked feverishly to adjust their deflector shields, to defend against these attacks, so that only minor damage might result.

The colonial interceptors were destroying the Mimasian fighters at an extremely swift rate. The colonial fighters in return were being swiftly destroyed by the big powerful surface laser weaponry.

The tenuous cometary gas cloud surrounding Mimas, flashed with brilliant lights as fighter craft from both sides exploded. The colonial Battle Cruiser's weapons pods and the big Mimasian surface lasers spat streaks of intense energy at each other. They flashed like brilliant lightning bolts throughout the cloud of gas and dust.

General Tilos T. Brennan-Chives approached Mimas with his fleet of one thousand troop transports, the eerie flashes and streaks of light showed clearly through the cometary gas cloud. The General could see for himself that the battle was hard fought and fierce. The General put his troop transports into a safe parking orbit, more than one million kilometres out from Mimas and then sent an encrypted communique to Colonel Bannon.

"Colonel Bannon. We are in a parking orbit and awaiting your signal to proceed. When the path is clear, send the designated all-clear passphrase for us to proceed. General Tilos T. Brennan-Chives"

The General then waited for the signal from Colonel Bannon to approach.

By now, only the colonial Battle Cruisers were left. The colonial fighters and the Mimasian fighter craft had all been destroyed. Colonel Bannon ordered his IFCs to join in the battle. Up until now, the deflector shields on the Battle Cruisers had held out quite well, any resulting damage had been minor. Now, however, all of that minor damage was beginning to add up and slowly, but surely the Battle Cruiser's deflector shields began to fail. One by one, the Battle Cruisers began to suffer from the effects of the collective damage.

The computers on board the colonial Battle Cruisers were still adjusting their deflector shields, but the shields themselves were becoming weaker and weaker. Each time one of the big surface lasers struck, more and more damage resulted. The repeated heavy blows by the big surface lasers began to take their toll.

Soon one of the Battle Cruisers lost its deflector shields, they gave way and eventually, there was a large explosion as a Battle Cruiser was struck again and again. The starboard side of this particular Battle Cruiser then erupted with explosions. A series of flashing blue electrical arcs shot out from its severely damaged electrical systems. Within mere seconds, there was an immense burst of brilliant blue light, as its four plasma drives exploded simultaneously. The Colonel had seen the Battle Cruiser explode and began to wonder if his Armada could do the job.

The Colonel sent out a general command to his Battle Cruisers, "To all Captains. If your ship is no longer capable of taking a pounding, withdraw from the battle to a safe distance! Repeat! If your ship is no longer capable of taking a pounding, withdraw from the battle to a safe distance!"

The Colonel checked one of his scanner screens, the one which showed the whereabouts of his Battle Cruisers, each identified by their hull numbers. A handful were withdrawing from battle, but most were not. The Colonel touched the screen, on one of the withdrawing Battle Cruisers and that ship's damage report came up on the Colonel's screen.

Colonel Bannon quickly scanned the damage report, *"Sweat Mother of God! Jesus! Bloody good call"*, he thought to himself, approving of that ship's withdrawal from the fight.

The Colonel then went back to the task at hand.

General Tilos T. Brennan-Chives had watched as a handful of Battle Cruisers came limping out from the cometary cloud of gas and dust surrounding Mimas. The General had also heard the command from Colonel Bannon for ships to withdraw if necessary and understood that the battle for Mimas was far more deadly and devastating than he'd considered.

"Colonel Bannon. Is the invasion of Mimas achievable? Repeat. Is the invasion of Mimas achievable? Do we still have a mission?", the General questioned across his communicator.

The answer was slow in coming back, "General Sir. It is too early to say. We are still fighting hard. I will keep you informed. Colonel Bannon over and out."

One by one, on various colonial Battle Cruisers, weapons pods began exploding off into space, as deflector shields began to give way. Occasionally there were immense explosions of brilliant blue light, as yet another Battle Cruiser blew into cosmic dust, in the silent void of deep space. The cometary cloud of gas and dust surrounding Mimas with far too thin to carry the sounds of the explosions. Colonel Bannon's own Battle Cruiser, his flagship, was buffeted by an immense shock wave. He quickly turned to his port-side scanner screens. The Colonel was just in time to see the results of the four immense plasma drives of an IFC, exploding in an immense blaze of blue brilliance. The region of the cometary gas cloud surrounding Mimas in which it had been, momentarily glowed brilliantly.

"Shit! That was close!", he thought to himself, *"All of those lives lost!"*

Colonel Bannon was now beginning to worry about the mission, his craft were destroying many of the Mimasian surface laser installations, but nowhere near enough of them. There were just too many of them. He then checked all of his scanner screens, he was losing far too many Battle Cruisers, far too quickly. As he watched, one by one there was a series of massive explosions. Then the craft he'd been watching disappeared in flashes of brilliant blue light.

He then ordered his remaining craft to withdraw beyond the range of the big surface laser weapons, "To all Captains. Withdraw beyond the range of the Mimasian surface lasers! Repeat. Withdraw beyond the range of the Mimasian surface lasers!"

The remaining Battle Cruisers and IFCs then withdrew from the battle.

General Tilos T. Brennan-Chives watched as the Armada withdrew from battle and one by one, Battle Cruisers and IFCs emerged from the cometary cloud of gas and dust surrounding Mimas.

"Colonel Bannon. Status report required! Status report required!", the General requested.

"General Sir. We've lost a lot of ships and I'm making a temporary tactical withdrawal to take stock and consider our options. I will get back to you very shortly. Colonel Bannon over and out", the Colonel replied.

The General was worried that the battle was over and that Mimas was unstoppable.

The Colonel quickly took stock, counting his remaining craft. He had lost a large part of his Armada. Now he had only one hundred and sixty Battle Cruisers and twenty six of his IFCs left. All of his fighters, except the fifty armed with the fusion missiles had been destroyed. It was such a terrible loss of life and he simply could not justify any further losses.

Colonel Bannon then decided, that it was now the right time to use them. He turned his scanners onto the surface of Mimas. Slowly he began to plan out precisely where he wanted those missiles to strike, one hundred of them in all, each carrying a two megaton warhead.

Colonel Bannon then contacted his last fifty interceptors. They had been lying in wait beyond the range of the Mimasian short-range scanners, all nicely cloaked. He gave them their orders and their respective targets.

Then the Colonel sent a message through to his superior commander, General Brennan-Chives, "General Sir. Our last resort measure has become necessary, it is to be quickly implemented."

General Tilos T. Brennan-Chives received the message and he fully understood it, "Colonel. You have the go ahead! Repeat. You have the go ahead!", then the General watched Mimas closely on his scanner screens.

The Colonel then sent out his command to his last fifty interceptors, "Pilots. Your mission is a go! Repeat. Your mission is a go!"

The pilots were quick to respond and they did so immediately.

Ahriman had watched the Armada withdraw, he was pleased with the results so far, as most of the human craft had been destroyed. However, he wanted them all destroyed, after all, if you totally crush an enemy, he is no longer a threat to you. He had also noticed the transport ships on his scanners. These weren't a threat to him at all, as they appeared to be very lightly armed. He would destroy them as soon as the Armada was completely destroyed. However, something in the back of his supremely evil mind, told him something was terribly wrong. Something was amiss. What had he missed?

From out of nowhere, fifty colonial interceptors appeared on his short-range scanners. They all converged on his world from fifty different directions. Ahriman simply didn't know what to make of it.

As Ahriman watched, he questioned, "Suicide missions? These fighters will be blown to pieces?"

Ahriman watched as the fighters approached and they entered the cometary cloud of gas and dust surrounding Mimas. Then just before reaching the range of his big powerful surface lasers, they all swung away back into the depths of space, quickly accelerating away with immense velocities.

The colonial fighters had launched their fusion missiles. Ahriman did not know this. He could not see the missiles on his scanners. They were too small and obscured by the cloud of gas and dust. There wasn't any time for

Ahriman to even guess what was happening. Then Ahriman's entire world suddenly vibrated violently, as multiple massive shock waves passed through Mimas. Too many shock waves to count. The shuddering continued to increase in magnitude for many long moments and Mimas was ringing like a bell, before the shock waves finally, ever so slowly began to dissipate.

From deep in space the sight was quite spectacular. The whole of Mimas was suddenly wrapped in an immense ball of brilliant blue light. An intense heat, likened to a billion suns burned deeply into the surface of Mimas's ice shell, as the one hundred fusion warheads released their energy with unequalled fire and fury.

The cometary cloud of gas and dust that had surrounded Mimas, was quickly blown off into space by the shock waves of the one hundred exploding fusion warheads. The heat of these fusion explosions vaporised vast regions of Mimas's icy surface. Massive quantities of vaporised gas and dust particles suddenly billowed outward into space, quickly replacing the shroud of gas and dust that had been blown away by the explosive shock waves.

Colonel Bannon again turned his scanners onto the icy surface of Mimas. Most of the major installations and laser defences were now totally destroyed. Very few, if any were left and even Mimas's massive ion drive had itself shut down. Colonel Bannon quickly sent out the order for the Armada to attack and destroy Mimas's remaining defences. His Armada then once again, entered into Mimas's tenuous cometary cloud of gas and dust, attacking the surface installations once more.

Dual laser beams and particle beams in the colonial Battle Cruiser's and IFC's weapons pods blazed into action once again and the surface of Mimas erupted in destruction once more. The return fire was hardly existent, as very few of the big surface lasers had survived the nuclear onslaught and many that had, simply malfunctioned.

Nonetheless, as the Battle Cruisers and the IFCs advanced, they were struck heavily. With accurate and rapid firing, the few remaining big surface lasers managed to destroy another five of the colonial Battle Cruisers. Then the big surface lasers were themselves finally all destroyed and all resistance to the advancing Armada halted completely.

Ahriman was insane with rage. His interceptors were all destroyed. His surface defences were also destroyed. He could no longer repulse any attack. To make matters worse, his ion drive had shutdown and he could not even retreat. Ahriman gave out an order to defend the interior against invasion, then he returned to his royal chambers to think. He could still win! He just had to think of how, very soon he had the answer he needed!

Colonel Bannon ordered his remaining craft to patrol the skies above Mimas and to scan the surface continuously, anything that might appear to be the slightest threat was to be destroyed.

Colonel Bannon then sent a single message through to General Brennan-Chives, "General Sir. The fields have been ploughed and are ready for planting."

General Tilos T. Brennan-Chives knew exactly what that meant and he quickly ordered his troop transports to move in and land on Mimas. His chosen landing zone was in the northern region, so designated as it was directly opposite Herschel Crater and the massive ion drive system, which had been designated as the southern region.

This was also the region where most of the interceptor launch tubes were located. It was hoped, that these would provide access to the Mimasian interior. Once they'd touched down, the General sent his scouts over to the nearest launch tubes. His scouts were to check each launch tube thoroughly, to assess whether they were suitable access points to the interior of Mimas. While his scouts did so, his engineers quickly assembled laser tunnelling equipment, ready for use.

The General's scouts returned, informing him, that they could use the launch tubes, if they were cleared out. They had checked them to a depth of more than one thousand meters. Upon hearing this, the General immediately sent out teams with the laser tunnelling equipment to the launch tubes. After which, he sent out more of his engineers to assemble special docking equipment over the launch tubes.

Very quickly, everything was prepared and many of his troop transports began docking above the Mimasian launch tubes. It had taken more than a day for his engineers to set it all up, but the General was now unloading his Colonial Troops, into the now sealed and air filled launch tubes, one hundred of them were quickly occupied.

As fast as the General's troop transports were unloaded, they were ordered to return to the Earth, to pick up another load of troops. Quickly his men had moved down the launch tubes and into the fighter bays, which were now completely empty. These now empty fighter bays provided more than adequate space for his troops to set up military base camps.

The Colonial Troops had not yet met any resistance, but only now did they come across some sealed access corridors. They were now more than two kilometres deep into the Mimasian ice shell and the first wave of a million troops was now on Mimas. Each of the one hundred launch tubes chosen now contained ten thousand fully armed troops.

Back on Earth, the second wave of Colonial Troops was now boarding the troop transports and would soon be on their way to Mimas. The little ice moon Mimas, with its surrounding cometary cloud of gas and dust, was currently drifting just beyond the outer regions of Cis-Lunar space, a few million miles from the Earth.

The first wave of troops already on Mimas were making room for them. They blew the air tight doors to the sealed access corridors and entered them. Still meeting no resistance, they continued penetrating deeper and deeper into the Mimasian ice shell. Every kilometre along the access corridors, sealed air tight doors were found and opened, still, they met no resistance. Kilometre after kilometre they penetrated, sealed door after sealed door they'd broken open. Yet no resistance was to be found!

It wasn't very long before the advancing troops had reached the fused and vitrified rock shell of Mimas. Throughout their advance through the ten-kilometre-thick ice shell, they had not met any resistance at all. When they reached the rock shell, they were confronted by a sheer wall of solid fused rock. There weren't any air-tight doors nor even any form of opening, just solid fused rock. The surface of the rock shell was smooth like glass, vitrified and extremely hard. Their laser tunnelling equipment was required and quickly moved up, without it the rock shell would have been impenetrable.

It was taking time and slow going, but by now the third wave of Colonial Troops were boarding the transports back on the Earth. The second wave had already been offloaded and now two million troops were slowly moving through the one hundred launching tubes. These troops were armed with the most advanced modern weapons and body armour. They were prepared for what was to come.

They all carried, high powered rapid-fire, pulsed lasers. These weapons were small, powerful and fast-firing. If their firepower was concentrated, they'd bore through thick steel plating and armour.

Some of the Colonial Troops, however, carried as backups, earlier more primitive weapons. These weapons included pump action shotguns, loaded with heavy, solid grain rounds, sub-machine guns and even rocket-propelled grenade launchers. Some of the Colonial Troops even carried razor-sharp single and double-edged swords. Sabres and Katanas were particularly popular.

As the laser tunnelling equipment began to tunnel into the fused rock shell, other transport craft from Cis-Lunar L-Five began to deliver heavy laser beam and particle beam tanks. These same transports also delivered small, yet fast flying hover attack vehicles. These vehicles could fly low over land at very high speeds. They were also armed with high powered lasers and could even fly at higher altitudes in a low gravity environment.

The laser tunnellers were boring deep into the rock shell. The Mimasians had blocked the access tunnels quite effectively. As for how far, no one could say. They bored deeper and deeper into the rock shell. At the boundary where the Mimasian ice shell and rock shell touched, the ice rock interface as the engineers called it, they built a very elaborate system of airlocks. The engineers were ensuring, that the Mimasian interior, would not lose its atmosphere to the vacuum of space.

Before long, the third wave of Colonial Troops had been offloaded on Mimas and now all of the troop transports were on their way back to the Earth to pick up the fourth wave. Each of the one hundred launch tubes now contained some thirty thousand Colonial Troops. Altogether, approximately three million Colonial Troops were deployed on the generation ship, Mimas.

Mimas was now slowly coasting towards the Earth, captured by our mother planet's gravitational field. Colonel Bannon's men had calculated, that Mimas would end up in orbit, at about one million miles from the Earth. Mimas would become the Earth's second moon.

The laser tunnelling equipment worked feverishly. With incredible efficiency, these new laser tunnel boring machines could tunnel at a rate of almost one kilometre per day. Already, after just eight days they'd tunnelled some eight kilometres into the rock shell. Eventually, they had located the other ends of the access tunnels.

No longer did the powerful laser beams cut through the solid rock, they flared brightly into an already existing tunnel system. There were the sudden screams of Mimasians, who were still working to seal the tunnels. They were quickly extinguished as the lasers disintegrated them. The humans from the Earth had now broken through.

On the surface of Mimas, the fourth wave of the Colonial Troops was already landing and the fifth wave would soon be on its way from the Earth. There would soon be four million Colonial Troops in the launching tubes, ready and waiting to fight. Meanwhile in the access tunnels, for the first time resistance was met.

Laser tunnelling machines became weapons of war and burned their way through the Mimasian defences. The tunnels soon filled with the stench of burning Mimasian hair, flesh and bone. The Colonial Troops pushed quickly down the tunnels, then around ten kilometres deep, they reached a network of many supply tunnels.

The Colonial Troops entered the network of tunnels and fanned out. The sounds of sporadic laser fire echoed through the tunnels. The screams of dying Mimasians and humans were everywhere. Blood and guts stained the tunnel walls. The blood and gore was ankle deep in some sections of the tunnels. The stench of burning death was everywhere!

Very quickly the supply network was taken over and then occupied by the Colonial Troops. The battle for its control had been fierce and bloody, in the end, the humans had prevailed. General Brennan-Chives then quickly moved his headquarters, from just beneath the surface of Mimas's ice shell, to the supply tunnel network ten kilometres into the rock shell. They were now, in all twenty kilometres into Mimas and still about fifteen kilometres from the Mimasian interior.

The General's one thousand heavy battle tanks were moved up quickly and his smaller, laser armed hover attack vehicles soon followed. The Mimasians supply tunnel network, quickly became a supply hub and base of operations for the Colonial Troops.

By now, the fifth and final wave of Colonial Troops was arriving and very soon, General Brennan-Chives would have all of his five million troops deployed on Mimas. The Colonial Troops were then sent into the tunnels towards the interior of Mimas. Fierce resistance was met and a series of running, bloody battles ensued. The General's forces pushed forward relentlessly, killing and destroying all of the Mimasians found in their paths.

Pushing and fighting all of their way along the tunnel systems, quickly the Colonial Troops traversed the kilometres that led to the interior of Mimas. Securing section after section of tunnel, as soon as they were taken. The General's forces managed to push more than ten kilometres further into the rock shell of Mimas. They were now within five kilometres of the Mimasian interior.

They had reached the same level of tunnels, at which the Saturnian miners, had found the large tunnel ventilation system. The General's troops had also found them and now they quickly secured their access. These tunnels also doubled as an immense transport and supply network for the Mimasians. Five kilometres deep, below the interior of Mimas, this network of tunnels crisscrossed every which way throughout the Mimasian rock shell. It was here, that the resistance to the General's advancing Colonial Troops was the fiercest.

The Colonial Troops advanced further towards the interior surface of Mimas. They killed and slaughtered Mimasians all along the way. In some sections of tunnels, the carnage was so great, that the General's troops found it necessary to stop and remove the still-smouldering Mimasian corpses. Some sections of the tunnels were so badly blocked with mangled, twisted and charred bodies, that the laser tunnelling equipment was needed to burn their way through.

The stench of *roasted, barbecued* death, pervaded the entire tunnel network of Mimas. It was truly horrific and yet still, the Mimasians threw themselves into the fight, with a complete and total disregard for the loss of life and limb. It was as if the very hand of their Emperor, Ahriman, was pushing against the backs of each and every Mimasian soldier, forcing them to fight to the death.

The advance of the Colonial Troops halted temporarily, to secure their positions, move more troops forward and remove the bodies of the dead. Any injured or fallen Colonial Troops were returned to the Earth as quickly as possible, for proper treatment and or burial.

The Mimasian bodies, on the other hand, were piled up and then disintegrated by the laser tunnelling machines. After clearing the secured tunnels of the injured and the dead, General Brennan-Chives then ordered his Colonial Troops, to move forward towards the interior surface of Mimas once more. The battle for Mimas continued unabated.

24. Under an Alien Sun.

Fiercely battling, kilometre after kilometre, the troops advanced and eventually, they came to the metal grills, just before the openings to the interior of Mimas. These grills had been fitted with gates and the laser fire from behind them had greatly melted them. To advance further, the Colonial Troops had to launch rocket-propelled grenades through the openings.

Explosions were heard beyond the openings and loud wailing and screaming followed. The Mimasians had never seen grenades before. The shrapnel from the grenades had cut through the flesh of the Mimasian defenders. Across the many gated grills, hundreds of Mimasians had been hit, many were dead and even more were wounded. Many of them were lying on the ground, slowly bleeding to death in agony.

The Colonial Troops, not knowing what to do with the wounded enemy, dispatched them swiftly and put them out of their misery. No one in the colonial forces had any knowledge of Mimasian anatomy, nor how to effectively treat their wounds.

Soon the General's troops had breached the interior surface of Mimas. They quickly finished dispatching the wounded Mimasian soldiers and began to set up their own defensive positions. Except for the heat, the soldiers liked the environment here, it was a dry heat and the gravity was low. This would be a good battleground for them.

They'd only have to contend with the enemy, an enemy that was far larger, but physically weaker than themselves, however, it was also an enemy that could fly. As the Colonial Troops swarmed out of the tunnel network, the sounds of flapping wings signified the approach of the Mimasian armies.

Thousands upon thousands of Mimasians began to swarm towards the armed forces from the Earth.

The Colonial Troops opened fire with their lasers and Mimasian troops began falling to the ground below them in screaming agony. Many of the Mimasians swooped to the ground around the human invaders and took up their own positions. Laser fire was then exchanged by both sides. Some Colonial Troops clashed in close-quarters combat. The air was thick with the cracking sounds of rapid-fire impulse lasers, the sporadic bursts of machine gun fire and the sudden blasts of shotguns.

Both human and Mimasian troops were dying by the hundreds, under the heat of a controlled fusion reaction, that was the alien Mimasian Sun. From out of the ground beneath the Mimasians, came sudden bursts of intense laser light. The laser tunnelling equipment had carved out sloping tunnels, allowing the colonial tanks to ascend to the interior surface of Mimas.

The Mimasians fled as the laser beam and particle beam tanks emerged. Very quickly the one thousand colonial heavy battle tanks had emerged onto the interior plains of Mimas. Following these were one the thousand hover attack vehicles. Very soon the entire armies of the Earth were all within the rock shell of Mimas and pushing out onto its interior surface. Try as they might, the Mimasians simply could not stop them.

General Tilos T. Brennan-Chives had quickly moved his mobile head quarters to the interior surface of Mimas. The battles taking place on the interior surface had all stopped when the tanks had surfaced.

The Mimasians for their part, had massed their armies around the humans, but at a much safer distance from them. Sporadic fire took place across the distance between the two opposing armies and when the Mimasian armoured divisions arrived, all hell broke loose. The Mimasians attacked almost without any discipline or any real tactics. They just pushed their armour divisions forward into the fight and the colonial forces responded.

General Brennan-Chives also sent patrols much farther into the Mimasian tunnel network, in an attempt to secure more of the network of tunnels inside the rock shell of Mimas. As both of the opposing armies fought vicious, bloody battles on the plains above, so they would also fight equally viciously in the tunnels beneath them. The Mimasian soldiers continued to throw themselves at the Colonial Troops, with little if any fear in their eyes and yet, when cut down by laser fire, or machine gun rounds, they wailed and screamed like any other wounded beasts. The war was continuing unabated and could only intensify further as it progressed.

Ahriman was in his royal chambers, he had been informed that the invasion had taken place. Humans had penetrated the rock shell and were now in the interior of his world. As a consequence, many of his commanders were slain by him personally and subsequently replaced. Ahriman delighted in the bloodshed, even though his world had been invaded. He knew something that the humans did not, that he could not be killed. Win or lose, war was the very air that Ahriman breathed and relished!

Ahriman was an immortal, supremely evil, discarnate entity. Even if his flesh died, he would yet live. Ahriman would just find another body, another host, perhaps even a human host and simply possess it. Even if his armies were all destroyed, even if every Tarlak was slaughtered and none were left, he would still win.

Ahriman, by possessing the flesh of a human being and travelling to the Earth, could take over their entire world and through it, the entire solar system. There he could survive, even thrive and turn the humans to evil, subverting them from within. Just as he had, with the ancestors of his Tarlaks. Ahriman relished the chaos and the blood-letting of this war and he cared not one iota for his creations, the Tarlaks. Yes even in defeat, he would yet win!

The Mimasian tanks were moving towards the colonial forces, hordes of Mimasian troops followed on foot and further hordes of Mimasians flew in the skies of Mimas, all under the hot alien Sun. The colonial tanks all switched on their shields and prepared for battle. The hover attack craft all turned on their shields and were soon prepared as well. The tanks began to advance towards the Mimasians. Laser beams and particle beams on both sides blazed and the colonial tank shielding withstood the attacks.

The colonials had been concentrating their firepower. Nearly three hundred Mimasian tanks began exploding across the battlefields of Mimas.

More and more Mimasian tanks moved up and the tank battle continued unabated. The General's tanks continued pressing forward. The exchange of laser beam and particle beam fire continued. The Mimasian tanks began concentrating their firepower. Tanks on both sides exploded into flames, mostly Mimasian tanks.

The General then ordered his hover attack craft to launch and enter the battle. His ground forces needed their air support. Flying swiftly into the battle with their lasers blazing, they quickly cut many Mimasian tanks and troops to pieces. The Mimasians it seemed, did not have any equivalent to hover attack craft. As the Mimasian main battle tanks became scarcer and scarcer on the plains of Mimas, the Colonial Troops began to swiftly advance. They pressed their advantage!

After many hours of doing battle, all of the remaining Mimasian main battle tanks were destroyed and only the Mimasian soldiers remained. Close to two thousand burning Mimasian tank wrecks littered the battlefields of Mimas. Over four hundred tanks and nearly three hundred hover attack craft on the colonial's side had survived the onslaught. The General used his field glasses to survey the battlefields, he was unhappy with the losses, but his forces had won the day.

The lull in the battle was short-lived, as the millions of Mimasian troops surrounding the human invaders, attacked without any armoured support. The millions of Colonial Troops then moved forward to meet them. As the colonials approached their enemy, many Mimasians leapt into flight. This was their natural element! From both the ground and the air, their lasers blazed. A massive volley of return fire from the colonials killed many of them. Soldiers began to fall, the majority were Mimasian, death and carnage was everywhere and its stench soon followed.

As the armies of both sides collided, the battle collapsed into close quarters combat. The Mimasians were well armed, but they were no match for the well trained humans, who had been both raised and trained in far higher gravity, three times higher. The colonials had the advantage of far superior strength in hand-to-hand combat, despite the Mimasian's much greater bulk and size.

The colonial tanks and hover attack craft also took their toll. The plains around the tunnels where the General's army had emerged, were littered with many hundreds of thousands of dead, for most of that number, the dead were Mimasian.

With the aid of their armoured divisions, the colonial armies drove the Mimasians before them. The Mimasians retreated mile after mile after mile. After several days of fighting, the battle began to subside and shortly thereafter it was over. The blood bath had finally stopped. Now the Mimasians no longer attacked, instead, they fled before the colonial armies and retreated deeper into the rock shell.

General Brennan-Chives ordered that his troop casualties be counted and body counts of the enemy be taken. It was many hours before the results were known. The number of human casualties was truly staggering, consisting of two hundred thousand dead and another half million wounded. The wounded were taken to both Cis-Lunar L-Five and the Earth for medical treatment as soon as they could be evacuated. The deceased were returned to the Earth for burial.

Of the Mimasian soldiers, there were more than a million dead. There weren't any wounded, the Colonial Troops had dispatched any that were alive. The Mimasian bodies were collected and piled up and the laser tunnelling machines were used to disintegrate them.

The tunnel systems in the rock shell of Mimas had been cleared of Mimasians, for nearly a one hundred and fifty-kilometre radius, all around the colonial army's entry point. The Colonial Troops now controlled one-third of the inner circumference of Mimas. This region was almost totally secured.

The Mimasians were massing for one final assault. The enemy could barely find enough lasers for their more than ten million troops. Many of them were armed with knives, swords, clubs, cudgels and even farming tools. They marched into battle under-equipped and with little chance of survival. The Mimasians did not seem to care, there were even many Mimasian females amongst their ranks.

The hands of Ahriman were at their backs once more, pushing the hapless Mimasians to their deaths.
General Brennan-Chives carefully studied the hordes of advancing Mimasians. The General was stunned, not by the enemy's numbers, but more by how ill-prepared they actually were.

"My God! Do they even care if they live or die?", the General asked himself silently.

They massed on three sides of the colonial-controlled regions. The General had arranged his troops and armoured divisions accordingly. Swiftly the Mimasians advanced. The General then sent his tanks and his hover attack craft into the battle.

The big laser beams and particle beams of the colonial tanks blazed, cutting down the advancing Mimasians in their thousands. The hover attack craft flew into the flying masses of the enemy, their lasers blazing. The Mimasians in the air were slaughtered in their thousands, falling to the ground, their bodies were burning masses of flesh and bone.

The battle tanks and the hover attack craft, their weapons blazed constantly. The ground all around their enemy erupted in destruction. Scores of thousands of Mimasians were lying on the ground, the dead and dying and yet, the hordes of Mimasians behind them, still advanced. They trampled over the bodies of those less fortunate in their thousands and stampeded their own wounded to death! General Brennan-Chives was astonished! He'd never seen such carnage!

It was only then that the General sent his own troops into the battle. Most of their well-equipped enemy were either dead or dying. The troops ran into the enemy masses, their weapons blazing. Flying Mimasians fell from the skies as the troops blew their flesh away with laser fire. The Mimasian troops advancing on the ground were cut to pieces and died in their droves. Many of the Colonial Troops also died, but not nearly as many as the Mimasians. After many, many long hours of battle, the remaining Mimasians then fled in front of the advancing Colonial Troops.

General Brennan-Chives had ordered another casualty count and another enemy body count. Several long hours later the result came in. The General had lost another two hundred thousand troops and another half a million wounded. The General quickly ordered the wounded troops to be evacuated to the Earth and Cis-Lunar L-Five for medical care and treatment. The

Mimasian body count though, was so horrendous, so high in fact, it took several further hours for the count to come in.

"Six million dead and zero wounded? No! That can't be right! Is this true? Are these figures accurate?", the General had questioned.

The General's aid assured him that the figures were correct, "General, Sir. These figures are accurate. The Mimasians just keep on pushing forward, Sir. Many of their dead, were trampled to death by their own kind. It's like they're driven, almost suicidal!"

Those words bored deeply into the General's mind, *"Driven. Suicidal"*, what does that mean?

The General's mind was haunted by the sheer numbers of the dead Mimasian and those words simply did not help him at all!

Like all of the rest before them, the tunnelling lasers were used to disintegrate the Mimasian dead.

Over half of the interior of Mimas was now under colonial control. Again the Mimasians began to mass. They hadn't any lasers left, only knives, swords, cudgels and quickly improvised weapons. They were driven to do battle by the evil mind of Ahriman. He controlled their minds and gave them a blood lust to make them fight. Worse still, Ahriman was beginning to affect the humans as well. His evil mind was having a similar, although somewhat lesser effect on them. That was also part of the reason that the humans dispatched the wounded Mimasians and took none captive. They too were being driven!

The General's forces were advancing towards their enemy. They pushed forward through the network of tunnels inside the rock shell of Mimas. The Mimasians were pushed back by the advancing colonials. Once the Colonial Troops had occupied a section of the tunnel network and came to an opening, they would surface. The Colonial Troops on the interior plains would then move up, catching the Mimasians in a crossfire.

With the Colonials in front of them and even more Colonials at their backs, the Mimasians had nowhere to go and were slaughtered in their thousands. In this way, the plains in between were secured. Then the process was repeated, over and over, with a ruthless efficiency that even Ahriman himself admired.

Many of the Mimasian city structures had been secured, the Colonial Troops, however, did not occupy them. The troops preferred to camp in the open plains or in the tunnels, rather than the decadent and squalid Mimasian cities, with their ever-present stench of death and evil. To Ahriman, however, this was a great disappointment. Something that he would have to change!

The Colonial Troops kept pushing towards the Mimasian masses, which in turn retreated further and further towards the far side of Mimas. In this section of Mimas was the immense ion drive. On the outer surface was an immense crater, Herschel. In the centre of that crater, there was a six kilometre high mountain peak, rising from the crater floor. That was the thruster exhaust system of the immense Mimasian ion drive.

On the interior surface of Mimas, these outer surface features were emulated. A great mountainous ring rose from out of the rock shell. The Colonial Troops watched this broad mountainous ring in awe as they pushed closer and closer to it. They could not see it from the point where they had entered Mimas, but now it loomed large before them.

Being on the inside of an immense sphere, with a horizon curving upwards, the full extent of this mountainous ring was now clearly visible. This mountainous ring was perfectly circular, well over one hundred kilometres in diameter. This mountainous ring, rose five kilometres high from the interior plains of Mimas.   On the inside of this mountainous ring, there was a large body of water, a Southern Circular Sea around thirty kilometres in width. In the very centre of which, existed an island mountain, rising more than six kilometres in height. This Southern Island Mountain was the base from which the entire generation ship, Mimas was operated. This mountain was where Ahriman's lair was to be found.

This Southern Circular Sea was one of only two large bodies of water inside of Mimas, the other being an identical sea in the opposite northern hemisphere of Mimas. Otherwise, there were only small lakes and rivers, fed by springs of icy water from Mimas's outer ice shell. This Southern Circular Sea could only be sighted from the hemisphere into which the colonial forces were now beginning to advance. The hordes of Mimasians were retreating towards it, with the Colonial Troops in hot pursuit.

Ironically, as they had approached this ring of mountains before them, no one had even noticed that this pattern was repeated in the opposing hemisphere, from whence they had just come. The second near an identical Northern Circular Sea, was also inside another ring of mountains and had within it, its own northern island mountain. The colonial troop's focus had been so intense and their battle so demanding, that no one had noticed the geography of the Mimasian interior at all. They had all pushed forward, so hard and so fast, that no one had looked back behind them.

The icy peaks of the ring of mountains fed small rivers flowing into the parched Mimasian plains. Although the rivers were quick to dry up and evaporate. Nonetheless, the regions forty kilometres from these mountains contained the most luxurious growth of flora and fauna yet seen inside of Mimas. The steep sides of these mountains, on both the outside and on the inside of this mountainous ring, were also covered with an extensive growth of flora. Many strange and unusual animals could be seen amongst the distant foliage.

It was only a matter of hours before the colonials had pushed all of the remaining Mimasians into the unearthly forests. Very soon they would be ready to pursue them. Mimasian males, females and young alike fled swiftly into the forests, moving quickly to the mountains beyond. The animals of the forests quickly fled before the malevolent Mimasians, who used to hunt them extensively, with great and unmatched cruelty.

Ahriman himself had become incensed, his creations, his precious Tarlaks, now feared the humans more than he, himself. Ahriman no longer had his metaphorical hands up against their spines, forcing his Tarlaks forward into battle and bloodshed! His Tarlaks would now flee and they would flee in his direction. The Mimasian's primal fear was too great for Ahriman to control and overrule!

The complex tunnel network in the rock shell of Mimas ended abruptly at the forest's edge. The Colonial Troops underground came to the surface and were confronted by the forests. That they, unlike the troops on the surface, had not yet seen. This tall mountainous ring appeared to be an effective defensive barrier. The colonial forces couldn't gain access to the other side of the ring, without scaling the mountains themselves.

As the Mimasians arrived at the mountain slopes, they climbed higher and higher in their attempt to flee the colonial forces. Then when high enough up, on the slopes of the mountains, they took to flight, to fly over the tall mountain peaks. The Mimasian females carried their younglings with them, clutching them tightly to their breasts. Some of the younglings were too heavy and fell to their deaths as their mothers could not bear their weight. A few Mimasian mothers persevered until exhausted and then both youngling and mother fell out of the skies to the jagged rocks below them. Many Mimasian mothers, however, managed to make it across the mountainous peaks.

The Colonial Troops quickly rushed through the forests and the animals of the forests quickly hid themselves from these new and unusual creatures. Creatures that the denizens of the forest had never seen before. Some of the more intelligent species watched curiously as the humans ran past, somehow aware, that their Mimasian antagonists had been routed. It wasn't very long before the colonial forces had reached the slopes of the mountains.

Although small in the distance, the Mimasians could be seen far higher up and even in flight across the mountain peaks. The Colonial Troops began to climb higher in their pursuit, in Mimas's low artificial gravity, they moved swiftly up the slopes.

Upon reaching the ice line, it soon became obvious that they couldn't climb any further. Their extra strength in the low gravity couldn't help them climb the steep icy slopes. General Brennan-Chives then ordered his one hundred laser tunnelling machines, to be moved up the mountain slopes, to a level well above the sea level on the other side. The sea level on the other side, being about one and a half kilometres below the snowline.

The laser tunnelling machines were carefully lifted up the mountain slopes and once in place, they began to operate. Very quickly they began to bore deeply into the mountains. At the rate of a kilometre per day, it would take perhaps a week or even longer to reach the inside of the mountainous ring. The amount of time depended on the density and the type of rock they were bored through. Through the one hundred tunnels, the Colonial Troops would then quickly move in and attack the Mimasians. Until then, the Mimasians had themselves several days to rest at the very least.

One by one, the powerful beams of intense light burst out of the rock, on the inner side of the ring of mountains. The molten rock then soon began to harden. This was followed by the Colonial Troops pouring through tunnels and onto the mountain slopes, on the inside of the mountain ring. All of the Mimasians that they'd been pursuing, were massed along the lower mountain slopes, just above the coast of the circular sea and they had nowhere where else to run or hide.

Upon hearing the Colonial Troops far above them, some of them took flight in an attempt to fly to the island more than thirty kilometres away. A deep cold moat specifically designed by Ahriman himself, so that his own people, the Tarlaks, could never revolt against him.

The Mimasians could fly, but they couldn't fly as far as the island mountain. The Mimasians could fly maybe twenty kilometres at the most. Even now, many days after their high-altitude flight across the mountain peaks of the southern mountain ring, they were still recovering. Their flight muscles still aching from the strain.

The Colonial Troops set up their camps on the mountain slopes high above the Mimasians. They watched as many of the Mimasians attempted to fly across the Southern Circular Sea, to the island mountain on the far side. Without exception, each and every Mimasian that made the attempt fell out of the sky into the deep dark, icy-cold waters of the circular sea. Many of them drowned, but a far greater number of them were swiftly killed and eaten by the savage, shark-like creatures that inhabited the Southern Circular Sea. This carnivorous feast stirred up something in the cold deep dark waters.

The Mimasians on the coast began to climb the mountains once again and were approaching the colonial troop positions. They were being driven by large and unusual reptilian-like creatures, that had emerged from the circular sea. They were long, scaled and squat-legged like crocodilians, but with a spinal sail running down their backs like dimetrodons. They began killing and eating the Mimasians, who then ran and took to flight to escape them. These reptiles began to climb the mountain slopes, stopping only when the slopes became too steep.

When the Mimasians reached the colonial troop positions, straight away battle began. The Mimasians with their knives, swords, cudgels and improvised weapons against the much better armed and equipped Colonial Troops. Laser and gunfire struck the Mimasians hard, flesh and bone was blown away from their bodies.

Many of them fell backwards down the mountain slopes and were scavenged by the reptiles. The close quarters combat became intense and many of the troops had drawn their swords, to fight the Mimasians on a more equal footing. The humans with their much greater body strength and their far superior training, began slashing and slicing the Mimasians to pieces.

This battle continued for many long hours and the Mimasians were being slaughtered in their scores of thousands. They had nowhere to go, they had savage reptiles at their backs and the Colonial Troops blocking any possible escape. The Mimasians were fighting for their very lives and it was a losing battle. It was a hopeless situation and the Mimasian females knew it, they began to kill their own young and then began committing suicide themselves. Some of them even joined their males and fought to their deaths beside them.

Within forty eight hours the battle had ended. The Mimasians had been almost completely slaughtered. General Brennan-Chives asked for a casualty report on his troops and yet another body count of the defeated Mimasian forces.

When the casualty figures finally came in, the General was shocked once again. Not so much by the colonial troop figures, which themselves were very high, but by the Mimasian estimates. Another two hundred thousand of his troops had died, with another half a million wounded. However, as many as twelve million Mimasians had been slaughtered.

The sheer numbers were ridiculous, staggeringly high figures. The General's aid confirmed the accuracy of the figures and that of the Mimasian losses. The General's aid then stated, that they had included roughly three million Mimasians, that had been observed attempting to fly across the circular sea, only to perish in its icy cold deep dark waters.

"Lieutenant, are you absolutely sure about these figures? I simply cannot believe how many Mimasians were killed!", the General had questioned.

"Those figures are on the conservative side, General Sir. Our people have observed around three million of them, attempting to fly across that sea, only to fall out of the sky and drown or be eaten. Their females killed off their own children and then committed suicide themselves", the Lieutenant had replied, then he asked, "Sir. Why didn't they just surrender? Instead, they just kept fighting till they were all dead. It doesn't make any sense at all!"

"Who knows, Lieutenant, maybe that's just their way? Perhaps, when we catch their leader, he might tell us why", the General replied.

The General had less than three million troops left out of his five million-man army and he hadn't yet taken the Mimasian's stronghold, their main base. The Island Mountain. The General decided to have the entire island mountain scanned, to ascertain how well it was defended. The result was, that it was ringed by high-powered lasers and deflector shields. The laser defence bunkers were all mapped out and the General had his hover attack vehicles moved forward. They were soon all on the inside of the ring of mountains and ready for battle once more.

The General had a feeling that these defences would be similar to the original ones on the Mimasian icy outer surface before they had modified them and built them up. He was confident that his hover attack craft would be more than capable of destroying the enemy's laser bunkers and that their shields would be more than adequate to protect them. He gave his orders to the pilots and they were soon on their way, flying across the Southern Circular Sea.

The hover attack craft approached the island mountain from every angle, each one assigned with a designated list of targets. They flew in extremely swiftly and before the Mimasian defences could react they attacked. Their high-powered lasers blazed away and the sides of the island mountain erupted in destruction. Molten rock exploded from the steep mountain slopes and fell quickly to the coastal waters below. Lasers mounted in the bunkers on the slopes of the island mountain returned fire.

Some of the hover attack craft were hit, but their shields held and they swiftly attacked again. More and more of the Mimasian laser bunkers were destroyed and the hover attack craft were hit again and again. Eventually, some of their shields began to fail and then some of the hover attack craft were blown out of the Mimasian skies. However, it wasn't very long before the last of the Mimasian laser bunkers was destroyed. Very few of the hover attack craft had been destroyed in the process.

General Brennan-Chives quickly instructed his engineers to develop a way for his troops to reach the island mountain. It was the only stronghold left on Mimas. His troops controlled all of the rest, only here were there any Mimasians left. Materials were shipped in from Cis-Lunar L-Five, for the engineers to utilise. More engineers and workers were also brought to Mimas. Quickly a small fleet of troop transports began to take shape.

Soon one hundred troop transports had arrived at the coast of the circular sea. The General's troops began to board them, one hundred in each. The fully armed Colonial Troops were then deployed onto the island's shores and began to search for tunnel entrances. They had not met any resistance as yet on the island. It wasn't long before they had found several large entrances into the mountain stronghold.

It took quite some time, several days in fact, but eventually, General Brennan-Chives had deployed a hundred thousand Colonial Troops onto the island mountain. They quickly began to enter into the network of tunnels. Only very slight resistance was met as they secured each section of the tunnels and only the sounds of sporadic laser fire were heard. The Colonial Troops soon found that all of the Mimasians they'd killed, had been either technicians or high-ranking Mimasians.

Their tools, the clothing they wore and their height clearly showed this. They were also armed with hand lasers and advanced weaponry. There were many Mimasians in the stronghold, but not that many that the Colonial Troops couldn't handle them. None of the Mimasians in the stronghold appeared to be infantry troops, none at all.

The Colonial Troops quickly took control of the lower tunnel network and began ascending into the higher network of tunnels. The main tunnels gradually spiralled upwards, branching out here and there at each level, then spiralling upwards once more to the next higher level. This pattern was repeated throughout the entire central mountain peak.

The Colonial Troops had moved quickly and soon gained control of the uppermost levels, including the scanner chamber, command and control centres. Soon the entire island mountain complex was completely under the control of the Colonial Troops.

The leader of the Mimasians had not been located and there was only one more tunnel and that the Colonial Troops had yet to secure. They reported the situation to General Brennan-Chives and then twenty Colonial Troops marched off into the final tunnel. The very same tunnel that led to Ahriman's royal chambers.

25. Immanent Danger.

The twenty Colonial Troops moved swiftly but cautiously down the final tunnel. After about fifteen minutes they came to the end of the tunnel and entered into a large cavernous chamber.

One of the Colonial Troops noticed the blood-stained walls, "Hey, on the walls! It's dried blood. What are those? Are they squashed corpses?"

"Don't be ridiculous! Who decorates their walls with squashed corpses", another trooper replied.

One of the other colonial troopers replied, "I really don't like the look of this place."

Another colonial trooper stated, "Rick, you're just being too superstitious mate. Get a grip!"

The soldier named Rick then quickly inquired, "Hey, what's that over there?"

Ahriman moved slowly across his royal chambers, his limbs didn't make a move, he moved simply by the sheer power of his mind. The Colonial Troops were all stunned into silence. They all watched as the tallest Mimasian they had ever seen approached. Ten of them panicked and quickly moved forward, attacking the tall dark approaching figure. Their lasers blazed, coherent beams of intense light leapt towards Ahriman and he laughed out loudly at them.

"Fools! You dare attack me!", Ahriman launched his thoughts directly into their minds.

The air around Ahriman suddenly glowed red. The beams of intense blue laser light stopped short of their targets, being completely absorbed in the eerie red glow. The Colonial Troops stood there, shocked and stunned, as the overly tall Mimasian continued to slowly advance towards them. Then

Ahriman swung his right arm and the ten Colonial Troops who had attacked
him, flew backwards against the chamber's blood stained walls.

As the other ten colonial troopers watched, the ten unfortunate men on
the chamber walls began to explode backwards against the wall, their bodies
twisting, rupturing and bursting. Loud screaming and wailing filled the
chamber as the men died the most awful of deaths. Blood and body fluids
began to flow backwards onto the chamber wall, spreading out and re-coating
large portions of it.

Then the bodies of the ten twisted and mangled men were flattened
against the wall, as if by a huge, powerful invisible press. Then their bodies
were stuck there, like some macabre, gross tapestry. Ahriman's almost
uncontrollable laughter echoed throughout his royal chambers and inside the
minds of the remaining ten colonial troopers.

The remaining ten colonial troopers stood still, they had tried to flee, but
they could not move. Ahriman held them tightly with his powerful,
malevolent mind. The air around them began to swirl.

They could sense the growing malevolence in the very air about them and
they all froze with terror. The sheer might of Ahriman's soul-crushing mind
was brought to bear upon them. They fought back hard, struggling against
Ahriman's oppressive soul, their willpower pushing and straining to the very
limits of their human endurance. All to no avail.

For long moments the struggle of minds continued. The evil Lord of
Mimas, Ahriman, was surprised by the power of their human minds. They
were not so simple as his Mimasian minions, far more complex, more wilful,
arrogant even. They had a level of disdain for him, that even he found
shocking and insulting.

How dare they hold him, Ahriman, in contempt! Although genetically
compatible with the humans of Mars, these Earth humans had very different

minds.

It wasn't very long, however, before he had complete control over all of them. These particular humans minds were all new to him and Ahriman just needed to study their minds, just that little bit longer and then twist them to his will. The ten soldiers broke under the strain and were now his to command, puppets, quickly he tested his level of control.

Ahriman willed six of the Colonial Troops to pair off and then attack each other. The first pair struggled against Ahriman's commands, yet try as they might, they could not refuse. They both drew their pulsed lasers and fired at each other. The brilliant pulsed beams blew flesh and bone away from their victims. Then they both fell to the chamber floor, dead. Ahriman was pleased with the results.

The next pair of Colonial Troops then drew their weapons, one a pulsed laser and the other a shotgun. Ahriman had far better control this time. They were like marionettes to his mind and he treated them as such, making them both do as he commanded. Practice makes perfect as they say and Ahriman was practising with his victims. Again and again, flesh and bone were blown away, as the two Colonial Troops fired their weapons upon each other. Then they too, like the pair before them, collapsed to the chamber floor, dead.

Ahriman was very pleased with the results so far, he motioned the next pair of Colonial Troops forward. One of them had tried to resist him, he was most stubborn, but to no avail, he took up a sword from the scabbard of his fallen comrade. The other one was far more compliant, drawing his own sword straight away when commanded. Soon the pair were fighting each other, their blades clashing swiftly, echoing throughout the royal chamber. Ahriman enjoyed the spectacle immensely.

Ahriman had complete control of their minds. The two colonial troopers moved to his will, with a level of compliance that showed Ahriman, that these Earth humans were no match for his mind.   Ahriman pushed the two troopers into slashing and chopping each other to pieces. Ahriman numbed their pain and forced them to continue, slashing and chopping. Even with blood pouring from deep open wounds, they were forced to fight on and on.

Ahriman then used his mind to delay the inevitable physiological reactions and forced the two troopers to continue fighting. On and on they fought, until finally the extent of their wounds caught up with them, causing one of them to collapse to the chamber floor. Then the other trooper dispatched him, by cutting off his head with a single deft slice, then he, himself collapsed to the chamber floor, dead from his own devastating wounds.

The remaining four soldiers then drew Ahriman's attention. He now had complete control of their minds and they would do whatever he demanded of them. What next? More fun and games? No, perhaps something more constructive this time. Ahriman then ordered the soldier named Rick to send a message over his communicator.

Rick did exactly as he was commanded, "Advance patrol to General Brennan-Chives. Advance patrol to General Brennan-Chives", he repeatedly spoke into his communicator.

Soon, General Brennan-Chives answered the call, "General Brennan-Chives here. Advance patrol, what do you have to report?"

Rick then replied, "General, Sir. We have secured the island mountain, including the Mimasian royal chambers. The Mimasian emperor has been captured and we have him in custody."

The General replied excitedly, "Good work man! Keep the Emperor under guard. I'll be there myself, very soon."

Ahriman smiled a wry smile, his old plans failed, new plans arise, he would yet succeed. A General would make a wonderful stepping stone as a host.

General Brennan-Chives quickly left his command post on the slopes of the southern ring of mountains. His command vehicle flew him towards the island mountain in the centre of the circular sea. Soon his command vehicle had landed on a broad ledge, close to a tunnel opening in the side of the mountain. An infantry Colonel was standing there waiting for him to arrive.

"General, Sir. I'm Colonel Yansy. You could say, that I'll be your guide to show you around", the Colonel informed the General.

General Brennan-Chives inquired, "How well do you know the Mimasian strong hold, Colonel?"

Colonel Yansy replied, "Sir, not that well. I've spent some time finding my way around the place and I have made a rough map of the complex. At least the parts that I've seen."

The General inquired further, "Well then, what can you tell me about this place?"

Colonel Yansy replied, "Well, Sir. The command centre is close to the top. The scanner and the communication centres are just below that. Below the mountain, inside of the rock shell, we've secured their ion drive. As far as we can tell, the water in the circular sea is used to cool the drive's generators."

The Colonel continued, "General, Sir, the generators are enormous and the actual drive itself is immense. We have our technicians studying it as we speak. The ion drive's controls are activated from a control centre, just below the mountain. As far as our technicians can tell, the whole drive system is probably six or even seven million years old. It could even be older. Honestly, we don't really know for sure, Sir."

General Brennan-Chives interrupted the Colonel, "That's all very well, Colonel, but I'd like to know about the Mimasian Emperor. What can you tell me about him?"

The Colonel replied honestly, "Well, Sir. I can't tell you much about him at all. However, I do know that his royal chambers are on the highest level."

The General then replied, "Good then, Colonel. I'd like to see this, Emperor. This gargoyle that wanted to destroy our whole civilisation."

The Colonel replied simply, "I can take you there, Sir. Right now if you wish."

"Right now, Colonel", the General instructed, "I'd like to see this bastard!"

The General was led through the labyrinth of tunnels inside the island mountain. In point three gs, the walking was quite easy. They were quickly moving through the larger tunnels as they steadily spiralled up through the lowest levels inside the mountain. It didn't take them too long to figure out, that the Mimasians had flown through these tunnels a lot faster than they could walk. The General was thinking that having a few Segways around the place would be very useful.

Before long, the two men came to a network of interconnected chambers. Colonel Yansy was quick to lead the General into one of them. In these chambers, their logistics personnel had set up a supply depot. The Colonel then commandeered a hover jeep. The hover jeep was small, but it was fast. To reach the upper levels they'd need it. General Brennan-Chives was soon on his way once more. Colonel Yansy was driving with his map spread out across the hover jeep's dashboard.

As they climbed through the spiralling tunnels towards the upper levels in their hover jeep, they noticed that the spirals were beginning to tighten and that the tunnel's steepness was beginning to increase somewhat. The network of branching side tunnels became fewer and farther between, these tunnels themselves became smaller as they got higher.

The sides of the tunnels themselves were very smooth, almost glassy smooth, vitrified. At every ten meters, circular ribs ran around the full circumference of the tunnel. These ribs protruded about a half meter out from the walls.

After quite a while they reached the upper levels and they were soon inside the Mimasian command centre. General Brennan-Chives asked the Colonel where the Mimasian Emperor was.

Colonel Yansy checked his map and then replied, "General, Sir. The Emperor's royal chambers, should be at the end of that tunnel", he pointed to a small spiralling tunnel off to one side.

The General then inquired, "Haven't you been in there yet, Colonel?"

Colonel Yansy then replied honestly, "No, Sir, not yet. We sent twenty troopers into the royal chamber earlier today. They've kept communications open and have informed us, that the royal chambers are secured. The Mimasian Emperor is in custody and under guard. They are currently waiting for you General."

General Brennan-Chives then interrupted, "So you decided to meet me first and then bring me straight here before you, yourself have even seen him?"

"That is correct, Sir", replied Colonel Yansy.

"Well, then, Colonel. I won't keep you in suspense. Let's go and see this so-called Emperor for ourselves shall we", replied the General.

The two men then moved off into the spiralling tunnel that led to the royal chambers. Walking quickly towards their first meeting with the Emperor of the Mimasians.

Gideon and Sandra had both watched the colonial Armada battling the Mimasians, in the cometary cloud of gas and dust surrounding Mimas. They had kept an even closer watch on the raging battles, inside of the interior of the little ice moon. Now Gideon felt something, something terribly wrong and Sandra felt it too. Gideon and Sandra called Winchilly over and tried to explain it to her. Winchilly could not understand, all she knew was that the Mimasian Emperor was supremely evil.

Gideon and Sandra told her, that they had to confront him. That they were compelled to do so and would have to do so very soon. The trio sat cross legged in deep concentration in their quarters on Mars. Their combined minds reached out into deep space, they were reaching out to find Colonel Bannon's Battle Cruiser. When they located it, patrolling the space around Mimas, they sent their minds into it.

Gideon spoke with his mind to Colonel Bannon, *"Jim, it's Gideon here. Please adjust your gravity plating. Switch your interior gravity down, point four gs should be fine"*, Gideon had requested.

Without thinking, Colonel Bannon lowered his ship's internal gravity. Gideon and Sandra then linked to Winchilly, their minds concentrating on the Colonel's Battle Cruiser. Then there was a sudden small flash of blue light inside of Colonel Bannon's Battle Cruiser.

Gideon, Sandra and Winchilly, suddenly appeared on board the ship, Colonel Bannon looked stunned. "How did you do that?", the Colonel enquired.

"We teleported, Jim, it's one of our new talents and we brought Winchilly with us", replied Gideon.
Sandra was very quick to tell the Colonel, "We haven't got time to explain, Jim. Take your Armada away from Mimas. As far away from Mimas as you possibly can."

Colonel Bannon enquired, "Why? What's happening? Have the Mimasians routed us?"

Gideon then replied very calmly, "No, they haven't, Jim. We haven't got enough time for explanations either. Just trust us on this one, Jim. Take your flagship and your whole Armada to Mars. Look after Winchilly for us, take her to the Aries colony. You should all be safe in high Martian orbit", Gideon requested.

In a small flash of brilliant blue light, Gideon and Sandra were suddenly gone. They had left Winchilly behind and she explained the situation to Colonel Bannon. The Colonel then ordered his Armada to break Mimasian orbit and lay in a course for Martian high orbit.

26. Confrontation.

On Mimas, half a kilometre away from Ahriman's chambers, there was a small flash of blue light. From out of nowhere, behind General Brennan-Chives and Colonel Yansy, two figures appeared.

When the flash of light had occurred, the two officers quickly turned around, just in time to see them both appear.

General Brennan-Chives exclaimed, "What in the hell!", then demanded, "Who the hell are you?"

Gideon then responded, "Doctor Gideon Reas and Sandra Danker from the Aries colony, Sir."

General Brennan-Chives then inquired, "How the hell did you get here?"

Gideon answered, "We teleported here, but we don't have time to explain that, Sir. General, Sir, you must not go any further. If you do, you'll both be in grave danger."

"What rot is this? We've secured the Emperor's royal chambers! My men have him under guard as we speak!", the General exclaimed.

To this, Sandra replied, "No, Sir, the Emperor's royal chambers are not secured. There are four soldiers guarding the Mimasian Emperor, however, they are now protecting him from attack. They are his soldiers now!"

The general replied, "You mean to say my men are traitors? That is simply inconceivable! Why the hell would my men join the enemy? An alien enemy!"

Sandra replied, trying to explain, "No Sir, what I meant is, your men are possessed. The Mimasian Emperor controls them now. They no longer have any will of their own."

General Brennan-Chives screamed at them, "Possessed! Have you two gone mad? Are you a pair of raving fucking lunatics? I will not hear any more of this rubbish! Colonel, let's go and see this, this alien fucking Emperor."

Gideon then moved in front of them both and spread his arms wide to block their path, "General, Sir, you must not! You haven't the slightest inkling as to what is in there! The Mimasian Emperor is completely evil and he is powerful! He can and he does possess people. Those four soldiers in his royal chamber, they are possessed! They are his now!"

The General was beginning to get angry, "Doctor Reas, Miss Danker! I'm ordering you both to leave. Now get the fuck out of my way!"

Sandra replied, telling him, "You can't order us around, General. We are both civilians", then continued, "General. If you go any further, you'll both lose your souls. The Mimasian Emperor will possess you both! Then he'll use you as his new host, as a stepping stone to power on the Earth!"

Then the General angrily replied, "I have had enough of this fucking bullshit! Colonel Yansy, bring up some military police. Have them both arrested!"

Colonel Yansy quickly responded, "I've already taken that liberty, Sir. Our military police will be here very soon."

General Brennan-Chives then replied, "Very good then, Colonel. Now maybe we'll be able to get moving again. I have an Emperor to interrogate!"

Gideon shouted at the General, "Have you ever wondered why your troops dispatched every wounded Mimasian that they came across? Have you ever wondered why your troops failed to take a single Mimasian prisoner?"

"The battles were far too bloody, there was no time for niceties!", the General replied.

"Really, General! So that's the official military doctrine now is it? Dispatch all of the wounded enemy on sight! Kill all of the enemy prisoners upon capture! Slaughter their elderly, their woman and their children! That is against the Geneva Conventions you know. Those are all war crimes, General!",

Gideon replied.

To which General Brennan-Chives replied angrily, "Doctor Reas! These are fucking aliens! The Geneva Conventions do not apply!"

"Wrong, General! The Geneva Conventions don't stipulate anything about the enemy being an alien species! The Geneva Conventions, do still apply!", Gideon retorted.

The General then replied, trying to justify his troop's actions, "What do we know about Mimasian physiology? Those wounded aliens would have died in agony. My men did them a service, they were all mercy killings! All of them!"

"No", Sandra responded calmly, trying to lower the tone of their conversation, then explaining, "The Mimasian Emperor has been inside your heads, from the moment you bored through the rock shell and reached the interior of Mimas."

Gideon then calmly continued on from Sandra, "The Mimasian Emperor's been pushing your armies forward, driving them all forward, hard as hell. He's been inside their heads! Every soldier you have. Your troops have been slaughtering Mimasians because he enjoys slaughter!"

"Don't be ridiculous!", the General replied incredulously.

Colonel Yansy agreed with the General, "Now the pair of you are just sounding plain stupid!"

"You really don't get it, do you, General? This was their Emperor's plan! His plan from the moment our Armada defeated his forces in space!", Sandra shouted.

"His plan!", the General spat back, questioning, "So his plan was the annihilation of his own forces? His plan was genocide of his entire species?"

Gideon tried to explain, "Their Emperor doesn't care about the Mimasians. They were just his minions. His defeated minions!"

Sandra calmly added, "Their Emperor has been cleaning house General. Making room for his new minions! Our people General. The Emperor wants us!"

General Brennan-Chives and Colonel Yansy both looked at the pair with increasing disbelief.

Gideon responded in a far softer tone, "General. The Emperor is not a Mimasian. He is something very, very different."

"Then what is he? What is he then?", Colonel Yansy asked.

"We don't know, General", Sandra replied honestly, "Something very powerful. Something very dangerous, a very ancient evil", then remembering Winchilly's reactions, "Whatever he is, the Martians are terrified of him! Absolutely terrified!"

"You don't get it, General", Gideon began again, then he continued, "That thing in there. It sacrificed every single Mimasian. Every single one of them, just so it could get someone with authority in here. So it can possess them. Its plan is ever so simple."

Sandra took over and explained, "It will posses you both and then it will travel to the Earth. Once its there on the Earth, it will possess others. Moving up the hierarchy, into higher and higher positions of power. Until it is in control of the entire Earth!"

"Sheer nonsense. Bullshit and poppycock!", the General spat back, he was nowhere near convinced.

The sound of footsteps was approaching them from far down the tunnel system.

Gideon and Sandra conversed among themselves telepathically for a short while, *"Gideon, what can we do? We have to stop them!"*

"Yes, I know but we can't use our minds against them", he replied.

"We might be able to block the tunnel?", inquired Sandra.

"We could, definitely, but the General would just have it cleared again", Gideon answered.

Sandra replied, *"Whatever we do, we'll need to do it soon. Very soon!"*

Gideon then asked Sandra, *"What are we going to do when we confront the evil one? We haven't even figured that one out yet."*

Sandra looked around and then answered, *"We haven't even solved this problem yet."*

Ten armed men quickly approached, they were all military police, when they arrived the General gave them their orders.

"Arrest these two civilians. Take them back to the Mimasian command centre and keep them there. Use force if you have to!", General Brennan-Chives had ordered.

Gideon and Sandra both looked at each other with raised eyebrows, at the General's last remark.

"Use force? The General is clueless. Didn't he just see us teleport in here", Gideon silently remarked to Sandra.

Sandra replied equally silently, *"He's not thinking straight. His mind is being influenced already."*

General Brennan-Chives and Colonel Yansy, then both walked off quickly towards the Emperor's royal chambers. The armed military police then took custody of Gideon and Sandra. They then began moving them back towards the former Mimasian command centre.

It wasn't long before General Brennan-Chives and Colonel Yansy came upon the Emperor's royal chambers. They quickly entered and began to walk towards the middle of the large cavernous space.

The two men suddenly noticed that two soldiers had quickly moved up on either side of them. Both the General and the Colonel noticed that none of the four soldiers bothered to salute either of them.

One of the soldiers greeted, "General, Sir, we've been expecting you. Our master will be most pleased with your arrival."

General Brennan-Chives caught this comment quickly, "Your master?", he questioned rhetorically, then replied, "Soldier. I am your commanding officer, you haven't any other master. Why have you not saluted your commanding officer?"

The soldier then replied, "We do not salute inferiors such as yourself! Our Great Lord Ahriman is our Master, our Ruler and Emperor of Mimas. Ruler and Emperor of this entire Solar System."

Suddenly the full horror of their situation dawned upon the General. For the first time, both he and Colonel Yansy looked around the royal chambers. It didn't take them long to see the mutilated bodies of the ten slaughtered soldiers squashed and flattened against the chamber walls as if plastered there. The red stains of blood and other colourful body fluids on the chamber walls had begun to dry.

They then quickly noticed, the older red stains of blood covering the walls of the royal chamber and the many older decaying Mimasian corpses fattened and pressed against the chamber walls. On the chamber floor, off to one side were yet more bodies. The twisted, mangled and butchered bodies of the other six soldiers were noticed and seen. The two officers then looked at each other.

"What the fuck?", was the thought that ran through both of their minds.

General Tilos T Brennan-Chives exclaimed, "My God! Doctor Reas was right! We should have listened to him!", but it was already far too late.

Colonel Yansy did not reply, his eyes were transfixed on the overly tall Mimasian, standing in an opening, at the far side of the royal chambers.

Rick the soldier pointed to the opening, he then ordered, "Move dogs! Lord Ahriman awaits you!"

The two men responded too slowly, so the soldiers persuaded them with the butts of their pulse laser rifles.

General Brennan-Chives and Colonel Yansy started to move slowly towards Ahriman, who watched as they slowly approached. Ahriman had a constant niggling fear in the back of his mind, he had sensed surges of power in the universal field and he knew that someone had been teleporting. He also knew that the manipulators of the universal field were now somewhere inside of Mimas.

When the General and Colonel Yansy were within thirty feet of the Mimasian Emperor they felt the air around them swirl with malevolence.

The four Colonial Troops quickly snapped to attention and saluted the Mimasian Emperor, Ahriman.

Ahriman laughed and remarked in his deep guttural voice, "I could get used to this, standing to attention and saluting! This wonderful show of respect. So professional! Grovelling without grovelling, such noble beasts your people are!"

Ahriman then smiled an evil wry smile, informing the General, "Soon to be mine, all of your people will be! My new minions!"

General Tilos T Brennan-Chives shouted defiantly, "Who in the hell do you think you are?", then his voice was suddenly silenced by the strength of Ahriman's mind.

Ahriman then brought his will down upon them both with its full, soul-crushing force. Their minds began to scream in abject agony, as he slowly crushed their souls. Their situation was completely, so utterly wretched and hopeless.

Ahriman took his time, he was enjoying the moment and then after many,

many long minutes, they were his and Ahriman had full control of them. Then Ahriman's evil mind sensed something wrong, something terribly wrong.

Gideon and Sandra had been walking quickly towards the Mimasian command centre. Armed military police, both in front and behind of them, handcuffs pressing tightly against their wrists. They could feel the screaming, tortured minds of General Brennan-Chives and Colonel Yansy. They suddenly realised they would have to act swiftly. Something was compelling them to take action, they didn't understand what it was, they just needed to act and to act now! The benevolent side of the universal field had been slowly expanding their consciousness, slowly evolving their minds and their abilities. Now they had reached the pinnacle of that process.

In a flash of the mind's eye, Gideon and Sandra both suddenly knew what they would have to do. Their minds suddenly reached the ultimate level of their enlightenment. The total knowledge of all that had ever happened in the entire universe was now suddenly at their disposal. It had all been unlocked.

Gideon and Sandra, now fully realised exactly what they were and became fully aware of their awesome abilities. This awakening had come upon both so suddenly, that they had both collapsed onto the tunnel floor. The ten bewildered military police stood over them, they were wondering what was wrong with them.

The entire universe swirled within their minds, civilisations of the past, the present and the future, flashed before their mind's eyes. Entire Galaxies, Stars and Planets, began to flash continuously, in and out of their minds. The knowledge of everything from the first event, up to the very present and the many possibilities for the future, were all suddenly within their grasp. After a very short while, which had seemed to be an eternity to them, they began to slowly recover and awaken from their psychic rebirth.

Gideon stood up, he then helped Sandra to her feet, the military police were still wondering what had happened.

"My God Sandra. I had no idea we would progress to this", Gideon telepathically told Sandra.

Sandra simply replied, *"Neither did I Gideon, neither did I."*

They looked at each other for long moments and then their attention turned back to the group of bewildered military police standing around them, all of them with their jaws still agape. There was a strange aura about them like the couple were almost glowing. The military police watched as Gideon and Sandra both slipped off their handcuffs and dropped them on the tunnel floor.

Gideon spoke to the soldiers, "I know that you have your orders and all that, but I'm afraid we'll be on our way now."

To which the leader of the group of military police replied, "You two aren't going anywhere, that we haven't been ordered to take you."

Sandra then spoke both apologetically and politely, "I am so very sorry gentlemen, but there really is little that you could possibly do to stop us. Goodbye."

With a brilliant flash of blue light, Gideon and Sandra both disappeared, the military police starred at each other in disbelief.

Ahriman led General Brennan-Chives and Colonel Yansy into a large cavern on the other side of the opening. The evil Lord Ahriman then sat on his large rock throne, it was made of the blackest obsidian and polished to a glass-like finish. Two colonial soldiers stood on either side of him. The General and the Colonel were standing in front of him. Behind them, within the clear sight of Ahriman, there was the opening to the throne room. A sudden flash of brilliant blue light occurred in the middle of the opening.

Ahriman watched as two humans suddenly appeared amid the flash of light, one male, the other female. Fear struck deeply into his ancient evil soul and he quickly suppressed it.

Ahriman spoke to them with feigned confidence, "Your return was not unexpected humans. Of course, I will make you regret doing so."

Quickly Gideon replied, "You know exactly why we are here, Ahriman."

Ahriman replied, still feigning confidence, "I know why you are here, but you shall both fail. I will possess both of you as well, just as I have with this General."

Sandra then spoke, "No, Ahriman. It is you who shall fail. We cannot allow your existence to continue any longer. We have been sanctioned, to rend your evil soul, such that it shall never recover."

Ahriman's power began to surge. The air in the throne room began to swirl and the smell of purification began to pervade the entire room. The very air was becoming malevolent. Filled with hatred, torment and countless other evil combinations.

Tendrils of evil thought began to invade Gideon's and Sandra's minds. Ahriman tried desperately to turn them to evil, to instil into them a blood lust and an insane desire to kill, to make them just like himself. If turned to evil, he could still use them both! If not as possessed minions, then perhaps as equally evil allies.

It wasn't working and so Ahriman stepped up his attacks on their minds. This time, in an attempt to crush their very souls, so that he could try to possess them. If not as allies, then minions they would become. Gideon and Sandra let their minds expand and they began to surge with raw power, within seconds Ahriman's mind was expelled from theirs and his mind reeled back in shock.

The very air around them now swirled and surged with benevolence. Ahriman was shocked by their sheer power and quickly stepped backwards over his obsidian throne, almost falling over it as he did so. For the first time in many, many aeons, Ahriman knew that he was in trouble.

Ahriman then exerted his will over the human soldiers under his control. They aimed their pulsed laser rifles at Gideon and Sandra. Bright beams of blazing blue light spat out of the lasers towards their targets. The air in front of Gideon and Sandra burst brightly into a brilliant blue glow, as the laser beams were absorbed. Gideon and Sandra could not help the soldiers, who had already lost their minds and their very souls to Ahriman. They were gone forever and could not be recovered.

Seeing that the soldiers could not them, Ahriman tried to use brutal shock and awe as a tactic. As they watched, one by one, each of the soldiers, under Ahriman's directions, then quickly turned their pulsed laser rifles upon themselves. The four soldiers died slowly as the laser beams cut through their flesh, avoiding any vital organs until the very last seconds. The soldiers collapsed to the floor of the throne room, dead. This was meant to shock Gideon and Sandra, to the point where their anger would boil over and in so doing, aid Ahriman in turning their minds to retribution and evil. This tactic also failed, as Gideon and Sandra felt nothing but sadness and compassion for the fallen soldiers.

Swiftly Sandra's mind expanded into an impenetrable sphere around Ahriman's throne room. Closing in his evil soul so that he could not escape. Gideon then approached Ahriman. His mind sent out extremely powerful tendrils of thought. Invading Ahriman's mind with benevolence and thoughts of peace and love, all of which were abhorrent to his evil soul. Gideon could use violence if absolutely necessary against Ahriman, but he had hoped, that he wouldn't have to.

When Gideon was within twenty paces, Ahriman struck, raising both of his clawed hands high above his head. Electrical energy began to discharge from the three sets of paired fingers on each of his hands. Like powerful bolts of lightning, electrical arcs shot towards Gideon. The bolts of lightning struck hard and Gideon was thrown to the floor. Again and again, Gideon was struck and he screamed out in agony with each and every strike.

Sandra entered Gideon's mind and absorbed some of the pain, while at the same time, helping to increase his strength. Slowly, much to Ahriman's surprise, Gideon began to stand, even though Ahriman kept on attacking him. Then when Gideon was on his feet and steady once more, he fought back. Ten brilliant blue beams of high energy spat from out of the outstretched fingers, on each of Gideon's hands. Ahriman was then struck very hard and violently, he quickly flexed his wings to take too flight in order to escape.

Ahriman flapped his wings feverishly as Gideon struck at him, again and again. The brilliant beams of energy began tearing gaping holes in Ahriman's wings. It wasn't long before Ahriman was back on the floor of the throne room writhing in agony.

Ahriman could not stand! Gideon's onslaught had been far too much for him and Ahriman's flesh was beginning to burn. Soon the last Mimasian body inside of Mimas was reduced to a pool of burning flesh and bone. The burning continued and the ashes of Ahriman's bones stained his pool of blood with streaks of greyish white. The Mimasian Emperor was now finally dead. Ahriman's body was no more.

Slowly Gideon and Sandra began to relax. Then they noticed that General Brennan-Chives and Colonel Yansy were still standing in their original positions. They had not moved, not by the smallest amount. They should have both dropped to the floor the moment Ahriman had died, but they had not. Ahriman still had control of them. Sandra kept her mind expanded around the throne room.

"He's still here Gideon! He's still here!", Sandra telepathically shouted.

"I know Sandra. Keep him contained. We can't let him have another host", Gideon silently replied.

Quickly, Gideon began to expand his mind outward until his mind encompassed the whole of Mimas. He began scanning the minds of all of the remaining colonial armed forces personnel from the Earth. There were a lot of them, nearly three million and the process was very time-consuming. None of them had been possessed yet, other than General Brennan-Chives and Colonel Yansy. Sandra could not keep the throne room encapsulated forever. Gideon would have to work quickly, very quickly.

In rapid succession, Gideon used his powers of telekinesis and teleportation. One by one the Colonial Troops vanished in small bursts of blue light. On a remote mountainside on the Earth, a corresponding series of bursts of blue light began to occur.

One by one, Colonial Troops began to appear on the slopes of a large mountain in the Earth's equatorial regions. It took quite a while, far longer than Gideon had wanted, but eventually, all of the remaining Colonial Troops on or inside Mimas had been teleported back to the Earth.

Nearly three million Colonial Troops all stood there, all looking bewildered, all looking at each other, their memories completely wiped of their experiences on the ice moon Mimas. How they had managed to get back to the Earth, they simply did not know.

They all remembered being on troop transport ships heading somewhere, then they were here. What happened to their destination? Had their transports taken them here instead? Where was here? The Colonial Troops did not yet even realise, that they were back on Earth.

The entity that was Ahriman began to stir. It had been a very long time, many aeons in fact since he had suffered the indignity of being discarnate. He had no host! He was no longer clothed in flesh! The entity that was Ahriman was enraged and his rage consumed him. He would have his revenge. The two humans, with their newly awakened psychic prowess, would pay the ultimate price! They would be his new hosts! They could not stop him now, he was a discarnate immortal being! By killing his host, they had brought themselves undone!

Inside Ahriman's throne room, a glowing red ball of malevolence suddenly burst into existence. It flew first at Gideon, who was caught off guard momentarily before repelling him. Ahriman was surprised at how easily Gideon had pushed him back. He was a novice in comparison and should have been far less capable. He then flew at Sandra, who upon seeing Gideon's reaction, had prepared herself accordingly. Her stance was firm and her resolve was stronger than Ahriman had anticipated. Even with her mind concentrating on containing Ahriman, Sandra was still able to push him back and repel him.

Then Ahriman remembered Sandra's words when she and Gideon had first entered his throne room, *"No, Ahriman. It is you who shall fail. We cannot allow your existence to continue any longer. We have been sanctioned, to rend your evil soul, such that it shall never recover."*

Ahriman considered those words, very carefully, *"We, who was this, we?"*, he asked of himself, then he questioned himself further, *"Sanctioned? By whom was this, we, sanctioned? What was the source of this sanction?"*

Then Ahriman came to the sudden realisation, that Gideon and Sandra were not alone, although they knew it not. They had hidden backup and Ahriman's very existence was now at stake.

Ahriman began darting feverishly around the throne room, darting here and there, looking for a weak point, trying to escape. Sandra using her powerful mind, contained him. Ahriman was trapped and now he knew it. The threat to his existence was very real.

Gideon had teleported all the humans on Mimas, back to the Earth. All except General Brennan-Chives and Colonel Yansy. Ahriman tried to attack Sandra in an attempt to break her deep concentration, but he could not approach her. He had another idea, one last chance to escape.

Ahriman had one chance left, he needed to use a human body to get to the Earth quickly and to increase his powers through flesh. He did not want to spend millions upon millions of years drifting through space again. Not every human being had been removed from Mimas, there were still two left.

Quickly he entered the body of General Brennan-Chives. In Mimasian flesh he could not teleport, humans, however, they were different. With his knowledge and their present level of physical and psychic development, he should be able to teleport to the Earth. First, however, he would have to escape from Sandra Danker's powerful psychic energy field.

Using his powerful will, he sent Colonel Yansy into motion. Suddenly, with incredible swiftness, Colonel Yansy leapt towards Sandra. The move was totally unforeseen and Sandra was caught by surprise. Sandra was knocked to the floor and Colonel Yansy landed on top of her. Sandra was now locked into a physical battle. Her mind was still trying to concentrate on keeping Ahriman trapped in her psychic energy field, within the throne room.

Sandra needed more practice, her powers were great, but fighting a possessed human was breaking her concentration. Even though her mind, was now the mind of a spiritual master, she hadn't had enough time to adjust to the change. Slowly her concentration weakened and Ahriman with sudden swiftness, began to teleport to the safety of the Earth in General Brennan-Chive's body. There he could hide amongst the Earth's billions on human inhabitants.

Gideon's mind was thinly dispersed over the whole of Mimas. He sensed Sandra's problem and with a supreme swiftness, moved accordingly. Gideon quickly drew in his mind and then encapsulated Ahriman, in General Brennan-Chive's body, before he could escape from Mimas.

Gideon's psychic energy field dragged the evil Ahriman, kicking and screaming, back to the throne room. Just in time to find Sandra prevail against Colonel Yansy. The Colonel flew backwards under Sandra's psychic thrust and he was embedded deeply into the rock wall, completely dead.

Sandra then joined her mind to Gideon's and now Ahriman, in General Brennan-Chive's body, was encapsulated in the intense psychic field of both the newly developed spiritual masters. General Brennan-Chive's body began to dissolve into fluid and slowly flowed onto the throne room floor. The discarnate entity that was Ahriman, was now insane with rage. Ahriman's entity glowed a deep bloody red, with the hatred of a trillion devoured evil souls. Immense discharges of electrical energy began to shoot out from his evil soul. It was all to no avail.

Gideon and Sandra both concentrated on condensing their psychic energy fields. They shrunk their energy field down in size, all the while increasing its intensity. Ahriman screamed in discarnate agony, continuously, he did not stop. The evil Lord of the ice moon Mimas knew that he was finished. The entity that was Ahriman was being compressed into an infinitesimally small pinpoint of no return.

With a discharge of immense power, Ahriman vanished swiftly from existence. Gideon and Sandra had teleported Ahriman's evil soul, through millions of light years of space, into the vastness of intergalactic space, between distant galaxies.

In so doing, they had spread Ahriman's entity across a vast volume of space, a volume of tens of thousands of cubic light years. The entity that was Ahriman was now so thinly spread out over intergalactic space, that he would cease to exist and could never hope to recover. Ahriman was rent asunder, he was now gone forever.

"Is it over now, Gideon?", Sandra asked.

"Yeah, I think Ahriman is finished", Gideon replied, adding, *"There is no coming back from that. He will never return. He won't harm any living thing, ever again."*

"That is great, but now, what about Mimas?", Sandra had asked.

"You know me, Sandra. I'm a terraformer scientist. I've got a few ideas for Mimas. Would you care to help me?", Gideon replied.

"Yes, my love, you know I will", replied Sandra.

Then both they went to work on the ice moon, Mimas.

27. The Purging of Mimas.

Gideon and Sandra both sat levitating, two feet above the floor of the royal throne room, facing each other as their minds expanded outwards. They could see the Earth as Mimas approached, having nearly settled into Earth's orbit a million miles away. Quickly, Gideon and Sandra concentrated their minds on Mimas itself, as they attempted to learn everything they could about the little ice moon, that was in reality a generation ship.

"Sandra, if we're going to purge Mimas clean. We have to know as much as we can about it", Gideon explained to Sandra.

"We will have to move Mimas, Gideon. I don't think we dare leave it orbiting the Earth", she replied. "You're probably right, but first, let's get to know this place", Gideon replied.

Sandra agreed and together their minds scanned Mimas.

Evil pervaded the very structure of Mimas, from its icy surface right through to its fusion reaction Sun, at its very core. Ahriman's filth and stench was everywhere. Countless centuries of rule by the evil Lord Ahriman had perverted everything, absolutely everything inside of the little ice world.

Before Gideon and Sandra could turn Mimas over to any other intelligent beings, human or otherwise, Mimas would have to be purged and cleansed. Gideon and Sandra also decided, that they would change the interior environment of the Mimas as best they could. Changing it from hot dry hell world, into a complete paradise.

Swiftly they scanned Mimas, the ice shell would be the easiest to purge and they then moved on to the rock shell. That wouldn't be so easy. The rock shell, at least closer to the surface, had been the Mimasian living quarters, being directly exposed to their evil and decadent lives. Between there and the ice shell, however, was just more rock and the tunnel network. Those in themselves would not be too difficult to cleanse.

On the interior surface of Mimas, there were also many lifeforms, which they had to look into and take into consideration. Some of them might even be salvaged, if the Mimasian influence wasn't too deep. Lifeforms in the circular sea surrounding the southern island mountain, that had been Ahriman's fortress, were exceedingly dangerous. The carnivorous reptilians, that resembled dimetrodons and the savage shark-like fish would need to be dealt with.

Inside the labyrinth of tunnels within the rock shell, they did not find any living things. There, they found many Mimasian bodies, that hadn't been disposed of by the Colonial Troops. These need to be eliminated as well. On the interior surface, they found many living creatures. These ranged from single cell creatures to more complex creatures, some with the intelligence close to that of apes. Then of course, there were the many species of Mimasian flora.

Gideon and Sandra decided to exterminate every dangerous carnivore inside of Mimas. When purging Mimas, they would remove every vestige of evil and malevolence that Ahriman and his hordes had tainted. In addition to this, they both decided, that they would permanently disable every weapon they found inside of Mimas that was still functional.

They also believed that the Mimasian ion drive would have to be disabled at some point, but not before Mimas was relocated, to its new location somewhere far from the Earth. All signs of the war and death would be removed as best as they could, to leave the little ice moon completely cleansed.

Gideon and Sandra began to cleanse Mimas. They started with the

Mimasian interior. A blue-green glow began filling the air. The dangerous carnivorous animals of the Southern Circular Sea and other developing malevolent species were vaporised in an instant, it was a painless death and they didn't feel a thing.

Pools of dried blood and all of the bodies of the fallen dead, both Mimasian and those few humans who had not been returned to the Earth, were also vaporised. All of the weapons of war were fused and disabled by an intense heat so that they could only ever be used for scrap.

Next Gideon and Sandra expanded into the Mimasian rock shell. Again all of the fallen warriors vanished, vaporised in an instant. Weapons systems were quickly disable and turned into scrap. The evil of Ahriman was being forced out of the very rock. The blood stained walls of the tunnel systems were cleansed and every remaining vestige of evil was removed.

The Mimasian interior life support systems were all checked and their automatic repair systems activated. The generator for the Mimasian controlled fusion reaction Sun was then checked and its systems overhauled by its automatic maintenance systems. All of these changes were triggered by their powerful psychic minds. The couple excelled at telekinesis and made changes at will.

Gideon being a terraformer, concentrated on the Mimasian interior, its biomes and its lifeforms, both flora and fauna. Sandra being an engineer concentrated on the more technical aspects of the changes they were making. They both came together to consult on those changes that required the both of them.

Next, they both moved into the Mimasian ice shell. This was quickly cleansed and their purging minds penetrated deep into space beyond. The cloud of gas and dust vaporising from the frozen Mimasian surface, suddenly glowed a deep blue-green and then the ice moon temporarily disappeared from view.

Mimas was suddenly swallowed up by the expanding bright blue green sphere of their purging minds. Mimas then reappeared again, in almost the same position some five minutes later. The pulse in brightness had been observed by the entire inner solar system. Mimas had been purged of all of the evil that Ahriman and his Mimasian hordes had wrought upon it.

Gideon and Sandra then began to think about Mimas's position in space. Mimas could not be left orbiting the Earth. It would give the human species something from the war to gloat over, their spoils of war. That could not be allowed. Mimas had to be move once more.

"Gideon. Mimas will be in the Earth's orbit very soon. Do have you any ideas on where to shift it to?", Sandra enquired.

"Well, Sandra. I've been thinking that the Mimasians caused a lot of problems. Not just for our human civilisation, but also for the Martians. So I was thinking, maybe."

Sandra was way ahead of him and was quick to interrupt him, "I know exactly what you mean, Gideon and I think I know what you want to do."

Gideon then confirmed what she suspected and together they put their plan into operation.

Gideon and Sandra then concentrated their minds on the immense Mimasian ion drive system, which then started operating once more. Carefully they placed Mimas on a trajectory towards Mars. One million miles from the Earth, the little ice moon Mimas continued on its course as if it would enter the Earth's orbit. Then slowly Mimas picked up speed and very soon the little ice moon was rounding the Earth and its Moon, heading on a trajectory for a Mars intercept.

Gideon and Sandra were flexing their psychic abilities. They had defeated the evil Lord Ahriman, but they would have another task to perform very soon. They looked over the interior of Mimas and then decided upon their modifications. First, they divided Mimas into three zones.

The zone where they were, that contained the immense Mimasian ion drive system and the Hershel Crater, was designated as the southern hemisphere. At the opposing end of Mimas, which contained another almost identical ring of mountains, another circular sea and another island mountain, they designated as the northern hemisphere. Everything in between the two mountain rings was designated as central or equatorial.

They decided to leave the Southern Ring Mountains unchanged. They also decided to leave its associated circular sea and island mountain unchanged as well. All of the carnivorous sharks and reptilians in the Southern Circular Sea had already been purged and that, they both figured was enough for the southern hemisphere of Mimas.

They now looked upon the northern hemisphere of Mimas. The Earth's armies had entered from the exterior surface of that hemisphere. The tunnels within the rock shell had led the Colonial Troops to the interior surface of Mimas, on the outside of the northern ring of mountains.

Curiously they both noticed, that there were tunnels from the Mimasian surface, that led towards the northern island mountain. Those particular tunnels stopped short on the inside of the northern ring of mountains, only reaching as far as the Northern Circular Sea.

It was apparent that Ahriman had blinded the Colonial Troops to those tunnels and that he had directed them towards the tunnels leading to the greater Mimasian interior. The quickest path to himself, so that he could possess a human of high rank and take control of the invading army. Gideon and Sandra both found that very interesting. What was so special about the northern island mountain, that Ahriman himself, would blind the colonial armies from locating it? They very quickly found out.

Gideon and Sandra both paid special attention to the northern island mountain and carefully inspected it. This entire island mountain appeared to be some kind of emergency escape ship, with its own ion drive system. An ion drive system that appeared to be disabled so Ahriman could never have used it to escape. Its very use would have torn a hole through the northern polar region of Mimas and left the Mimasian interior open to the vacuum of space. Sandra and Gideon had considered, that perhaps, that was why the emergency escape ship's ion drive had been disabled. It was also likely that was the very reason that Ahriman did not want the colonial armies to find it.

The northern island mountain, the escape ship, was also surrounded by its own circular sea and its own ring of mountains. These features were almost identical in basic structure to those in the southern hemisphere of Mimas. The Northern Circular Sea was not infested with sharks and finned crocodilians.

This they found to be quite curious. Eventually, they both came to the same conclusion, that the entire northern island mountain and the interior of the Northern Ring Mountains, had long been abandoned and were simply left in that state.

They knew not why it was abandoned and as Ahriman and his Mimasian hordes were gone, they realised, that they probably never would. Although Gideon suspected that Ahriman, considered that the emergency escape ship, could be used as a weapon against him. So perhaps Ahriman himself, had the escape ship disabled and abandoned. Gideon could never know for sure.

Next Gideon and Sandra concentrated on the region, midway between the northern and southern mountain rings, the central or equatorial zone. Likening this to a temperate and equatorial region within the Mimasian interior. Here they quickly realised, that the very central region of Mimas had originally been designed as a circular Equatorial Sea.

It was now a broad dry plain as the rivers from both the southern and Northern Ring Mountains dried up long before reaching the Equatorial Sea basin. Likewise, the springs that fed the plains on either side of the Equatorial Sea basin and the springs within the Sea basin itself were woefully insufficient to fill it. The interior of Mimas was a perpetual semi-arid desert.

"*Why?*", Gideon and Sandra thought to themselves.

Sandra quickly had the answer and explained it to Gideon, *"It's a combination of the artificial Mimasian Sun's output and insufficient water pressure in the springs themselves."*

Gideon understood, he was after all a terraformer scientist by trade, *"So if we adjust the Mimasian Sun's output to be slightly lower, then the rivers from the ring mountains will the reach the Equatorial Sea. They won't all evaporate. The Equatorial Sea basin will slowly fill."*

Sandra then added, *"There are deep tunnels and valves underneath both of the circular seas and underneath all of the springs as well. That's what controls the depths of the circular seas and the water pressure of the springs. These all source their water from the Mimasian ice shell."*

Gideon quickly caught on, *"So if we adjust the valves on those deep tunnels supplying the springs, we can increase their water pressure. The springs in the plains on either side will then overflow and form small rivers, that will eventually flow into the Equatorial Sea basin. If we combine that with the springs in the seabed itself, the Equatorial Sea basin will fill much quicker."*

"Exactly, Gideon. There must be a control system for all of this", Sandra, who herself, by trade was a spacecraft design engineer, explained.

"Which means there must be settings that we can use to turn Mimas into a paradise", Gideon surmised, adding, *"The original designers of this place must have been geniuses."*

"Yes, Gideon and look what that bastard Ahriman turned them into", Sandra replied.

"Sandra, it seems very likely that the Mimasians weren't really up to the task of running this generation ship. We can fix this!", Gideon concluded.

"Yep, let's renovate this place", Sandra agreed.

Gideon and Sandra scanned Mimas once more, this time they were looking for the Mimasian infrastructure control systems, specifically the flow controls to the Mimasian springs. Having scanned the entire ice moon from north to south, the controls were found in the bowels of the southern island mountain, two levels up from the ion drive systems controls.

"We should have started at this end", Gideon mused.

"You're probably right, Gideon", Sandra agreed.

Gideon and Sandra then carefully looked over the controls.

Sandra being the engineer was quickest to make sense of the controls, *"Such a simple system! These are the flow controls to the Southern Circular Sea. It's a simple slider control system. Sliding it up increases the water flow and its depth, sliding it down decreases the water flow and its depth. It's so simple! Although, I can't see anything here that controls the flow to the Northern Circular Sea."*

"The flow controls for the Northern Circular Sea are probably under the northern island mountain, in a control room just like this one", Gideon replied.

"Really! How'd we miss that?", Sandra questioned.

"Probably because we were both looking for the flow controls to the springs in the central regions", Gideon replied.

"You're probably right, Gideon. Speaking of the flow controls for the springs. They're

right over here", Sandra replied as she tapped on another control console and then noted, *"We have the full set as well. Flow controls for the Equatorial Sea basin and the plains on either side."*

"Are you sure, Sandra? I mean, we don't have to recheck the northern island mountain again do we?", Gideon asked, double checking.

"No. No. It's all here, Gideon. Three simple sliders", Sandra replied, pointing to each flow control in turn, *"Southern springs, Sea basin springs and Northern springs. Mind you, these are the master flow controls. If you want to control each spring individually, I suspect they're over there on those other three control consoles. The three consoles that are crowded with slider switches"*, Sandra pointed across the room.

Gideon looked across the control room to where Sandra pointed. There were three large control consoles literally jam packed with sliding switches. At least two hundred switches on each console.

"Okay, Sandra, so there are literally hundreds and hundreds of springs", Gideon noted.

"I expect so, Gideon. Now let's slide these up a notch, shall we", Sandra replied.

"Wait! Wait! Wait!", Gideon cautioned, asking, *"How do you know where to slide them to?"*

"There's a scale of sorts, Gideon. It's really very simple. Slide the switches right down and the springs stop flowing. Slide them up and the water flow increases", Sandra noted.

"Yes, but how far up, Sandra?", Gideon asked.

"Right to the top on all three. That's the flow required to fill the Equatorial Sea basin and flood the plains on either side. We definitely don't want to do that!", Sandra replied smiling, then she adjusted the three slider switches to a particular mark on the console, *"This position, seems to match our Equatorial Sea's hypothetical shoreline."*

"That's it? That simple?", Gideon enquired.

"Yeah. It's a very simple system, Gideon", Sandra replied, adding, *"The*

Mimasians had it set to the second lowest level. The springs were all flowing, but the Sea basin was dry. If I didn't know any better, I'd say that that was an accident that happened aeons ago and was never corrected."

"What about those other three consoles then?", Gideon asked.

"Granularity. Those control the springs on an individual basis and likely override this console", Sandra surmised and after glancing at their slider switches more closely, *"They're all set to their midpoint setting. So basically, they're not in use."*

"So it's done then? The Equatorial Sea is now beginning to fill?", Gideon enquired.

"Sure is, Gideon. Sure is", Sandra replied.

True to Sandra's word, the Mimasian Equatorial Sea basin was beginning to slowly fill.

Gideon looked further around the control room and noticed another console on the other side of the room, *"Sandra. What about that console over there? What do you think it does?"*

Sandra's mind drifted over for a closer look, *"Wow! Another nice simple console. The builders of this place, Gideon. I like their work. I really do!"*

"Yeah, but what does it do?", Gideon questioned.

There were a number of slide switches and Sandra started adjusting their levels.

"Sandra. Do you really think that's wise?", Gideon queried.

"It's okay, Gideon. I've got this", Sandra replied, pointing to and explaining the slider switches, *"That's the air pressure. I've stepped it up from seven hundred millibars to one thousand millibars. I've also adjusted the gas mix to be more Earth-like. You know what I mean, oxygen, nitrogen, carbon dioxide and water vapour. That sort of thing."*

"Okay. That does make sense. The air in this place is a bit thin", Gideon replied, agreeing with Sandra's changes.

Sandra tapped on the console with her astral index finger, *"This one should be much quicker."*

The thin Mimasian air slowly thickened to one thousand millibars. The water vapour levels increased and instead of the occasional, scattered wispy clouds, there were now more complex and full-bodied cloud structures. In some regions, rain began to fall for the first time in aeons and the rivers began flowing from both of the ring mountains with far greater volumes of water. All flowing towards the Equatorial Sea basin.

The entire interior of Mimas was beginning to transform from a mostly desert and semi-arid desert biome to something that would be far more temperate, with the regions closer to the Equatorial Sea possibly even becoming tropical.

Having begun the process of transforming Mimas into a paradise, Gideon and Sandra both ended their meditative trance and awoke. Sandra could sense something in the very back of her mind. Gideon began to sense it as well. At first it made no sense whatsoever.

"Gideon. What is it?", she asked.

"I don't know, Sandra. It's as if someone wants us to do something", he replied.

Sandra slowly began to understand the message formulating in her mind, "Gideon, behind Ahriman's throne, buried deep inside the rock shell."

Now Gideon could also see them, "Yes, I can see them. Can we teleport them through?"

The benevolent side of the universal field had shown Gideon and Sandra where to search with their minds. They both locked onto the objects in question and then with a flash of light, they'd brought them through into the throne room. Complete with their crystalline cryogenic life suspension tanks.

Through what appeared to be frost-coated, clear crystal aluminium they could see, two-winged, yet humanoid creatures, one was male and the other one was female.

"My God. Sandra, you do know what they are, don't you?", Gideon asked.

"Gideon, they're what the Mimasians were, before Ahriman took control of them", Sandra replied.

They looked at the two creatures in suspended animation.

"Why would Ahriman keep them? It makes no sense", Gideon enquired.

Sandra replied, speculating "A genetic base stock maybe? You know, just in case Ahriman messed up genetically with his Mimasians."

"Ahriman's Mimasians looked pretty genetically messed up to me, Sandra", Gideon remarked.

"Well then, Gideon, I guess we'll never know, but nonetheless, here they are", Sandra replied.

"Maybe these were the original builders of Mimas", Gideon mused.

"Perhaps. Perhaps not", Sandra replied, "We'd have to ask them to get the answer."

These new aliens had very light, pale-coloured skins. Six slender fingers on each hand, that were set in three pairs per hand, but completely without claws, just fingernails. Their arms and legs looked very human and in the correct proportions with their bodies. Although they were smaller than the average human, at a mere five feet tall.

Their wings were both large and a delightfully creamy flesh colour. At the base, the wings formed into a long prehensile tail, with a flat rounded end, not pointed and spade-like, like the Mimasians.

Their skins were smooth, with little, if any body hair at all. On their heads, their hair flowed in long blond, wavy locks, being held back by headbands made of a fine golden flax.

Their faces were almost angelic in appearance, small, with very delicate features. They didn't have any horns or brow ridges and their teeth were small and indicated, that they were probably vegetarians. Their eyes were a deep crystal blue, with a slight hint of purple and showed the sparks of intelligence.

For millions of years, they'd been locked inside the rock shell, captives of Ahriman. Ancient reminders of what they had looked like, in contrast to what Ahriman had made them into.

"This complicates matters, Sandra", Gideon remarked.

"You think, Gideon?", Sandra questioned in reply.

"I think we'll need some guidance from the Martians on what to do with these two", Gideon noted.

"Agreed", Sandra replied, then looking around the alien's cryogenic life suspension systems, she noticed a plaque with some kind of script written upon it, "Look Gideon", she pointed to it.

Gideon looked to where Sandra was pointing, "I can't be certain Sandra, but for some reason, I'm reading that script as saying, *'Thol'*."

"Is that what they are?", Sandra asked of no one in particular, "Thols?"

28. Options and Complications.

On his way to Mars, Colonel Bannon received an urgent message from Eros.

"All of the remaining Colonial Troops on Mimas, have been located on a remote mountainside on the Earth, in the nation of Bhutan. How they got there, we do not understand. Mimas has changed course again. Mimas has not entered the Earth's orbit as expected and is now on a Mars intercept trajectory. Information leads us to believe, that Doctor Gideon Reas and Sandra Danker were somehow responsible. We are assuming that Doctor Gideon Reas and Sandra Danker are on Mimas. Note: All of the troop transports, are still on Mimas."

Colonel Bannon didn't understand why Mimas had changed course, nor why it was once again heading towards Mars. The Colonel had one idea though, Gideon and Sandra must be responsible. How he did not know, but the Colonel knew he was right, he asked Winchilly.

"Winchilly, what do you make of this?", he asked, after passing Winchilly the message.

Winchilly feigned reading the message, instead reaching into the Colonel's mind for the relevant information, then she replied telepathically, *"Gideon and Sandra are responsible, it is within their psychic potentials."*

Exactly his own thoughts on the matter, the Colonel inquired further, "What do you think they're doing with the ice moon?"

Winchilly replied surprisingly quickly, *"They said, to take this ship and of course, that means us, to my world. That is where they will go. They will come here."*

The Colonel looked at her, then inquired, "Mimas is currently on course to Mars. So what happens next must be happening here?"

"I believe so", Winchilly replied.

It was now well over a week later and Colonel Bannon and Winchilly watched as Mimas continued on its course towards Mars. Mimas continued out-gassing, as it was still in the inner solar system and closer to the Sun. Mimas with its cometary cloud of gas and dust, was currently the most visible object in the entire solar system. Winchilly swept the Battle Cruiser's scanners along Mars's orbital path. From the Aries colony in high Martian orbit, past the planet itself and onwards towards Mars's leading Trojan point and then back towards Mars's trailing Trojan point.

There was no sign of any enemy craft. None at all had been seen since the Colonial Troops had mysteriously reappeared back on Earth. An event that was still quite unexplainable for the Earth's governmental agencies. Strangely enough, the event was not being reported in the news feeds either.

With no word yet from Gideon or Sandra, they could only assume that the war was over, even though they had no confirmation as yet, nor any details on the matter.

Winchilly then pointed the Battle Cruiser's scanners back towards Mimas. Colonel Bannon could see it far more clearly now. Mimas was a small object in the distance, surrounded by a huge, nebulous cloud of gas and dust, billowing out and being pushed back into a long tail by the Sun's solar wind.

Colonel Bannon changed course for Mimas and then sent a message to Eros and the Aries colony.

"Mimas is now on its approach to Mars. We will investigate and report back later, on what the situation is. Colonel James J Bannon."

Colonel Bannon skilfully piloted his Battle Cruiser into high Mimasian orbit. A vast amount of data had been entering into his ship's computer memory banks. Terabytes of data, in fact. All about the Mimasian interior topography and its developing new environment. The Colonel had no idea how that was happening, but Winchilly insisted, that it was Gideon and Sandra accessing his ship's computer network directly with their minds.

At Winchilly's advise, Colonel Bannon then sent a message to Eros, stating that Mimas had been placed under control. Then in a sudden flash of brilliant blue light, Gideon and Sandra were back aboard the Colonel's Battle Cruiser.

"Jim. It's good to see you again", greeted Gideon.

"Jesus wept, Gideon!", a surprised Colonel Bannon exclaimed, before answering, "It's good to see you and Sandra as well, Gideon."

Sandra then greeted the Colonel, after which Gideon and Sandra turned to Winchilly. They both spread out their arms. Winchilly walked towards them and the three embraced each other. During this embrace, Gideon and Sandra sent vast volumes of information to Winchilly, telepathically. The young Martian woman almost swooned due to the vast volume of information, however, now she knew everything that had transpired inside of Mimas.

"The war is over! The threat is no more. The Mimasian Emperor, Ahriman is dead", Winchilly transmitted telepathically to the Colonel.

"More than dead! The Mimasian Emperor has been rent asunder", Gideon clarified.

Sandra then added, "There is no coming back from that. The Mimasian Emperor is gone forever."

"Jim, set course for Mars. We have some business to attend to", Gideon requested.

Yeah, sure thing, what's the nature of the business?", the Colonel enquired.

"Ah, Colonel, we'll let you know soon enough. We have important matters to discuss with our Martian friends", Sandra informed him.

Gideon and Sandra both looked at Winchilly, "When we meet your Elders, we will need your support Winchilly."

Winchilly smiled and agreed, *"I will do what I can to help."*

Several days later, the Colonel's Battle Cruiser landed on the Martian surface, just outside of the monoliths, to the south of the Elysium region. Once they had entered the monolith complex, Gideon, Sandra, Winchilly and the Colonel were quickly led to the Martian leaders. Colonel Bannon waited uncomfortably, but patiently, sitting on a cushion on the floor of the large room, while everyone else was in a telepathic conference.

Whatever was being discussed, the looks on the Martian's faces showed serious concern. The Martians may have been nonverbal telepaths, but their facial expressions spoke volumes. The telepathic conference went on for several hours and at many points, there appeared to be, what looked like tension and apprehension showing on their faces. Eventually, the faces of the Martians showed signs of understanding and they began to take on a more peaceful demeanour. Shortly thereafter the telepathic conference ended.

A worried Colonel Bannon asked, "Well then, Gideon, have you concluded your business?"

"We sure have, Jim. The Martian Elders have all agreed to our plans, which is quite surprising actually", replied Gideon.

"What plans, Gideon? You haven't told me anything as yet!", the Colonel exclaimed.

"We will, Jim, as soon as we get back to your Battle Cruiser. We will explain everything to you, absolutely everything", Gideon replied.

Once back inside the Colonel's Battle Cruiser, Gideon asked, "Are you ready to hear it all, Jim?"

"As ready as I'll ever be", the Colonel replied.

"First of all. The Mimasian Emperor is dead and so are all of the

Mimasians. Every last one of them. Their Emperor was a very powerful entity and he drove his minions to fight to their deaths, all of them. That's also why our own casualty figures were so high", Gideon informed the Colonel, then explained further, "Their Emperor was affecting our troops as well, Jim. He wanted to possess General Brennan-Chives and our own armed forces, then send them back to the Earth as his own all-conquering army."

"That would have been disastrous", the Colonel remarked.

"It could well have been. We humans were to become his new evil minions", Sandra added.

Winchilly then added, *"We Martians know of his power. We are all very lucky that he failed."*

"Okay. So that was their Emperor's plan. He's failed. Now what is your plan?", the Colonel asked.

"We've purged Mimas of all of Ahriman's and the Mimasian's evil influence", Sandra replied.

"We've also terraformed the interior of Mimas to a much greater degree, to make it far more habitable", Gideon further informed him, giving Sandra the full kudos, "Sandra was able to adjust Mimas's environmental control systems. Thicker atmosphere, more surface water, that sort of thing."

"After purging and terraforming Mimas, we weren't really sure what to do with it.", Sandra honestly admitted, adding, "We knew that we couldn't leave it orbiting the Earth. It would have become a war trophy. The spoils of war and we didn't think that was a good thing at all."

"That's why we had to bring Mimas to Mars. We needed to discuss this situation with the Martians", Gideon explained.

"Is being a war trophy really that bad?", Colonel Bannon questioned.

"It does set a bad precedent", Winchilly stepped in.

"Yes. Winchilly's right. If we have one war trophy, why not another war trophy and another and another and so on", Sandra remarked, explaining, "The spoils of war can lead to some people, wanting more spoils, more war trophies."

"And where do those war trophies come from, Jim?", Gideon asked rhetorically, answering himself, "As Sandra just equated, more war trophies just means more war!"

"Okay, guys. I get your reasoning, but why did you need to come to Mars?", the Colonel enquired.

"This is bigger than us, Jim. Mimas is a whole new world. We needed to ask the Martians, what would they do in our place?", Sandra replied.

"We were simply going to ask Winchilly's people what we should do. We wanted their advise", Sandra told the Colonel.

Winchilly then stepped in, *"It turns out that my people are very fearful of your people, Jim. Please do not be offended. I have no wish to offend you. We, my people, are very grateful for all that you have done. Especially for having freed us from slavery. However, my people are telepathic and we watched in horror, at how easily your people fight wars. How easily your people slaughtered the Mimasians, often without any mercy at all. It has become a great concern amongst my people. It frightens us!"*

Colonel Bannon looked at Winchilly with a combination of understanding and concern, he had sincerely believed, that the people of the Earth and Winchilly's people would become great friends.

The Colonel reached out to Winchilly, taking her hands in his, "I am truly sorry, Winchilly. My people had no wish to frighten your people. It is the sad result of this war", he then let her hands go.

"That's what we walked into during the telepathic conference, Jim", Gideon admitted.

"Okay. I can understand that. Your people are wondering if one evil is being replaced by another", the Colonel replied, then reassuring, "Let me assure your people, Winchilly. That this war was just an aberration. Winchilly, your people have nothing to fear from us. Nothing at all!"

"Nonetheless, Jim, my people fear your people", Winchilly replied sadly.

"Winchilly's people are afraid to share their world, Mars, with us", Gideon explained.

"They fear at some point, our people will enslave them. Just like the Mimasians did", Sandra added.

"We are now free after so many aeons. Slavery is now my people's greatest fear", Winchilly noted.

"Please, Winchilly. Tell your people that's nonsense. It will never happen", the Colonel stressed.

"You cannot see the future, Jim. You cannot speak for every Earth human. You cannot make us any guarantees, that we can accept", Winchilly replied, explaining, *"We have seen the dark side of your people, Jim and how easily it was influenced by the Mimasian Emperor, Ahriman."*

The Colonel was quiet for a long while, before replying, "Okay Winchilly. I can see the problem. Now what's the solution?"

"We did spend a lot of time discussing options", Sandra admitted.

"The first option was to close off Mars to colonisation, but that was considered far too impractical", Gideon informed the Colonel, explaining, "Mars has only recently been terraformed and we won't be opening up Mars for colonisation for a couple of centuries. The atmosphere still contains far too many volatile and noxious gasses and way too much water vapour. The ocean basins are still filling and still flooding. There are massive cyclonic storms that are just ridiculously dangerous, sometimes they link up a cover the entire planet. The new atmosphere and hydrosphere will have to settle down and develop safer and more predictable patterns and that will take centuries. Even then, Jim, with all of these terraforming issues, we ourselves, have absolutely no idea how to stop colonists from coming to Mars. They can just land on the planet and then set up homesteads during the closed period. Without military help, we simply can't stop them!"

"I can see how that would be impractical", the Colonel agreed.

"We considered completely closing off just the Elysium subcontinent", Sandra noted.

"Okay, that option sounds like it has legs", the Colonel remarked.

"Not really, Jim. Remember the age of Empires back on the Earth. That did not turn out so well for the indigenous peoples of Africa, the Americas, Australia or the Pacific Islands", Gideon replied, explaining, "It would be the same thing here. Whether we closed off the Elysium subcontinent or not, people would just come in and homestead anyway. That's just what we humans do. Short of violence, how do we stop them?"

Sandra then added in, "Think of the Aztecs, think of the Inca. Millions died, Jim, millions. Whole civilisations were destroyed."

"Okay, okay, Sandra. I can see the issues with that one", the Colonel agreed and then he was quiet again for long moments thinking.

"What about integration? Would that work?", Colonel Bannon suggested.

A cold shiver went up Winchilly's spine, a visibly physical reaction, that was noticeable to everyone in the ship's cabin.

"Winchilly?", the Colonel enquired with concern.

Sandra placed her hand on Winchilly's shoulder and then replied, "Don't you remember last century's psychic pogroms, Jim? Our own psychics were persecuted on Earth, just a few decades ago. Winchilly's people are all nonverbal psychics, Jim. Our psychics were at least able to talk and even still, look at how they were persecuted."

"No, no, you are right, Sandra. I should have considered that. I do apologise, Winchilly", the Colonel replied apologetically.

"So what does that leave us with?", the Colonel enquired.

"Mimas", Gideon and Sandra both replied in unison.

"Mimas?", the Colonel enquired.

"Yeah! Gideon and I have fixed it up quite a bit", Sandra explained, adding, "We weren't entirely sure why at first, but it was something we felt had to be done."

Gideon accessed the Battle Cruiser's computer network and put an image of the Mimasian interior on the screen for the Colonel to view.

"Wait. Wait now. That doesn't look anything like the images the General's people sent through to us. I was under the impression that Mimas was all semi-arid desert", the Colonel noted.

"You're absolutely right, Jim. There were only two seas inside of Mimas, a few springs here and there and a handful of small lakes and rivers", Gideon agreed, then explained, "Being terraformers and having these new psychic *'gifts'*, we thought we could improve on the interior somewhat."

Sandra stepped in, "We both knew that Mimas had to have an environmental control system somewhere. So we searched for it and when we found it, we changed the settings."

The Colonel looked at the screen and flicked through the images of the Mimasian interior. Circular seas were in both of the southern and northern polar regions. Another sea circled Mimas, around its equator. Rivers aplenty flowed from both poles to the equator and a there were lots of lakes.

Overflowing springs were in a great abundance as well. The plant life had responded to the increase in water and was growing prolifically. The entire interior of Mimas had been completely transformed.

Winchilly was smiling, the broadest of smiles, *"When, Gideon and Sandra had shown the Elders, what they had done to Mimas, my people were amazed."*

"Shown them?", Colonel Bannon enquired.

"Telepathically of course, Jim", Winchilly elaborated, adding, *"When my people saw those beautiful images, straight out of Gideon's and Sandra's minds, they all began saying, that Mimas was the solution. Mimas could be our new home!"*, Winchilly was excited.

"Under the stewardship of Winchilly's people, Mimas will become a paradise", Sandra noted.

"It's really ironic, Jim. The homeworld of their oppressors and enslavers now becomes their home", Gideon remarked.

"Well, it does sound fitting", the Colonel agreed, adding, "After countless aeons of pain and suffering, your people certainly deserve something out of all of this, Winchilly."

Winchilly smiled and nodded in reply.

"After the transports delivered the last of General Brennan-Chives Colonial Troops to Mimas, those transports were just left there sitting on the surface", Gideon commented, adding, "They're all still there now, just waiting for crews and passengers."

Sandra then quickly added, "And those transports are sitting right on top of the tunnels, leading into the interior of Mimas. They're the only way into the Mimasian interior. Those tunnels are a perfect access control point."

"That does kind of make sense", the Colonel agreed, explaining, "No one can get into the interior of Mimas, without going through a tunnel and that would require permission. Kind of like an immigration border checkpoint."

"Which is exactly what we would require", Winchilly agreed.

"It's not quite as simple as that though. Mimas is way too close to the Sun.

Mimas is now like a huge comet, bleeding its ice shell off into space", Gideon noted, then he informed the Colonel, "We need to place Mimas back in Saturnian orbit. Back in the very same orbit it came from. Mimas belongs there."

"There is also another complication", Sandra informed the Colonel.

"Complication?", the Colonel enquired.

"Inside of the Southern Central Mountain Peak, embedded deep within the rock behind Ahriman's throne, we found something, Jim", Gideon informed him.

Sandra continued on from Gideon, "A pair of crystalline, cryogenic suspension pods. Very advanced. Very, very old."

Gideon continued on from Sandra, "We brought them both out, through the rock."

"The pods contained a pair of alien beings. One was male and the other one was female. Thols", Sandra finished.

"Thols?", queried the Colonel.

"These, we believe, are the original species that Ahriman took control of, possessed and mutated into the Mimasians", Gideon explained, as he put an image of them both onto the screen.

Winchilly commented, *"The Mimasians called themselves Tarlaks. Those are not Tarlaks."*

Colonel Bannon looked at the screen curiously, "They look like Angels!"

"Which is really kind of ironic, considering that Ahriman mutated them into devilish gargoyles", Gideon replied.

"Are they still alive? Still viable?", the Colonel enquired.

"Oh yes. Very much so", Sandra noted, "Their cryogenic suspension pods are in extremely good working order. They are very much alive."

"Which in itself is amazing, as they are probably well over six million years old", Gideon noted.

"What on Earth are you going to do with them?", the Colonel asked.

"That is undecided, Jim. My people have yet to make a decision about them. We will study them first. If we can determine that their minds are as gentle as their bodies portray, then we then will release them and nurture them", Winchilly replied.

Sandra was somewhat excited, "Perhaps even resurrect their species."

"Let's not get ahead of ourselves, Sandra. We've only found the two of them and that will become a genetic variation issue", Gideon reminded her.

"So far, Gideon. There may be more of them embedded in the rock behind that throne. Who knows how many", Sandra countered.

"True enough. We will need to do a deep scan of the rock again, when we get back there. If there are any others, we will find them", Gideon agreed.

"When will the Martians be leaving for Mimas?", Colonel Bannon asked.

"Again that is undecided. Most of my people are in favour of it, but it has not yet been officially decided", Winchilly replied.

"Winchilly's people are still pawing over the data that we've sent them, as well as the telepathic information that we exchanged with them. However, based on the telepathic conference, I expect the decision will be made very soon", Sandra replied.

"Yes. My people are naturally very cautious. First, they will send scientists and engineers to assess Mimas. If the assessments are favourable, they will send people to retrieve the troop transports. Then my people will migrate to Mimas", Winchilly explained.

29. Assessing the Renovations.

The following day Winchilly received a request from her people to send one of the troop transports down to Mars. The Martians wanted to use the transport to fly their scientists and engineers to Mimas, so that they could access the ice moon's suitability as a possible new home.

Winchilly relayed this request to Gideon and Sandra who in turn, relayed the request to Colonel Bannon. A thousand troop transports were still sitting on the surface of Mimas. Gideon and Sandra gave Colonel Bannon the location of a troop transport that was located directly above one of the handful of Mimasian tunnels that had not been closed off.

Colonel Bannon then ordered a couple of his pilots to deliver the troop transport to the Martians, at the monoliths just to the south of the Elysium subcontinent.

Winchilly's people made quick work of it. Once the troop transport had arrived at the monoliths, the Martians removed most of the troop seating. Then they loaded a large number of scientific instruments and other equipment onto the transport. Once this was done, over eight hundred of their scientists, engineers and technicians boarded the troop transport ship, for transit back to Mimas. However, none of the Martians were actually pilots, as the Martians had no pilots.

The Martians asked if Colonel Bannon's pilots could take them to and fro, from Mimas. The two selected pilots quickly realised, that this could be a major problem, if later, the Martians wanted to actually move to Mimas. All of the troop transport's pilots were back on the Earth. Gideon and Sandra had sent them all there, along with all of the Colonial Troops.

The two pilots conferred with Colonel Bannon, who asked them to teach the Martians how to fly the troop transports. The plan was, to teach a group of Martians to fly the transports and they would then train their fellow Martians to do the same. The two pilots, however, believed that they needed to stay with the Martians for much longer, in order to ensure that the new Martian pilots would be proficient enough for such a task. They needed to ensure that the Martian pilots, had the necessary level of skills to carry out both the task of piloting the transports and the training of newer pilots. Colonel Bannon agreed to the pilot's secondment to the Martians, until such time that the Martians were fully proficient.

The fact that four of the eight Martian trainee pilots, were in fact young Martian women, had absolutely nothing to do with the two colonial pilot's decision making processes. The four female Martian trainee pilots on the other hand, being telepathic, of course knew otherwise and they thought that the situation was quite amusing. Colonel Bannon was of course completely oblivious to this particular situation.

Soon the troop transport was flown back to Mimas and landed above the tunnel that led into the Mimasian interior. Sandra and Gideon had been observing the troop transport's approach to Mimas. As soon as the transport had safely landed on Mimas, they both placed their arms around Winchilly and then they teleported across to the transport, taking Winchilly along with them.

The trio appeared suddenly inside the transport, in a small flash of blue light. At first this startled the two transport pilots, their trainees and the Martian scientists who were nearby.

"*How?*", the nearest Martian trainee enquired.
"*They have these skills that we do not. I know not how it works*", Winchilly replied.
"Doctor Reas!", one of the pilots greeted, it was Carl, the same pilot who

had crashed with Gideon and Sandra on Mars, before the Mimasians had revealed themselves.

"Carl. It's good to see you again", Gideon replied.

"Training some new pilots we see", Sandra noted, with an amused smile on her face.

"Why yes. Our Martian friends will need lots of pilots, if they're going to make use of all of these troop transports", Carl replied, his face only slightly red.

Gideon turned to the Martian Elder who was in charge of the expedition, "Sandra and I have altered the interior of Mimas quite significantly. We'll accompany you into the interior and explain those changes as best we can."

"Thank you, that would be most helpful", the Elder replied.

The trio then led the large group of Martian scientists and technicians into the ice shell of Mimas, while Carl and his fellow pilot, Marin, continued to train the new Martian pilots.

"We found these designs in your databases. Rather than simply walking everywhere, we thought they'd be a far more useful mode of transportation. So we built quite a few of them", the Martian Elder noted.

A large number of Segways were unloaded from the troop transport in flat packs and they were in the process of being assembled in the staging area within the ice tunnel.

"We have left only ten tunnels through the ice shell open. This central tunnel and nine others around it", Sandra informed them, adding, "When we get to the rock shell, those tunnels all come together and open up into a much larger space. From that huge chamber, a single larger tunnel extends all of the way through the rock shell and into the Mimasian interior."

"Is it open all of the way through?", the Elder enquired.

"Not at all, Elder. There is a bulkhead and a pressure door at the beginning of the rock shell tunnel and another bulkhead and pressure door a few hundred yards further in. Together they form a rather large airlock that can be sealed off if necessary", Sandra informed him.

The group then Segwayed swiftly down the ten-kilometre-long ice tunnel, taking a little over thirty minutes to almost reach the rock shell.

"Perhaps, Elder, your people should have studied our jeep designs", Gideon remarked.

"Perhaps. We will send your recommendations to our technicians", the Martian Elder replied.

The ice tunnel slowly began to change from a straight line into a gradual spiral, that eventually opened up into a rather large broad circular open chamber, situated along the rock wall. The size of the chamber was enormous. As they entered the open space, they could see the other nine ice tunnel entrances, evenly spaced around the perimeter of the chamber.

In the very centre of the broad circular chamber, there was a single large tunnel that led into the rock wall itself. It was perpendicular to the rock wall and a very broad, gradual funnel-shaped opening led into it. Without looking back Gideon and Sandra Segwayed towards the tunnel and over the funnel-like entrance. Winchilly and her people quickly followed behind them without any hesitation.

As they rounded the edge of the funnel-shaped opening, they transitioned from the rock shell into the tunnel proper. Even though they were now perpendicular to the rock shell, they had noticed no changes in the gravitational forces. The very rock beneath their Segways, was always the down direction, no matter where they were situated.

"Gravity plating is built into the tunnel walls", Gideon explained, as they passed the first of the bulkheads and its pressure doors.

The Martian Elder simply replied, *"Yes. Understood."*

The Mimasian rock shell, was on average twenty five kilometres thick and it took well over an hour to traverse the distance to the service tunnels that branched off from it. They were still five kilometres from the interior and stopped for a short break.

The Martian Elder commented, *"Your jeep recommendation, will have my recommendation for approval, Doctor Reas"*, then he enquired, *"How far is it to the interior?"*

"About another fifteen to twenty minutes or so", Gideon noted.

"And these side tunnels?", the Elder asked.

"There are networks of tunnels under the Northern Island Mountain Peak. There is a corresponding Southern Island Mountain Peak in Mimas's southern hemisphere", Sandra explained, further noting,   "All of these tunnel networks are separated from each other, by the Circular Seas, Southern, Northern and Central."

"Circular Seas?", the Martian Elder questioned.

"It will make much more sense when you see them for yourselves", Sandra replied.

After a short break, they all continued their journey along the tunnel towards the Mimasian interior. A little over twenty minutes later, the tunnel began to change once more, levelling out and becoming a broad spiral. Shortly thereafter a side tunnel appeared, down which they could see light. Gideon and Sandra led the group down this tunnel towards the beckoning light. When they finally reached the end of the tunnel and entered the light, the sight of the interior of Mimas was breathtaking.

The group found themselves on a broad ledge on the flanks of the six-kilometre-tall Northern Island Mountain Peak. In front, below them was the thirty kilometre-plus broad, Northern Circular Sea. On the far side of this circular sea was a ring of mountains, the Northern Mountain Ring, the highest peaks of which reached an impressive five kilometres in height. These majestic mountains were simply breathtaking to behold and yet, somewhat disturbing, more than a few of the Martians found themselves suffering from vertigo and had to sit down.

"My apologies, Elder. I should have given you some warning. Mimas is an inside out world. It takes a little getting use to", Gideon replied apologetically, he had forgotten that the Martians were not use to the unusual horizons that certain colonies presented.

"No. No need to apologise, Gideon", the Martian Elder, replied, *"I don't believe that any amount of warnings or preparations would have helped. This is something that had to be seen to be believed."*

This sight, as spectacular as it was, was dwarfed by the vista beyond it. A few of the Martians who had found it necessary to sit down averted their eyes from the majestic view.

Winchilly, who had become accustomed to the cylindrical horizon inside of the Aries Colony encouraged her people, *"Please, be not afraid, the disorientation will pass. I assure you, it will pass."*

The interior of Mimas was a world on the inside of a roughly spherical shell and in this world, the horizon curved up and around them on all sides. Beyond the Northern Mountain Ring was a broad stretch of land. From the mountains, the land reduced in height, abruptly at first and then gradually, forming high hill country, followed by smaller undulating hills and finally plains.

A broad central circular sea perhaps thirty kilometres across stretched around the interior equator of Mimas. The Martians all stood in gaping awe of the vista before them and gradually even those who had been disoriented regained their feet.

"The first time I saw the interior of the Aries Colony, I felt the same", Winchilly remarked, then added, *"Tomorrow, they will be fine. They won't even know what the fuss was about."*

Rivers flowed from the Ring Mountains, down the valleys, through the hill country and across to plains to the Central Equatorial Sea. Scattered here and there across the landscape, were a large number of lakes, some were large, but most were small. Winchilly and her people looked out upon the vista before them. Above the bowl-shaped Mimasian interior floated clouds of varying types.

Billowing cumulus clouds drifted high above the Equatorial Sea. Cumulonimbus clouds drifted around the Northern Ring Mountains and rains were seen falling on some of the mountain slopes. Within the mountainous ring itself, above the Northern Circular Sea were lesser, more wispy clouds and there were thick mists along both the near and far shorelines.

The small Central Sun, a controlled fusion reaction, burned brightly in the very centre of Mimas, providing both warmth and light to this inside out world. A thick layer of ozone, high above the highest clouds, protected the land that was so close beneath, from the more harmful of radiations.

"My people have seen into the minds of our enslavers. This is not what we have seen. Mimas was almost a barren place, a desert place", the Martian Elder noted, asking, *"How is this even possible?"*

Gideon answered as honestly as he could, "We are terraformers, Elder, Sandra and I. We both believed that the original builders, would have put in place environmental control systems. So we searched those out and when we found them. We adjusted the settings to bring about these changes. We found we could transform this place, Sandra and I, so we did."

"Your gifts are stronger than any that we've seen. That much is certain", the Martian Elder replied, *"Perhaps, just perhaps, your both being terraformers has something to do with it, as you, yourself have just noted."*

Sandra remarked, "Elder. What you see before you is repeated on the far side of Mimas. We transformed the entire interior of Mimas from the Northern Hemisphere all the way to the Southern Hemisphere and everything in between."

"And then added in a few touches ourselves, like the Equatorial Sea", Gideon added.

"That was a dry seabed, just a desert basin, now it's a thirty-kilometre-wide stretch of sea circling the entire interior circumference of Mimas", Sandra commented.

Gideon added, "As a terraformer scientist, I was even surprised by how quickly the Mimasian flora responded to the extra rainfall. The plant life took off and began to respond and grow, spreading almost immediately. It was fascinating to watch. Truly fascinating."

"It is a very beautiful place, but is it safe, Gideon?", the Martian Elder asked.

"Elder, we purged the entirety of Mimas clean of Ahriman's evil. We removed all of the Mimasian's filth. We even eliminated any creatures that were dangerous or carnivorous. Any animals that could be a threat were eliminated", Sandra stepped in and assured him.

"The only things we couldn't easily remove, were the remains of the destroyed weapon systems, although we were able to completely disable them", Gideon admitted.

"It appears that we will need a recycling program then, assuming that we decide to stay

of course", the Martian Elder replied.

"And the remaining flora and fauna?", Winchilly enquired.

"We left it as we found it, Winchilly", Sandra admitted.

"We will need to check for ourselves, but any flora and fauna that we have on Mars, but cannot be found here, we will need to bring across with us", the Martian Elder noted.

"Any grains, fruits and vegetables from Earth, that you might fancy, we can organise that as well", Gideon commented.

"Thank you, Doctor Reas. That would be most helpful", the Martian Elder replied, then he added, *"We will set up our primary research base here and study every aspect of this world."*

"As small as Mimas is Elder, it is still a very large world. We will need flyers to access most of it", Winchilly noted.

"We do have some flyers on the transport. We can retrieve more from Mars if required, perhaps even construct and bring up a few jeeps", the Martian Elder replied.

"Elder. The most important thing in this world, at least to our minds, is at the top of the Southern Island Peak. The Thols", Gideon remarked.

"Yes. Yes. I must admit, that I am very interested in seeing these Thols", the Martian Elder replied, adding, *"I wish to see for myself, what the Tarlaks evolved from."*

"And whether or not we can bring them back into existence", Winchilly added.

"Yes, of course, Winchilly. The Thols are a priority", the Martian Elder agreed, *"Tomorrow, when the flyers are brought in, we will go there. We will assess them."*

"I simply do not understand", the Martian Elder commented, questioning, *"If Mimas could be turned into a paradise, why was it so arid, a virtual desert world? It makes absolutely no sense!"*

"We have some theories about that, Elder, but we'll never really know for certain", Gideon replied.

"It could be possible, that over time, the Mimasians lost any understanding as to how to manage their own environment", Sandra speculated.

"Sandra, the environmental control room was clean. That indicates that the room was maintained to some degree. At the very least it was cleaned regularly", Gideon noted, speculating, "Perhaps one of the cleaners, accidentally knocked the environmental controls to their lowest levels. Then following Sandra's reasoning, none of the Mimasians had any clue on how to reset the controls."

"That really doesn't sound very plausible", the Martian Elder replied, with a psychic chuckle.

"No, it doesn't, Elder" Gideon agreed, then added, "It's more than likely that Ahriman himself, wanted his world that way. The less habitable a world is, the less population it can maintain."

"That does sound far more plausible", the Martian Elder agreed.

Sandra stepped in, "We will never really know, Elder. Not for certain. The main thing is, to make Mimas perfect for you guys."

"Yes and we do appreciate that very much", the Martian Elder replied.

The next day, there were eight hundred Martian scientists, engineers and technicians, along with all of their equipment on the broad ledge and in the tunnels, overlooking the Mimasian vista. They quickly formed into groups, with each group being designated a section of Mimas to survey and study.

The Martian Elder's group was to proceed straight to what had been Ahriman's royal chambers, where the Thols in their crystalline cryogenic suspension pods could be observed. Gideon advised the Elder's team, that they would need to take some Segways with them as well.

The Martian Elder's team flew their flyers across the Northern Circular Sea and over the peaks of the Northern Ring Mountains. Once they on the other side of the mountainous ring, they had a far better view of the Mimasian northern hemisphere. The mountain slopes dropped away quickly and they were soon flying above hill country with valleys, rivers and quite a few small lakes.

The thicker Mimasian flora had hugged the mountain slopes during the times of Ahriman. With Gideon's and Sandra's renovations, however, this flora had begun to encroach upon the hill country. The hill country then fell away into plains, that gradually sloped down towards the Equatorial Sea. The sparse flora that had existed in the dry times of Ahriman, was beginning to quickly flourish in the newly terraformed environment. Scattered here and there, could be seen the destroyed hulks of military equipment, both Human and Mimasian.

Soon they were flying across the Equatorial Sea itself and they could clearly see that the southern hemisphere was, as noted by Gideon and Sandra, almost identical to the northern hemisphere. The overall tapestry was the same, only the finer details were different. Once they were across the Equatorial Sea, the Martian Elder's team found themselves flying over plains once more. Only this time the plains were gently sloping upwards, towards the hill country and the Southern Ring Mountains beyond. The pattern with valleys, rivers, and lakes was also very similar to the northern hemisphere. More destroyed weapons systems from both sides were also visible.

It wasn't long before the Martian Elder's team was flying up the slopes of the Southern Ring Mountains. This was a far older region of Mimas, the flora was thick and the mountain slopes were quite heavily forested. Somewhat more so, than was seen on the slopes of the Northern Ring Mountains. The group traversed the peaks of the Southern Ring Mountains and Gideon then led them directly across the Southern Circular Sea, to a broad ledge on the slopes of the Southern Island Mountain Peak. They all landed their flyers and stepped out to stretch their legs.

"This place looks very familiar", the Martian Elder noted.

"It should, Elder. The major features in both hemispheres are essentially duplicated. So both the northern and southern hemisphere will have a lot of similarities", Sandra explained, adding, "This ledge, the landing, that tunnel, are the same in both hemispheres."

"And as we need to spiral up the inside of this mountain peak, all the way to the top, we will be needing those Segways", Gideon informed the group.

"Then we had better start unloading our equipment then. Those Segways won't unpack and assemble themselves", the Martian Elder decided.

Once the Segways were unpacked and assembled, it wasn't long before Gideon and Sandra were leading the Martian Elder's team, along the long spiral tunnel that wrapped its way around the interior of the Southern Island Mountain Peak. At each level, smaller tunnels branched off in many directions, while the spiral tunnel continued its gradual climb towards the top of the mountain peak.

Gideon had been right to recommend using the Segways, as it quickly became apparent, that traversing the spiral tunnel by foot would have been completely impractical. It was also readily apparent, that the Mimasians had flown through these tunnels. It took several hours to traverse the long spiral tunnel all the way up to the top.

When they had reached the level of the Mimasian control centre, they all stopped and got off of their Segways. They were all tired from the journey across the interior of Mimas, but way too excited to stop and rest. Here was where the ice moon's scanner chambers and control chambers were. Further along, there was the final tunnel that led to Ahriman's royal chambers.

"From down that tunnel, you can scan the entire environment in space around Mimas", Gideon pointed down one short tunnel, then he pointed down another tunnel, "Down that one, you have the Mimasian control centre."

Sandra followed up, "From there, you can pretty much control the whole of the Mimas, except for the environmental controls."

Gideon then added, "Everything from the Mimasian fusion Sun to the Mimasian ion drive system, can be controlled from there."

Sandra then added, "The ion drive system has a secondary control centre at the base of this peak. The ion drive can be controlled from here, but must it be started from down there. The environmental controls are in a chamber, just one level up from the ion drive's secondary control centre."

The Martian Elder replied, *"Thank you, Gideon, Sandra. We are taking note. Our scientists and engineers will study these very soon"*, he then asked, *"Where do we find the Thols?"*

Gideon smiled, "For that, you follow us down that long tunnel over there."

Sandra took the lead and started walking towards the tunnel that Gideon had pointed to.

It didn't take too long for the group to traverse the tunnel to Ahriman's royal chambers. The tunnel opened up into a large chamber, on the far side of which was an opening that led into Ahriman's throne room. They all crossed the royal chamber and entered Ahriman's throne room. Ahriman's throne on the opposite side of the cavernous room, was of the deepest, blackest obsidian and highly polished to a mirror-like surface.

In front of the dark shiny throne, on either side, were the two crystalline cryogenic suspension pods, that Gideon and Sandra had extracted from the very rock behind the throne. The group quickly walked across the throne room, to the cryogenic suspension pods and were stunned by what they saw.

The Thols had very light, pale coloured skin. Six slender fingers on each hand, that were set in three pairs per hand, but completely without any claws, just their finger nails, short rounded and smooth. Their arms and legs were very human like and appeared to be in the correct proportion to their bodies, as a human might expect. Although, they were much smaller than the average human, at only about five feet tall.

Their wings were both large and had a delightfully creamy flesh colour to them. At their base, they formed into a long prehensile tail, with a flat, rounded end, not pointed or spade-like, like the Mimasians. Their wings were attached by powerful flight muscles, that wrapped around their chests and which anchored to a much larger than normal sternum. The female Thol had breasts like a humanoid being might, however, they were configured lower, below the flight muscles.

Their skin was smooth, with very little, if any body hair at all. Upon their heads, they had fine hair flowing in long, blond wavy locks. Hair that was being held back by head bands, made of what looked like, fine threads of golden flax.

Their faces were almost angelic in appearance, small, with very delicate refined features. They didn't have any horns or brow ridges at all and their teeth were small and indicated, that they were probably vegetarians. Their eyes were a deep crystal blue, with a slight hint of purple and showed the sparks of intelligence. Their eyes sat within shallow eye sockets. These two beings were as different to the Mimasians as was chalk to cheese and yet, there were very definite similarities.

"Oh my!", the Martian Elder exclaimed, *"I can see where the Tarlaks came from, but how and why did Ahriman turn such gentle creatures into those brutish demons? I will never understand!"*

To which Winchilly remarked, *"Evil is what evil does, Elder."*

"Indeed, Winchilly. Indeed", the Martian Elder replied, then questioned, *"Only the two of them?"*

"We are not sure, Elder. Sandra, let's find out", Gideon replied.

Gideon and Sandra concentrated on the rock wall behind the throne, in the same region where they had found the two Thols. At first, they found nothing, only the hollow spaces where the two cryogenic suspension pods had been. Sandra sighed and stopped searching. Gideon, however, did not. After several minutes of concentration, Gideon stopped as well.

"Well, Gideon? Did you find anything?", Sandra queried.

Gideon was slow to answer, then the grin on his face gave it all away, "About another seventy five feet deeper into the rock. There's another forty cryogenic suspension pods!", he exclaimed.

"Forty?", the Martian Elder questioned.

"Yes, Elder. Forty!", Gideon confirmed, speculating, "It could be that these first two are special, perhaps leaders. Those headbands could denote royalty! The others, perhaps they're common folk or maybe they're even members of their royal court?"

"Royalty?", Sandra queried.

"Potentially", Gideon replied, then noted, "It will take us quite a while to extricate these cryogenic suspension pods from the rock."

One by one, Gideon and Sandra focused on the cryogenic suspension pods and slowly extricated them from within the rock. They separated the cryopods out by the gender of the occupant inside. They placed them in front of the obsidian throne, on their left was the first cryopod they'd extracted, possibly a King. On their right, was the second cryopod they'd extracted, possibly a Queen.

When they had finally finished extracting the forty cryopods, they took stock. On the King's right-hand side, there were ten cryopods and on the Queen's left-hand side, there were thirty cryopods. All up, the cryopods contained eleven male and thirty one female Thols. Gideon and Sandra were both exhausted and needed to rest.

The Martian Elder was excited, *"Forty two Thols! Forty Two! We will need to study them of course and we will need to be very, very careful. Their numbers are so very small and they look so fragile, but with our skills, our technology, perhaps, just perhaps, we can resurrect their species!",* he was ecstatic.

Winchilly had a hunch and informed the Martian Elder, *"Elder, the way their numbers are, if you leave out the Royals, they're three to one, female to male. Whoever put them into cryogenic suspension, was hoping that one day they'd be revived and their species resurrected."*

The Martian Elder considered that for several long moments, *"You may be right, Winchilly! Their numbers match a ratio for quickly breeding up their population. Whoever built this generation ship, built into it secrets, that I doubt that even Ahriman himself knew existed. They were forced to build it perhaps, but nonetheless, they defiantly added in this marvellous little secret. Right behind Ahriman's very royal throne as well!"*

Winchilly had never heard the Martian Elder being so excited before and she let Gideon and Sandra know of it. Gideon and Sandra, being warn out from extracting the cryogenic suspension pods from rock wall, let Winchilly know that they could discuss it later, after a good nights sleep. They explained to Winchilly, that the next day was just as likely, to be as busy as the first one. Winchilly agreed.

30. Barriers.

The eight hundred Martian scientists, engineers and technicians had spread out across the interior of Mimas and were crawling over every inch of the ice moon. Was Mimas suitable for their purposes? Would the Martians be happy to live within the interior of Mimas? It was very difficult to tell, the Martians were not saying anything about their assessments. It was more than a week before any signs began to show as to how their assessments were going.

Mimas was now directly in line with Mars, a million kilometres away in the direction of the Sun, at Mars Sun Lagrangian point one. The cometary-like out-gassing from Mimas continued unabated, driven by the Sun's warmth and solar wind. This vast coma of gas and dust had spread out for millions of kilometres in every direction, completely engulfing Mars in its entirety.

The gas and dust spiralled into the Martian gravity well and much of the gas and dust was being absorbed by Mars, adding to its new atmosphere. All of the Martian colonies in high Martian orbit, including the Aries colony were engulfed by the cloud of tenuous gas and dust, their attitude control thrusters working overtime to keep each colony on station, pointing towards the Sun.

Gideon, Sandra and Winchilly had returned to the Aries colony in high Martian orbit. They were staying in an apartment in the northern end cap, close to its axis of rotation. The gravity in the apartment was far closer to that which Winchilly was used to. They were all eagerly awaiting news as to how the assessments of Mimas were going when they received a message from Colonel Bannon.

Gideon read out the message aloud, *"Mimas has settled into a stable position at Mars-Sun Lagrangian point one, approximately one million kilometres from Mars. We have noticed that the rotation rate of Mimas has increased from roughly two point four rotations per hour to a touch under two point eight rotations per hour. Colonel James J Bannon."*

"Well, that was to be expected", Sandra remarked, explaining, "Mimas settling into Lagrangian point one that is. We've all been inside Mimas's coma for days now."

"It also means that our Martian friends have complete control of its ion drive", Gideon noted.

Winchilly commented, *"Increasing the rotation rate of Mimas, indicates that my people have increased the centrifugal force. They've stepped up the artificial gravity to almost point four gs."*

"They would only do that to make the interior of Mimas more similar to Mars. That does sound like a good sign", Sandra noted.

"Perhaps, perhaps not", Winchilly replied noncommittally, cautioning, *"They may simply be testing the Mimasian control systems to the ion drive. It does not necessarily mean, that they will accept Mimas as our new home."*

"Yet, it is still a good sign though Winchilly", Gideon remarked.

Winchilly was still noncommittal, *"Perhaps."*

The next day a request came through from Carl Trigg, one of Colonel Bannon's pilots, who, along with his colleague, Marin, had been training the Martians to fly the troop transports.

Gideon received the message and then read out the request, *"Our Martian friends have asked me to forward this request. They would like to review a catalogue of food plants that we might have available. Fruits, vegetables and grains. That sort of thing. Carl Trigg."*

"Now that's very interesting. They'd only do that if they wanted to select foods to transplant to Mimas", Sandra noted, then asked, "Winchilly, what's your take on this news?"

Winchilly was still noncommittal, *"Perhaps, perhaps not. Any foods my people select could equally be used within the monoliths on Mars."*

Gideon agreed, "That is true enough, Winchilly. They'd be interested in new foods, whether they choose to move to Mimas or not. I know I would."

"This is so frustrating. Has Carl given us any hint at all, as to what they want to do?", Sandra asked.

Gideon replied, "They want to review our vegetarian food products. That's pretty much it, Sandra."

"Well, Gideon, since you're our lead terraformer! I'll leave up it to you to send over a copy of the relevant information to them", Sandra replied before leaving the room.

Winchilly looked at Gideon with a curious, questioning look.

"Sandra prefers certainty, not knowing, well she does find it quite frustrating", Gideon replied to the unspoken look, he then added, "I have to admit it as well, Winchilly. I also find it quite frustrating."

"Should I go to her?", Winchilly asked.

"Maybe touch base with your people first and see if you can get an answer", Gideon advised.

"I will do that. While I do so, Gideon. You should put together that information for my people to review", Winchilly replied.

"Agreed, Winchilly, agreed", Gideon replied.

The next day, Gideon had his data ready to send to Mimas, he looked at Winchilly and held up his data crystal, "What did you find out from your people, Winchilly?"

"When we get there. I will ask them", Winchilly replied, then asked, *"We go there now? Yes?"*

Sandra quickly stepped in, "You forgot, Gideon. Winchilly can't just jump onto a compucomm and talk with them. She has to go there physically."

"Oh. My apologies, Winchilly. It slipped my mind", Gideon admitted, then he reached out to both Sandra and Winchilly.

Once the trio were physically linked together, Gideon and Sandra concentrated. They searched for the Martian Elder on Mimas. They located him in Ahriman's throne room at the top of the Southern Island Mountain Peak. In a small burst of light, the trio disappeared from the Aries colony in high Martian orbit and reappeared a split second late inside of Mimas.

The Martian Elder turned around to look towards the trio when he sensed their presence.

Gideon held out his data crystal and the Martian Elder reached out to take it, "This crystal contains the catalogues you requested", he informed him.

The Martian Elder took the data crystal and passed it to one of his colleagues, *"Thank you. Our people will review the contents straight away."*

"When you've decided what crops and produce you require. Let us know and we'll deliver the relevant seed banks to wherever you wish", Gideon advised.

The Martian Elder nodded in response and Winchilly then asked, *"Elder, have our assessments been favourable?"*

"So far yes, Winchilly, but we are still undecided", the Martian Elder replied, then upon noticing Winchilly's apparent disappointment, *"To leave our home is a big decision, Winchilly and we must not take it lightly."*

Winchilly nodded in understanding.

Sandra looked over to the cryogenic pods on either side of Ahriman's old throne. Two of the Thols had been revived, the first two that Gideon and Sandra had discovered. They were squatting down on their haunches in front of their cryopods.

"Ah yes. We have revived the two leaders", the Martian Elder advised, *"It is very good that you have arrived at this time. Good timing indeed. We have been unable to communicate with them. Perhaps you might help?"*

The trio followed the Martian Elder as he walked over to the two Thols and the scientists attempting to communicate with them.

"These cryogenic suspension pods are very old, perhaps as much as six million years or more", the Martian Elder advised them, adding, *"This is not the technology of the Tarlaks either."*

"You said you can't communicate with them?", Gideon questioned.

"We had the same problem with the Tarlaks, when they first conquered our world all those many generations ago", the Martian Elder noted, explaining, *"We could not see their thoughts clearly at all and it took a long time for the Tarlaks to be able to speak to us, in a way that we could understand. Their own original language consisted of clicks, barks and guttural sounds. We seem to have a similar problem with these Thols."*

"Couldn't you just tweak them?", Sandra enquired, adding, *"You know, like you did with us."*

"Oh no. That wouldn't work, Sandra. You, your people, are very much like us", the Martian Elder noted, explaining, *"Before we were conquered, our people spent a million years or more, genetically tweaking your people's dna, to be more and more like ours. These Thols are far too different."*

Winchilly noticed that Carl Trigg and his fellow pilot, Marin, were helping the Martian scientists and drew Gideon and Sandra's attention.

"I thought you were training pilots, Carl?", Gideon queried.

"We were, Doctor Reas. Our Martian trainees learn very quickly. The first eight pilots we trained are now very proficient and they're currently training eight more each. So that's seventy two all up. If they do decide to migrate to

Mimas, we will need a lot more pilots though", Carl replied, before explaining, "The Elder thought that we might be able to help them communicate with the Thols."

Sandra noticed two Martian women close by to Carl and Marin, "And your new Martian friends?"

"Oh yes. They are both pilots. Our star pupils, in fact. Highly accomplished", Carl replied, praising the trainees, while he and Marin both began to blush.

The young Martian women both smiled in amusement.

Gideon approached Carl and quietly queried, "Star pupils, Carl?"

Carl smiled back and replied quietly as if no one would hear, "What can I say, Doctor Reas? I look into her beautiful emerald eyes and all I can see is stars!"

That statement seemed to elicit even more smiles and amusement from the two Martian women, who of course being telepaths, heard everything.

Sandra sent a thought to Gideon, *"Carl and Marin both appear to be quite smitten"*, Winchilly and the Martian Elder both picked up on the thought.

Gideon replied in kind, *"The young Martian ladies appear to be quite smitten as well."*

The Martian Elder sent the trio a few thoughts, *"This seems to be a common occurrence. Our young women find your men folk enticing"*, he then frowned, *"I myself find it strange and unusual."*

"Winchilly?", Sandra enquired, hoping that she might elaborate.

Winchilly's golden-tanned features suddenly showed a slight tinge of red and then she slowly tried to answer, blushing all the more as she did so.

"Martian men have highly ordered minds, very structured, very few stray thoughts", then she looked at Sandra and Gideon, *"Your minds are chaotic, controlled chaos,*

with stray thoughts everywhere. It is very intriguing and very alluring."

"You see", the Martian Elder replied, almost laughing telepathically, *"I see strange and unusual. Winchilly sees intriguing and alluring."*

Sandra replied, "I think, Winchilly's sweet" and then she reached out and hugged her affectionately.

The Martian Elder noted, *"The are other men from your world back on Mars, inside of our monoliths. They too are smitten with some of our young Martian women. Those young women are all smitten in return. Our sociologists are studying the phenomena."*

Gideon chuckled to himself internally, then looked at Carl and Marin, then looked at the two Martian women, "This reminds me of a very old saying, Carl. A fish and a bird may fall in love, but where will they build their nest?"

One of the young Martian women, Carina, looked confused and responded, *"Carl. What does this mean? We are neither fish nor bird. Either of us. I do not understand the meaning of these words."*

Carl replied, trying to explain, "It is a metaphor my darling. It is also something that we should perhaps discuss later."

Winchilly looked at Gideon and Sandra, *"Does not the same apply to us?"*

Sandra looked at Winchilly and replied, "That too, Winchilly, is also something that we will need to discuss later."

Gideon slowly and cautiously approached the two Thols, so as not to alarm them. The Thols looked at Gideon and began to *'speak'* in clicks, soft barks and melodic trills.

Marin noted, "Those clicking sounds, they're almost like the click language of the Kalahari Bushmen. Very rare these days. Not that many of them left", he was from South Africa.

Carl also noted, "Those trilling sounds are very similar to the trilling of magpies."

"Thank you both. I'm noticing that already", Gideon replied, as he squatted down in front of them and attempted to see if he could understand the Troll's thoughts.

Several minutes later, after yet more clicking and trilling from the Thols, Gideon slowly stood up, "I'm picking up fear, uncertainty and concern. Just emotions really. Not much else."

The Martian Elder commented, *"Yes. We can pick that up as well, but as you say, not much else."*

Sandra stepped in, "They want us to release their people!"

"How do you know that, Sandra?", Gideon asked.

"Didn't I tell you, Gideon? I'm multilingual. I speak at least eight languages", Sandra explained.

"You never mentioned that before, Sandra", Gideon responded.

"I never thought about it before, Gideon", Sandra admitted, then explained, "My father's language was German. My mother's language was English. Of course, my au pair spoke Spanish. So I actually grew up multilingual with three languages. I pick up languages ridiculously easily."

"Then why I am over here? I only know two languages, English and bad English", Gideon replied.

"Well then, Gideon, we certainly won't be teaching them bad English, will we?", Sandra replied.

Carl and Marin could be heard snickering in the background.

Sandra and Gideon swapped places and then Sandra crouched down in front of the two Thols. The Thols then clicked, barked softly and trilled at Sandra. Sandra listened carefully and intently while attempting to understand their thoughts.

"They are very scared and uncertain. They are extremely worried about their people as well", Sandra reported, adding, "They want us to free their people and they want an explanation. They are very confused and they don't understand what has happened to them. Why are they here? Where is here? Who are we? Meaning us. They just have so many questions."

Very carefully and very slowly, Sandra reached out to the female Thol.

Sandra gently touched and then stroked the female Thol's cheek, thinking to her, "Please don't be afraid. We found you here in these sleep pods. You and your people have been asleep for many millennia. We will help you."

The female Thol then turned to the male and smiled, then she clicked a few times and then trilled. Somehow she had understood and explained it to her mate. He smiled in return.

"I'm going to try something", Sandra commented and then she closed her eyes and concentrated on the female Thol.

Both Thols waited patiently, while Sandra sat crouched in front of them in deep concentration.

After several long minutes, Sandra opened her eyes and then spoke to the female Thol, "Please. If you can understand me, trill twice and only twice."

The female Thol then trilled precisely twice.

"What did you do, Sandra?", Gideon enquired.

"I'm multilingual, Gideon, gifted with languages. I'm not entirely sure how I did it, but I believe that I've given this female Thol, a language abstraction layer", Sandra replied, "She can understand us now. We won't understand their clicks and trills, but we should be able to understand their thoughts."

The Martian Elder approached the Thols, crouched down and thought to the female, *"Please. Do not be afraid. We are here to help you. Can you understand me?"*

The female Thol clicked, trilled and softly barked, the Martian Elder picked up her thoughts, *"Yes. I understand you. I will not be afraid. Please, do for him, what you did for me so that he will understand you as well."*

Gideon, Sandra and Winchilly were also able to pick up on her thoughts, as were the other Martians within the throne room.

The Martian Elder noted, *"This is a splendid thing. Sandra, please do the same for her mate."*

Sandra focused on the male Thol, while the female softly clicked and trilled to him, *"Be not afraid my love. These others will help us."*

Gideon thought to Winchilly, *"This is remarkable."*

"I did not know, that Sandra could do this thing", Winchilly replied.

"Neither did I, Winchilly. It seems that we each have our gifts and they are not all the same", Gideon remarked, *"and we, ourselves, don't know that we even have them until we discover them."*

A few long minutes later, Sandra opened her eyes and spoke to the male Thol, "Can you understand me? If you can, please trill twice and only twice."

The male Thol trilled twice and smiled a broad smile, he then turned to his mate and then clicked and trilled, *"I can understand them now. How is this possible?"*

Everyone nearby, except Carl and Marin, picked up on his thoughts and understood them.

His mate clicked, barked and trilled back, *"They have gifts that we do not. It seems to work. Let us be happy with that."*

Both Thols then rose to their feet, as did Sandra and the Martian Elder.

The male Thol gestured towards the other cryogenic pods in the throne room and asked in a short series of clicks and trills, *"What of my people?"*

Gideon replied, "Your people still sleep. They are all safe inside the cryopods."

"Will you awaken them?", the male Thol asked in short quick trills.

Gideon deferred to the Martian Elder, who replied, *"When we have found it safe to do so, then we will awaken them. This world we are in is still being assessed. We do not yet know, if it is suitable. We may awaken your people here or perhaps back on our world. That decision is yet to be made."*

"When will that decision be made?", asked the female Thol with a few trills and clicks.

"That decision will be made soon enough. Until then, your people are safe", the Martian Elder assured them.

The male Thol then smiled and replied, *"We have slept for a long time. We will be patient. We will await your decision. I am Patriarch Yanis and this is my mate, Matriarch Yarule"*, with a series of intermixed clicks, barks and trills.

The Martian Elder replied in thought, *"That is very good, Yanis. While you wait, there is so much that we must tell you and a whole world is waiting for you to see. This one we are assessing. We call it Mimas."*

Both Thols nodded in agreement.

31. The Exodus.

The following day, Carl and Marin took their first eight trainee pilots on a field trip. A request from the Martian Elder. They took the same troop transport, that had brought up the eight hundred Martian scientists, engineers and technicians to Mimas and flew it to the Martian monoliths, just to the south of the Elysium subcontinent on Mars. Once there, they loaded up with a thousand more Martian technical personnel, to further study Mimas and aid in their determinations.

The Martian Elder had also requested that Carl, Marin and their trainee pilots, train a sufficient number of new Martian pilots, to fly the thousand troop transports that were left abandoned on the surface of Mimas. After consultations with Colonel Bannon, back on the Aries colony in high Martian orbit, this was agreed upon. Carl notified Gideon, Sandra and Winchilly of this new development, as it appeared that the Martians were going to make their final decision very soon.

"If they need a thousand pilots, then they must be close to making a decision", Sandra noted.

"They'll need co-pilots as well, so that's a couple of thousand pilots, Sandra. It does looks very likely though, that they will all be emigrating to Mimas", Gideon replied.

Winchilly as usual was noncommittal, *"Perhaps, perhaps not. They may decide to emigrate here or they may have other plans."*

"Other plans?", Sandra enquired.

"Yes, other plans. My people could decide to salvage as much of whatever remains within Mimas, for use on Mars", Winchilly replied, noting, *"However unlikely, it is nonetheless a valid option for my people. They could make that choice."*

"Then how will we know when they've made their decision, Winchilly?",

Sandra asked.

"Gideon will be the first to know", Winchilly replied with a smile.

"Oh yes. The crops and produce. When they've decided upon what they need, they'll request the relevant seed banks", Gideon noted.

"And then they'll inform you, where they want them delivered. The monoliths on Mars or here inside of Mimas", Sandra understood.

Winchilly chimed in, *"That delivery destination will tell you my people's decision, even before they divulge it officially."*

Gideon and Sandra nodded in agreement.

There was chaos in the throne room. The two newly awakened Thols were beside themselves with concern and grief. They had both been looking over the other cryogenic suspension pods, searching for something that was very precious to them.

They searched frantically for their precious item, but to no avail, it was not to be found no matter how many times they searched. Their thoughts became frantic and the Martians were unable to follow those thoughts. So the Martian Elder summoned Gideon, Sandra and Winchilly to the throne room.

When the trio entered the throne room, they immediately saw the problem. The two Thols were frantically searching the other forty cryogenic suspension pods. The female Thol, Yarule, in particular, was extremely distraught. Yarule's frantic and chaotic thoughts could not easily be read by the Martians. Yarule was inconsolable and the Martians had no idea what to do.

Sandra approached Yarule and tried to calm her. Yarule continued searching frantically and appeared to be completely inconsolable. Sandra reached out and took Yarule gently by her arms. She looked directly into Yarule's eyes, then gradually enfolded her arms around her and hugged her gently. Ever so slowly Yarule began to calm down. Yanis stopped searching and watched Sandra and Yarule. He had not realised that other beings could empathise with them so closely.

Yanis gave off a few clicks and a couple of barks, followed by several trills, *"Our Son is missing! Where is our Son? Why is he not here? We, Yarule and I, we need our Son! We must find him!"*

Now the chaos began to make much more sense. The Thols were looking for their missing Son.

Sandra stepped back and looked at Yarule, sadly informing her, "We have only found these forty two cryogenic suspension pods. Yarule, there are no others."

Yarule gave out a loud wailing trill, then began to make soft sobbing sounds, unlike anything they'd heard from the Thols before. Yarule began crying and her tears flowed freely. Sandra put her arms around her and hugged Yarule once more. It took a very long time for Yarule to compose herself and then finally with tears still in her eyes, she gently stepped back from Sandra.

The Martian Elder approached the Thols and slowly explained, *"Our history tells us, that the Emperor of the Tarlaks, Ahriman, would posses the heir to the throne, each time his current host's body expired. Sadly, it is probable, that your Son was the very first in a very long line of hosts."*

The gravity of the Martian Elder's information began to dawn on the Thols. Yanis understood straight away, he stood up straight and became quite stoic. Yarule also understood but continued crying.

As she sobbed, she reached out for Sandra's gentle embrace once more and pressed her face into Sandra's ample bosom.

Sandra continued to console Yarule, gently stroking her long, blond wavy hair. Despite being different species, from different times, Sandra and Yarule were destined to become good friends.

Gideon informed the Thols, "This would have taken place as much as six million years ago or more. You and your people have been in cryogenic suspension for that long."

Yanis clicked and trilled, then added in a few barks, *"We understand. There is nothing to be done. It is sad, my mate is sad, very sad. I am also sad",* he placed his right hand on Yarule's shoulder, *"Yarule will recover, eventually. It will just take time."*

Even with his language of clicks, trills and soft barks, Yanis's sadness was clearly evident.

Sandra stepped back slightly and gently stroked Yarule's left cheek, "Are you okay Yarule? Is there anything we can get you?"

Yarule replied with a series of soft barks and clicks, followed by a few short trills, *"I am anything but okay, Sandra. My Son. My Son is what I want. Can you get him for me? No, you cannot. My Son is, many, many aeons dead. Forever gone!"*

"I have no children, Yarule. I cannot imagine how you feel", Sandra replied sadly, while continuing to stroke Yarule's cheek.

Yarule took Sandra's right hand in hers and lowered it, then trilled, clicked and softly barked, *"I am greatly saddened, but there is nothing to be done. We cannot undo the past. When our world fell to the evil one, we went into cryogenic suspension. Our Son was meant to be with us. Alas, he was not!"*

"Your Son may have been, at least at first. You are here now, so that could indicate that your cryogenic suspension pods were captured and moved. It is quite possible, that your Son was taken at that point", the Martian Elder speculated.

"And what of the evil one now? What has happened to him?", Yarule questioned.

Gideon replied telepathically to everyone in the throne room, *"Ahriman was defeated. He was far too dangerous. We could not let him live. He was rent asunder. We dispersed his evil essence across thousands of cubic light years of intergalactic space. He can never harm anyone ever again!"*

Yarule nodded and then trilled, *"Thankfully his evil is done! There will be no more of it!"*

Once the Thols had calmed down sufficiently and accepted their loss to some small degree, the Martian Elder assigned them some Martian guides to show them around Mimas. The Martian Elder then informed them both, how Mimas, a generation ship, had entered the solar system. How Ahriman and his Tarlaks had conquered the Martian home world in an unprovoked attack, severely damaging the planet's biosphere in the process and rendering the planet uninhabitable.

That only now, were Gideon and Sandra's people from the neighbouring planet, the Earth, terraforming Mars to bring it back to life once more. Gideon then explained, that in around a century or perhaps two, Mars would become a world very much like his Earth, festooned with life once more.

Carl and Marin had arrived back at Mimas with their eight trainee pilots and a further thousand Martian scientists, engineers and technicians. Their troop transport had been over crowded during the crossing, as it was also loaded with more equipment.

The Martians had insisted on bringing as much equipment as they possibly could and that their own discomfort was an irrelevance. Both Carl and Marin had disagreed, however, their two star pupils explained, that their people were use to harsh conditions and treatment, and that the troop transport was more than capable. It was over engineered on the side of safety, like most Earth manufacture ships.

The two pilots now had another problem. They both felt out of their depth but decided to persevere with their task, namely, training a couple of thousand more Martian pilots. They decided, that the best way to train all of the new pilots, would be for the seventy two pilots that had already been trained, to perform the training themselves. That would leave both Carl and Marin in purely supervisory roles. The fact that the highly intelligent Martians were quick to learn and pick up new skills certainly helped.

Their two *'star pupils'*, both young Martian women, suggested that it might help them if their psychic faculties were awakened. Then they could communicate with their Martian students far more effectively.

Carl and Marin both agreed to be tweaked. They then became members of a very exclusive little club, non-psychic humans, who had suddenly had their psychic faculties awakened. This was noticed almost straight away by Gideon and Sandra, as it was by certain others. It took several days for Carl and Marin to become accustomed to their new skills, with their *'star pupils'* helping them.

A few days later the Martian Elder handed back the data crystal of crops and produce to Gideon, *"Is it possible for us to receive seed stock for everything in this catalogue?"*

"Everything, Elder? That would be unusual", Gideon replied, informing him, "I will need to check on availability, but we can probably deliver most of the seeds we have in stock. Please, keep hold of the catalogue. I do have my own copy" and Gideon handed it back to him.

"After you have checked on their availability, please deliver the seed stocks here to Mimas", the Martian Elder advised.

"So you've decided then. You're people are going to migrate?", Sandra enquired.

"Yes, Sandra. We have completed all of our assessments. Mimas will suit our purposes very well indeed", the Martian Elder replied.

"Carl's latest reports indicate that the trainee pilots are almost ready. How soon will your people be making the move?", Gideon asked.

"Very soon, but first we need to awaken the rest of the Thols", the Martian Elder noted, then added, *"They need the companionship of their own kind."*

"Agreed. Yarule is still grieving over the loss of her son. Having thirty other women of her kind around to console her, will certainly help", Sandra replied.

"Yes, that is definitely a good idea, Sandra", Gideon agreed.

"Perhaps, we'll bring over the seed stocks first and place them in storage over in the Northern Island Mountain Peak", Gideon suggested.

Sandra added, "That is a good idea, Gideon, except, instead of us delivering the seed stocks, the trainee Martian pilots could fly over to the Aries colony and pick everything up. You know, practice runs. It will be good for them."

"I agree. Once you have determined their availability and made the necessary preparations, Gideon. I will then make the arrangements for our pilots to pick up the seed stocks", the Martian Elder replied.

"Then, Elder. I'd better get started straight away", Gideon replied.

A couple of days later, Carl and Marin organised a number of transport flights. The transport craft were actually troop transports, so first, ten of the transports were stripped of their seating and bunking to allow for the storage of goods. They organised one transport to fly to the Aries colony in high Martian orbit, to collect the crop and produce seed stocks. However, the Martians also had their own crop and produce seed stocks back on Mars. They also needed to transfer these as well, so one transport was organised to collect those from the Martian monoliths, to the south of the Elysium subcontinent.

The remaining eight transports were also sent to Mars, but to collect flat pack housing. Housing that was designed to be put into a suitable location and then it would unfolded itself automatically into its final shape. These houses were also self founding, creating their own foundations and damp coursing, as the first step in the process. The first Martian towns and villages would be constructed using that flat pack housing technique. They would literally pop up in a matter of hours.

As these flights were to be trainee pilot flights as well, Carl, Marin and the first eight Martian pilots would be at the controls of one transport each. They would each take eight Martian trainee pilots with them. It took several days for everything to be prepared, including the preparations of the required seed stocks and flat pack housing. Then the ten transports left Mimas for the respective destinations.

While the transport preparations were taking place, Gideon, Sandra and Winchilly were helping with the awakening of the remaining forty Thols. One by one, the Martian technicians awakened the Thols from their aeons long sleep. As each Thol was woken up, Yanis and Yarule, sat by their side and when they were lucid enough, they explained the situation to them.

After which, Sandra would approach the newly awoken Thol and concentrate on them, giving them a language abstraction layer. Once the language abstraction layer was installed, the Martian Elder then checked to see if the newly awakened Thol could understand him.

The Martians were extremely cautious with this procedure, only awaking one Thol every two hours. They then checked each Thol thoroughly, both physically and mentally, before moving onto the next cryogenic suspension pod. This entire procedure was going to take at least a week and during that time, Gideon, Sandra and Winchilly remained inside of Mimas, at the Southern Island Mountain Peak to help with the procedure. It was not something the Martians could do without Sandra's peculiar skill set.

The first two transports to return to Mimas were the transports carrying the seed stocks. All of the seed stocks were quickly unloaded, stored and catalogued, inside of the lower tunnels of the Northern Island Mountain Peak for future use. After those two transports were unloaded at Mimas, Carl and Marin, then flew them both back down to the monoliths on Mars. There they were also loaded with more of the housing flat packs being transferred to Mimas.

One by one, the transports started returning from Mars carrying the housing flat packs. Housing for well over two and a half million Martians was required, so many trips had been organised. On each trip, a different Martian trainee pilot got to fly the transport, as part of their training. Carl, Marin and the eight original trainees supervised them.

As each trainee pilot reached proficiency, they prepared another group of ten transports to fly to Mars, to help transport more of the housing flat packs. As this pattern repeated, they eventually had a hundred transports flying back and forth from Mimas to Mars. It took them almost a month of flying back and forth to bring all of the housing flat packs across from the monoliths.

During this time, the task of awakening the Thols had been completed. The Thols were now getting used to their new environment inside of Mimas. They had evolved in a gravitational environment that was roughly point nine five gs and found the Mimasian gravity much easier to deal with.

Carl, Marin and their two 'star pupils', returned to the Southern Island Mountain Peak after their successful transport missions, to find a large group of Thols on the broad ledge overlooking the Southern Circular Sea.

The Thols were all happily conversing in their own language of clicks, soft barks and trills, under the light of the artificial Mimasian Sun. They joyfully tested their wings in short flights around the flanks of the Southern Island Mountain Peak. The much lower Mimasian gravity was making their flights so much easier for them.

The Martial Elder asked, *"We have our housing?"*

"Yes. The technicians are now deciding on where to set up the towns and villages", Carl replied.

Looking at the Thols, Marin noted, "They look happy enough."

"Yes, they've been asleep for a very long time. We have asked them to be careful, at least until they get used to their new environment", the Martian Elder replied.

Winchilly who had been with the Thols, approached the group, *"We will need to set up our shelters first, before we bring our people across."*

"I expect that some of the housing will be set up at the Southern and Northern Island Mountain Peaks. Probably close to the tunnel entrances, on or around ledges just like this one", Carl noted.

"Quite probably, although we will set up many towns and villages in the central hills and plains as well", the Martian Elder responded.

Carl's *'star pupil'*, Carina asked, *"What more do we know about the Thols."*

Winchilly replied, *"Their solar system had two Suns. They called the larger one, a Yellow Dwarf, Cathol and the smaller one, an Orange Dwarf, Cythol. They called their homeworld, Homwol, which translates as trees. Their world had a single large moon and they called it Luns."*

"A system not unlike ours, except for the twin Suns. Cathol sounds like a G-type star and Cythol sounds like a cooler K-type. That kind of sounds like the Alpha Centauri system. Maybe?", Gideon speculated as he and Sandra approached.

"No, not Alpha Centauri", Winchilly replied, explaining, *"Our scientists have already asked about that possibility. The Alpha Centauri system has three stars. Their stellar system had only two stars. It had no Red Dwarfs."*

'So what does leave us with, as possible points of origin?", Gideon enquired.

Carl quickly responded, "There is only one other star system that fits the bill, Doctor Reas. Xi Bootis! That stellar system has a G-type primary and a K-type secondary. It's only about twenty two light years away as well."

"It seems you know your stars, Carl", Gideon remarked in reply.

"I was an astronomy major at university, Doctor Reas", Carl explained, adding, "Travelling at a modest thirty kilometres per second, they could have made that crossing in less than a quarter of a million years, assuming a direct route of course."

"Mimas is capable of much, much faster velocities than that, Carl", Winchilly noted.

"Yes, Winchilly, but they may have travelled to several stellar systems before finding one with suitable habitable planets like ours", Carl replied, noting, "We have no way of knowing the path that they took nor how circuitous it was."

"That is very true, Carl", the Martian Elder agreed, adding, *"They did not keep any navigation logs either."*

Sandra then remarked, "They also shared their homeworld with more than one intelligent sapient species as well. Most notably, a peaceful species called Carlins and from their descriptions, they had cat-like faces. There was another, much smaller mischievous species that they called Harricks. On their world, the Thols lived at the tops of very tall trees that they called Jula Jula, in very large and complex communal nests. The Carlins lived on the plains in a broad valley far below, in small villages. The Harricks lived amongst the forest undergrowth and were rarely if ever seen."

Winchilly shivered, *"The Thols also mentioned some sort of insectoid species. They called them Chittens. Six-legged, large pincer-like mandibles and they spat formic acid."*

"Yes, Winchilly. I nearly forgot all about that one. Fascinating, very dangerous, but very fascinating", Sandra replied.

"I did not find their tales of the Chittens fascinating at all, Sandra", Winchilly informed her, adding, *"I found them terrifying. The stuff that nightmares are made of."*

Sandra replied telepathically with an amused smile on her face, *"I didn't know that you had nightmares, Winchilly. Should you have one, Gideon and I will always be there."*

"Being eaten alive is a nightmare that many of my people have", Winchilly noted, shivering as she explained, *"It was something that the Tarlak nobles occasionally practised!"*

Sandra's smile quickly vanished and she replied telepathically, *"I am so sorry, Winchilly. I had no idea."*

"I'm going to organise some Sequoia and Karri seeds to be brought over", Gideon remarked, changing the subject and explaining, "Here inside Mimas, they should grow as tall as the Jula Jula trees that they remember on their home world."

"Elder, please check your fruit stocks for something called a Chillic", Sandra noted, "They were a fruit of some kind. Something the Thols really enjoyed eating."

"We can do that, Sandra. Winchilly, is it something that you recognise?", the Martian Elder replied.

"Actually it is, Elder. We have them on Mars and they also exist on the Earth as well. On the Earth, they're called peaches", Winchilly replied.

"That is strange, Winchilly? How is it I didn't recognise them?", Sandra enquired.

They are a variety we have back on Mars. I haven't seen them here inside of Mimas, but then again, I haven't been looking. On the Earth, there are many different varieties", Winchilly replied.

"I'm sure the Thols will be pleased to know that we have that covered", Sandra informed them all.

"Well, if these Chillics, Peaches, exist on the Earth and on Mars, and the Thols have memories of them, then it's likely that they originated on their homeworld, Homwol. So they likely exist here inside Mimas as well", Gideon noted.

Martian technicians were installing housing flat packs at selected locations around the interior of Mimas. Some areas were designated to be villages, other areas as small towns and yet and other regions as larger towns. On the broad ledge at the Southern Island Mountain Peak, several flat packs had been arranged appropriately to form a small township.

The flat packs were also self-founding, creating their own foundations. When activated, they automatically unfolded into two-story buildings that had up to four bedrooms. Sleeping quarters were on the top level, living quarters were on the lower level. Twelve had been designated for this particular location. Larger housing flat packs, which had up to six bedrooms, were also being set up in the other regions of Mimas. Especially across the broad plains on either side of the Equatorial Sea.

"It's kind of like origami, only in reverse", Sandra noted as she watched a flat pack unfold into a brand-new two-story abode.

"This is how most of our housing was constructed before the Tarlaks came", Winchilly replied.

"When will your people arrive?" Sandra enquired.

"While the technicians are '*popping*' up the housing, Carl and his team are transporting other required materials and items", Gideon advised, adding, "It won't be too long now before they bring the whole Martian population across."

"When the housing is all completed, my people will reconfigure the transports to carry people once more", Winchilly informed then, *"Once they've done that. Our people will come across."*

"Everyone Winchilly?", Sandra asked.

"Almost everyone, Sandra. Some of our people will volunteer to stay on Mars. They will seal off the Monoliths and remain behind as caretakers", Winchilly explained.

While they were talking, Yanis and Yarule flew over to them. There was a short series of clicks, trills and soft barks from Yarule, *"We have been flying around the flanks of this island. Many food sources have been found."*

"Fruits, nuts, mushrooms and other fungi", Yanis added with a few of his own clicks and trills.

Winchilly quickly replied, *"Don't eat them yet! Please brings us samples, so that we can test them, to make sure that they are safe."*

Yarule quickly responded with a few sharp clicks, some barks and a few trills, *"We would not eat them without testing them first. My people are collecting samples now, for that very purpose."*

Winchilly replied apologetically, *"I am so sorry, Yarule. It's just that the previous inhabitants of Mimas were Tarlaks and anything we find here, may have been tainted by them. Everything we find here will need to be tested."*

Yarule trilled and clicked, *"I do understand, Winchilly."*

Yanis noted in a long series of clicks, soft barks and trills, *"There are very tall trees here on this island. They are not Jula Jula trees but appear to be a very closely related species. I have a very small team of our people looking into those as well."*

"That does make sense, Yanis. Those trees may very well be the descendants of your own Jula Jula trees, having evolved somewhat over the last six million years", Gideon replied

"Perhaps. That is possible", Yanis replied with a few quick trills.

"Gideon has organised some more seeds. Tall trees from the Earth", Sandra informed Yanis and Yarule, "They're called Sequoia and Karri trees. Once we have a couple of forests growing, you may find them useful as well."

"Here, the gravity is much, much lower, so they will grow very much taller than they do on the Earth", Gideon added.

Yanis and Yarule both thanked Gideon before Yarule stepped forward and gave him a tight hug. Gideon returned the hug in kind.

Over the next few weeks, the transports were reconfigured for passengers and then the exodus from Mars began in earnest. A thousand passenger transports flew from Mimas to Mars, as the mass migration of the Martians took place. A thousand passengers per transport and the first million Martians were soon on their way to Mimas.

The passengers within those transports, upon landing on Mimas, waited very patiently for their disembarkation. There were a lot of them and disembarkation was going to take quite a while. Especially as there were only ten access tunnels through the Mimasian ice shell, still open for use. The transports each took their turn offloading their passengers.

Once they'd disembarked from their passenger transports, they gradually streamed into the Mimasian interior. They used a newly installed rapid transit system, that swiftly traversed the ten tunnels within the Mimasian ice shell. Ten kilometres later, they were within the ice shell and inside of the immense circular chamber, at the interface of the rock shell. There, they were batched into smaller groups of one hundred and transported through the twenty five kilometres of the Mimasian rock shell. The process took time but it was working, albeit quite slowly.

Once they were inside the Northern Island Mountain Peak, they underwent their final processing. Based on their abilities and professions, they were allocated housing in the various new villages and towns within Mimas.

Once their new housing was allocated, they were then transported to their new homes, where they were finally allowed to settle in. Each and every house that had been constructed had been provisioned in advance. The process was exceedingly slow, but the Martians demonstrated remarkable patience throughout. Patience and fortitude were the hallmarks of Martian society.

The exodus of the first million Martians from the monoliths to Mimas went quite smoothly, albeit very slowly. Then the passenger transports returned to Mars once again, to pick up the next million Martian people. The entire process of disembarkation and housing allocation repeated. Although it was still slow, it went as smoothly as before. The process just took time.

It wasn't long before the fleet of passenger transports returned once again to Mars, to transport the final half million Martians. On this particular trip, there were far more transports than the Martians required, so the excess transports had all of their seats removed upon arrival at the Martian monoliths.

Whatever had been left behind on Mars, that might be needed on Mimas, was stowed aboard those transports and transported to Mimas. At the end of the exodus, over two and a half million Martians had emigrated to their new homes inside the interior of Mimas.

Not all of the Martians had gone to Mimas. A little over twenty thousand Martians volunteered to remain on Mars, within the Martian monoliths as caretakers.

Around three dozen Colonial Troops had also gone native with new Martian girlfriends. Half of those Colonial Troops travelled to Mimas with their Martian girlfriends as part of the exodus, while the other half remained on Mars along with the Martian caretakers.

32. Reverse Course.

Colonel Bannon looked at his clock. It kept standard time in a twelve hour format. Next to it was a second clock, that had been given to him as a gift. That clock kept local Martian time. It was a twenty four hour clock with a strange wedge like gap in the centre at the very top.

The right-hand side of the clock had the numbers one through to twelve, running clockwise, with twelve being at the base, where six would have been on a twelve-hour clock. On the left-hand side of the clock, also running clockwise, were the numbers from twelve at the base to twenty four at the top.

Between twenty four and one, there was this odd, strange gap. It was precisely thirty nine minutes long and labelled *'Void'*. On Mars, a Sol was twenty four hours and thirty nine minutes long, so there was this odd period of time, thirty nine minutes long, that did not fit into any hour of the day. Colonel Bannon looked at the Martian Sol clock and just shook his head.

"Some things defy logic", he thought to himself.

Colonel Bannon's compucomm signalled that he had an incoming call, it was perfectly on time. The Colonel picked up the call, already knowing who was on the other end of the line.

"Gideon, Sandra. It's good to see guys. How's Martian exodus going?", the Colonel enquired.

"It's all going very well, Jim. Nearly all of Winchilly's people are now here on Mimas and being assigned housing", Sandra informed him.

"Though there are a small number of volunteers staying on Mars as caretakers", Gideon noted, "They'll stay there to maintain their old facilities. The monoliths have all been place under lockdown and we should put in place procedures to keep people away from them."

"Okay. We can arrange that, Gideon. So it looks like everything is going well then", Colonel Bannon replied, then asked, "They're happy with their new digs then?"

Sandra laughed softly with a broad smile, "Obviously, Jim! They are pretty much moving their entire civilisation to Mimas."

"And those other aliens. The Thols?", the Colonel enquired.

"We have found and revived forty two of them", Sandra replied, explaining, "They are a fascinating species. Very gentle. Very peaceful. Fascinating to talk with."

"I must admit, I'm happy to here that. Especially after the Mimasians", the Colonel responded.

"Tarlaks, Jim. The Mimasians called themselves Tarlaks", Gideon informed him.

"Tarlaks, Mimasians, it doesn't really matter now, Gideon. They're all gone", the Colonel noted.

"Jim. We should let you know. The Martians intend to fly Mimas back into Saturnian orbit", Gideon informed him, "They think that it's best for Mimas. They're going to put Mimas back in its original orbit around Saturn. Mimas was there for the last ninety thousand years, so they reckon it kind of belongs there. I tend agree with them."

"Okay. So I'll assume that's going to happen, something completely outside of my control", the Colonel replied, agreeing with the Martian's decision, but not being able to officially state it.

"Gideon and I are going to stay on Mimas for the next month or so, maybe longer. Your pilots, Carl and Marin, have requested their secondment to be extended indefinitely as well", Sandra noted.

"Indefinitely?", the Colonel questioned.

Gideon stepped in, "Colonel. The Martians have tweaked both Carl and

Marin. They are somewhat like Sandra and I now, both telepaths."

"That and the fact, that they've both met a couple of young Martian ladies", Sandra noted.

"Okay. Look, I'll do them a solid for now. I'll extend their secondment, so they are officially on the books and keep all their rank and privileges", the Colonel replied, adding, "but they will have to make a decision at some point. Are they remaining in the Colonial Forces or are they going native?"

"I'll pass that on, Colonel", Gideon agreed.

"I've had quite the problem with my men going native lately", the Colonel remarked.

"How so, Jim?", Gideon asked.

"Three dozen of my men have resigned their commissions and found their way down to the Martian surface and those monoliths", Colonel Bannon replied.

"Were they with the Colonial Troops that liberated the Martians?", Gideon asked.

"Yes, they were, Gideon. They were all commandos saving Martian lives during the liberation of Mars", the Colonel noted, adding, "It appears that they met some very grateful young Martian women and now they've run off to be with them. They're now all living inside those monoliths. As I said, Gideon, they've all gone native."

"I can understand them, Jim. After all, Sandra and I are with Winchilly", Gideon replied, "There is something about Martian women, Jim. Something very special. By the way Jim, I think you'll find half of those men, followed their Martian girlfriends all the way up here to Mimas."

"Yeah, well okay then, Gideon, it is what it is. Just keep me posted on any new developments and report back regularly. Colonel Bannon over and out", the Colonel signed off.

Colonel Bannon then pulled out a large pile of documents and began shuffling them into some semblance of priority, before starting to work on them.

Lord Folcrom Orpheus and Lady Folcrom Freyja watched Colonel Bannon, completely unseen. The two shadowy figures in robes of the darkest black, like shimmering raven feathers, stood inside his office. The Colonel had not seen them enter and could not detect their presence. They were completely unseen and invisible to him.

"The good Colonel knows way too much for my liking", Orpheus noted.

"Good, is the important word here, Orpheus", Freyja replied, noting, *"He is an important man. We need to adjust his memories very, very delicately, but not just yet. Mimas needs to be put back in place, in Saturnian orbit first!"*

"I've found what I've been looking for, Freyja", Orpheus noted, *"The bodies of eleven male and ten female Mimasians. They're all on ice back at Eros. They don't appear to have kept any others."*

"They didn't? Only twenty one of them? Are you certain, Orpheus?", Freyja questioned.

"Apparently, all of the other Mimasian bodies on Mars were cremated. They kept only ten of each gender as samples of the Mimasian species. Those twenty and the one they already had, Kildrark, makes twenty one", Orpheus replied, adding, *"The Mimasian dead on Mimas, were either left in situ or vaporised. They're probably still there as far as I know."*

"Good then. We'll start at Eros and redirect the Mimasian bodies back to the Earth. We should keep them, they're important, but somewhere where they can't cause any controversy", Freyja commented.

"Agreed, Freyja. We'll start the cover up on Eros", Orpheus replied, adding, *"When Mimas is back in Saturnian orbit, we'll come back here and do the same. Archive*

everything for our own copies, then everything else gets swept under the rug."

"We're going to need a bigger rug, Orpheus", Freyja replied, almost giggling, *"and what about Cis-Lunar L-Five?"*, Freyja enquired.

"I've organised some of our our other cousins to work at that end. It's all being dealt with as we speak, Freyja", Orpheus replied.

"What do we do about the Martians, Doctor Gideon Reas, Sandra Danker and those two pilots?", questioned Freyja.

"That's a wrinkle we need to iron out, Freyja. A particularly convoluted wrinkle I'm afraid", Orpheus remarked, admitting, *"I'm still trying to figure out how we should handle them."*

There was an ever-so-slight shimmering in the air in the office and the pair was gone. A split second later, they both reappeared within the world within the rock, Eros. Colonel Bannon shivered ever so slightly, this was a perfectly normal reaction. He turned around and reached for his climate control system console and adjusted his office's temperature. Slightly higher should do it he thought to himself.

The Thols had been making themselves useful inside of Mimas. One group, mainly their women folk, had started building complex communal nests, in the tops of the tall trees that forested parts of the flanks of the Southern Island Mountain Peak. Selected branches were cut and gathered from smaller trees along the coastline of the Southern Circular Sea. What looked like a species of willow tree, the long branches of which were both strong and flexible.

The Thols worked meticulously, weaving these branches around the top most boughs of the tall trees. Genetically, a type of Jula Jula tree. Carefully weaving the branches into place, to form large nesting platforms, walls and roofs. So tightly and thickly did they weave the branches, that barely any gaps could be discerned and barely any wind could pass through.

The Thols lined the woven rooves and walls with immense fan shaped leaves harvested from another plant, that grew far below them in the forest undergrowth. Layer upon layer, meticulously positioned and tied into place with thin local vines, harvested from nearby in the mid levels of the forest.

When they'd finished, both the rooves and walls were completely impenetrable to water.

Once finished with one large nest, more of a tree house really, the Thols then moved on to build another. Then another and another and so on, until they had enough tree housing for all of their number. After which, they linked all of their nests together, with strong, safe aerial walk ways.

The Thols could fly, so these walkways were not necessary for themselves, however, if they ever had non-Thol guests, those guests would need those walkways. Finally, the Thols built long ladders and spiralling stairs made of flexible willow-like branches and vines, so that their friends amongst the other species could climb to their tree nests and visit them. With the Thol's tree nest housing being so high in the tall Jula Jula-like trees, only the bravest of their friends might climb to those heights.

Before long, the Thols had built a whole complex of interconnected tree houses. This was the way, that Thols had built their homes since as far back as they could remember. Gideon, Sandra and Winchilly had watched the tree house construction with fascination, from one of the Southern Island Mountain Peak's higher ledgers with a pair of field glasses and were quite impressed.

Yarule flew over to them and landed on the ledge, then spoke with a few trills and clicks, *"What do think? Looks nice, yes? When will you come up to visit us?"*

Winchilly replied honestly, *"My people have no wings, Yarule and we do not do well with heights."*

Sandra then replied diplomatically, *"Your tree houses look beautiful, Yarule. I think, however, that the Martian folk may have difficulty climbing so high. It is not their way."*

Yarule looked sad, then replied with a few clicks and trills, *"For every problem, there is a solution."*

Gideon stepped in, pointing to some trees and replied, *"And there is a solution. Yarule, instead of climbing up the Jula Jula trees themselves, perhaps a strong, safe suspension bridge, from this ledge to those trees. Then from those trees, stronger, safer walkways to your nests."*

Yarule looked at where Gideon had pointed and took his words in, replying with soft barks, clicks and trills, *"A simple task it is for us. These things we can do. Yes, I will make it so!"*

"Thank you, Yarule", Winchilly replied, *"My people will find that much less daunting."*

Another group of Thols were helping the Martian engineers with the Mimasian ion drive system. The Thols had recognised it as their own technology straight away, as were the cryogenic suspension pods they'd been sleeping in. They had noted, that the Mimasian ion drive system, although it was their technology, was somewhat degraded and they had recommended, that they check it out thoroughly and test every single component. The Martian Elder agreed and requested that his technicians assist them in any capacity that they could.

The next day, the Thols had finished performing their checks and tests. The Martian technicians were very grateful. There were a lot of things, that they themselves had missed. The exercise had been a huge learning experience for them. The Thols had explained, that the most important thing, was to ensure that the ion drive's self maintenance and repair systems were running and functioning correctly.

One of the Thols had told the Martian technicians with a series of clicks, trills and soft barks, *"We may live in high tree nests, but we do know our way around an ion drive system. Especially one of own design and manufacture."*

That in itself elicited telepathic laughter from the Martian technicians.

Another Thol had remarked, *"Mimas is a complex creation. It would have taken our people centuries to hollow it out and create, perhaps even an aeon or two."*

That gave the Martian technicians a new level of appreciation for the Thols. At a point in the far distant past, the Thols had been highly advanced. Their civilisation had been every bit as capable, if not more so, than modern human civilisations, either Earth or Martian.

Several days later, after the ion drive's self maintenance systems had finished performing their job, checking and maintaining the ion drive, it was again reactivated and Mimas was again on the move. This time flying on a reverse course back towards Saturn. Gideon contacted Colonel Bannon to let him know that they were on their way.

"Good to see you again, Jim. Just letting you know that Mimas is on its way back to Saturn as we we speak", Gideon informed him.

"Yes, Gideon. My people just informed me of that a few minutes before you called", the Colonel replied, adding, "Our surveillance tells us, that the Mimasian ion drive appears to be working with a far greater efficiency. How did that come about?"

"Yes, Jim, that is correct. The Mimasian ion drive system was actually stolen Thol technology, so the Thols gave it a good once over. We should make much better time flying Mimas back to Saturn, than when the Mimasians did flying it in", Gideon confirmed.

"About that, Gideon. You will need to contact Titan. The man to speak to is Administrator Mark Spencer. He manages the Titanian and Saturnian colonies", Colonel Bannon informed him.

"I will definitely send him a message, Jim and give him a heads up. I'll let him know what's happening", Gideon replied, remarking, "The colonists out that way were badly hit. I don't want them all shitting themselves when Mimas approaches."

"That's what I'm talking about, Gideon. Just let them know, that you're just putting Mimas back where it came from. Keep them in the loop", the Colonel reiterated.

"Will do, Jim. Over and out", Gideon signed off.

As Mimas flew out of its position in Mars Sun Lagrangian point one, its cometary coma and tail continued billowing out and followed along with it. Soon Mars and the colonies in Martian orbit, were clear of the haze of escaping gases and dust particles. During Mimas's months positioned in Lagrangian point one, Mars had captured a great deal of the gases escaping from it and its new atmosphere had benefited as a result.

Administrator Mark Spencer had received a message from Doctor Gideon Reas, stipulating that the Mimasian war was over and that Mimas was being returned to Saturnian orbit. This was the first real confirmation, he had received that the war was over.

Mark Spencer walked out of his office and read the message out loudly enough for all those around him to hear, *"The Mimasians have been all defeated! The Colonial Troops have prevailed. The Mimasians are no more. We are flying the ice moon Mimas, back to Saturn and we will place it back in its original orbit around Saturn. Once that task is completed, we will meet you on Titan. Repeat. The Mimasians have been defeated."*

At first his people were quiet, they were shocked at the unexpected pronouncement, then when it had finally sunken in, they all began to clap and cheer. Mark Spenser held up his hand for silence.

"Get the word out! Let our people know we are all safe!", he told his personnel.

And that is precisely what they did, they quickly spread the word that the Colonial Troops had prevailed against the Mimasian threat.

As Mimas travelled further from the Sun, its surface temperature dropped as the Sun's warmth waned. Mimasian surface activity gradually diminished and by the time that Mimas reached the outer edges of the asteroid belt, out gassing had significantly decreased. Mimas's cometary like coma and tail persisted, but both were noticeably reduced in both size and density.

Mimas's tail, still pointing away from the Sun, grew shorter, thinner, and more tenuous. After crossing Jupiter's orbital path, the out gassing gradually subsided and eventually ceased. Mimas's cometary-like coma vanished entirely. By the time Mimas neared Saturn, its surface appeared cold and lifeless once again, with ice frozen as hard as granite.

Although Titan's head Administrator, Mark Spencer, had been given a heads up about the success of the Colonial Troops in winning the Mimasian conflict and that the ice moon, Mimas, would be returning to its original position in Saturnian orbit, he none the less organised his people to keep a close eye on its approach.

The Saturnian and Titanian colonists had suffered terribly when the Mimasians launched their attacks. Whole colony cylinders had been destroyed, thousands of colonists had died and Administrator Mark Spencer was extremely cautious of Mimas's approach. A close eye would be kept on Mimas at all times. Every morning when he entered his office, cup of coffee in hand, Mark Spencer checked the latest status reports on Mimas's progress.

Titan's head Administrator was not the only one watching Mimas approach Saturn. Folcrom Orpheus and Folcrom Freyja, also kept a close watch on the progress of the little ice moon as it returned to its original

Saturnian orbit. Placing Mimas back in its original orbit around Saturn, was perfect for their agenda and the agenda of their clandestine and occult organisation, the Council of Shadows.

33. The Council of Shadows.

The Martians, assisted by the Thols, very carefully moved Mimas back into its original orbit around Saturn. Apart from the major surface damage caused by the conflict, outgassing caused by the Sun's heat, had caused surface changes as well. Broad fissures were now clearly visible on the outer surface of the Mimasian ice shell and those would eventually need repairing.

The Martians had begun making plans for those repairs. They were considering the acquisition of a smaller centaur asteroid, to use as a source of raw materials for those repairs. Apart from those issues, you'd never have known that Mimas had flown all the way to the Earth and back again. Mimas was now in precisely the same orbit it had been in, before the conflict.

Gideon had been sending reports regularly to Colonel Bannon at the Aires colony in high Martian orbit. Each report was simply to keep the Colonel in the loop and did not require any reply. Gideon's latest report about Mimas being back in Saturnian orbit, however, did receive a reply. Gideon read the reply carefully. Then he read the reply over again, even more carefully. After which, he read it several more times. It made absolutely no sense. In the end, Gideon asked Sandra to read the reply as well.

"This doesn't make any sense, Gideon. Jim's questioning why we're here at Mimas. Jim's even questioning Mimas's flight back to Saturn. My God, he's even querying why Mimas needs repairs?", Sandra remarked, speculating, "It's as if Jim has no memories of anything that's happened recently!"

"Yeah, Jim's even questioning the existence of the Martians", Gideon replied, noting, "His reply 'Martians?', that says it all. I don't think he remembers anything at all Sandra. I've kept Jim in the loop with everything, absolutely everything and now it appears he has no memory of any of it."

"How can that be?", Sandra enquired, commenting, "It doesn't make any sense at all, Gideon."

Winchilly was following the discussion and stepped in, *"Gideon. Sandra. You are not the only Earth psychics. My people may have opened up your minds, your abilities, but there are humans on the Earth who are naturally born psychic."*

"So, Winchilly, what are you saying?", Sandra asked, then continued, "That psychics from the Earth have rewritten the Colonel's memories."

"That isn't possible, Sandra", Gideon replied, explaining, "Everybody knows that the Earth's psychics can't use their abilities off-world. That is a well-known fact. It's kind of like a rule. They don't even travel off-world."

"You can, Gideon, both you and Sandra. So it goes to reason, that there must be others that can as well", Winchilly explained.

"Altering memories can't be a very common ability. It would have to be subtle, very subtle and it would need to be very carefully done", Sandra replied.

"It isn't common at all. It is not something that my people would do", Winchilly replied.

"There are psychic academies back on the Earth. That's the sort of place where they might teach this sort of thing", Gideon speculated.

"They do have remote viewing teams as well. Constantly scanning the Earth's population for criminals and terrorists", Sandra replied, then queried, "but as far as I know, they can't work off-world? Not a single one of them!"

"Maybe not all, but perhaps some. Perhaps the most powerful amongst them", Winchilly replied.

"Well, assuming this is real, they've been in Martian orbit. From there, there are the Belter colonies, then Jupiter and finally, Saturn", Gideon remarked.

"So they could be on their way here? To us?", Sandra queried.

"Potentially", Gideon replied, he then added, "Assuming this is even real."

Gideon and Sandra arranged to fly from Mimas to the colony on Titan. They arranged to use one of the troop transports to do so. The transport was to be piloted by Carl, with Marin as his co-pilot. Carl and Marin both took their *'star pupils'* along with them.

Winchilly had introduced them to Sandra and Gideon, as Carina and Shareen. They flew to Mimas rather than teleport, so as not to let on that Gideon and Sandra had psychic abilities. They both wanted that information to be limited to a select few.

As they approached Titan's main colony, the view through the troop transport's screens and portals was largely obscured by the haze and smog of Titan's thick atmosphere. Rich in complex organic compounds and tholins, Titan's thick atmosphere was itself a navigation hazard. Both Carl and Marin were relying on their transport's instruments, to navigate their way through the smog, the colony's beacon keeping them on track.

When they were close enough to see through the haze and smog, they could see a series of domes scattered across the landscape of Titan in a tight cluster. There were at least a hundred of them within their sight and as they flew closer, even more that they could see further off in the distance. The domes were all constructed with exotic plasteel alloys, that could resist the extreme cold of Titanian conditions. They were all extremely well insulated.

Within the domes, were farms, park lands and open spaces, all illuminated by artificial lighting. Most of Titan's main colony was buried deep underground, with only the domes and the spaceports showing on the surface. This was one of things that had protected them from the Mimasians, that and the thick hazardous atmosphere of Titan.

The transport touched down on one of the landing pads at the colony's main spaceport. A broad umbilicus reached up from the landing pad and connected to the transport's main underside hatch. A tight hermetic seal was formed against the transport's hull and soon a scissor lift was rising up within the umbilicus. The group aboard the transport, opened the transport's underside hatch and stepped out onto the scissor lift. The scissor lift then descended once again into the bowels of the landing pad.

Everyone aboard the transport had disembarked and they were met by a group of armed security personnel. The security officers took them via a transport pod to the very centre of the colony, to the administration offices. The three Martian women were all wearing hooded robes and gloves, so as not to cause any alarm. After arriving at the administration offices, the group was then led to a conference room, that was close by to Administrator Mark Spencer's office.

Gideon, Sandra and Winchilly entered the conference room, with Carl, Marin, Carina and Shareen following close behind. Upon entering the conference room, they found the colonial Administrator, Mark Spencer and his secretary, Linda, waiting for them. Gideon introduced his group to the Administrator and they all took there seats.

It was at this point, that Winchilly, Carina and Shareen removed their hoods and took off their gloves. There was a sudden gasp of shock from Mark Spencer and his Secretary Linda. Without saying a word the Administrator gestured to the Martian women.

"They are humans from Mars, Martian women, Mr Spenser", Gideon replied to the gesture, before sending a silent telepathic message to his group, *"Do not mention the Thols, this will be difficult enough as it is."*

"Martian humans?", Administrator Spenser questioned.

"Martian humans and Earth humans are very closely related species",

Sandra explained, adding, "There's very little difference between us genetically. Our two species are ninety nine point nine nine nine percent the same."

"Over ninety thousand years ago, the Mimasians destroyed the Martian biosphere and kept the Martians enslaved, right up until our people recently liberated them", Gideon explained.

"Mimasians!", Mark Spencer exclaimed, "We know them well enough. We found this one, among a few others floating in space, while we were looking for our own survivors", he clicked a remote control and an image of a deceased Mimasian appeared on a wall screen.

"Yes. That is a Mimasian, however, they called themselves Tarlaks", Winchilly informed him telepathically.

The Administrator and his secretary were both taken aback and Sandra had to step in and explain, "The Martians are all nonverbal telepaths. They don't speak, they use telepathy."

"Oh. Okay. Please understand. This is quite a shock for us", the Administrator apologised, explaining, "This entire incident with the Mimasians has been quite an ordeal, quite shocking. We are not use to seeing aliens at all. First the Mimasians and now", he paused, "Martians!"

Winchilly empathised, *"We do understand. The Tarlaks were an evil species and they have caused much harm. They were, as you say, alien. We, however, are not. Extra-terrestrial yes, but genetically, not very different at all."*

Carl added in, "There are no more Mimasians left Administrator. They all fought and died to the very last. Every single one of them."

"So we do not need to worry about the Mimasians any more?", the Administrator enquired.

"That is correct Administrator", Gideon confirmed.

Gideon got right down to business, "Administrator. The Martians are the very reason we came here."

"The Martians?", Mark Spencer questioned, "Mars has very little to do with the Saturnian colonies."

Winchilly quickly stepped in, *"Administrator. Mars is undergoing terraforming. Humans from the Earth will be colonising Mars in the near future."*

Sandra then quickly added, "It's been only a little more than a century since the psychic pogroms on the Earth. Winchilly's people have serious concerns about our colonisation of Mars. The Martians have left Mars and they now live inside of Mimas."

"Inside of Mimas?", the Administrator enquired.

"Our whole civilisation has moved from Mars to Mimas. We now live inside of the ice moon", Winchilly explained, adding, *"All two and a half million of us."*

"Two and a half million? Did you say two and a half million Martians? Living inside of Mimas?", the Administrator repeated questioningly.

"Yes, Administrator", Sandra confirmed, explaining, "That is why we are here. The Martians are a very peaceful folk. They have taken over the interior of Mimas as their new home. They wish to live here in Saturnian orbit, in peace. They have all suffered terribly at the hands of the Tarlaks for a very long time. Well, over nine hundred centuries of suffering!"

"And what is it that you need from us then?", Administrator Spencer asked.

"It's very simple really, Administrator. Just let the Martians live in peace. Perhaps enact a new law, to keep people away from Mimas, so that the Martians can do just that, live in peace", Gideon requested.

"Administrator. The Martians were enslaved for over ninety thousand years! Their technology enabled us to defeat the Mimasians!", Sandra explained, adding, "Allowing the Martians to live in peace, without our interference, is the very least we can do. We owe them that much."

The discussions continued for almost three hours. In the end, they had an agreement. The Administrator agreed to new enact a law, barring colonists from approaching Mimas. Saturnian colonial law would treat Mimas as a *'privately owned'* colonised world and the laws of trespass would apply. A world that could not be approached without the express permission of its owners, who, of course, lived on or more correctly, inside of Mimas. The identity of those owners or more specifically, the fact that they were Martian was not revealed. Permission to approach Mimas could only be obtained by an official request, made in writing to the Saturnian Colonial Administrator's office on Titan. Administrator Mark Spencer's office.

In order to make this possible, Mark Spencer suggested setting up a communications hot line to Mimas, so that communications could be made when required. As the Martians themselves were all nonverbal telepaths, that would require a permanent Earth human presence inside of Mimas to run the communications hot line. At least until the Martians themselves, had learnt enough English to be able to communicate by typing.

Gideon, Sandra, Carl and Marin all volunteered, much to the delight of their Martian women. However, Winchilly pointed out that there were other Earth humans inside of Mimas, who had come across from Mars during the Martian exodus. After the meeting had concluded successfully, the group from Mimas were taken back to the space port and their transport. Once they were all back aboard the transport and seated, Carl and Marin then flew the transport back to Mimas.

Lord Folcrom Orpheus and Lady Folcrom Freyja, had watched the meeting in the Administrator's conference room completely unseen. The two figures in their robes of the darkest black, like the shimmering of raven feathers, stood inside the room, carefully observing the meeting. Their psychic obscuration fields hiding them in plain sight. They were completely unseen and undetected. The people in the conference room could look directly at them and not even suspect that they were there.

"This Doctor Gideon Reas is doing half of our job for us", Freyja silently remarked.

"Indeed he is. It appears that we need to do nothing with regards to Mimas and the Martians", Orpheus replied, but cautioned, *"We should do something about those Mimasian corpses though."*

"We could cause them to be shipped back to the Earth, just like we did with the other ones that were on Eros", Freyja suggested.

"Yes, yes, Freyja. That is a given", Orpheus agreed.

"What about the Saturnian and Titanian colonists?", Freyja enquired.

"I'm of two minds about that, Freyja", Orpheus admitted, explaining to his younger cousin, *"We should do what we've been doing everywhere else. Adjust their memories to bury the entire incident. Here, here, however, we may have an opportunity."*

"An opportunity? What are you suggesting, Orpheus?", Freyja enquired.

"I'm thinking Freyja, that we get clever, we kind of let them keep their memories. Let them even memorialise the events", Orpheus replied, considering, *"but maybe, just maybe, make it so they just don't talk about it and simply obfuscate their memories of what really happened."*

Can we actually do that, Orpheus? I mean, we will still have to alter their computer records, won't we?", Freyja questioned.

"Well maybe, potentially. I'll give it some thought", Orpheus replied, explaining, *"With the Martians living here now, a different methodology is required. That much is certain."*

"These Martians Orpheus, they have such gentle minds and they have suffered greatly. We should help them if we can", Freyja commented.

"That will shall, Freyja, that we shall", Orpheus agreed.

Gideon, Sandra and the group had returned to Mimas and all were back at the Southern Island Mountain Peak. On the broad ledger overlooking the Southern Circular Sea. Now a small yet busy village, they discussed the agreement they'd reach on Titan, with the Martian Elder. The Thols had all moved into their high tree houses, further around the flanks of the Southern Island Mountain Peak, but were still present in the village, clicking, softly barking and trilling away in conversion.

"It's actually a very simple arrangement, Elder", Gideon began to explain, "Administrator Mark Spencer has agreed to recognise Mimas as a *'private'* colony, essentially private property. There are precedents from the Earth that can support this option. Administrator Spencer is in the process of setting up the relevant regulations to make this possible."

"A private colony?", the Martian Elder queried, asking, *"How does that work in practice?"*

"As a private colony, no one can legally land on or access Mimas without the express permission of its owners. That would be your people, Elder", Gideon explained, adding, "To do so without permission would be considered a crime. A crime called trespass, that is punishable under the law."

Sandra stepped in, "We are going to set up a communication link with Titan. A link directly to the Saturnian Colonial Administration office. If anyone wants to come to Mimas, they first have to officially apply through the Administrator's office on Titan, in writing. The Administrator then contacts you and you make the decision, yes or no."

"So all access decisions come to us here?", the Martian Elder requested confirmation.

"Yes, Elder", Sandra replied, "You decide, who you let into Mimas."

"These arrangements do seem acceptable", the Martian Elder responded.

While this discussion had been taking place, two unseen figures had been listening in and observing the local scene. Their psychic obscuration fields hid them from everyone in the village, on the broad ledge, beside the tunnel entrance to the Southern Island Mountain. While listening to the conversion, Freyja had been distracted by the Thols. Neither of them had seen a Thol before.

"Orpheus. These Thols are a fascinating species", Freyja remarked, while watching the Thols flying about the ledge and conversing with their clicking, soft barks and trilling, *"Their trilling language is almost lyrical. So melodic!"*

Orpheus looked more closely at the Thols, *"They were the genetic base from which the Mimasians were created. How far the apples deviated from the tree is unfathomable"*, he correctly surmised.

Freyja, still fascinated by the Thols, walked away from their observations of Gideon and Sandra's discussions with the Martian Elder, to observe the Thols more closely. As Freyja approached a small group of Thols, they suddenly took to the air, flapping their wings wildly and trilling loudly, it was an alarm call.

Everyone in the village reacted to the alarm call and approached the Thols. Freyja took several steps back and then checked that she was still hidden, still obscured. Freyja signed with relief, her psychic obscuration field was still working, she was still hidden.

Turning to Orpheus, Freyja remarked silently and telepathically, *"It's okay, Orpheus, my obscuration field is up, they can't see me."*

Orpheus was not so sure, he gestured to Freyja to step back further away from the Thols, they were so different in so many ways. Freyja stepped further back, as Orpheus had requested.

Yarule clicked, softly barked and trilled wildly, *"There is something here. Something new. I know not what, but it has a scent to it. An odd scent!"*, she informed the approaching people, then pointing to Sandra, *"It smells female, similar to you, but no, not quite the same. It is the same, but not the same, it is different!"*

Freyja looked to Orpheus and silently apologised, *"Sorry, Orpheus. I appear to have slipped up."*

"The Thols picked up on your scent, Freyja. Time to pay the piper!", Orpheus replied, as he allowed his psychic obscuration field to dissolve and he slowly appeared from out of nowhere, in full view of everyone in the village.

Freyja did likewise and then the pair stood before everyone in the village, clothed in robes of the darkest shimmering black, like crow feathers.

Everyone took a step back as Gideon quickly asked, "Who the hell are you?"

"I am Lord Folcrom Orpheus. This is my protege, my cousin, Lady Folcrom Freyja", Orpheus introduced himself and Freyja.

Sandra then asked, "Why are you here?"

"We observe. We make changes. We ensure stability. We clean up messes!", Freyja replied.

"You're from the Earth, aren't you? Are you remote viewers from the psychic academies?", Gideon enquired curiously.

Orpheus smiled, "Yes and no, Doctor Reas. We are, different!"

"How did you get here?", Winchilly asked.

"We jaunted, blinked as I like to call it", Freyja informed her, "It's what you guys call teleporting. Although I must be brutally honest, you guys make a right mess of it. So damned loud. There's no subtlety to your techniques at all. The entire solar system hears you every time!"

"Be nice, Freyja!", Orpheus mildly chastised, "They are new to all of this after all and they haven't been formally trained."

"True enough, Orpheus", Freyja agreed, adding, "I keep forgetting that, being self-taught is the pits."

Sandra then shook her head lightly, then commented, "I thought, that is we thought, that the Earth's psychics couldn't use their gifts off-world."

"Most of us can't. Only a few of us can", Orpheus replied honestly, adding, "You can, but then again, the pair of you weren't naturally-born psychics were you", Orpheus then turned to the Martian Elder, with a look that beckoned an explanation.

Seeing the look on Orpheus's face, the Martian Elder stepped in, "*We did make some alterations. Tweaked, as you might call it. Our first attempts had quite some, shall we say, surprising results.*"

"You have not adequately answered my question, Orpheus", Sandra quickly stated, then asked again, "Why are you really here?"

Orpheus looked around frowning, "Humanity, that is to say, Earth humans, are not ready to know about Martians or Aliens. They're simply not ready."

Orpheus looked at the Martians and the Thols nearby, "The Mimasians were bad enough, but now we have Martians and Thols as well. Humanity is simply not ready for any of this! This entire Mimasian incident has caused a huge mass panic back on the Earth and in Cis-Lunar L-Five. Back on the Earth, my people are working very hard making corrections for this entire incident. Some of us are even off-world, working to resolve the issues that have cropped up here."

"By correction, you mean rewriting people's memories don't you, burying everything, covering it all up!", Gideon tossed back almost angrily.

"Yes, Doctor Reas. We do rewrite people's memories as necessary, we even adjust computer records and files as we see fit. You will not find me nor any of my people apologising for that either. It is necessary!", Orpheus admitted unapologetically.

"But why? Why is it necessary", Sandra questioned.

"Did I not mention the mass panic back on the Earth and in Cis-Lunar L-Five? Our species is simply not ready for these kinds of events. We won't be for another three to five centuries at least. So we hide it, we cover it up, we bury it deep and sometime in the future, when humanity is ready, we will release all of it. We are keeping detailed records of this entire incident. In fact, we keep detailed records of every incident that we find necessary to adjust", Orpheus informed them all.

"Anyway, Sandra, you guys can't talk", Freyja interjected, adding while pointing to Gideon, "Your Gideon here, blinked over three million Colonial Troops from Mimas back to the Earth and dumped them on a tropical mountainside, with their memories wiped! Good work there by the way, Gideon, that saved us doing the job."

Gideon admitted sheepishly, "Yeah. I did kind of do that, didn't I."

"It wasn't all that good, Freyja. The population of Bhutan almost quadrupled overnight", Orpheus commented, "The memory wipe side of things helped, but it was really hard to cover that mess up."

"In my defence, Orpheus, we were dealing with an evil Mimasian Emperor, hell-bent on destroying all of human civilisation. So I may not have fully considered the consequences at the time", Gideon tried to explain.

"Geez, Gideon, lighten up, don't worry about it! Orpheus was just being a bit picky. He'll get over it", Freyja informed him.

"Picky, Freyja? Picky? You do remember, don't you? It took a large team of us a week to clean up that mess", Orpheus reminded her, "We were jaunting soldiers everywhere by the dozens and rewriting memories hand over fist. I can't even remember how many officials had to have their memories rewritten. Not just on the Earth either, but up at Eros as well. So, Freyja! Not picky!"

"Officials? Eros?", questioned Gideon.

"Your good friend, Colonel Bannon. He couldn't just leave Mimas and fly off to Mars with his Armada could he? He had to keep the Security Council at Eros in the loop, didn't he, as part of his procedures. That also meant informing the Security Council about Sandra and yourself, including your abilities", Orpheus informed them both, adding, "We had to rework more than a few people's memories on Eros as well. Quite a few, in fact! The pair of you should be thankful."

"Okay, okay, fair enough", Sandra butted in, then asked, "but how on Earth, are you going to cover up an ice moon, Mimas, flying around the solar system?"

Freyja laughed and pointed to Gideon again, "Thank, Doctor Reas for that one. Gideon's Martian terraforming project, had Chariklo and Chiron flying all around the solar system. People will remember that and they won't remember Mimas at all. Especially now that Mimas is back in its original orbit, precisely where it came from. Thanks for that by the way, Gideon. Our people are in the process of adjusting the relevant memory associations as we speak. Everyone will forget that Mimas moved."

"That's crazy! That was more than a decade and a half ago!", Sandra tossed back.

"It makes no difference at all, Sandra. Time is completely irrelevant", Freyja replied.

"What about the Saturnian colonists? Surely you can't hide all of those deaths", Sandra questioned.

Orpheus casually replied, "Again, you guys have helped out immensely. Mimas is now a private colony, off limits and protected under trespass laws. Memory-wise, all we need to do is turn this war into a natural disaster."

"A natural disaster? How the bloody hell are you going to do that?", Gideon asked.

"Please, Doctor Reas. Give us come credit. We've been doing this for a very long time. We are actually quite good at it", Orpheus relied.

Freyja stepped in, "First we obfuscate their memories, then we alter them to remember the entire incident as a massive natural disaster. One that affected the entire Saturnian orbital zone and beyond. The incident was of course, regrettably, beyond our current level of technology to deal with. The greater the level of their trauma, the easier it is for us to rework their memories. The human mind prefers to bury trauma. It is actually far easier than you might think and as Orpheus has just noted, we've been doing this for a very long time."

Orpheus then added, "They will remember the disaster. Of course, they will and they may even memorialise it, but they won't remember that it was a War. That will all be obfuscated and subconsciously buried. Deeply buried. We have cousins working this very same magic, so to speak, at both Cis-Lunar L-Five and Eros, at the Earth's trailing Trojan point."

"Who gave you the right to decide this?", Gideon asked.

Freyja smiled broadly and simply replied, "Pops did. Well grand pops technically."

"Pops?", Sandra queried.

"Our Great Grandfather, Folcrom Tafazah", Freyja clarified, explaining, "Pops set up the psi corp, the psychic academies, the remote viewing teams, the whole shebang. Although, he did have a bit of help of course."

Sandra remarked, "We are aware of history Freyja. Tafazah did all of that, just after the psychic pogroms, just over a century ago."

"You don't know all of it, Sandra Danker. Not by a long shot", Freyja replied.

"Freyja, you've said too much already!", Orpheus gently chastised.

"Why, Orpheus? You know you're going to induct them. We both know it", Freyja responded, then thinking directly, silently to Orpheus, *They are way too powerful not to induct, Orpheus. They are seriously powerful! We cannot leave them with idle hands!"*

Orpheus answered the thought with his own, *"Agreed, Freyja. Idle hands are the Devil's workshop."*

"Idle hands need to be kept busy, Orpheus!", Freyja replied bluntly.

"Induct us?", Sandra queried.

"Orpheus did say that they were different, Sandra", Gideon reminded her.

"Bingo, Gideon! Bingo!", Orpheus commended, then explained, "Pops, as Freyja recalls him, did set up the psi corp, the psychic academies and the remote viewing teams on the Earth. Every psychic on the Earth is by law inducted into the psi corp at a very early age, directly into the psychic academies. Those psychic academies are run by psychics, level nine or higher, as are all the remote viewing team members. All level nine psychics or higher."

"And you two?", Gideon asked.

"Just getting to that now, Gideon. Tafazah was a very clever man. He set up the whole remote viewing team system to watch over and protect the Earth", Orpheus reiterated, adding, "But who watches over the watchers? Tafazah thought long and hard about that one, so he created another group. A separate hidden group, whose entire purpose was to watch over his creations, the psi corp, the psychic academies and the remote viewing teams. All of it! A group, that could work off-world as well as on the Earth."

"And you two belong to that group?", Sandra questioned.

"We do indeed, Sandra. Tafazah realised that he needed to watch over the watchers, so he created another, hidden organisation for precisely that purpose", Orpheus confirmed, explaining, "All of its members are psychics, level ten or higher and every one of us, is a descendant of Folcrom Tafazah himself. We are all his scions!"

"Pops believed in keeping this in the family", Freyja noted, adding, "He didn't believe that he could trust such an important task to anyone else. So our group was firstly made up of his children, then his grandchildren and now, his great-grandchildren."

"Which brings me back to my original question. Induct us?", Sandra circled back and asked again.

"Freyja is correct. It is likely that I'll induct you both, if and only if, you are suitable", Orpheus replied, informing Sandra further, "Neither of you, are naturally-born psychics, nor descendants of Folcrom Tafazah. So this would be a first. This is something that we've never done before."

"That means, we're both level ten psychics or higher", Sandra tweaked.

"That is correct, Sandra", Freyja confirmed, thinking to herself, *"Exactly how high a psychic level are you two?"*

"Wait a second! If this hasn't been done before, shouldn't you check with your group first? You know, make sure your doing the right thing?", Gideon enquired.

Freyja smiled and giggled, "Cousin Orpheus is kind of the boss."

"It's good to be the boss", Orpheus replied, adding, "It gives me a certain degree of leeway with this sort of thing."

Orpheus stepped forward and approached Gideon, "Do not be afraid, Gideon. I just need to assess you."

"Assess me?", asked Gideon.

"We call it the cold hard stare", Freyja replied, "I was assessed in exactly the same way. By Orpheus himself, in fact. It is harmless."

"Okay", Gideon cautiously agreed.

Orpheus reached deeply into Gideon's mind and began to assess his psychic potential, his personality and his motivations. After several long minutes of intense focus, Orpheus stepped back.

Orpheus let loose a subtle sigh of relief, thinking to himself and Freyja, *"Thank the Gods he's suitable, Freyja. I couldn't even get an accurate handle on what psychic level Doctor Reas actually is. This man is literally off the charts!"*

Orpheus reached into his shimmering black robe and a hidden, invisible pocket opened up. He reached into this pocket and pulled out a long hooded robe of shimmering black, like the black sheen of raven feathers.

Orpheus passed the robe to Gideon, "Please take this robe. It is yours now. It is the robe of a Folcrom. You may adorn it, in any which way you wish."

Freyja smiled and noted while clapping, "Excellent, Gideon, you appear to be suitable."

Orpheus then approached Sandra and performed the same procedure, the cold hard stare on her. After several long minutes of intense focus, Orpheus stepped back. Again Orpheus reached into his invisible pocket and pulled out another hooded robe of shimmering black, just like the first one.

"Orpheus, was she the same as Doctor Reas?", Freyja silently enquired.

Orpheus quickly thought back, *"Sandra Danker is off the charts as well! I have no idea how the Martians did this! I don't even think, that they themselves, fully comprehend it either."*

Orpheus passed the robe to Sandra, "Please take this robe. It is yours now.

It is the robe of a Folcrom. Adorn as you see fit."

Freyja smiled broadly once more while clapping, "Two for two! Both suitable! This is a great day indeed!"

Orpheus then pronounced loudly, amplifying his voice, "I welcome you both, Lord Folcrom Gideon Reas and Lady Folcrom Sandra Danker, to the Council of Shadows!"

Freyja then began loudly clapping and exclaimed, "Welcome Brother! Welcome Sister!", then she followed up with, "It's a shame we're not back on the Earth. Induction ceremonies are usually followed by a huge celebration and a feast. It is sad really. I do love a good celebration", a huge smile beamed across her face.

Carl then quickly asked, "What about us? Marin and I?"

Orpheus replied honestly, "Carl, Marin. I'm sorry to tell you, that neither of you is suitable. You are both only level fives, if that."

"Only level fives? How does that work out then?", Marin questioned.

The Martian Elder responded, *"When we altered Gideon and Sandra, we did not know at the time, what the results would be. We all found ourselves quite surprised by those results. They were, unexpected, to say the least. So when we altered both yourself and Marin, we had a far better understanding of the results and we were, far more cautious, shall we say. We gave both you and Marin, telepathic communications only."*

Both Carl and Marin frowned, but quickly let it go when their Martian girlfriends Carina and Shareen stepped in telepathically to comfort them.

"So what do we do now?", Sandra enquired.

Orpheus smiled back, "Oh, you two will work that out for yourselves. You've already been doing some of our work for us. So you'll figure it out."

"Just follow the guidelines and the rules Orpheus has implanted in your minds. It is very simple really", Freyja informed them both.

"Oh, by the way. Always keep us in the loop and if you need anything from us, anything at all, just call out our names up here", Orpheus tapped his right temple, so that they both understood, adding, "and we will come a jaunting, just as quickly as we can."

Then there were two tiny flashes of blue light and both Orpheus and Freyja disappeared.

They were both gone!

"Extraordinary!", the Martian Elder exclaimed telepathically.

"What did Orpheus mean? You'll work it out for yourselves?", Winchilly enquired.

"That probably has something to do with all of these guidelines, rules and regulations, I've got surfacing in my mind. Orpheus transferred across detailed files, directly into my head", Gideon replied almost angrily, he had a slight sense of being violated.

"Not to mention all of these endless checklists and tasks, Gideon. I probably have the same files as you. Their Council of Shadows keeps themselves very busy", Sandra replied.

"Yes, Sandra, I can see those as well", Gideon replied, then remarked, "It looks like we have a very busy future ahead of us Sandra."

Sandra let loose a slight giggle and then asked, "Do you see it, Gideon? Do you see it?"

Gideon frowned and replied, "Yes. Yes, I see it, Sandra."

Sandra commented loudly so everyone could hear, "Folcrom Tafazah was responsible for starting the entire push towards terraforming Mars. It's kind of like he's been Gideon's boss from the grave since day one."

"Yeah, Sandra. It seems like my entire life's work was originally Folcrom Tafazah's plan all along", Gideon agreed, then remarked, "and now we've been inducted into this, his Council of Shadows. They've just kind of made it official. We now work for them."

Winchilly then noted telepathically, *"As you are now both members of the Council of Shadows. You will both need to figure out what that means."*

"Indeed we will, Winchilly, indeed we will", both Sandra and Gideon replied in unison.

Orpheus and Freyja had not actually left Mimas. They'd simply jaunted a short distance away and then obscured their existence once more. Far enough away that the Thols would not pick up on their scent. No one noticed their presence. They both observed very carefully, wanting to make sure that they'd made the right decision, inducting Gideon and Sandra into the Council of Shadows.

"They seem to be on the right track, Freyja. They are all obligation and responsibility. I don't think we could have chosen a better couple", Orpheus remarked.

"Sandra and Gideon do make a nice couple don't they", Freyja noted in reply.

"They almost didn't get together, Freyja", Orpheus replied, explaining, *"They were captured and detained on Mars by the Mimasians. Before that, they'd been highly professional, not even attempting to let each other know, how the other one felt."*

"So their ordeal, their captivity on Mars changed everything for them? Brought them both together?", Freyja questioned.

Orpheus almost chuckled and then pointed to Winchilly, *"That young Martian woman over there, Winchilly, she facilitated them coming together."*

"I'm not sure that I follow you, Orpheus", Freyja admitted.

"They're not a couple, Freyja!", Orpheus replied, informing her, *"They're actually a throuple, Sandra, Winchilly and Gideon."*

"A throuple! That probably explains why Winchilly is pregnant", Freyja replied.

"Really? Do they know?", Orpheus enquired.

"Not yet, but they will soon enough", Freyja replied, *"I think we've chosen well, Orpheus. They'll become very valuable council members. We should go now and let them get on with it. They have so much to learn and so much to do."*

"Agreed, Freyja, agreed", Orpheus replied.

Then there was an ever so slight shimmering in the air and then they were both gone.

No one noticed them leaving and that was just the way they wanted it.

www.ingramcontent.com/pod-product-compliance
Lightning Source LLC
Chambersburg PA
CBHW050914030726
47503CB00007BB/2283